# Stephanie

*By the same author*

Ross Poldark
Demelza
Jeremy Poldark
Warleggan
The Black Moon
The Four Swans
The Angry Tide
The Stranger From the Sea
The Miller's Dance
The Loving Cup
The Twisted Sword

Night Journey
Cordelia
The Forgotten Story
The Merciless Ladies
Night Without Stars
Take My Life
Fortune is a Woman
The Little Walls
The Sleeping Partner
Greek Fire
The Tumbled House
Marnie
The Grove of Eagles
After the Act
The Walking Stick
Angell, Pearl and Little God
The Japanese Girl (short stories)
Woman in the Mirror
The Green Flash
Cameo

The Spanish Armadas
Poldark's Cornwall

# Stephanie

## Winston Graham

Carroll & Graf Publishers, Inc.
New York

Copyright © 1992 by Winston Graham

All rights reserved.

Published by arrangement with the author.

First Carroll & Graf edition 1993

Carroll & Graf Publishers, Inc.
260 Fifth Avenue
New York, NY 10001

Library of Congress Cataloging-in-Publication Data

Graham, Winston.
  Stephanie / Winston Graham.
     p.    cm.
   ISBN 0-88184-939-1 : $19.95
   I. Title.
  PR6013.R24S74   1993
  823'.912—dc20                                   92-42462
                                                  CIP

Manufactured in the United States of America

To George Astley

My most grateful thanks to Dr David Jackson,
whose help and advice have been quite invaluable.

Also, at an earlier stage, to Dr Denis Hocking,
my friend for so many years.

# BOOK ONE

BOOK ONE.

# *One*

## I

The Portuguese colony of Goa was taken over by India in the spring of 1961. In 1974 the leading hotel group in India, observing the long stretches of unspoiled beach, the rich vegetation and the good climate of the recent possession, decided to put up a luxury hotel there. It was built on the site of one of the old Portuguese forts erected to protect the colony from Turks, Frenchmen, Englishmen, pirates and other undesirable visitors. There were also wells there, and it had been used as a watering post for sailing vessels calling in on the long voyage back to Portugal.

The hotel, built with elegance and good taste in such a way as to merge into the countryside, was a great success, and nine years later a number of spacious, self-contained luxury bungalows, each in an acre of garden, were added on the slopes above the hotel. On 13 April 1984, which was a Friday, in one of these superior bungalows, a man and a woman were making love.

It was four o'clock in the afternoon, the sun beat down out of a sky from which all the colour had been sapped, a fresh breeze was drawn in off the yellow Arabian Sea. The hotel flag fluttered tautly. A surf had grown up along the great flat arc of the beach, creating a fine mist so that one could only see about the first two miles of the lightly bronzed sand.

Presently the girl moved out of the air-conditioned bedroom, parting the lace curtains as she went to sit on the verandah. The man joined her and rang for tea. Out here the heat met them, but it was not overpowering; the breeze filtered through the eucalyptus trees and the palms, keeping the air warmly light.

They were silent for a while, content with savouring their mutual pleasure, having nothing more to say to each other than what in the passion of the moment had already been said.

A tall rather bony man with dark wiry hair receding at the temples, Errol Colton looked to be in his early forties but was in fact thirty-eight. He had a mobile, humorous, sophisticated face with an expression that suggested he had seen a lot of life and found most of it wryly amusing.

Stephanie Locke, who was twenty-one, also looked older, in spite of her slender, loose-jointed build. She was tall and pretty with a narrowly oval face, bright eyes and a quick and easy smile. When she ran, but only then, her knees seemed too close together. There was a vitality and a volatility about her which was not without a sense of strain, of nerves near the surface. Her fair hair, loose now, was normally done in a ponytail.

The sound of a car in the drive told them their tea was being brought up in a taxi from the hotel.

'I could have made it here,' Stephanie murmured as the little dark-skinned waiter appeared coming up the pathway balancing a laden tray.

'It's my view', Errol said, yawning, 'that you should never do anything you can get someone else to do for you.'

'Except in bed,' she suggested.

'Well, wench, I don't yet include that under the heading of a chore . . .'

The smiling waiter brought in two thermoses and sliced lime and sugar (and hot milk just in case they had changed their minds), and some biscuits and slices of plum cake. Errol signed, and the waiter bowed and, still smiling, left. She poured the tea. It was a peaceful moment. After the taxi had driven away, the only sound was the faint rustling of the wind.

He yawned again.

'Sleepy?'

'Not more than is physiologically normal. But it's too early for a nap, and life's too short.'

'Race you to the end of the beach,' she suggested.

'Uh-huh.' The beach was six miles long. 'I might potter out and take some more shots.' Errol was a keen and expert photographer and had brought three cameras with him.

'If you do,' she said, 'I may stay in and write to Daddy. I owe him something more than a postcard.'

Errol squeezed some lime into his tea. 'Give him my love.'

'You don't even know him.'

'The man who produced you must be worthy of affection . . . He knows *about* me, I suppose?'

'Of course.'

'And approves?'

In spite of their intimacy they had talked very little about their personal lives.

'You've asked me before. I honestly don't *know*. I don't see much of him and . . . It's a different ball game from when he was young. Would you want your little Polly to play fast and loose?'

'Not at her present age. But yes, it'll come to that, I suppose – always assuming that coming away on a holiday with me can be called playing fast and loose.'

'More or less, by Daddy's standards. After all, you're a married man, old enough to be my uncle, and you mean me no good.'

Errol rubbed his ear. 'Who knows what may come of it yet? After all, I bought you a brooch in Bombay. There can be worse wages of sin than that.'

'It's *lovely*. Did I remember to say thank you for it?'

'You certainly did.'

'One thing I knew I'd forgotten. I should have said: "You shouldn't've."' She had risen to get a scarf, and she stooped and kissed him. He wrapped his arm around her bare legs.

'You weren't exactly innocent when I met you.'

'As I've told you often enough, there was nothing serious for me until I saw you blowing on the horizon like a . . .'

'A sperm whale,' he suggested.

She giggled. 'Yes.'

When tea was finished he took off his thin black Chinese silk

15

robe and put on a shirt and a pair of shorts. She lit a cigarette and rested her bare feet on the verandah rail.

'He's a cripple, you've told me.'

'Who? Daddy? Yes.'

'How does he manage to write those articles on gardening if he can't do any gardening himself?'

'Oh, he can. He buzzes around in his electric chair. And he's always potting and repotting things on the bench – or superintending planting . . . But d'you mean you've actually *read* articles by him?'

'I've seen 'em. And didn't he do a thing on television?'

'Last year. A short series.'

'I think I looked in once – before I ever met you. Suzanne was watching. She likes that sort of thing. Dark-haired, rather stout. You must take after your mother.'

'He gets fat because he can't take exercise – it's simple enough. But yes, my mother was blonde.'

'She left him, you said. I've often thought that must take a bit of doing – walking out on a cripple.'

'I wish you wouldn't call him a cripple – he's just lame, has to use a chair, that's all.'

'Well, call it what you will. She left a lame man with two young daughters.'

'He was only slightly lame at the time – walked with a stick. But yes, she fell in love with this Brazilian. It was the big thing in her life, apparently. Daddy told her she was free to go.'

'In spite of you and – what is it? – Teresa. In spite of you and Teresa? I call that a bit thick.'

'Don't you think you should come off your morality plinth, Errol? After all, you're spending a lot of money bringing a dumb little undergraduate to India and lavishing presents on her while your underprivileged wife languishes at home. And you're taking risks –'

'What risks?'

'You said your board of directors didn't approve of your mixing business with pleasure.'

'Did I? Oh, to hell with that. Incidentally, I don't see Suzanne as at all underprivileged. She lives extravagantly and well and I spend most of my spare time with her when I'm at home.'

'Which must be seldom.'

'Let's see, did you meet her once?'

'I saw her with you at that concert at the Sheldonian.'

'She's a great one for music. I'm almost tone deaf, you know.'

Stephanie put out her cigarette, watched the last smoke curl up as the end was crushed in the ashtray.

'She's your second attempt, love. Tell me about your first. Didn't you dump her in Greece?'

'That sort of thing.' Errol was not a man to show either annoyance or embarrassment. 'It reminds me, I must get something to take home for Polly, as it's her birthday soon. I wonder what those fellows on the beach have for sale.'

'Oh, pretty shoddy stuff.'

'I'm not sure. That thin little scarecrow I took photos of – he had a couple of brooches that didn't look bad.' Errol picked up a case containing two lenses. 'I might go up to the fort first, see if I can get a telescopic view of the headland. Will you be all right for an hour?'

'You left me to my own devices in Bombay often enough. I didn't get into trouble. Remember?'

He grinned.

She said: 'When you smile your eyebrows peak up in a most devilish and attractive way. I wonder you haven't had three wives.'

'I shall yet.'

'You know what my father calls you? He hasn't met you but I suppose he knows I wouldn't fall for an ordinary bloke.'

He bent over her. 'What does he call me?'

'Errol Flynn.'

He studied her, without a smile this time.

'It won't do. I never conquered Burma.'

'What does that mean?'

'It was a joke. You're too young to understand.'

'Tell me.'

'Never. It's nothing – Ah!'

She attacked him and he had to grasp her hands. They wrestled and almost upset the tea things.

'Tell me!'

'Help! Help!' he called, pulling himself free and retreating into the bedroom. 'It was only a film he was in. I swear it isn't worth repeating. Stop it, woman!'

'Explain!'

She grabbed at him again and they collapsed onto the bed. Laughing still, his eyes kindled, he pinned her back upon the bed and pulled the bathrobe vigorously off her, so that she was wriggling naked in his arms. He kissed her, and with fierce gestures grasped her flesh, pressing it, kneading it, smoothing it, inciting it. When she lay back for a moment defeated and breathless he stood up, tore off his own clothes and came back upon her and took her again with an avid relish that left the afternoon's lovemaking well away.

# II

Later they played tennis for an hour, a game they both knew pretty well. He had all the heavy guns, but with her nimbleness of foot and long legs she was all over the court returning everything he sent across. He won the first set 6–4, but in the second, tiring, he found himself trailing 2–5. Thereupon he changed his tactics and began to play heavily sliced shots which, when they bounced, leaped away at disconcerting angles. Perhaps it was not he who beat her in the end but her own sense of fun. Seeing a lob come over and knowing it was going to break extravagantly, she would begin to laugh and so muff the return. He won 7–5. Bitterly complaining that he had cheated her, she was led away for a long cold beer and a rest in the amber light of the setting sun.

They dined late, off Goan prawn curry and chicken Basquerie and pineapples and ice cream. The warm air made the darkness more intense outside the circle of the lights.

He said: 'Let's see, we've three more days. Tomorrow's free.

Sunday morning I've ordered a taxi to take me into Old Goa. I want to photograph the ruins and the churches. It was quite a city once.'

'I know.' She would have liked to go with him, but he had clearly not included her in the idea, so there it was.

'You'll not be bored?'

'Bored? When there's all this sun and this sea?'

'Tomorrow . . . let's bathe first thing and then go into Panjim. Coming through, it looked a tatty little place, but I'm told there's one good eighteenth-century church, and there's a fishing village at the end of the peninsula I'd like to see – can't remember its name – Dona something. I'll get the same taxi.'

'Sure. Fine.' She felt sun-and-sea soaked and tired and beautifully relaxed and slightly tipsy. There was no good wine, so they had drunk gin and tonics. Her normally talkative nature was lulled. Life was extravagantly good, and she was happy to drift along with him gently steering.

It was not to turn out quite to plan. Errol woke the next morning with sinus trouble and a splitting head: too much sun, he supposed, so they cancelled the trip; he spent the morning in bed, and she went on the beach alone.

From the hotel you walked past the swimming pool and the arranged deck chairs, and it was forty-odd steps to the beach. Errol was quite content with the pool, but he had humoured her in this, and they sat each day under one of the bamboo and raffia umbrellas within a few yards of the sea. She went to her usual place and spread a towel, lay on her face half in sun, half in shade.

They had been away ten days: it would be just over two weeks in all, and it had done her a power of good. Oxford had become a bit of a rat race. The crowd she went with – Tony and Bob and Fiona and Zog and the rest – all had more money than she had and a pretty well insatiable appetite for spending it. She'd had a wonderful first two years. She had found herself bright enough to keep up with the work and yet still be able to have the fun of going to parties all over the place and sitting around in endless late-night conversations. She had turned down the option of a year abroad at the end of the second year. A good many of her immediate contemporaries reading Modern Languages had been away this year, but as most of her close friends were reading other subjects she had decided to stay with them, as it were, and carry straight on. Her languages were so good already that she thought with a bit of cramming before Schools she ought to be sure of a reasonable second. Thank God the University had not yet split the second class, as she had heard they might.

And after the 'reasonable second', supposing she got it, what then? She thought she could probably land a job as an interpreter. Her father was completely bilingual in French, and she had become the same. If the worst came to the worst, she knew that Errol would find her a job. Always supposing that before then she had not married him, or they had not split up. She was aware that either might easily happen.

It was through Zog that she had met Errol. (Zog was not his real name but everybody called him that because he was Albanian and was some not-too-distant relative of the former King.)

Zog knew Sir Peter Brune, the rich scholarly aesthete, who had an estate near Woodstock, and had got her invited along with Tony Maidment and Fiona Wilson to one of his well-known weekends. Errol Colton was a fellow guest and was alone because his wife had flu. Stephanie had seen this attractive young-middle-aged man, and had noticed his eyes kindle when he first looked at her. She was not unused to being looked at admiringly but this was a little different. His look was not a stare for he had the good manners to glance quickly away, but it was very concentrated. And when he was introduced to her he knotted his eyebrows and looked at her and spoke to her as if no one else in the room existed. Nor it seemed did anyone else at the party or in the world exist for him except her for the rest of the weekend.

And it went on. Telephone calls, flowers, letters. She hadn't the guts – or the iron will that would have been necessary – to resist him. Nor did she very much want to. He was dynamic and wickedly attractive. Also he was funny. Most of her boyfriends, of whom only two had been more than friends, were too young and too solemn for her. She had a light, quick-firing intelligence which Errol's agreeable sophistication exactly matched. Within two weeks they were lovers and they met whenever they could arrange it. (He was often out of England.) But this trip, this holiday together, was, as it were, the first public announcement.

He had not hesitated to invite her, although he said it was against 'company rules'. He was clearly deeply smitten – 'besotted' was his word – and could not pass up such a chance. She had accepted in the first place for the simple personal reason that she wanted to be with him, but the excitement of visiting India was a strong secondary incentive.

So it had happened, and it had been a wonderful two weeks' enjoyment without a future or a past. There was already something between them more than the sexual urge, strong though that was. They sparked each other off, sometimes with brief quarrels, but always, it seemed, the sparks were flying without real anger – and laughter at the end. A true relationship was beginning.

All the same, though she lived a free and easy life, she didn't particularly fancy herself as a home-wrecker. Errol's reassurances to the contrary still left her feeling uncomfortable. Just now and then when she was alone she thought about it.

'Morning, miz,' said a voice. She rolled over and sat up.

It was the thin little Goan they had spoken to before. Though there were virtually no beggars on the beach, there was a persistent procession of people trying to sell you something, from bananas and soft drinks to saris and carpets, from copper and brass trinkets to jewellery and mosaics. Errol had a cheerful but immensely firm way of getting rid of them in the shortest possible time, but he had consented to look at this young man's tray and fumbled over a ring and a brooch or two before sending him on his way.

'Sir coming?' said the young man, looking at her and then hopefully at the hotel.

'Not this morning, Krishna.'

'Good rings,' said Krishna, showing the jewellery of his teeth. 'Very good, very cheap. See? Look this. Beautiful brooch.'

'Thank you. I'm just going to swim. And I wouldn't want anything unless Mr Colton were here.'

'Sir come later?'

'Not today, I think. Perhaps tomorrow.'

'You like take one back for him, see? This. See this. Suit you, miz. Beautiful stone, eh?'

'Beautiful, yes. But not today. Thank you, Krishna.'

The young man lingered in a way few of them dared to linger when Errol was around. Stephanie got up and shook the sand off her towel. Two Goan girls had come up unnoticed and were sharing a corner of her shade, squatting, whispering together and smiling at Krishna. Stephanie folded her towel and hung it on the raffia roof of the sunshade. Then she walked towards the sea. After a few yards she stopped and turned to look at the hotel. The sun wafted in her face, burned her feet; the surf was hissing as it crawled in over the sand. Krishna was walking back, starting the long trek towards his village; the girls still squatted whispering to each other.

What had she left there? A paperback, a pair of sunglasses, a cotton hat, a thin wraparound dress, a purse with a few rupees in it. If they went, they went; but she didn't think they would. The Goans were known for their honesty as well as their good manners. She plunged into the sea with a crow of delight.

A half-dozen Indian women were bathing near her still wearing their saris. What price emancipation?

When she came back twenty minutes later the girls had gone as if they had dematerialised, but her possessions were untouched. She dried her feet and looked at the blood oozing from her heel where she had caught it on a piece of half-buried driftwood. Very careless.

Her body had almost completely dried already, her hair was half dry simply from three minutes' walking back along the beach. Her heel was stinging. It was nothing, the merest cut. But this being India, did one take extra precautions? Errol had some antiseptic stuff. Worth a walk? It was nothing. And she could see if he was feeling better.

She climbed the steps to the hotel but disdained the taxis

always waiting to whisk guests up to their bungalows, and negotiated the steep path, cutting corners off the conventional road. The swim had invigorated her and she felt ready to try the four-minute mile.

In the drive outside their bungalow two cars were standing, one an Ambassador, the maid-of-all-work car and taxi that proliferates throughout India, the other a sleek black Mercedes. Such a new and shiny Mercedes is as rare in India as a Rolls in a Welsh mining village. A chauffeur in a dark suit was sitting at the wheel. As she went up the steps she heard voices.

Errol was entertaining two Indian guests. One she had met in Bombay, and was a business associate of Errol's, Mr Mohamed, who had visited him at the Taj there. He was a stout bearded silent man who wore too much jewellery. The other man, clearly the owner of the car, was a different and superior type. A tall smooth man with a long neck and an oval head on which the greying hair was slicked back so smoothly that he looked more bald than he really was. He wore a suit of cream shantung silk with a black silk shirt and a cream tie, a diamond tiepin, diamond cufflinks and a black silk handkerchief. He exuded a quiet importance. He might have been the maitre d'hotel at an exclusive London restaurant, or chief adviser to some oriental dictator.

He and Errol were seated. Mr Mohamed was standing holding some documents, which were clearly under discussion.

Silence had abruptly fallen at her entry.

She said: 'Oh, sorry. I didn't know anyone was here.'

'Oh, come in, come in, darling. My friends called unexpectedly. Of course you know Mr Mohamed. Mr Erasmus is a colleague from Hong Kong.'

Mr Mohamed bowed from the waist. Mr Erasmus slightly inclined his head. She saw the table was spread with maps and what looked like shipping lists, and a wallet was open with some money in it.

'Sorry,' she said again. 'I cut my foot and thought I'd get some antiseptic for it.'

'In there, darling; second drawer, I think.'

23

'How's your head?'

'Not too agreeable yet. But improving.'

Mr Erasmus said: 'May I please know the young lady's name.'

'Of course,' Errol said. 'Miss Locke. Miss Stephanie Locke.'

Mr Erasmus eyed her with cold, polite interest. His skin looked so smooth he might just have shaved, or did not need to shave. He spoke perfect English, but his eyes were too slanted to be European.

Presently the stinging antiseptic was on, and a plaster, dusted with antibiotic powder, over the cut.

'You have had a tetanus injection?' Mr Erasmus asked.

'Oh yes, thank you. Errol insisted before we left.'

'Stop and have some coffee while you're here?' Errol suggested, dabbing his head with a damp towel. But it was a half-hearted invitation and she smilingly refused. Couldn't wait to return to the beach, she said.

'You'll stay to lunch?' Errol said to the men, but again it was perfunctory. Mr Mohamed deferred to Mr Erasmus, who said: 'Thank you, I must catch the afternoon plane to Delhi. Mohamed, I expect, will be returning to Bombay.'

The fat Indian bowed formally from the waist as she left. The tall man inclined his head.

# III

She spent an hour in and out of the sea and then climbed the hill again to meet Errol for lunch. He was better but his normal friendly yet devilish smile was tight-lipped and, she thought, forced.

'Have they gone?'

'They've gone.'

'Sorry I crashed in. I'd no idea.'

'Neither had I.'

'Who was the new man?'

'Just a colleague.'

'I didn't think he liked me.'

'He's only interested in business.'

'Well, I certainly didn't like him.'

They walked down the hill and through the hotel to one of the outside restaurants looking directly over the sea. They hadn't spoken on the way down.

When a waiter had taken their order she said: 'Is he the sort of boss?'

'Who?'

'Mr Erasmus, of course.'

'He's the head of the South Asian division of our group. That's all. We're only loosely associated.'

'He gave me the creeps.'

'Oh, lay off it. He's all right. In a business like ours you have to meet all sorts.'

'Your business?'

'The travel business, of course. We're expanding all the time. You have to be international these days if you want to move on.'

His voice was abrupt and unfriendly. He was clearly still out of sorts. They hardly spoke then for a time, but a bit later he rounded on the obliging young waiter who had not brought quite what was ordered.

When the man had gone scuttling away Errol said: 'They're too slow. It does them good now and then to get a kick up the backside . . . I see you don't agree.'

'Well . . . a lot of famous men have done it, I know, but . . .'

'Done what?'

'Been rude to waiters. It always seems to me unsporting because they can't answer back. Of course if they're *really* inefficient or rude to you . . .'

'Which he wasn't? Maybe you're right. But you know with these cluster headaches I get very irritable, my dear.'

'These what?'

'Cluster headaches. It's a form of migraine. Due, I'm told, to changes in my indole-peptide metabolism. Haven't you noticed?'

'Should I have?'

He laughed. 'Probably not. Except that I kept blowing my nose and scratching my head last night.'

'So what can you do for it?'

'Not much. Pain killers. But it's soon over – usually less than a day. And not serious . . . Does it put you off?'

'Put me *off*? Why ever should it?'

'My mother could never stand people with ailments. Said it made her feel unhealthy to mix with 'em.'

In fact she rather warmed to this confession of physical weakness in a man so dominant. No doubt it explained his brusqueness today and the lack of that impish humour she found so engaging.

She said: 'Sorry I blundered in this morning.'

'Sorry I glowered. I assure you they were no more welcome! I just wanted to lie in the dark!'

'You're better now?'

'Yep. Did you see the cash on the table?'

'What? Cash? Yes. It's not my business.'

'Nor is it. But you see we're thinking of opening a theme park in Agra, and –'

'Ugh! . . . Sorry . . .'

'It isn't as bad as it sounds. Just a development. The Indians themselves are in favour of it.'

'But that surely means *big* money.'

He laughed. 'Today we were only dealing with their commission. In India transactions can't be arranged any other way.'

After lunch they dozed for a while in a couple of the chaises longues, the Caryota palms and the banana trees wafting sun and shadow over them as the fronds moved in the breeze. Presently he threw his paperback down and said he thought he'd like to see Krishna again.

'He was looking for you this morning.'

'I'll bet.'

She went with him; the sun was still hot as they strolled across the beach. There were a few more people about than in the morning but unless you walked at high-water mark you didn't meet anybody.

A group of dark-skinned native boys were hauling in their fishing boat on wooden rollers. It was a primitive craft, long and very narrow, with a high prow, and it did not look as if any nails or screws had been used in its construction. Everything was lashed together with thongs. Stephanie and Errol stood watching while the catch was brought in in baskets and separated out and assayed. They laughed and talked with the men – Errol was very good at this. He took a lot of photographs, and then they went on their way.

A mile further along was the beach encampment, which closed down and was carried away every night, and brought back and erected every morning. Here the beach sellers congregated in tents or behind raffia screens, or stood beside trestle tables full of carefully arranged trinkets. Old pewter pots and pans and inkwells and bubble pipes, copper bells from Benares, wooden idols from Khajraho, silk scarves from Madras, silver bangles and brass rings from Delhi, carpets from Kashmir, endless saris and rugs and paintings and cheap skirts and shirts and sandals.

They had no need to ask for Krishna; the bush – or beach – telegraph had been at work and he came trotting to meet them, his battered old suitcase under his arm. He squatted on a sandhill away from the others, and soon the three of them were fingering his wares.

The brooch Errol fancied had three rubies in it and was the prize of Krishna's collection and for which he wanted eight thousand rupees. That was about four hundred pounds, and if the stones were as good as they looked it was dirt cheap. Even if they were not as good as they looked, it could hardly be expensive. (Always supposing the rubies were not pieces of glass. Krishna swore on his mother's grave that they were not.) Errol was pretty sure the stones were real, so bargaining began. Eventually at 5,250 rupees Krishna would go no further, so Errol tentatively agreed the price.

'Mind, I'm not at all certain I shall have it,' he said, putting the brooch back among the others.

'Take it,' said Krishna eagerly. 'Take it, eh? Keep it tonight, eh? Pay in morning.'

At a second attempt Errol lit a cigarette. The smoke blew

swiftly away. 'Okay, I'll pay you in the morning – or let you have it back. In the morning, about midday, eh?'

Although it was not for her, Stephanie wore the brooch home. The setting was ornate but nicely worked.

'You said you'd meet Krishna at twelve,' she said. 'Aren't you going off photographing churches?'

'Oh, well . . . Well, what the hell. These little men are here to please us. They're used to waiting. I say . . .' He stopped. 'That stall. They're selling hash cookies. I can smell 'em from here.'

'You mean – it's what it sounds like?'

'Yes. You must have tried them at St Martin's, surely.'

She pushed her hair back. 'I've smoked a joint now and then. Not had anything in this form.'

'Let's try 'em. We'll keep them, have them for dessert. I'm getting tired of ice cream. May add a touch of the exotic to our lovemaking.'

'I haven't noticed anything lacking so far!'

He laughed again, his good humour restored, and kissed her neck and went to buy a box.


# IV

Next morning it was she who had the headache, he who was bright and cheerful. It had been a strange adventure in the night, when substances seemed to float and vision was enhanced and laughter and hysteria were interchangeable. Mischievously he had persuaded her to take more than she wanted, and to humour him after the day's embarrassments she had eaten too many. She not infrequently took a fair amount to drink: it came from inner impulses of recklessness, a sudden sharp pleasure in kicking over the traces; but in these flurries of alcohol she had never been altogether without control of herself. Last night she had been, and this morning the aftermath was unpleasant.

It had been a strange sexual encounter too, in which angels and devils seemed equally to scream and moan, in which sensations became double sensations and perversity was all. One floated, half-drowned, on a butterfly sea of orgasm which was deliriously beautiful but wayward and tormented. At the very edges of ecstasy was pain.

Errol was almost too much on form this morning, and took another hash cookie after breakfast to keep up the euphoria. He examined the brooch in the bright light of morning, then scrabbled in a suitcase and took out a jeweller's glass. After a bit he shook his head.

'They're rubies all right, but they're not top class. Too dark. He swears they're Burmese, but they probably come from Thailand. And there's a flaw in the middle one. I doubt if I'd be asked to pay more than four hundred pounds for the brooch in Bond Street.'

'So you'll not buy?'

'Doubt it. Unless I could beat him down to two hundred. These people have an exaggerated idea of values.'

'Shall you let him have it back this morning before you go?'

'No. Make him wait. I should be back by four.' He ruffled his hair, looking her over appreciatively, at the casual feminine grace with which she sprawled in her chair. 'And what mischief will you get up to while I'm gone?'

'Wish there was some. No, I've got books to read. Actually *read*, darling, to improve myself – you know – in the hope that I might get a second in June.'

'If there were some other things you could graduate in,' he said, 'you'd certainly get a first.

## V

It wasn't easy to concentrate on Cervantes in the original Spanish with the brilliant glitter of the sun and the sea. Soon she would be back in Oxford in a petrochemical atmosphere and under draughty skies – with Schools not far away. At eleven she bathed in the pool and then, still wet, with a thin beach coat over her arm walked across the beach to dry. At once Krishna appeared.

'Mr Colton has gone out for the morning taking photographs,' she said. 'He'll be back this afternoon and will see you then.'

Krishna trotted beside her for a while, his face anxious. He explained that the brooch was really his father's, and his father blamed him for having let it out of his sight. The value was so great – to them – that it represented the family fortune. If anything should happen to it . . .

'Nothing will happen to it,' she said; 'it is quite safe.'

He was not able, Krishna explained, he was not allowed into the hotel and he did not even know their names.

'Colton,' she repeated. 'C.O.L.T.O.N.'

'Col-toon.'

'He will be home by five.' All the same she wished Errol had not taken the brooch on approval. Had he ever really had any intention of buying it? Certainly Krishna, having come down so far in price, could never reduce it again, by half. Errol had a mischievous streak, she well knew. It didn't matter much if he played tricks on her; it was a bit callous to practise them on this ragged young Goan.

She lunched at one of the other restaurants today – it was hotter than usual, and one sought the breeze. The menus at all the restaurants were very much the same, and she had tiger prawns, for which she was developing an insatiable taste.

The hotel was preparing for some sort of jamboree. Endless streams of waiters and workmen were carrying and rearranging tables and putting up balloons round the swimming pool. Monstrous effigies, inflatable and grotesque, were being erected on poles and swung gently in the warm air. Long barbecue trestles were rattling into place. There would, of course, be dancing. Every night there was dancing to a live band, but this was obviously some special occasion. The Indians – and the Goans – never lacked for an excuse to make merry.

A fairly cosmopolitan bag of guests at the hotel: English, French, German, Swiss, Indian; none, fortunately, in a special majority over the others. Being a gregarious type, she would have chatted to most of them, but Errol seemed to want to keep all his laughter and high spirits for her, and have other people stay at a distance. Now that they saw her on her own, two English couples separately came across to talk to her, and she had a very unstudious afternoon. Tea came and went, and it was five before she walked up to her bungalow and realised that Errol was over-due. She hung about a bit and thought, well, damn it, he might have telephoned. Another bathe? In the afternoon breeze the sea was prancing; it would probably be unsafe to swim because of the undertow, but jumping through the breakers was always exhilarating. She must be careful not to be rescued, though. Young Goan lifeguards were usually on the watch with an old tyre and a length of rope, and they seemed particularly eager to rescue ladies who appealed to their sense of the aesthetic.

As soon as she came out of the sea and saw Krishna waiting she wished she had used the pool instead.

'He is not home yet,' she said. 'He will come soon.'

Krishna glanced anxiously at the sun, which had less than an hour to set.

'I do not take the money home, Father beat me with rod. He will say we are in ruin!'

'Mr Colton should be back very soon.'

'*You* bring the money, miz?'

She squeezed the water out of her hair. 'I am sorry to tell you this, Krishna, but I do not think Mr Colton will buy the brooch after all. He has decided, I think, that it is not what he wants.'

Krishna sucked his teeth in dismay. 'The money?'

'I do not think he will keep the brooch.'

'Then the brooch? Where is it?'

'In our apartment.'

'The money . . .'

'No money.'

'The brooch. You get brooch, miz, *please*. Father beat me with rod.'

She picked up her flimsy wrap and put it on to protect her shoulders from the sun.

'I am going up now. He should be back. If not I will tell him to meet you at the steps at seven.'

'Dark then.'

31

'The lights from the hotel will show up the steps.'

'Master come, miz. You or Master. Father beat me with rod. We are ruin.'

She shook him off with difficulty, feeling annoyed with his persistence and annoyed with Errol. Of *course* the brooch was safe with them, but the young idiot of an Indian had trusted them without knowing anything about them. For all he knew they might be leaving on the morning plane, taking the brooch with them. How could he challenge them?

She went to the desk to see if there was any message, but there was not. She took the taxi up to the bungalow but nothing had changed. The air was moist and cloying now. She pulled off her bikini and took a shower, then found some ice in the fridge and poured a large gin. She felt better for this. Be damned to hash. Good luck to them as liked it, but it was not for her.

From the balcony she watched the sun go down. *When barréd clouds bloom the soft-dying day* – who had written that? The barréd clouds were there tonight – a thin black wafer bisecting the sun as it sank into the opal sea; but it would be quite hard to think of a tropical day as soft-dying; too abrupt and dramatic for that. Even the sun seemed to go too fast. At five past six its rim touched the horizon, and in a little over two minutes it was gone! Royal purples, iridescent greens and peacock blues glowed in the turning waves.

In her handbag, as she took out a handkerchief, was a bill for next month's rent of the flat in Broomfield Road, by agreement paid in advance, and this as yet unpaid. It was rather a grand flat for an undergraduate, tastefully furnished, good prints on the walls, but she had moved into it a year last January, thanks to a sub from her father. She had shared it with an Australian girl, Jennifer Price, but Jenny had gone back to Adelaide last Christmas when her mother unexpectedly died, and had not returned. Having just met Errol, she had not made an immediate attempt to find a new flatmate because it was marvellously convenient to have the place to oneself. However, she simply couldn't afford to keep it on on her own, hence the unpaid bill; and she had refused Errol's offer of help (kept mistress?); so she must find someone fairly quickly. The obvious person was Anne Vincent; she would come like a rocket, but there were drawbacks. Anne was in her first year and had a crush on her. There was a Lezzy feel about the relationship and Stephanie didn't want to fan it.

After the sun, a short luminous afterglow, some stars came out, and it was night. Another drink; shut the windows. So far as she had been able to discover, there weren't any flying insects by the sea in Goa, but there was no point in going out of one's way to attract them.

Seven o'clock came. She closed the paperback she had been leafing through, took off her beach wrap, slid into a frock, combed her hair. Then she thought of Krishna. The wretched little man would be waiting at the bottom of the steps. Damn Errol! Quite often he had been unpredictable in his comings and goings before, but not as bad as this. She'd have to take the beastly brooch down herself.

If she could find it. She tried the drawers but no luck. A brooch was easy to put away in some unobtrusive corner. Maybe the provoking man had taken it with him.

The only other possible place was his briefcase under the bed. She yanked the case out, feeling felonious and wondering if he would come in and catch her. Well, serve him right. The case was one of those with a combination alphabet to unlock it, but in Bombay she had seen him press an E, two Rs, an O and an L. She did the same and the case flicked open.

A *wad* of money, mostly in hundred-dollar bills, nearly fell out. A pile of documents too, on a variety of styles of paper, from good vellum to the flimsiest of cheap decorated Indian paper. Diagrams, maps of various parts of the world, details and dates of consignments. Names of ships, airlines, names and addresses, hotels, towns, Hong Kong, Singapore, Peshawar, Shanghai, Kuala Lumpur.

Then she saw the brooch. It had been dropped in loose and was at the bottom of the case. She grabbed it, put it on the bed, turned to shut the case. One last look: peeping Tom. Most of the papers seemed to be records of consignments, for Greece, for

33

Holland, for England. But there were attached memos, here and there. One read: *No worry about customs here. Just pay the officers!* Mainly it was flax they were shipping. An odd thing to be concerned with and in such quantity. Wasn't it?

Stephanie shut the case and with a toe slid it back under the bed. She thought she would run down and give Krishna the brooch back to quell his anxieties and then come up and finish dressing. Not that anyone dressed much in India. When they came down for the first dinner Errol had remarked: 'I believe mine must be the only tie in Goa.' But she would brush her hair again, make up her face.

Errol had to be home soon. What would she say to him? Not very much. She was trembling. Silly, she needed another drink. Maybe she needed to get altogether stoned tonight. And to stay permanently stoned until she returned to England. Not on hash, but on good honest gin.

She drank the next down quickly and felt it warming her with a protective glow. A protection against an ugly suspicion. There must be some mistake.

She picked up the brooch and pinned it to her frock, then took it off, fished out a bit of tissue paper and wrapped it. Better to let Krishna see they had been caring for it.

She stepped out of the bungalow and began to walk down the stepped slope to the hotel. The breeze caressed her face. There must be some mistake?

In her two and a half years at Oxford she had mixed with a fair assortment of people, students, dons, many from outside the university. Particularly in the last year she had become friendly with this inner group of rich students, Bob and Tony and Zog and Fiona and Arun Jiva and the rest, and through them she had come to see some of the seamier side of undergraduate life. Nobody was vicious but a number were pretty wild. Some took drugs, some took drink, a few, like Zog, nothing. But she had become familiar with the jargon of the day.

Flax she knew to be the in name for heroin.

# VI

She was halfway through dinner when he slid into the seat beside her.

'Hi. Remember me, eh? Sorry, I got delayed at the office.'

'Hello.' She looked at him, half smiled, then went on with her dinner.

No one could call him good-looking, but he had such tremendous bony, whimsical charm, such appeal, and tonight he had a clean glowing look as if he had spent the day in restful ease and was all ready to enjoy the night. She swallowed a mouthful of food, to stop the bile from rising in her throat.

The music ended and he looked about, nodding to one or two fellow guests. He patted her hand and said: 'Now you're cross. Never mind. I'll make up for it . . . Oh, I see, no waiter service tonight. One has to go to the burning ghats.'

It was his name, and a good one, for the barbecue meats laid out and simmering at the trestle tables. He went off, picked up a plate, and presently came back with it filled with a variety of curries.

'Did you have a good day?' he asked.

'Very good. The usual, of course.'

They ate in silence for a time. The band anyway was noisy enough. Some people who had finished their supper were already dancing. Others had broken off between courses. The white-coated waiters drifted silently in and out of the tables removing used plates.

'I got some super photographs,' he said. 'The Sé is pretty splendid – that's the cathedral – neglected but all the more photogenic for that. I took some nice ones through the wheel of a broken handcart . . . And the Church of St Cajetan – Romanesque, you'd think. The old monastery – not much left but the tower. And some of the colour-washed houses make good subjects. Little enough colour in the people, though.'

He went on talking but she did not have much to say. Seeing she had finished her meal he said: 'Dance?'

'Later. Mind if I smoke?'

'Like another drink?'

'Yes, please.'

He went away and came back with a bowl of fruit. A waiter brought them drinks and Errol sent them back because one of the glasses did not please him.

Stephanie finished her cigarette. 'I took the brooch back to Krishna.'

He did not say anything until the waiter had returned with fresh glasses. His eyes looked very light coloured in the arc lamps. 'Whatever made you do that?'

'He was round me all day with a pathetic tale that he'd be beaten by his father if he didn't take back the brooch or the money tonight, so I –'

'And you believed him?'

'Yes. Well, yes . . . I waited until after seven. I thought maybe you'd taken off for England and left me to pay the bill.'

'Could you have?'

'No.'

He laughed. 'These little black devils.'

The fun around the pool was becoming furious. Urged on by a dozen people in fancy dress, a chain was forming, each holding another's middle, and jogging round the pool to a South American beat.

'It's an eastern Lambeth Walk,' said Errol. He knitted his eyebrows. 'But the brooch was in the case, my pet. How did you get it?'

'Opened the case. I saw the combination when you got your passport out of it in Bombay.'

'Did you now. I'll be the son of a gun.'

'Warning to you, dear. If you will desert your mistresses they may turn nasty.'

'Well, you'd have had plenty to pay the bill with in there!'

'So I noticed.'

'Notice anything else?'

A fractional hesitation was all she allowed herself. 'Nothing that made much sense. What is flax?'

'Flax is flax, dear. A staple food. Haven't you heard of it?

Makes linseed, textile fibres, candlewicks, God knows what else. You ever heard of a flax wench?'

'No.'

'They were about at one time. Still are in some countries. Manmade fibres don't have it all their own way. It's a very profitable commodity, otherwise we wouldn't handle it.'

'We?'

'I and my companies.'

'I thought you were into theme parks.'

'We're into a lot of things. Business is business. Okay?'

'More or less.'

'What d'you mean, more or less?'

'Are you bending the law a bit somewhere?'

'What makes you think that?'

'I caught a glimpse of a note which said not to worry about customs officers because they could be bought.'

'My word,' he said. 'You have been busy in my absence!'

She flushed. 'Bluebeard's wife, opening the forbidden door.'

'Maybe. But what the hell? We're none of us angels.'

'And anyway, it's none of my business, eh?'

'You said it, but yes . . . Rest assured it's all very minor and innocent. And you're in no way involved.'

When he had finished his meal they danced and drank some more, but he did not offer her any more cookies. Afterwards she refused to sleep with him. She wouldn't make the conventional female excuse.

He didn't like that at all, but she was not giving way. She wanted a long time, a long time to herself, to think.

# *Two*

## I

Naresh Prasad walked down the crowded street towards the tea shop where he was to meet his friend Shyam. He knew himself to be in an awkward situation but did not doubt his ability to talk his way out of it.

It was really only a question of not being able to repay the loan for another month or so. In the privacy of his own room – though Bonni had been there, as she always was, whining under his feet, as was the privilege of a wife – rehearsing in his mind what he had to say, he had felt confident. His reasons for not being able to repay the money this month had seemed reasonable, his excuses excusable, his regrets and pleas could not be disregarded except by a man with a heart of stone. And Shyam Lal Shastri, his old schoolfriend, though noisy and a bit of a bully, was in essence a generous man and would not let him down.

But as he crossed the street, picking his way among the rush-hour traffic, the honking ramshackle taxis, the bicycles, the crowded buses, the thousands of pedestrians hurrying like himself, milling in ant fashion about the shops and the streets, or squatting talking in the gutter amid a babel of noise and hot dust, he had a moment's unease wondering whether Shyam might just possibly cut up rough. Shyam Lal Shastri had been known to cut up rough as a young man and was credited with having stabbed a youth to the point of death in a crowded cinema in a dispute over a girl. It would be a pity if he cut up rough.

The tea shop was at the entrance to a bazaar and opposite a big advertisement for the latest sensational movie, showing – four times life-size – a beautiful Hindu girl being carried off by

38

a bandit. The tea shop was crowded and dark, and it took a minute for Nari to accustom his eyes after the slanting glare of the sun. Then he saw Shyam sitting at a table with a middle-aged bearded man in a white newly pressed cotton suit. At first he thought, he hoped, they were not together but when Shyam saw him he spoke to the older man and the older man nodded.

They were already drinking tea and munching arrowroot biscuits. Nari greeted them both and the middle-aged man was introduced to him as Mr Haji Noor Mohamed. For a moment or two Nari chatted brightly to Shyam, who was the same age as himself and was stout and pockmarked but darkly good-looking if you liked the extrovert type. Mr Mohamed had no small talk and sat silently sipping his tea and watching Nari with deep-set assessing eyes.

No one invited Nari to take tea, so he ordered some for himself. There had been a meeting of the Congress Party yesterday – for some anniversary, and Nari wondered if Mr Mohamed had come from out of town to join the celebrations. The dress was right, but the wearer of it belonged to a different faith.

Out of the blue, as it were, quite without any good reason at all, it seemed, just when they were discussing the ill effects of smog in Bombay and what they must do to clean up the city, and the constant influx of new inhabitants – many thousands a day flocking in from the surrounding countryside – and how some firms were moving their premises to Poona where it was cheaper and cleaner and no union problems, and how lax the city council was in dealing with the matter of over-population – just when the conversation was proceeding very smoothly Shyam broke off and said: 'Have you brought the money to repay your debt, Nari?'

Nari looked, and felt, insulted. That they should be expected to discuss his private affairs in front of a complete stranger . . .

'Look, Shyam, with all the good will in the world towards you, I do not think it is suitable –'

'It is very suitable,' interrupted Shyam. 'Mr Mohamed knows all about our little arrangement, for it is from him that I borrowed the money to lend to you.'

'You . . . borrowed the money . . . ?'

'From Mr Mohamed. How else would I find such money myself?'

This was a bit of a thunderbolt, and Nari found it hard to believe that Shyam should have done any such outrageous thing. Shyam came of a good family. His father was a Brahmin and they had land somewhere in the hills between Bombay and Ahmadnagar. A bit of a thunderbolt.

'Mr Mohamed, I will tell you, is not a professional money-lender. Oh dear, no, nothing of the sort. He is a gentleman of private means whom I have known for some time, and when I told him of your predicament – your temporary predicament – he was quite willing to help – temporarily – a young lawyer in distress. That is why I have brought him with me this afternoon so that when you repay him in person you can thank him for his generosity. And only eight per cent interest! Not any of your twenty-five or thirty per cent interest such as a moneylender would charge!'

Nari burned his lips on the scalding tea. A little went down and helped to nerve him for his exercise in apologetics.

'Alas,' he began, 'my life has not gone according to my plans this month. My wife, Bonni, has been ill, and you know what doctors charge. Then I have had the misfortune to have one of her relatives – an aunt – staying with us, and the old lady has eaten me out of house and home. Furthermore . . .'

He listed the other misfortunes that had befallen him which unhappily made him unable to repay any of the loan this month. Next month would be far better. Next month he would not have to face again any of the expenses he had just listed which had come on him so unexpectedly and undeservedly of late.

When he was at school the English teacher had used a quota-tion – was it from Shakespeare? – *The lady doth protest too much*, and it crossed Nari's mind that this was what he was doing now; but he could not stop. Under the contemptuous gaze of his school chum and the penetrating but expressionless stare of Mr Mohamed he could not control his tongue and he went on, justi-fying, apologising, excusing.

When at last he fell silent – a local silence amid the mindless hubbub and clatter of the café – Mr Mohamed lowered his gaze and began to turn round and round a thick gold ring on the second finger of his left hand. He had altogether six gold rings on one hand and five on the other, most of them set with stones or seals. He also had a gold bracelet, a gold wristwatch and a gold tiepin.

He said in a guttural undertone: 'You have been playing poker again.'

Nari swallowed something thick in his throat. In the last month he had only been to the Hotel Welcome three times and he could not understand how this stranger could possibly know. Who had told him? Shyam did not know. Could Bonni have spoken to someone? Or was it just a bluff?

'Twice,' he admitted. 'But once I went to take tea with my friends there, and the other time I lost nothing of consequence. I sat down at the table for barely half an hour, just to be friendly, with my friends, you understand.'

'Then why have you no money?'

'I have tried to explain, sir. And I am only a clerk. My monthly salary is –'

'I know what your monthly salary is. The whole of it for four weeks –'

'I have to live, sir, and maintain a sick wife.'

'You should have thought of that before you borrowed money to pay your gambling debts.'

The three men stared at each other.

Shyam said loudly: 'Look here, Nari, we must have this out, see? Two months now you have owed me this money. Mr Mohamed has lost patience. You must pay up or suffer the consequences.'

Nari had about 150 rupees in a secret pocket inside his shirt to protect it from pickpockets. He dug this out and laid it on the table.

'This is all I have now. This is all I have in the world! We are in rented rooms and there is nothing I can sell. On Friday week I shall have my pay, but on that I have to live for all the next month – to keep a wife, to pay the rent, to eat enough to stay alive . . .'

His voice trailed off as he saw neither of the men was interested.

Mr Mohamed made a contemptuous gesture towards the money. 'Put that away. It is of no consequence, that trifling sum. I too have my masters, and it will be necessary to pay them the whole sum this week and no more delay.'

Nari looked from one to the other. 'What can I do?'

'You should have thought of that before.'

'You cannot send me to prison! It was a friendly loan from a schoolfriend! I signed no paper! I could be convicted of nothing!' Gaining confidence, he gathered up the notes and thrust them back into his shirt pocket. 'I am sorry, sir. I did not know you had lent this money, and I will certainly repay it next month.'

Mr Haji Noor Mohamed waved away the flies that had settled on the table where Nari in his agitation had spilled a drop of tea.

'Not to prison,' he said. 'Oh, not to prison. We could not do that . . .'

'Well, then,' said Nari, feeling better. 'But I promise next month –'

'We will send two men,' said Mr Mohamed. 'They will break your legs.'

The noise outside was now deafening. A traffic jam had built up and all the horns were blaring, men cursing, bicycle bells ringing. A policeman was thrusting his way through the crowd to see what was amiss.

What was not amiss was Nari's hearing. Although Mr Mohamed spoke low the young man could not fail to hear the words spoken. At first his mind would not credit them. Then he broke out in a sweat which even in that heated atmosphere seemed cold.

He turned his eyes affrightedly to his friend Shyam Lal Shastri, but Shyam had a finger inside his mouth picking one of his back teeth. His expression was sullen and emotionless. If it meant anything it meant there was no help being offered by him.

42

'You . . .' Nari choked. 'How could that be? . . . No one would do such a thing . . .'

There was no reply. Nari knew, alas, that such things could happen; among the gangs and petty criminals of Bombay such things could certainly occur. Behind the racecourse, and in the back streets where the prostitutes lived and down by the docks. But not – it did not, could not happen to an educated, respectable, law-abiding solicitor's clerk, just because by misfortune he had fallen in debt to the tune of a few thousand rupees.

Mr Mohamed was getting up. He was a short man when he rose, a stout man with short legs, but no less formidable for that. A gold earring glinted.

'I shall be going. Think the matter over, Naresh Prasad. I will give you twenty-four hours more. Return your answer to Shyam Lal Shastri at this time and this place tomorrow. I bid you both good day.'

Neither of them had the nerve to try to stop him leaving. He moved stockily out among the tables, among the clatter of tin cups and the shouts of thirsty drinkers and the yapping muzzled dogs, and was soon lost sight of among taller men.

Nari slumped down in his seat, feeling faint and sick. Bile rose in his throat and was only just choked back. Shyam sat quietly beside him, brushing away the flies again.

'By all that's holy!' Nari broke out. 'You have put me into this position! You, my old schoolfriend, that I trusted and hoped would help me! Who is this man? How dare you borrow money from such a one with the pretence of lending it to me yourself –'

'Shut up!' snapped Shyam. 'This is all your own doing! Gambling on your salary is begging for trouble. What else did you expect? A lawyer's clerk with a wife to keep and many of her relations too, how could you expect to play poker and not run into such trouble? You are a fool, man! I tried to help you but what do you do? Go back to the tables and squander more! How much more are you in debt? How much more?'

'Shyam,' Nari said, 'I owe nothing except the seven thousand rupees. But that is enough –'

'It is more than enough!'

'Tell me – this man – he will not carry out his threat? It is far outside the law –'

'Oh yes, he will, Nari. I regret, very much regret, to tell you that he will. It is not an agreeable situation –'

'There are moneylenders,' Nari said wildly. 'I must find one tomorrow morning! What's the matter? Why do you shake your head?'

'Of course you can find one. But this will only put off the day of reckoning by a month at most. Then you will soon be owing ten thousand rupees instead of seven thousand.'

'Then what can I *do*? What do you suggest?'

'It is not for me to suggest,' Shyam said. 'You have only yourself to blame.'

'That's not true!' Nari was furious. 'Yes, I have been extravagant – it is hard not to overstep the mark on the pittance I get. But it was you who lent me the money, not that man! You should be the one to suffer for such a wicked deed! . . . Here, where are you going?'

'Home. I am not here to be insulted. You must find your own way out of this.'

Nari clutched his sleeve and the chair fell over. The man next to them protested and shouted that he was a clumsy fellow, and by the time Nari had pacified him Shyam was out in the street.

Nari ran after him, again grasped his arm. Shyam tried to shake himself free but this time could not. He faced about.

'Leave me alone!'

'That I cannot do! What am I to do now? Tell me, what am I to do? You are my friend. We have known each other for twenty years . . .'

A beggar, a holy man, half-naked and smeared in grey ash was trying to attract their attention and their pity, holding his begging bowl in both hands and pushing it between them. Nari ignored the man but Shyam gave him half a rupee. Out here the heat of the city, generated through the day, had become overpowering, and blue petrol fumes were everywhere.

Shyam said with his usual coldness: 'Seventeen years to be

44

exact. I did not meet you until I was nine. And that was a bad day for us both.'

'What can I do?' Nari asked again. 'You must *advise* me! These thugs – they will kill me. *You* are responsible!'

'Let me tell you once again it was your own stupid fault! A petty clerk trying to live like a king! I helped you out of my kindness of heart. Out of my kindness of heart, I tell you! I thought you could save enough to repay Mr Mohamed. But you did not reform. Now . . .'

Nari waited. A boy without legs crouched on a trolley was trying to sell them a newspaper.

'Now there is only one possibility which is only just occurring to me. But are you the man for it, I wonder? This is not boy's work I am thinking of.'

'What is it? Tell me. Please tell me. I will do anything to get out of this dreadful predicament!'

Shyam scratched his pockmarked nose. 'No, on considering you, I do not think you have the strength of character.'

'At least tell me, so that I can say yes or no! That at least you owe me! What is it you're suggesting?'

The other young man shook his head. 'I can tell you nothing now. But I will think it over.'

'There is no time!'

'Yes, there is. Meet me outside the India Coffee House at one o'clock tomorrow afternoon. I will have made enquiries and will know more then. Ask for an extra hour off. There will be time then for you to consider it before we meet Mr Mohamed at five.'

# II

Bonni's marriage to Naresh had been arranged by their parents, and, since she came from a village in the foothills behind the city, it had been thought a good match. Nari was studying law and would soon be qualified and able to take a partnership or to set up on his own. In the meantime a clerkship with an established firm gave him time to study and a small but manageable income, and they had two rooms and a verandah to begin their married life.

But Bonni was soon dissatisfied. She was a pretty girl with a pretty girl's love of colourful, pretty things and she found Nari a disappointing husband. Once the first flush of his interest in her had gone he was out most nights instead of studying, and spending money which should have gone to keep them both in a degree of comfort. She went to the movies with girl friends and whined complaints at him when he came in late. Presently it became clear even to Bonni, though he tried to hide it from her, that he was not clever enough or industrious enough to pass his law exams, and it seemed probable that he would remain a typing and filing clerk for the rest of his days. Bonni did not produce children, and complained of anaemia and general neglect. Nari's complaint was that Bonni had an endless succession of relatives to stay, that the flat was never without one or two, chattering and whispering and sleeping on the charpoy on the balcony. One week it was her mother, then an aunt or a cousin or a sister, or sometimes all three. They whispered together in corners when Nari was about, criticising him. It was a woman's world in which a single man was dominant but alone.

Tonight he came in early but spoke only a few words to Bonni before going to the bedroom. A sister, Kamala, had arrived that afternoon, and she was a woman Nari particularly disliked. When Bonni came into the bedroom and asked if he had eaten, if he was ill, he said no and he was not hungry, he just wanted to be left alone.

The night was a long one and he scarcely slept at all, turning and tossing, with semiwaking nightmares of men with shining shaven skulls creeping up the stairs with hammers to break his legs. Bonni moaned in her sleep every time he turned over. In the end, just when dawn was showing up the dust on the encrusted fanlight, and the sparrows were beginning to chirp and chatter, he fell into a deep slumber and was wakened by Bonni shaking his shoulder and telling him he would be late for work. He stumbled to his feet, rinsed his face in some lukewarm water, made a pretence of shaving, and then bent over the potatoes and radishes his wife had prepared for him. He was hardly able to force the food down, his knees weak with fear and his stomach churning. When Bonni asked him for money to pay the baker he snapped at her and dropped a few rupees on the table saying it was all he had. He was down to his last anna, he said. Then he drew on his jacket and went out into the early heat of the day, leaving behind him a discontented woman exchanging complaints and criticisms of him with her ill-favoured sister.

It was an hour's journey to the centre of the city from the suburb where he lived, and the train was more madly crowded than ever. Its sweating mass of humanity packed the carriages with scarcely room to move an elbow, and coming home he knew it would be worse, with travellers virtually fighting to get on the train at Churchgate Station. He walked to his office which was close by in a sidestreet off Vir Nariman Road near the High Court.

The morning went slowly. Mr Srivastavar, one of the six partners in the law firm, and Nari's immediate boss, was not in the best of tempers, which was not surprising as Nari's typing yesterday had been full of mistakes, and also he had filed some letters under the wrong name. Mr Srivastavar told him that if he did not improve he would be sacked. There was plenty of unemployment, he pointed out, among the lesser educated students of Bombay, and replacing one unsatisfactory worker would be the simplest thing in the world.

Nari took the rebukes meekly and apologised and said he would do better. But he did not dare to ask for an hour off. If his business with Shyam was not completed in time he would have to be late back and make up some story about an accident.

The last hour dragged by at last and he slipped out quickly for fear some other member of the staff should come with him; then he walked to the India Coffee House and stood behind a parked car and waited for Shyam Lal Shastri.

One o'clock. Ten past one. Twenty past one. At twenty-five past he saw Shyam strolling through the crowds, coolly, as if there was no hurry. Nari rushed up to him.

'You are late! My God, you are late, man! What has kept you?'

47

Shyam was wearing a brilliant purple shirt and clean white trousers. He looked as if he did not have a care in the world. Nari grasped his arm and Shyam looked down at Nari's hand with contempt.

'Let me loose or I will tell you nothing. There, that is better. Do you want to talk here, in this crowd?'

'Wherever you please, so long as you tell me what I can do!'

Shyam looked around and sniffed. 'Well, it makes no difference. We shall not be overheard. Are you a man or just a weakling? That is what I must know first.'

'Tell me what you have come to tell me.'

'I can give you the opportunity – through friends of mine I can give you the opportunity to break free of your shackles, to discharge your debts, to become a free man again. How would you like that?'

'What do I have to do?'

Shyam laughed in his face, showing his gold teeth, the spittle at the corners of his mouth.

'Almost nothing. You will have a pleasant trip to England, all expenses paid. Your debt will be cancelled here and you will receive a handsome bonus in England for your trouble. How does that appeal to you?'

Nari stumbled over the broken pavement, and a motor-bike, accelerating away, narrowly missed him.

England? This did not make sense. Where was the catch? He had always wanted to go to England.

'You have cousins there, *bhai*?'

'Yes. Two. But –'

'So then you can visit them! What better? You will have to take several weeks off. If you wish to go you will leave perhaps at the end of the month. Tell me if you wish to go.'

Nari stopped. People were brushing around him, talking, arguing, shopping, begging.

'I must carry something?'

Shyam laughed again. 'Quite so. Good guess. But nothing big. Do you wish me to go further?'

They had been walking down the street and were now at the

48

corner of a wide square, with policemen directing the traffic. The morning smog had cleared and the sun beat down out of a sky stretched pale by the heat.

'Mark you, you are still quite uncommitted so far,' said Shyam. 'You are free to say no to my friends. They will bear you no ill will. You can walk away right now – although at five this afternoon you will be expected to produce the necessary for Mr Mohamed, and you know the consequences if you do not.'

'I wish to go further,' Nari said, speaking with a thick tongue.

'Then come with me. It is only two streets away. Have you ever met Dr Kabir Amora?'

Nari shook his head.

'I think you could still withdraw,' said Shyam, 'but then they wouldn't like it because they would think you might talk. And if they thought you had talked then you would be in the deepest trouble it is possible for any man to be in. Two broken legs would be nothing, my dear old chap.'

Nari stopped again.

'What must I carry? Tell me. You are my friend – or have pretended to be.'

'Just little packets. But let Dr Amora explain.'

# III

'*Swallow* them!' screamed Nari. 'What are you asking me to do? It is not possible!'

'It is not even difficult,' said Dr Amora. He was a short man with a white, opaque left eye and a chain of holy beads round his neck. 'You will see. Many have done it. Few have failed. It is only a matter of practice.'

'*Practice!*'

'Yes. With grapes. We have two weeks before you need to go. We will start tomorrow.'

Nari glared wildly round the bare little room, seeking some escape. There were a few empty medicine bottles on the table,

49

an open attaché case containing pillboxes, a consultancy couch with broken springs, a framed diploma. There was a heavy smell of jasmine in the air, and a holy garland hung round the neck of a small statue of a monkey god in a corner. How could this man, a Punjabi by his accent, be doing such work, have any religious beliefs at all – even of the most depraved kind?

'I could not do it! And retain them in my stomach for more than twenty-four hours! Never!'

'They will remain in your bowels, not your stomach,' Dr Amora said. 'And about that you have no cause to worry. You will first take half a dozen pills. They are the pills used by astronauts to slow down the bowel motion. You will pass no motion for four days. It is quite simple, I assure you. It is quite foolproof. There is no need to worry.'

'And if I say no! If I refuse! If I want no part of this!'

Amora exchanged glances with Shyam, then he shrugged. 'Your friend will have told you you have now gone too far to say no. Now you know too much, Naresh Prasad. You have become one of us.'

The windows were shut, the scent of the jasmine oversweet, like an anaesthetic.

Dr Amora shifted his stomach to a more comfortable position. His wall eye stared straight ahead. 'This time tomorrow at one? We will be starting with a few grapes.'

Shyam put a heavy, now friendly arm round Nari's shoulders. 'Think what you gain, *bhai*. Your debts discharged! Four weeks in England to visit your cousins! And a thousand pounds sterling in cash to spend or to bring home – am I right, Kabir? I am right – a thousand pounds sterling in cash to spend in England or to bring home! Many men would give their ears for such a chance!'

'And if I am caught? Ten years in a British jail!'

'You won't be caught! This is too clever a device.'

'What am I swallowing? If one of the packets breaks open the contents will kill me!'

'They don't break open,' said Dr Amora. 'It has never been known to happen.'

50

Nari felt faint, he felt he wanted to die. The heat in here was intense, claustrophobic.

'I do not know if I can do it. I do not think I can swallow –'

'Tomorrow at one,' said Dr Amora. 'We will be starting with a few grapes.'

# *Three*

## I

It was a sunny day towards the end of April when James Locke
had the telephone call from his daughter. He never had an over-
coat but wore a motoring cap and a muffler to protect himself
from the chill wind. He was in a distant part of his garden looking
at two specimens of the rhododendron Loderi Venus which he
had grown from cuttings and which were almost ready to plant
out in their permanent places. It was a good piece of land here,
with a few tall beeches and pines and a nice woodsy acid soil of
around pH 4–5. Not moist enough, but judicious spraying did
the trick. About him were a number of his earlier plantings,
*macabeanum*, which had flowered for the first time last year,
*falconeri*, not too happy in spite of all its cosseting, a fine mag-
nolia, Leonard Messel, in full bloom, another, *campbellii alba*, a
big tree now but one for which he knew he would have to wait
some years yet for the first bud.

He had a cordless telephone attached to his wheelchair and
as soon as it buzzed he wiped his soiled hands and picked it
up.

'Daddy?'

'Hello, poppet. Safely back, then?'

'You know I am. Rang from Heathrow. Remember?'

'Perfectly. I consider the last thirty miles of your journey the
most hazardous.'

'Ho-ho. Look, I could come home this weekend.'

'What's stopping you?'

'Only you, if you have anything on.'

'Not a stitch. You know I'm a lonely old man.'

'Oh, come off it. So you don't mind if I hazard my life on the Oxfordshire roads?'

'Not in such a good cause.'

'Brilliant. See you Sat'day. Lunch on Sat'day?'

'I'll tell Mrs Aldershot.'

'How is she, by the way?'

'Very well. I see her approaching.'

'Daddy, why don't you marry her?'

James Locke was thinking of the appropriate reply when his daughter rang off. He hung up the telephone and pressed the electric button to activate his chair. He met Mrs Aldershot where the path came out of the woodland and the herbacious borders began.

Locke was now nearly sixty-five, markedly handsome though becoming stout, with greying hair streaked with white, a slim aristocratic nose and lips, a man who looked more a cleric than a gardener, certainly far more the bookish epicure than the war hero he had once been. A limp, which thereafter had been his, grew worse and in the last four years he had been in a wheelchair, though perfectly capable of getting out of it, to take a bath, to go to bed, to tend his garden, to write his gardening articles, to sit at table. He was seldom ever quite out of pain, but the discomfort was minimised if he took pills and did not try to stand or walk too much.

Mary Aldershot was forty-five, his housekeeper, long divorced, still attractive, capable in all domestic things, strongly opinioned on a few. She had been with Locke almost since his wife left him. He called her Mary but she still called him Mr James. Stephanie would not have had the cheek to put such a suggestion to her father face to face, but over the telephone it was easier.

In fact James had asked Mrs Aldershot to marry him four years ago and she had refused.

'Was that Miss Stephanie?' she asked. 'I took up the phone until I heard you answer.'

'She's coming for lunch on Saturday and staying the night. She may, I suppose, stay Sunday night too, but the chances are

53

she'll drive back on Sunday evening, leaving here at some ungodly hour when all decent girls should be safely asleep.'

'Duck,' said Mrs Aldershot. 'She loves that, and Maker's had some lovely ones in last week.'

'Be sure there's plenty on them.'

She patted his shoulder. 'As if I would not. And smoked salmon. Cheese. Cheese and fruit – would that do to end? What about Sunday?'

'We'll think it over. How long's lunch today?'

'Twenty minutes.'

'Caviar, I suppose.'

'Wait and see.'

'Be off then. If you ring your bell I'll be in one of the greenhouses.'


# II


Janet Locke, a clever febrile artistic wayward young woman, had left her husband when Teresa was nine and Stephanie six. She had met Frederick Agassia, a rich young Brazilian, at a function in London and presently the attraction was too much for her and she very regretfully abandoned James and their two daughters and went away with Agassia to Rio. Five years later she was killed in a car crash, so James became a widower *de facto* as well as *de jure*. In those days he had been much more mobile; but the desertion had cut a deep ravine in his mind which he was careful not to show.

Of his daughters Teresa was the cheerful conformist, Stephanie the cheerful rebel. These days, of course, everyone had affairs at the drop of a hat, marriage being the non-U word, but Stephanie's overt liaison with this Errol Colton was a little too reminiscent for comfort of her mother's sudden upsurge of passion for Frederick Agassia.

True, that had seemed to last. He had reluctantly gone through with the divorce, and, so far as he knew to the contrary, Janet and Frederick had been living in unalloyed bliss when the bus

54

driver coming towards her dozed off to sleep. So it could be that Stephanie, side-stepping her mother's early marriage, had found the love of her life at almost the first shot. James very much wanted to meet Errol. He knew, of course, that even if he disliked him on sight he would be unlikely to influence Stephanie – she being a girl who knew her own mind. Nor, God help him, would he ever attempt to.

But Errol Colton had been married twice already and presumably was still living with his second wife and daughter; he was well-to-do in some not precisely defined way connected with tourist development, and he was a lot older than Stephanie. How much more easy and unperturbing Teresa was, meeting and quickly marrying a talented young accountant, settling in suburbia and thoroughly enjoying it, expecting her first child in July. She and her husband seemed quite uninfluenced by the modern fashion which would have condemned their way of life as stuffy and old-fashioned.

Stephanie arrived in her yellow Mini at 12.30, and, since it was another fine day, James whirred himself down to the gates to meet her. Since going to Oxford she had seen very little of her father, even though he lived a bare fifty miles away. All the same, their being together was always pleasant, and whenever she left she told herself it wouldn't be so long next time. But it was.

At the house he ran his chair up the ramp to avoid the three steps and kissed her and hobbled with her into the drawing room. Presently Mary Aldershot came in and they shook hands and all had a drink together. Then the older woman went off to prepare lunch, refusing Stephanie's cheerful offer of help.

It was a large enough house for Mrs Aldershot to have her own set of rooms. Dinner she had every night with James; at breakfast and lunch they kept to their separate apartments. Over lunch Stephanie chatted brightly about her fabulous trip to India, her *lovely* trip to India, and was only waiting for an opportunity to go again. James had been once, briefly, to Calcutta and had found the poverty appalling. Travelling as Stephanie had travelled, she had seen little of it, and she thought conditions had much improved since her father was there.

James had sensitive antennae where his daughters were concerned, and he thought there was a shade of darkness in Stephanie he had not perceived before. In spite of her tan she did not look particularly well. Of course, for two years now she had lived a life that at one time would have been called rackety. She moved in a fast set, kept unearthly hours, took quite a lot of drink. Young, optimistic, with perfect health, she had taken life in her stride. Well, the clear bell of her nature was still ringing, but somewhere there was a hairline crack. Errol was referred to casually and without the least discomposure, but James's perception was that he was not mentioned often enough. Since there had always been great frankness between father and daughter, it seemed unlikely that she was restricting her references to spare him embarrassment.

As always when home, she was full of interest in the garden and they spent a couple of hours after lunch looking at the things he was growing, and discussing them. Even though it was still only April, the mild winter had brought things forward and there was a show of early bloom.

Looking at her, blonde ponytailed, slim and elegant and leggily feminine, James was visited by a sudden rush of affection for his younger daughter. He had been in love with his wife, and Stephanie was in many ways like her, impulsive, overtalkative, nervously acute, with a glowing aliveness and a total inability to dissemble. He was not often a man to show his feelings, but sometimes they bubbled up and made him emotional. He turned away from Stephanie to hide his expression and glowered at a Tai-haku cherry which was holding back from bloom as if undeceived by the false sunshine.

'Do you know about drugs?' Stephanie asked, plucking at a weed.

'Drugs? What sort? The forbidden sort? No. Why?'

'There's a fair amount in Oxford, of course. Not just among undergraduates but in the town. I've tried smoking a joint a few times and eating some other stuff but it doesn't seem to work for me. At least, it works after a fashion but I get a filthy head the next day.'

'Ah,' said James. 'Good thing, I suppose.'

'Yes. Maybe.'

They talked about plants for a bit, then James brought the subject back.

'I've lived an average life and seen a fair share of the seamy side. But, honestly, where drugs are concerned I'm a newborn babe. I don't know the first thing about them.'

She smiled slowly. 'You're the wrong generation.'

'Pretty well, yes. They were certainly never a major problem. Though I did know one youngish woman . . .'

'Oh?'

'Husband killed in the war, so she went to live with her brother, who was a doctor. Somehow she got her hands on the morphine. Started injections, two a day – went up to four, then to six, before he found out.'

'What then?'

'She went for a cure. Came out after two months. Completely cured – for a bit. Then went on the streets to get the money to buy the stuff. I'm not sure what happened to her in the end.'

'There was a case in Headington last month,' Stephanie said after a minute. 'Nothing to do with the university. A chemist's assistant. He was hooked – on heroin, I think – and took an overdose and died. It didn't make the headlines.'

They moved between two shrub borders. 'Damned birds,' said James. 'They've taken nearly all the forsythia.'

'I thought you liked birds.'

'In their proper place. But they're mischievous little buggers . . . Why this sudden interest in drugs?'

'It isn't a sudden interest. I just feel maybe if I take no notice of it I'm living with my head in the sand. Time I woke up, observed the world as it is today, took an attitude.'

'Attitude?'

'Well, not like the Statue of Liberty! But this is the new scene for our generation, isn't it, and I thought maybe I should make up my mind about it.'

'Whether to take them or not?'

57

'No, *no*. I'm not even *interested*. Whether I'm actually *against* them – in other people, I mean.'

'Pro or con?'

'Pro or con. I've always taken the view that what other people do is not my business. If somebody finds that smoking a reefer gives them a lift and enables them to enjoy life more fully, well, then, that's their affair. Isn't it? We go our own way, live our own lives. None of this "for whom the bell tolls" rubbish. Correct?'

'Correct enough.'

'It's too bad if the marijuana smoker finds it not doing its stuff any longer and drifts into the hard drugs, really gets hooked and finally kills himself. Along the way there's a lot of suffering and crime, but there's a lot of suffering and crime in the world anyhow. What business is it of mine?'

'Indeed. None at all, I might say.'

'You might say . . . Of course I like my drink. So do you. But I don't see any signs of addiction in you, and I hope I shall not see any in me. But some girl at St Martin's might get addicted to good old mother's ruin, and her downfall, if less dramatic, could still take place. Couldn't it? There she is, a soak, sitting on the pavement outside a pub with a bottle in her hand, too gassed to find her way home. That isn't the new scene; that's the old scene. A great one in Victorian times! But is it any more my fault or my responsibility or your fault or your responsibility than the man with the syringe or the pills?'

They had moved as far as that part of the garden given over to the purely acid-loving plants.

'These are new *yakushimanum* hybrids,' James explained. 'It's been one of the finest rhododendron finds of the last forty years, and it's going to give rise to scores of new plants, all small and sturdy, and of almost all colours. Unfortunately, most of the hybrids don't have the marvellous leathery-tomentose leaves of the parent. I have high hopes of a couple of them.'

'What a name! Where does it come from?'

'Japan. It's an island there, Yakushima. Stephanie.'

'Yes?'

'I'm not sure yet why you feel you have to take a pro or con attitude to the particular problem at this particular time. As a direct decision not as a generality? Is that what you mean? Something has come up and you need to make a choice.'

He studied the curve of her cheek, which was all he could see just now. She said: 'I suppose you could say that.'

'Some special friend of yours is in danger of getting hooked, and you want to know how far you'd be justified in trying to stop him?'

'Not altogether that.' Stephanie fingered the furry brown underside of a rhododendron leaf. 'Rather more than that. I'm thinking of the distribution side.'

James activated his chair to move around her so that while apparently looking at a plant he could get a better view of her face.

'Distribution. Ah yes, well, that's rather another kettle of fish.'

'Why is it?' she said. 'Tell me why it is.' Her tone was sharp, aggressive.

Surprised, he said: 'I would have thought that evident, wouldn't you?'

'Well, just tell me why.'

'The drug barons make their illegal millions out of the poor suckers who buy their stuff. I've always regretted that the death penalty never operated for people like that.'

The sun was shining in her eyes. Her mouth looked pinched. She said quite angrily: 'But there are two standards, aren't there? These men who smuggle in marijuana and heroin are breaking a manmade law, and so are those who push it on the streets and so are those who use it. But this is just an arbitrary law, dividing one kind of addiction from another. You want the death penalty for the drug barons but not for the drink barons or the tobacco barons. You wouldn't consider being even in the same *room* as a man who imported cocaine from Colombia, but you'd mix, and be pleased to mix, with a Guinness or a Haig or a Wills! Where's the difference?'

James looked at her for a few moments, then pressed his button. 'Let me show you the new daffodils.'

They went on. He said: 'Are you angry with me, Stephanie, or with yourself?'

She laughed, but there was not much amusement in it. 'Did you ever play pelota, Daddy?'

'I played squash.'

'Yes, well, you're the wall I'm banging the ball against.' She bent and kissed his forehead.

He said: 'So in fact *you* are having to make a choice?'

'Not a *choice* so much as a value judgment. Nothing more than that.'

'Well, here the con's pretty heavy, isn't it. As I told you, I'd string up the distributors.'

'Every one?'

'Every one.'

'That's a lovely daffodil.'

'Golden Ducat. It's been on the market ten years or more now. Only slight disadvantage is the flower is so heavy it's sometimes too weighty for the stem. I believe they're breeding that out; but of course here I haven't the facilities.'

'You say you lost touch with your friend who took to morphine. Was that a long time ago?'

'Oh, before I married. I did go and see her once in the clinic. Not an agreeable experience.'

'She knew you?'

'Oh, she knew me well enough. She was just thin, frail, irritable, eyes shrunken, not able to keep still, much changed from the attractive woman I'd known.'

'Have you heard me speak of Sir Peter Brune?'

'Brune? I know his name. He gives a lot of money away. And he wrote that definitive book on – was it? – Aristophanes.'

'I met him last autumn. Well, he's got this lovely house called Postgate, north of Oxford, not far from Woodstock. As it happens, that was where I met Errol. I like him very much – Peter Brune, I mean. A thoroughly nice man. And he's a great benefactor of St Martin's, so they like him there too. Someone told me that he financed a clinic for drug addicts in Reading. I might . . .'

'Might what?'

'Ring him next week, ask him if I could visit it. To see what people are like there.'

'It's so important to you?'

'Yes, it is. There are certain things. I want to make up my mind about things. This might help a bit. It might even help a lot.'

'Did you think of seeing Henry Gaveston?'

'What, the Bursar? The Col? What would he know about it?'

'About drugs specifically, I'm not sure. But he has close links with the police, and he's likely to be fairly well briefed on most aspects of the seedy side of undergraduate life.'

'I thought he was SAS?'

'He has been. Among other things. If you wanted a view of the drug scene in Oxford he'd be sure to know.'

'Yes?' said Stephanie, doubtfully. 'Yes, I might do that.'

'But see your Peter Brune first. He might just be able to do the trick for you, whatever trick it is you want.'

# III

Mrs Aldershot did not dine with them that night. She had been quite adamant, so James acquiesced on condition they should all go out to Sunday lunch together.

As well as knowing a lot about plants James knew a lot about wine, and Stephanie, when she was home, always regretted not coming home more often. This was civilised drinking. They started with a Sancerre, moved to a Montrose, and ended with a Coutet. On this occasion, feeling the need, James had rather gone to town. It not only unlocked Stephanie's tongue but his own.

Towards the end of the meal he said: 'And your affair with Errol Colton – it's really serious?'

'Daddy, of course it's really serious! I'm not a tart! I wouldn't rush off to India with some boyfriend just for the fun of it!'

'Begging your pardon, then. But Errol, I gather, has a wife. May it not become embarrassing?'

'Oh, yes, maybe. It *might* have been. But . . . I think it may be over now.'

'*What?* Your affair with Errol?'

'Yes,' she said in a small voice.

'*That's* a surprise. Since when?'

'Since we came home.'

James sipped his chilled Sauterne. 'So you're not in love with him any more?'

'I didn't say that.'

'Is he out of love with you?'

'Nor that either! But I think we're just coming to the end of the line – to the end of *a* line anyway!'

He said no more for a time. This was the big surprise of the weekend. It was not one he found unwelcome so long as Stephanie was not damaged by it. He thought she was pretty upset. But if they were still in love . . . The idea that young people should sacrifice their affair with each other to preserve a marriage seemed a highly improbable scenario these days.

He held his tongue, afraid to say the wrong thing, waiting for her to continue if she had the mind to.

Eventually she said: 'I'm talking too much. Nothing has been decided.'

'Between you?'

'Not exactly. Chiefly by me. I'm in – deep water.'

'Have you met his wife?'

'Just to say hello. She's very dark, rather brooding. Nice, I thought. But that was before things blew up.'

'His first wife was Greek, wasn't she? I think you told me.'

'Yes. His daughter Polly is his first wife's daughter.'

'If you break up, will he go back to his wife?'

'It isn't like *that*, Daddy,' Stephanie said in some irritation. 'He's never left her!'

He shifted in his chair, for his ankles were aching. They always did when his children were home because he moved out of his chair more.

Stephanie said: 'Perhaps I've been a bad picker, like you.'

62

'I wasn't a bad picker. It was only later on that she picked someone else.'

'Sorry. Pity she didn't go on with her painting. I think some of them are good.'

'So do I,' he said, eyeing a still life on the dining room wall. 'Trouble is, painting's a full-time life of its own, whether you're good or not so good. Maybe she had too many interests.'

'I couldn't paint a shelf,' said Stephanie. 'You've told me I'm a bit like her, but not in that respect.'

'Does Errol paint?'

'No. But he's a nut on photography.'

'I should have liked to meet him.'

'I was going to bring him home. Now it's doubtful, to say the least.'

James saw her eyes. 'It still means a lot to you?'

'Yes – well, yes. I've said so.'

'Who knows? Since I haven't an idea what's troubling you, I can't predict. But it might come all right again.'

Stephanie rubbed the back of her hand across an eye. 'I doubt if you two would have suited each other, anyhow.'

'Whom is that meant specially to insult?'

She smiled. 'I certainly don't know what to make of him half the time! And as for you, I've known you a bit longer, but you still puzzle me.'

'Say on.'

'Is there any more of that Coutet? . . . Thanks. *In vino veritas.* My tongue is loose . . . But you are such a *gentle* man, so mild, so good-mannered, so elegant; butter wouldn't melt. But it *must* have melted at one time.'

'What d'you mean?'

'Well, that perfect *array* of medals in the case in the hall, you didn't get them on a Christmas tree.'

'I was young and rash –'

'Maybe. But does character change all that much, just in the course of a few years?'

'In those days I was acting *out* of character,' James said, but his daughter did not seem to hear.

63

'For instance. For instance, Daddy, when this man came over from Rio and stole your wife, did you not make a – make a fight of it? . . . Or did you? I was too young to remember.'

James lit a cigar. 'There is port but –'

'No, this is delicious. And I'm sure it won't keep till tomorrow!'

He said: 'For a few years when I was young I got into the habit of fighting. It seemed to come easy to me. Maybe some old cutpurse lurks in the family genes. When it was over, then I put all that side behind me. Had to. In answer to your question, did I fight when your mother said she was going to leave me . . . I did my best to keep her, or my worst, if you look at it that way. Yes, I fought, but in a civilised way. it was all very civilised but very bitter just the same.'

'Thank you, Daddy. I'm sure you don't want to go into details. I asked Teresa a couple of times but she's only three years older and doesn't have a much better memory of it than I have.'

'I'm afraid I've been a very lax single parent.'

'Lenient, yes. Except where grammar and syntax were concerned.'

James laughed. 'Well, it seemed with two daughters on my hands, I couldn't guide them morally, but I did expect 'em to write the Queen's English.'

'I remember so well things you dinned into us. "The verb to be never has an object." "A relative pronoun must be next to its antecedent." "Tommy sits next to his uncle." I wonder if Teresa remembers! I must ask her.'

They finished the Coutet. James's cigar was half-spent. Stephanie lit a cigarette. They had moved from the dining room to the drawing room where a fire burned. The girl stretched her legs gratefully. In this warm cosy atmosphere she was more easy than she had been for many weeks. All the grievous, heart-wrenching problems remained unsolved, but just now they were outside the walls of this house. Here was a sort of sanctuary.

James said: 'When a woman takes it into her heart and her head and her guts to fall in love with a man, there's not much one can do to restrain her. You ought to know! When it happens, as in my case, it was *another* man, there are very few barriers one can put up. Even her love for her children didn't quite weigh heavily enough in the balance.'

'I think you loved us more than she did.'

'That's an assumption based on the event. I don't think it follows.'

'It was a funny old visit Teresa and I paid her. They did their best to make us feel welcome; but it was all rather brittle. It's a brittle city.'

They sat silent for a while. 'Well, just in case you don't know it,' Stephanie said, 'I love you very much.'

'This must be the drink working on you,' he said brusquely, seeing the tears in her eyes and feeling them in his own. '*In vino lachryma*, as they say in dog Latin.'

'Talking of dogs, why don't you keep one?'

'They make messes in the garden. But that isn't why I don't marry Mary Aldershot.'

Stephanie crowed with laughter.

'Incidentally,' James said, 'this concern for my welfare is quite exceptional. I must boast to Teresa about it, try to make her jealous.'

'How is she?'

'Heavily preggers. But enjoying it, I think.'

'One thing about Teresa, she really does enjoy everything.'

'Don't you?'

'Not everything. Not by any means everything.'

'Including, no doubt, your impending break up with Errol Colton.'

'Very much including that,' said Stephanie.

# *Four*

## I

Stephanie said: 'Could I speak to Sir Peter Brune, please?'

'Who may I ask is calling?' She recognised the voice of John Peron, Peter Brune's secretary and general assistant.

'Stephanie Locke.'

'Mrs Locke?'

'Miss Locke. I spent a weekend . . .'

'Of course. My apologies. I am not sure whether Sir Peter is on another line, but will you hold?'

She waited, examining the fingers of her right hand which showed a stain from nicotine. Why did one over-smoke when one was in a dilemma?

'Stephanie?' The unmistakable, cultured, amused-sounding voice with its slight Welsh accent.

'Sir Peter. I –'

'My dear, how nice to hear from you!' He sounded as if he meant it. 'It's time you came to see us again. Were you ringing me to remind me?'

She laughed. 'Hardly . . . I just wanted –'

'How is Errol? I believe you've been off somewhere with him.'

'Yes. He's well.'

'I bear some of the responsibility for it all, since you first met him at my house.'

'I absolve you.'

'Where was it – India – you went?'

'Yes. It was very good. Sir Peter . . .' She hesitated.

'As the shop-gals say, can I help you?'

'I'm not sure. Now it comes to the point, I'm not quite sure

66

why I'm bothering you. It is true, isn't it, that you run a clinic
– or finance a clinic – for the treatment of drug addicts?'

'Not exactly. But I know what you mean. You're probably
talking about the Worsley Clinic outside Reading. I'm on the
board of that.'

'And that treats . . . ?'

'Well, it was not started exclusively for the treatment of drug
addiction but that is its main purpose nowadays. Advanced cases.
Often people are sent to us when ordinary hospitals have had a
go and failed. Lord Worsley started it years ago, when addiction
was a minor blackspot, but it's grown with the problem. Privately
financed. We try to charge people according to their means.
There's always a minimum of twenty-five per cent getting the
treatment free. Was this what you wanted to know?'

'Partly. Thank you.'

'Clearly you don't have a problem yourself. Some friend?'

'No. Not that exactly either.' She struggled to find the words
that would explain sufficiently but not explain too much. She
pictured him sitting there, fingering a cuff link. A big man but
spare, sallow-skinned, deeply lined cheeks, a sardonic charming
mouth, grey hair, probably in his late fifties, not quite the obvious millionaire, not quite the obvious scholar. Long years of
wealth had given him a sense of importance he was quick to
deny. 'I *have* a sort of a problem, but it's one of conscience
or something. I want to make up my mind. God, that sounds
prosy . . .'

'Take your time. I'm in no hurry.'

'Look,' she said. 'I've lived a fairly mayfly sort of life, enjoying
things, not caring much. Drugs were for other people to worry
about. Well, somehow it won't do any longer. One should, I
think, have a point of view, at least. Whether it's something one
mildly dislikes, like a drunk in the street, or – or something
much more.'

'It's no easy problem. There isn't any pure black or pure white
about it. Just endlessly different shades of grey.'

'I expect that's right. But I'm so totally ignorant and I think
it's time I woke up and saw for myself.'

67

'Saw what?'

'I don't know. Just have the opportunity to visit somewhere like the – the Worsley Clinic. See what people look like. See what it means in terms of a human life. You may think it silly but I just don't want to form any judgment from hearsay.'

'With some special purpose in mind?'

'Yes, I suppose so. Lord knows, I'm not the hot gospeller type. I shan't be in the front of any procession. But there's a sort of choice in front of me over the next few weeks. I'd like to be certain – or more certain than I am now. Indeed, I'd like to be very certain. Understand?'

'Not with the greatest clarity. What do you want me to do – arrange for you to visit the Worsley Clinic? In what capacity?'

He waited.

She said: 'I thought . . .' and stopped. 'Well yes, if that's the best way . . . Yes, I'd like to visit the Worsley Clinic. But in what capacity I don't quite know. I haven't any friend there. Clearly they don't want people snooping around at all hours. But I thought –'

'Oh, it can be arranged. The head man is a Dr Charles Bridge. I can telephone him, say you're a friend of mine (which incidentally you are!), say you are studying the subject for a thesis. That do?'

'Brilliant.'

'But I'd warn you, you won't see anything dramatic. Clinics are, well, clinical places . . . Would you like me to come with you?'

She was startled. 'That *would* be kind.' She stopped. 'But Sir Peter, I think no. I don't want any red carpet. I'd just –'

'I promise you they'll be far too occupied to put down a red carpet for anybody. But it's up to you.'

'Well then, thank you. But isn't it too much trouble for you? Aren't you busy buying property – or whatever millionaires do in their spare time?'

He laughed. 'I have a few modest commitments on Wednesday. But I'll ring Bridge in a few minutes and see if he can arrange something tomorrow – I'm certainly free in the afternoon. I'll get Peron to ring you back. What time d'you lunch?'

'I'm due out fairly soon. Back well before two-thirty.'

'We'll ring you at three.'

# II

She blew out a breath as she put the telephone down and resisted the temptation to pull out another cigarette. In spite of a happy self-confidence bolstered by the fact that she knew herself to be intellectually above average and that she found herself attractive to men, she had not relished making the telephone call and the request. Peter Brune was an important man inside the college and out. He had endowed a new library for St Martin's and given them some vast sum for repairs needed to the roof and clock-tower. She had seen him at High Table three or four times, usually dining with the Principal, but she was only a lowly student in the body of the hall. There was talk of his receiving some honour from the university this year. Apart from his benefactions he was also, as her father had remarked, a notable Greek scholar. It was just chance that she had got invited to Postgate, and during the weekend there, though always charming, he had had a variety of other guests and hadn't had all that much time to talk to her.

So the telephone call might have been looked on as a presumption. Instead it had gone well, and his offer to accompany her was specially flattering. Sir Peter was not married, apparently never had been, and, if there were those to suggest he was not the marrying kind, that made it all the more complimentary that he should be so obliging.

After all the nagging worry, she felt disproportionately relieved to have done something about it. Just for the time being it was as if she was unloading the agony of choice. This could only be temporary, for the choice had finally to be hers. Nothing useful might come out of this visit, but for the present she could hope there would.

Not easy, those last days in India. They had slept together

twice more, but each time she had withdrawn within herself and he, aware enough, had become increasingly irritable. She also thought he was aware enough of why, though not perhaps the extent of her knowledge or suspicions. Smack, scag, dragon were the words most commonly in use for heroin, but flax had recently become the local, fashionable word. She remembered Fiona Wilson laughing at her once for not knowing. And Arun Jiva, who was there, had also smiled.

It was not just that, though, which convinced her. So many of Errol's odd comings and goings – and the men he met – had slotted into place.

So what did one do? Every night she had examined her own feelings. What did one do? Close your eyes, forget it, put it behind you (am I my brother's keeper?) and let the affair run on as long as it may? He's an engaging lover, a wonderful companion. Let it run.

Or break off with excuses. You want to concentrate on Schools. It has been fine while it lasted. (Find someone else, perhaps. Quickly, find someone else and tell him so.)

Or break it off and tell him why. He must have some idea, her disillusion dating from when it did, and her untactful questions.

Or shop him.

Unlikely. He had never personally done *her* any harm, however much harm he might be doing to others. Doubtful if the police would believe her anyway. She just couldn't see herself in that role. And yet . . .

She had thought more than once of consulting Teresa. As sisters they had been drawn close together by their mother's defection. The difference in age did not seem to matter. They had shared confidences, confessions, arguments, laughter, loneliness. Once or twice they had ganged up against their father, though heaven knew it was seldom necessary; he was such an old softy where they were concerned. Only since she went to Oxford had they drifted apart, and Teresa's marriage had widened this. Yet there was no lack of sympathetic understanding between them – absence was all.

Still, she could not *ring* and say: 'Teresa, I've had rather a

70

shock – it's about Errol . . .' Confidences over the telephone at a range of fifty miles. It wasn't on. Go up to London and have lunch together. That was the way.

Maybe understanding had been a *little* less complete of late. Before going to India she had rung Teresa, and had felt instinctively some lifting of Teresa's eyebrows at the news. Although a conformist, Teresa was certainly not a prig, but the idea of her young sister going off to the ends of the earth with a married man she had only known since Christmas was no doubt a bit of a surprise. Could she now, only a few weeks later, see Teresa and confess she had made a horrible error and had discovered Errol to be a common criminal? It would be humiliating, to say the least.

The doorbell rang and her heart jumped, telling her plainly enough that she was not emotionally or sexually free of him yet. If ever.

But it was not Errol. Only Anne, twenty minutes early as usual.

'Stephanie, dar-ling.' A fond embrace. Anne Vincent was twenty, not bad-looking in a coltish way but with not much idea how to make the best of herself. Brilliant at Maths, if she would only work; in her first term she had become undisputed chess champion of St Martin's. But of late she had grown enamoured of the smart set to which Stephanie belonged. Stephanie was not sure whether she would do the girl more good by cutting her completely or by remaining friendly and using her influence to make her behave. Certainly the flatmate bit would not be a good idea, even for a relatively short time. Anne's kiss confirmed that.

But she ought to get someone, and not many undergraduates had enough money. (If you got two it would be the end of privacy – which she much needed if she was going to make any sort of a showing in Finals.)

'Am I early?' said Anne. 'Never mind, we can have a drink first and you can tell me about your holiday.'

Usually when people say that, they don't really want to know – unless you've had a miserable time – but one of Anne's more engaging qualities was that she really did seem interested in what you had done. They sat in the kitchen over a coffee while

Stephanie showed her a designedly small selection of the photographs with which Errol had bombarded her. Though she had only seen him twice since their return, the photographs had flooded in from him as soon as developed.

'Smashing snaps. They really are. Errol's a kingpin, isn't he. How is he, by the way?'

'Very well.'

'Has he been over this week?'

'He came last Thursday.'

Anne sipped her coffee. She made too much noise doing this. 'I suppose everything's fine between you?'

'Yes, lovely, thanks.'

Anne's china-blue eyes wandered wistfully round the kitchen. 'You're staying on in the flat?'

'Well, at least till after Schools. I haven't made up my mind what I'm going to do then. If I get a reasonable degree I may try to stay on for postgraduate work. It's tempting. Life in Oxford is quite agreeable.'

'Yes. Yes, isn't it. I've got this room in Parkville Road, as you know. Mrs Asher. She's really quite good, does well for you, and not too fussy. Of course it isn't the same as having a perch of your own. I think my family would sub me if I found the right sort of place. Is Errol moving in with you?'

'Good Lord, no! He's got a *wife*. And a house in the Chilterns and a flat in London. Why ever should he move in with me?'

'I don't know. I just thought . . .'

Stephanie got up. 'I expect to keep this just for myself, at least for the time being. Where are we going to eat?'

As they left the flat together Anne said: 'Tell me, how soon are you going to make arrangements for the college ball?'


# III


In the afternoon John Peron rang to say Sir Peter Brune would pick her up at nine tomorrow to take her to Reading. She had hardly put the telephone down before it rang again.

'Stephanie? Good afternoon to you. It's the Bursar speaking.'

'Oh . . . good afternoon.' She wondered what was coming.

'Your father rang me this morning. Said you were interesting yourself in the drug scene.'

Hell! 'Well, in a way, yes. I – after I graduate I might take up social studies' – what a lie! – 'and it seemed to me I've not ever really thought about some of its modern aspects – including the drug scene.'

'Ah. Your father seemed to think you needed advice. He said you were ringing Peter Brune.'

'Yes, I did that this morning. He's taking me to the Worsley Clinic tomorrow afternoon.'

'Good. Well, you're in good hands there. It occurred to me, though, that if you wanted to see more of it in the raw, so to speak, I might provide additional background.'

'That's very kind, Bursar. In what way?'

'Well, as you'd expect, I have contacts with the local police and social workers.'

'The police?'

'I don't think, in this case, though, you'd want to be put in touch with the law, would you? They tend to be a bit heavy handed. There are a couple of social workers I know who I think might be useful to you if you really want to get an all-round picture of the scene. One, Sandra Woolton, particularly, I'm sure could help if you were interested.'

'. . . Thank you.'

'You know all about squats and communes and that sort of thing?'

'I've read about them. Yes, I've a fair idea.'

'Sandra was on cannabis for a time, but came off it. Of course, that's fairly mild. Do you want to know more about the hard stuff?'

'Anything connected with it, really.'

'Well, shall I give her your telephone number?'

'Thank you very much, Bursar.'

As she hung up she felt annoyed at ever having mentioned the subject to her father. He shouldn't have fussed. Indeed, he

73

shouldn't have interfered. It was not like him, and in a sense it infringed on her independence.

## IV

They left next morning at nine, travelling in Peter Brune's chauffeur-driven Daimler.

Brune said: 'I'm still not quite sure why you want to see the inside of a place like this. It's really very unimpressive. But if nothing more, it's an outing.'

She laughed. 'You'll feel I've brought you on a fool's errand? But it's not just idle curiosity.'

'I'm sure it wouldn't be with you. But . . . you're not into drugs at all yourself, are you? You look far too healthy.'

'No, I've never taken to them . . . It's something quite different.'

She had an impulse to confide in this man. It would be a tremendous relief to have a sage and worldly-wise man's advice. But it would be cowardice to do so. This was between herself and what for want of a better word she must call her conscience. No other person could advise her. Events might help her to make up her mind but not by confession. Besides, telling Peter Brune was effectively making the choice, for he might feel it imperative to tell the police, otherwise he became an accessory after the fact.

Building on her impromptu lie of yesterday she said lightly: 'I'm thinking about doing social work when I've graduated; but I realise I've only existed in a small corner of life.'

'Well, my dear, you're still pretty young. You've a long way to go.'

'I hope so. The Bursar rang me yesterday offering some help and advice.'

'What, Colonel Gaveston? Henry?'

'You must know him well, of course.'

'For more than twenty years. But did you telephone him too?'

'No. I mentioned to my father that I was thinking of speaking to you, and he must have rung the Bursar. He's going to put me in touch with some social worker who's very much into the drug scene. Or so he says.'

'I don't think I've ever met your father. I've seen him on television. Does he approve of your new interest?'

'Approve perhaps is too strong. I don't think he minds so long as I am not in any way hooked myself.'

They drove on in silence. Peter Brune looked older in the light of day. Yet his whole face was good-humoured, the lips turned as if they waited to smile.

It looked like a country house when they reached it, which no doubt was what it had been. Laurels and rhododendrons – not at all, she thought, the sort her father grew, probably the despised *ponticum* – tall trees, a fairly strong wire fence, presumably to keep the curious out rather than to stop anyone inside from escaping. Attached to the main building was a flat-topped, large windowed, wood-framed extension which looked like a laboratory.

A spacious tiled hall, a sister in a blue uniform, then the smell of antiseptics. Dr Bridge was a short dark man with a clipped moustache and a bald domed forehead.

'Miss Locke. Welcome.' His handshake was crisp and dry and very brief. They talked for a minute or two, then he said: 'I'm sure Sir Peter will have warned you that much of our work is confidential – that is, between nurse and patient – and all but a very few of our patients (who are too ill to move) are here voluntarily and can terminate their treatment whenever they wish. Therefore it's important that nothing should happen which would give them the impression that they were being observed by an outsider. So may I ask you to put on this blue overall so that you may pass as a trainee nurse?'

It was a quick tour – Bridge gave the impression of doing everything in a hurry, even his voice was rapid and undertoned and confidential. As she was shown round Stephanie half listened to what he was saying about the withdrawal of the drug, the replacement with oral methodone, group therapy, the part played by psychiatry and general counselling.

'Treating a drug addict is a very wearing and testing experience

75

for the doctor. You have to make ethical judgments – moral judgments, if you like – that can't really be justified by any sort of social values that you're familiar with. Many doctors give up after a few years, unable to stand the strain.'

Dr Bridge explained that about sixty per cent of the patients being treated had been on analgesic drugs, mainly heroin; twenty per cent had been on cocaine; the remainder a mixed bag, chiefly cannabis.

Three rooms with six beds in each, two of men, one of women. (Bridge said men as addicts were in a majority.) In the first room all the patients were under some sort of sedation and mostly asleep, but in the second they were restless, an old man scratching and yawning, another sweating, a third, a boy of fifteen with his knees tucked up under his chin and crying with pain. In the women's ward two, quite young, were emaciated skeletons, clean and docile enough, but as thin as if they had just been taken from Belsen. Then there was a children's ward and a few private rooms. (Bridge looked at Sir Peter, who spread his hands equivocally and deferred to Stephanie, who at once nodded.)

Bridge said: 'A few of our better patients are receiving treatment and therapy so I can't include them. Here we have a few bad cases. If you'll just come as far as the door, I will give you a glimpse.'

# *Five*

## I

On the way back there was silence again for a while, except for the hum of the car.

Eventually Stephanie said: 'Well, thank you very much, Sir Peter.'

He smiled. 'Would it not now be appropriate to drop the sir?'

'Of course. Thank you.'

'I must confess it's pleasant these days to meet a young lady who observes the formalities. I'm old enough to find it irritating to be addressed by my Christian name by every Tom, Dick and Harry who happens to have a nodding acquaintance.'

She laughed. 'Well, thank you for arranging this for me – Peter. And for sparing the time.'

'I hope it has done the trick for you – whatever that was.'

'Whatever that was. Well, I tried to explain when I rang you. I just wanted to see what I could.'

'And what have you seen?'

'A number of sad people. As you predicted. Some of them – some of them . . .'

'It probably isn't very different from visiting a hospice for people with cancer.'

'Except that this is preventable.'

'Yes. Very true.'

She said: 'Those last rooms were – not nice. That woman screaming. She might have been being tortured.'

'So she was in a way. Partly of her own choice . . . Of course, some of it was put on for our benefit.'

'Those children were a more cheerful sight – though it's

77

horrifying that they should be there at all. Out of range of the patients Dr Bridge was pretty downbeat.'

'In a job like his you have to face the facts.'

'That so many regress? He said a ten per cent cure rate was optimistic.'

'Over the long term probably, yes. But short term the rate is over fifty per cent.'

Stephanie bit her lip. 'I suppose short term is important.'

'I think so. Dr Cranford – the other chief, who wasn't there today – puts it in perspective. Before the days of the wonder drugs sanatoria treating consumptives had a low rate of permanent success. But a good many patients benefited and were able to go out and live useful lives for a limited but extended time.'

'I can see that point of view. The difference is that these people we've just seen – their illness has been self-inflicted.'

Peter Brune smiled at her. 'It's all due to the old principle of free will. You have to realise that in a susceptible person morphine and its variants – of which heroin is the most powerful – produces one of the most subtle and enjoyable sensations known to man. It doesn't help people to be cleverer or more efficient, or to have greater stamina – even in the short run – but I understand it's a tremendously pleasant sensation of relaxation and warmth and comfort – and often it's accompanied by a tingling sensation in the personal regions which isn't altogether unlike a sexual orgasm. People choose to indulge in this sensation in the first place as an act of free will. Then eventually – like someone eating fatty food all his life – they have to take the consequences.' He made a disclaiming gesture. 'But sometimes it doesn't go all the way and the consequences aren't so dire.'

'How do you mean?'

'Well, for quite a few people a fixed dosage of, say, heroin or cocaine becomes a necessity of their daily life. But they never need to increase it. Of course they get withdrawal symptoms if they don't have it, but with it they can live pretty normal lives, work, marry, act like responsible citizens.'

'I didn't know that.' She hesitated. Again the impulse to confide. Her father had been too close to her.

She said: 'What's your attitude towards people who distribute the hard drugs?'

'D'you mean the pushers?'

'No, the bigger men. Those who supply the pushers.'

He looked at her again, blew out a breath. 'I grew up to be tolerant of the way men make their money. I think of the "judge not, that ye be not judged" business. But all the same . . .'

'All the same?'

'Yes, all the same. There are degrees of frightfulness, aren't there.'

The big car hummed through a still almost bare countryside. Stephanie was often surprised at the lateness of the trees, how they clung to their leaves so far into autumn and were loth to bud again until spring was half-over.

Peter Brune laughed. 'Of course if my pet theory were followed it would do away with the drug barons.'

'What is that?'

'It's not an original idea, of course. Just take the ban off drugs. Allow them to be on sale in shops, like candy or fish fingers.'

She looked at him. '*All* drugs?'

'Not all at once. Begin with marijuana and the amphetamines. If that achieves its object, then move on to what is called the hard stuff later.'

She stared at the chauffeur's head, wondered if he could hear. 'I know the argument. But I'm . . . surprised that . . .'

'It should come from me? Well, look at it this way. A man on, say, heroin, which is the most addictive and the most expensive, he needs about a hundred pounds a day to buy his requirements from pushers. If he could buy it legitimately, even with a heavy government tax, it probably wouldn't amount to thirty-five pounds a week, so he wouldn't need to commit a crime to get that sort of money. The police today calculate that eighty per cent of crime is drug-related. Therefore if you allow the free sale of drugs, what will happen? You create – or greatly enlarge – a drug culture. You destroy – or greatly reduce – a crime culture. And you save vast amounts of money.'

'Yes, but –'

He smiled at her again. 'Dear Henry Gaveston, I know, does not agree with me at all. Probably your father would not. But I have come to take a rather jaundiced view of human nature, my dear. If people want something they will generally get it. If it is such a need as a drug need they will go to any lengths to get it. Also in considering these things there is the awful lure of the forbidden. What Poe calls "The Imp of the Perverse". Many people wouldn't bother to try drugs – to persist with drugs, for you do have rather to persist at the beginning – if there wasn't this challenge to them. Yes, if you legalised drugs there would be a huge increase of junkies lying in the street. But old people would be able to go out at night without fear of being mugged.'

Almost home. From this altitude you could see many of the gleaming spires.

She said: 'And d'you think if that happened your clinic would be more or less full as a result?'

'It isn't my clinic, by the way . . . Well, it's anybody's guess, but I'd expect the need of ten times as many clinics – and ten times less work for jails. Addicts are irresponsible but they're seldom violent. Analgesic drugs tend to make people sleepily contented, not aggressive as an alcoholic would be.'

'Not even when suffering withdrawal symptoms?'

'They'll feel extremely unwell, I agree – until they get the next fix. But it varies enormously from person to person.'

After a moment she said: 'It would be a funny world. May I ask how you came to take an interest in drugs in the first place?'

His big mouth moved into the half-smile it was always promising. 'Guilt, I suppose.'

'Guilt?'

'Of a sort. I suppose it's behind a lot of my so-called philanthropic ventures. My father began life humbly enough. He inherited a firm from *his* father making machine tools; but between the wars he turned to small arms; he patented one of the first automatic weapons. Ever heard of the Brune Repeater? No, it has long since gone. But he expanded rapidly and made a fortune selling his weapons abroad. When the Second World

War came along he simply quadrupled his fortune by being patriotic!'

'But does that mean –'

'It doesn't mean I have any special emotional tie-in with drugs. Any more than I have with paraplegics at the Gladstone Centre or cancer patients at the Royal Marsden – though the last may have some relevance . . . But I'm convinced from the firm's records that, in the thirties particularly, my father was fairly unscrupulous whom he sold arms to; so I like to make up a bit of leeway on his behalf in the Heavenly Register. Actually I met Lord Worsley when he was still alive, and he interested me in the project. But as you know, it's only one of my interests . . .'

'Of course. Which include large gifts to the university and to St Martin's.'

'Oh, those. But those are special. In memory of 1951–53. When I was up, I mean. I still think of them as among the best years of my life, if you'll forgive the cliché.'

They were in Oxford now. In a few minutes they would be turning into Broomfield Road.

'Mind you,' he said, 'I don't talk as freely as this to everyone.'

'Thank you.'

'Do you often provoke confidences?'

She laughed. 'I don't know.' And then: 'Do you know Errol well?'

'Is it the next on the right, or the one after?'

'No, three more.'

'Three more, Parsons,' Brune said in a louder voice. 'Then it's to the right.'

'Very good, sir.'

He leaned back. 'Do I know Errol well? No, not well. But I've known him – oh, ten or fifteen years. I met him first in Corfu. I have a house there, you know.'

'No, I didn't know.'

'You must come and spend a holiday with us. Have you been to the island?'

'No.'

'Most of it is ruined, but it has great natural beauty, and there are a few secluded spots. My house is about three miles from the sea.'

'Thank you. I'd love to come sometime.'

Peter Brune's eyes narrowed as if coming into the sun. 'I knew Errol's first wife, Elena. They ran a hotel on a popular beach. He's very good company . . . But who am I to tell you that?'

Stephanie laughed again. 'Well, yes, I agree.'

'I used to go to the island twice a year, in May and September, so I saw quite a lot of them. Then he left Elena – who doesn't accept divorce, so according to her he is still her husband. I believe he and Suzanne went through some sort of a ceremony in England. Have you met Polly?'

'His daughter? No.'

'Quite the Greek beauty. Or will be in a few years. But why d'you ask?'

'I wondered. He seems very well off now.'

'He's in the leisure business, and travel, I think – and that sort of thing has rocketed in the last few years.'

They had turned into Broomfield Road, and the car stopped at number 17.

'I'm really very grateful,' Stephanie said. 'Will you come in and have a drink before you go on?'

Peter glanced at his watch. 'Well, I think probably . . .'

'There are one or two questions I still want to ask you.'

He looked quizzically at her. 'Put like that, how could I refuse?'


## II


After Peter Brune had gone, Stephanie took a second much-needed drink and got out her books: Schools loomed like a thunderstorm rumbling in the middle distance. She had not so far actually skipped a tutorial but she had recently admitted to Bruce Masters that she had simply not been working. They both knew this wouldn't do if she were to make a decent showing at the end of May. How be concerned with an academic life when real life clutched at you, red in tooth and claw?

Yet she felt in a way relieved for having partly shared her problem with somebody else. Was Peter Brune's sardonic solution either credible or remotely acceptable? Surely not in a civilised country. Yet the converse, the situation as it was developing now, was scarcely less acceptable. And the drug importers were making millions out of the situation. No wonder Errol was rich! What did one do about it? What *could* one do about it? It was perfectly plain that she had at least to break with him. His money was evil money. The flowers he had sent her, the theatres he had taken her to, the luxurious first-class trip to India, all bought with evil money.

She pulled across an old exercise book and saw a quotation from Seneca she had scribbled down last year: *Actio recta non erit, nisi recta fuerit voluntas . . . An action will not be right unless the will be right; for from there is the action derived. Again, the will will not be right unless the disposition of the mind be right; for from thence comes the will.* Would her action, if she took action, be right, and for those reasons? She threw the book across the desk and picked up Cervantes. She read for a while, and then the bell rang.

She swore under her breath and went to the door, half fearing it might be Anne Vincent. And it was.

'Darling, I'm not stopping,' Anne said. 'I've brought you some fresh strawberries. They were in the market, flown in from somewhere, and I couldn't resist them.'

'Oh thanks. Thanks a lot.'

'And a carton of cream. Regale yourself while you wage war on the books.'

Saying all the time that she wouldn't come in, she came in, and saying anyway she mustn't stop, she perched on a corner of the desk and chattered away.

'What's wrong with your leg?' Stephanie asked.

'What? Oh that. Didn't I tell you?' Anne stared at the bandage above her knee. She affected the prevailing fashion for sweeping skirts, so this part of her anatomy was seldom seen. 'I fell off my bike in the High. Some bloody fool with a car squeezed me into too small a space, and I was so concerned to tell him what I thought of him that I didn't look where I was going. I thought it would need stitches but Dr Hillsborough said it would be okay.'

'Bad luck.' Stephanie put the water on for coffee; there was no way now of avoiding a session, and if it was brief it did not so much matter. 'That the old man or Jeremy Hillsborough?'

'Jeremy. He's quite dishy now, isn't he, now he's wearing contact lenses.'

'Is that what it is? I didn't know.' In fact Stephanie, who had been three times to the Hillsborough surgery for minor ailments, didn't really find Jeremy Hillsborough dishy at all. She supposed there was always a special appeal to a susceptible girl like Anne in a moderately good-looking unmarried doctor of thirty-odd. To Stephanie there was an air of extra confidentiality about the lanky Jeremy that jarred. If you went to him with a sore throat you felt he expected you to confess you had missed two periods and what would he advise?

'Do you know Jeremy's friend, Dr Arun Jiva?' Anne asked.

'Oh yes. Reasonably well. Chiefly he's a friend of Tony Maidment's. Why?'

'Nothing really. He's no looker, is he. People laugh at him with that pince-nez. Is he a Paki?'

'No, Indian. At least – I don't know whether he's a Muslim or a Hindu. I'm surprised you haven't met him before.'

'Oh, I've seen him about often enough, but I went to one of Anthony Barr's breakfasts this week, and he was there. Holds himself aloof.'

'Well, he's older, isn't he. And takes himself seriously.'

'Right. D'you like him?'

'He's quite pleasant.'

'He seems to have lots of money. Some of these orientals have, of course. Tell me, Steff,' Anne said, 'talking of money, do people try to borrow from you?'

'Here? Sometimes. Not often.'

'There's this girl Charlotte Harris. Shares with me and Penny at Mrs Asher's. She's always in money trouble; she's borrowed from me three times – not big money, but I'm not all that well-heeled – swears she'll repay next week, never does. I think it a bit thick.'

'Have you asked her?'

'More than once. But I don't like to be too hard. Of course she says it'll be all right in a week or two, I give you my oath, et cetera. You know. Oh, is that coffee? Thanks.'

Stephanie said: 'I think you've got to write it off as a bad debt. Put it down to experience.'

'Right. Yep, I suppose so. Hell, I wish I didn't take sugar, I know it's bad for the complexion. It's one reason I'd like to get away from Mrs Asher's.'

'What, the sugar?'

'Oh, Steff. No, you know.' Anne wafted the steam delicately away with her hand. 'What used to be called morality has gone out of the window long since, of course. You sleep as you want and with anyone you fancy. Penny spent the night at Magdalen last week! . . . But borrowing money without any real, serious intention of returning it – that's still morally wrong, isn't it?'

'It is in my book,' Stephanie said.

'Right. But it really is disagreeable. My parents lash out cash to enable me to live like a lady, not to subsidise some wet, feeble girl who lets her own grant dribble through her fingers.'

The coffee was helping. For once she began to feel like work. Just as soon as Anne could be edged out . . . She might even be able to concentrate.

Anne fidgeted with the bandage then let her skirt slip down. She glanced at the mantelpiece.

'Talking of Tony Maidment, you must be going to his twenty-first, aren't you? You know him so much better than I do.'

'Well, yes. I accepted but it's been so frantic since I came back that I've forgotten to put the card up. Is it next Sunday?'

'Right. I expect it'll be quite a do. His mother's rolling, and he's the third baronet or something.'

'Or something.'

'I confess I was scared witless that I might not get an invite, me

85

being only in my first year and really only knowing him through you. But it came. I'm thrilled. What are you going to wear?'

'I haven't thought. Anne, I don't want to sound blasé, but things really have been rather wild since we flew back from Delhi. I had to see my beloved parent. As you know he's more or less confined to a wheelchair, and I've been neglectful. Then other things crowded in – not least the fact that I've been skipping work and Finals are only a few weeks away . . .'

She hoped Anne would take the hint.

She did at last. She was eased off the corner of the desk and towards the door, where she turned and said: 'Is Errol going with you to Tony's party?'

Stephanie was suddenly unreasoningly angry. She swallowed down her first reply and made an effort to speak in a controlled way.

'Darling, does it matter to you?'

'No, but –'

'Look, you don't go *with* people to a birthday party. You don't make up a group to go together the way you do for a college ball or a commem. ball. I've been invited and I shall go. You've been invited and I imagine you'll go. I don't even know whether Errol has been invited, but I don't think he'll be there because he will probably be in Holland. That satisfy?'

Anne blinked. 'Oh, yes. Oh, right. I only asked.' The bite in Stephanie's voice had not been altogether disguised.

Stephanie said: 'Because I'm having an affair with Errol doesn't mean we have to live in each other's pockets. Get that?'

'Right. Oh, right.'

The anger was blowing itself out as quickly as it had come. She was startled by it herself, as if only now consciously realising the degree of the tensions within her. 'Let's see, what time is it on Sunday?'

'Eight. Shall I pick you up?'

'No, thanks. Thanks all the same, Anne. Let's go under our own steam. If the party tends to drag I might come home early – I've so much work to do.'

'Right,' said Anne for the twelfth time as she was ushered out.

# Six

## I

Errol Colton came back from one of his meetings in London and parked his BMW in the drive. He slammed the door and went into the house and immediately up the stairs to his study on the first floor. It was a room covered with his photographs. Every wall was full. On the desk in a rack were letters which had arrived and were waiting for him – among them one from Stephanie, whose distinctive handwriting it was easy to recognise. In happier times he had likened it to a succession of telegraph poles striding across the page.

At first he did not look at any of the letters but with unsteady sweaty hands unlocked a drawer and took out a snuffbox, a small mirror, a straw and a razor blade. He put some white powder from the box on the surface of the mirror and assembled it in a thin line with the razor blade. He put the straw into each nostril in turn and sniffed until all the powder was gone. Then he put the things away and began to read the letters, though he could not concentrate on anything. Stephanie's was only a single sheet of paper and he had barely glanced at the contents when his wife came in.

She was an elegant young woman with raven-black hair and a slightly hooked nose which did not seem to detract from her good looks. Her expression was not welcoming.

'You didn't let me know when to expect you.'

'What? Oh, I wasn't sure.'

'Are you going to use the car again?'

He poured himself a brandy. 'The car? I don't think so.'

'Don't you usually put it away?'

'Later.'

He was down around the mouth, and a bad colour.

'There's something to eat if you want it,' she said coldly.

'Er – no thanks.' He sipped at his glass.

'You look green. What's wrong? Is it one of your headaches?'

'I'm okay.'

'Well, you don't look it.'

Conversation had been no more fluent than this over the last week. It spouted and died, with no common interest in keeping it going.

She said: 'The men haven't been about the pool. We want it for the Perrys on Sunday.'

'Have you rung them?'

'Of course. But you'd better ring again.'

'Remind me in the morning.' He put down Stephanie's letter and went to the window. Following a heavy shower, the declining sun, so pale after India's, was glistening on the wet gravel drive and the leaves of the laurels which screened the house from the road. He waited for the white powder to steady his nerves. 'Polly get away all right?'

'I drove her back.'

'She seems to be settling down.'

'Yes, she's settling down.'

He glanced at Suzanne, trying to concentrate on the normal. 'Megson's have agreed the date of the exhibition.'

'What exhibition?'

'Of my photographs. It's June the eleventh.'

'Good.'

'We'll probably give a party afterwards. My club's a lot cheaper than Claridge's and just as pleasant. It'll be my first West End show.'

'I know,' she said with the same lack of enthusiasm.

Five years ago he had taken a great fancy to her and had charmed her into living with him and then marrying him. She had not been slow to be charmed, being an actress with dark good looks and a fine body but an awareness that none of the managers thought her talented. Her ambition to become a second

Janet Suzman was rapidly failing, and Errol Colton had an engaging manner, a prosperous lifestyle and potential in plenty.

She could not complain that the potential had not been realised. Two years ago they had moved into this Georgian country house; they had built an indoor swimming pool, a tennis court and a croquet lawn and there were parties every other weekend. They had cars enough and more than their fair share of help; his daughter was a weekly boarder at Westonbirt; they had a pied-à-terre in London, they went frequently to first nights, and she could go as often as she wanted – though not accompanied by him – to the opera. It was very much of a success story.

Fairly soon Suzanne had discovered that she had married two men. One was Errol fronting himself to the world, or in pursuit of a woman, or entertaining guests, or joking with his daughter; the other was the man at home, where he was untalkative, indrawn, buried in his photography, moroseness never far away. The life he *wanted* to live was clearly that in which he promoted and projected himself, but this could only be maintained part of the time: then the batteries switched off. In spite of his muscularity, his maleness, his craggy good looks and volatile energy, she sometimes thought of him as a weak man. Underneath the macho image was someone who could turn and waver as the wind blew.

From the beginning she had resented his infidelities, but she saw it was part of the image he had created for himself. But this girl from St Martin's had seemed more serious. She had seen Stephanie once, and thought her a high-living, high-flying, care-for-nothing sort of girl, just the type to hold a special fascination for Errol; but the most scaring thing about her was her *youth*. Suzanne was only thirty-four and was well aware of her own good looks and elegance. But she was also aware that in the prosperous ambiance she was living in she had allowed herself to put on a bit too much weight. This girl Stephanie had not yet reached the age when she even had to *think* about it. Thin as a wand, leggy, high-breasted, she was prancing through life like a mettlesome colt, unbridled, undisciplined. What a woman to lasso and bring kicking to the ground!

This trip to India had brought it all out into the open, made it in this strange inversion of modern morals curiously more 'respectable'. Stephanie's father, it seemed, was quite well off, but Stephanie herself might not be averse to marriage to a property tycoon. It was a good life he could offer her. Nor could one write down his own physical magnetism when he laid it on the line.

Last weekend had produced a bitter quarrel. In the quarrel Errol had dropped some hint that he might be breaking up with Stephanie, but with him you could never tell truth from lies. Now he had been away two nights and had come home in no conciliatory mood. He looked as if he had been in a road accident. Leave him alone now. Get out and say no more.

She stayed and said more.

'I need money. Last weekend was expensive.'

'You must have saved while I've been away.'

'Can you give me any reason why I should have?'

'How much d'you want?'

'Five hundred would about cover it.'

'What're you doing, feeding the staff on caviar?'

She glanced at the letter lying on his desk. 'Has the girl been with you in London?'

'Of course not.'

'Does she write to you every night?'

'I've said all I want to say about that. There is nothing new to add.'

'Is she still playing hard to get or hard to get rid of?'

He turned on her angrily and then controlled his anger. The coke was helping. She watched his face change, saw the cocked eyebrow, the mouth guarding itself just in time.

'Want a drink?'

'I've had one.'

'Well, have another.'

In the silence he went across and poured her a gin, splashed it with tonic, handed it to her. 'There's no ice here.'

She took it without speaking.

'What did you say you wanted?'

'Five hundred.'

He took out his cheque book and sat at the table, wrote in it. The chair creaked as he tore off the cheque and turned.

'I've made it seven fifty.'

'Thanks,' she said.

He frowned wryly. 'You look like Helen of Troy in a sulk.'

Her face did not change. 'It wasn't Helen of Troy who was let down. You ought to know with your Greek connections.'

'Ah, yes. Ah, yes.' He was feeling better every minute, a little more confident of his ability to find a way through the horrifying mess he was in. 'I think I will have something to eat, now you suggest it. What have we got?'

'Cold chicken. Smoked salmon. Or Janice can make you an omelette before she goes.'

'The salmon will do. And see the bread's cut thin; with plenty of butter. Is there any Vouvray?'

'I'll see.'

She turned to the door, holding the cheque between thumb and forefinger as if wet. She had not touched her drink.

'Suzanne.'

'Yes?'

'Maybe there is something more I should say. I was going to leave it for a while.' He hesitated. 'One makes mistakes. It's not always easy to admit them.'

'Such as?'

'Such as my affair with Stephanie. It's coming to an end. But it's not going to be easy for either of us.'

'You dropped a few guarded hints on Sunday. Is there any reason I should believe them?'

He shrugged. 'I'm more than ever sure.'

'Is she?'

'I think so.'

'Have you seen her?'

'Not this week. I'm seeing her on Sunday. At least, I expect to.'

'How nice for you both. Is this to be the great parting or the great reconciliation?'

They stood for a moment in another silence. Again he turned to the photographs, as if they were the one comforting and pre-occupying diversion from reality. They all had to be sorted, chosen, before being mounted for the exhibition. He had to choose about seventy from more than a thousand, covering several years of his life. He thought to consult Suzanne about some of those of her that he wanted to show, but this was not the time.

'I'm going to this birthday party of Tony Maidment's – Sir Anthony Maidment – it's his twenty-first at his home at Sutton David. Sunday evening.'

'How should I know? Are you taking her?'

'Of course not.'

'Then why aren't you taking me?'

'Because I expect to *see* her there. That's when I intend to make the final break. I shall tell them that you have flu.'

'Thank you very much.' She picked up the drink now and sipped it. It was all too familiar, this fluctuation in his moods. When she saw him coming across from his car his face had alerted her to the prospect of some catastrophe. When she came into the room he had been sharp-edged as a knife. Now he was pulling out the stops for some sort of reconciliation. She was not deceived. She refused to be deceived. Because she wanted to be reassured she wouldn't allow herself to be reassured.

She said: 'Don't you care for her any more?'

'It isn't as simple as that.'

'It can't be.'

He met her look only for the second time since he came in. His eyes had their concentrated, attentive look, as if for the moment he was thinking only of her questions. Whether it was a trick or a trait it was difficult to resist. His sense of fun was even trying to break in, but failing – some darker bruising loomed too large in his mind.

She folded the cheque. 'And after this, if it does come to an end, what next?'

'Next what?'

'Next woman. Girl. The next one you're going to fancy.'

He shook his head from side to side. 'I don't know. Christ, each time I tell myself . . . One lives and learns. It may be never.'

For the moment he believed it. After she had gone he stared at the closed door and the sweat broke out on his forehead again. He dabbed it away. Maybe it really would be never.

# Seven

James Locke was on the Chelsea Flower Show Committee, and on the Monday of the following week he drove to a meeting of the organisers at the Royal Hospital. This year he had been invited to be one of the judges of the rhododendron exhibits. Since his own garden ran merely to twelve acres and had only been in existence twenty years, he felt this a signal honour. Among the other judges would be men and women who owned and tended some of the great gardens of England and whose ancestors had travelled to the Himalayas and Sikkim in search of new species. Some of these people still living had given their names to hybrids which had become known throughout the gardening world. James often thought that if you wanted immortality – at least the only kind in which he believed – you were much more likely to attain it by hybridising a particularly successful family of camellia than bothering to get your name in history books or have statues put up in Whitehall. Even a good rose had an extended life. Who, for instance, of her generation – though she was now defunct – had lasted longer than Frau Karl Drushki?

After the meeting he hobbled painfully to his car and drove to his club for a luncheon appointment with his old friend Colonel Henry Gaveston.

The hell with central London was that even with a disabled sticker it was almost impossible to get near enough to be within limping distance of the Hanover Club. In the end he parked on a double yellow line in Davies Street near a bus stop and hoped for the best.

Henry was waiting for him. A tall, ramshackle man, stooping,

94

with a war-damaged shoulder and left hand, a lined and scarred face (scars coming from life and not from battle), yet handsome in an aquiline way with silver-grey hair that tended to fall across his forehead. They had been at school together and through some of the war, though Henry had been in the Irish Guards until the SAS came into being.

He had had a distinguished army career, serving after the war in Aden, Cyprus and Northern Ireland, but had retired early under a cloud, having proved too tough in Ulster to keep in line with government policy. Half-Irish himself – his mother had come from County Limerick – he had met terrorism with an iron fist of his own and was consequently now on the murder list of the IRA.

He was a Fellow of St Martin's and had been appointed Bursar five years ago. He lived near Thame a few miles east of Oxford, dressed untidily, almost scruffily, and new undergraduates were warned of his habit of inviting them out there for the week-end and then expecting them to spend most of it working in his garden. He had married late, had a son still at university and a wife as untidy as himself who wrote biographies and was at present in America on a tour to publicise her latest work.

They did not join one of the general tables but lunched alone at a window table overlooking the garden. To talk to, Henry did not seem a hard man, any more than you would have supposed James to have been a brave one. They were two elderly gentlemen, lifelong friends, benevolent, easy talkers, easy in each other's company, enjoying a meeting to reminisce, to swap confidences, to try out one of the better club clarets, to glance around the gracious Georgian dining room, to raise a hand in greeting to friends who came in and out.

Over the fish they talked of plants and gardens, of Evelyn Gaveston's travels in America, of young Charles Gaveston's preoccupation with the tenor saxophone. 'Of course at his present rate he'll be independent of government grants or subsidies from me. In the group he's formed he's already making more money than I am paid for being Bursar of an Oxford college! But Evelyn and I would have liked him to spend a few years in the Guards first, whatever his choice afterwards. Young men can't wait.'

'We didn't,' said James. 'But then there was a war on.'

They discussed a *sciadopitys verticillata* which Henry Gaveston had been growing for ten years but which had never got its roots down firmly enough to survive without a stake. 'It needs guying,' said James.

'Yes, but why *should* it?' demanded Henry. 'It comes from a hilly district in Japan. It's perfectly hardy. I've got no lime. Yet it flops around in every gale like a drunken sailor on a Saturday night.'

'Ground soft?' suggested James. 'So guy it. Get some of your conscripted young guests to do it one weekend. Otherwise you'll lose it.'

'Hell,' said Henry. 'If you had to guy every pine tree my garden would look like a village fête.'

They discussed their old colleague Jock Armitage, who had announced his decision to resign his seat at the next general election.

'Don't think I could ever have gone into politics,' said James. 'I always see both sides of things. I don't claim this as a virtue; it may well be a weakness; but whereas in a war I can very easily say, "My country, right or wrong", in a political crisis I couldn't always say, "My party, right or wrong".'

'Both sides,' muttered Gaveston, as the pork chops were served. 'That's what I could see in Ireland, for I love the Irish – most of 'em. But a few are dastardly, and them I would *stamp* on. World opinion be buggered.'

They talked of Scotland having won the Grand Slam and the game they had seen at Twickenham together earlier in the year. Only when the cheese was served did they come to the real purpose of the meeting.

'Young Stephanie,' said Gaveston. 'You really worried about her?'

'Not exactly worried but concerned. She came home the weekend before last, and I thought her more wired up than I've ever known her. We had a very good weekend – everything went

96

apple pie – but underneath she was a bag of nerves. I didn't fancy it at all.'

'And you think it's to do with drugs?'

'That or a broken love affair. Or both. I don't know how they interlock, or if at all. You saw her?'

'I've seen her on and off for the last three years! A very nice gal, if I may say so, James, and you well know my susceptibilities. She's been kicking up her heels recently – got into rather an odd set, in my opinion . . . though I don't think there's much harm in 'em really. So long as *you* were able to pay the piper . . . I assumed you knew about it and were willing to let her go on a slack rein. She never got into any trouble in the college, and I didn't feel it was my business to interfere. Girls will be girls.'

'But you saw her last week?'

'Yes. After you telephoned I rang her and arranged for her to meet a woman called Sandra Woolton who's a social worker and knows as much about drugs as anyone in Oxford. I understand they met and Sandra took your girl to a squat that she knows of near the river. They'll let her into these places because for a while she was one of them. Then they went on to a pub Sandra knows of where dope is fairly freely traded in the back rooms, so that Stephanie could see how it all worked: needles and vomit and the rest; the place was raided after Christmas but it has all started up again. Now they've an elaborate system of warnings, with two Doberman pinschers to hold up the police for a few minutes while the dope is flushed away.'

James picked at a bit of cheese. 'And when you saw her yourself?'

'That was on Friday. She'd been with Sandra the night before. She was just coming out of hall so I walked partway back to her flat.'

'And what did you think of her?'

'As you say – wired up. Talked too much. But James . . .'

'Yes?'

'I don't know if you're worried about this, but I could certainly detect nothing in her manner to suggest that she was on anything herself.'

'Well, no, not really –'

'I also asked Sandra, who's far more up in these things than I am, and she's certain there's no sign of Stephanie being on anything at all.'

'I didn't think so. But thank you for the reassurance.'

Henry eyed his old friend. 'I don't think I should worry, old boy. She's had this love affair you were telling me about which is in process of breaking up. She's been slacking in her work. And Schools are less than four weeks off. Believe me, she's not the first student to get het up. It would be a bit surprising if she were not!'

James nodded and sipped the last of his wine.

'So I don't think there is much to be even concerned about,' Henry said. 'If in Stephanie's case it were really what it seemed on the surface, just a wish to know more about drugs and to make judgments about them, then I'm glad you let me know so that I could counteract Peter Brune's heterodox influence.'

'Heterodox influence?'

Gaveston pushed his boyish grey hair out of his eyes and laughed. 'Oh, only in a manner of speaking. Peter's a dear man. I've known him for ever – which is almost as long as I've known you. But in spite of helping to finance this clinic he has wayward views about legalising drugs and so abolishing the rackets that exist. Well and good, it's a point of view. But all he ever sees, I'm sure, are his clean and carefully hospitalised patients in the Worsley Clinic. He is in some ways the typical liberal, working out the theory of a problem and coming to typically liberal conclusions. The world to such people is governed by theorems, and life must fit into these theorems, not be human and messy and contrary and individual and cross-grained and greedy and weak. So in their own minds they organise a perfect world, and if like Peter they are very rich, they can live in a way that pretends it exists. Ordinary people, alas, know different.'

They got up and moved to go downstairs for coffee. James waved away several offers of help, and proceeded from table to table until he got out to the landing and found the lift.

Downstairs they met a few friends, but presently these drifted off and James Locke and Henry Gaveston were left to themselves to talk of the old days. Last year James had gone to France, Mrs Aldershot driving, and had been to some of the old places he had been active in during the war. Most of the people he knew were gone, some dying instantly during the war, more having been taken off in the natural course of time. A number remained, some who had sheltered him at the risk of their own lives and that of their families, others who had been active in the *Maquis*. When the principals were no longer there the children remembered. It had been a fruitful reunion.

Only Henry probably knew the truth of James's last drop into France. To the world he said he had landed badly and damaged both ankles in a ditch, which was true enough. But as he crawled out of the ditch he had been arrested by the waiting Gestapo, beaten insensible and thrown into a hut for the night preparatory to being taken away to one of their 'interrogation' centres. In the night his guard, seeing James unconscious on a trestle with blood dripping from his head, had thought it safe to doze off. Coming round just before dawn, James had strangled the guard with his left elbow and right thumb and crawled away from the camp leaving a trail of blood that he eventually staunched, and lying up all next day in a spinney within sight of the Gestapo huts. Then he had trekked for the next two days, mainly on hands and knees, through woods and fields until picked up and given food and shelter by some French villagers.

Over the years this all somehow became too heroic for James, who told his friends the abbreviated story. Not that many bothered to ask. It was: 'How are the ankles, old man? . . . Bad luck. I suppose nothing can be done surgically? . . . Oh, it has been done . . . Too bad! Well, I suppose, yes, hmm, it's good you are able to get about as much as you do in spite, isn't it.'

'A funny thing about war,' Henry said, snipping the end off his cigar. 'For professionals like me it's different. We volunteer to fight – or to be able to fight if the necessity arises. We're trained for that purpose. Our life is devoted to it. That's why a regrettable incident like our little adventure in the Falklands – which would never have happened if our Foreign Office had not given the Argentines the wrong impression – when it *had* to be launched it was a brilliant operation, daring, highly risky and magnificently executed, a notable achievement. So I regret the casualties less than in the World Wars. Of course I regret every single drop of blood that had to be shed – but every drop was volunteer blood, spilt by professionals in the fulfilment of their professional duty. To me one of the ultimate obscenities of war is the conscript army – invented by the French, you know – in which decent little men with no instincts to fight are virtually dragged from their houses and compelled to murder each other. That is civilisation in its grave.'

James sipped his port and stared across the room. 'I agree with every word. But I was thinking while you spoke. Harrison, the greengrocer in our village, died last year – eighty-five or -six, I suppose. He was just old enough to be conscripted into the army in the First World War and he saw the last twelve months of it in France in the South Wales Borderers – had an absolutely hellish time; he came in for everything, trench warfare at its worst. After the war he returned to the village, aged twenty, settled into his father's shop, married, came in for the shop, lived quietly – quietly hen-pecked, I suspect – until he died. Never went abroad again, never wanted to. Collected stamps and kept pigeons. I'd known him for years, so I went to see him a week or so before he died. When we'd talked for a few minutes the conversation got round to the war – his war. And d'you know what he said to me? He said: "I wouldn't have missed it for anything."'

Henry laughed. 'Whatever generalisation you make, there's always human nature to set you back. That's why Peter is so often wrong. Seriously, James, we must do this more often, even when there's no suitable excuse. I suppose it's always a big effort for you, making the journey to London? Damn it, we only live fifty-odd miles apart. Will you come to lunch when Evelyn's home?'

'Of course.'

'In the meantime I'll keep a special eye on Stephanie over the next few weeks – until Finals, in fact. It'll have to be a quiet eye, so that she doesn't see it and resent it, but I think I can manage that.'

'Thank you.'

'She's a very bright girl and very bright girls tend to live on their nerves. I'll have a word with Bruce Masters, see what he says. And thank you for lunch.'

'Food's better here now,' said James. 'Seems often to be the case in London clubs that as the food improves the conversation deteriorates. Afraid I'm not here often enough to judge the other side of the cake.'

Henry Gaveston said: 'I wish talk were better in Oxford. People there stick too much to their own hobbyhorses.'

They got up together. James collected his two sticks from the porter and Henry accompanied him to his car. There was no warden waiting or sticker on the screen. Henry had other business in London and made off with his erect but loose-jointed walk. In spite of his retirement, James knew he still had contacts with the army and the Ministry of Defence who used him as one of their experienced advisers. Certainly there was no one more experienced in combating terrorism than this shambling Bursar of St Martin's.

Driving a car, even an automatic, was not easy for James, but, the right ankle being the less painful of the two, he managed fairly well. Mary had been going to drive him up and do some shopping while he lunched, but she had gone down with a bad cold. It was his custom when he returned after driving himself to leave the car by the front door for her to garage later, at the rear of the house, but he decided to put it away at once. In any case his ankles were now so painful with the undue exercise that they were unlikely to get worse.

He drove through the open garage doors and noticed that his wheelchair was where he had left it this morning. Unusual – but useful as it turned out. He eased himself from the car with a grunt, unshipped his sticks, sank gratefully into his chair and pressed the button.

The first thing he saw when he came round to the front of the house was the police car. A Rover, he noticed, white with blue stripes. It probably denoted some particular division (traffic, was it?) but he wasn't up in police matters, having, to his recollection, not spoken to an officer for the last five years.

There was no one in this car, so presumably the occupants were admiring his garden or taking tea with Mary if she had recovered sufficiently to be in a hospitable mood.

The concrete ramp enabled his chair to circumvent the steps, and in a moment he was in the hall. Mary had heard him, and it only needed her face to tell him there was ill news.

'Something wrong?' he asked, his chair gliding silently across the carpeted hall.

'Mr Locke?' A man in civilian clothes came out of the drawing room.

'Yes?'

'Oh, I'm Inspector Summers. Good afternoon, sir. I have been here a little while, waiting for you to come back.'

'We rang the Hanover, Mr James,' said Mary, 'but you had just left.'

'Ah well, come in, Inspector. Though I see you are in. Has Mrs Aldershot been attending to you?'

'Thank you, sir. After you, sir.' In the drawing room was a blond young policeman holding his cap.

Inspector Summers was six feet one and looked tired, as if with the early onset of middle age.

James wheeled his chair round to face them. Deliberately he adopted a light tone.

'My driving licence expired? I seem to remember –'

'No, sir. I wish it were only that. We were rung up some little while ago by the Oxfordshire police, and it has become my disagreeable duty to call on you this afternoon –'

'Something to do with my daughter?'

Summers looked up slowly. 'Is there a reason why you should assume that, sir?'

'A very good reason. She is the only relative I have living in Oxfordshire.'

'Oh, I see –'

'Has she met with an accident?'

Summers coughed. 'I'm very much afraid so, sir. She was found dead in bed this morning.'

# BOOK TWO

# One

The Boeing 737 from Brussels made a conventionally perfect landing at Heathrow and began to taxi towards the waiting terminal. Among its passengers was a smartly dressed but undernourished-looking Indian. He wore a white ribbed wool long-sleeved pullover, a green silk shirt with a pastel green patterned collar and an emerald green tie with a thin yellow stripe. Over it was a long-waisted grey jacket; and he had black cord trousers, white socks and black sandals. A young man with deep-set, liquid, sad eyes, a long neck, an aquiline nose, curly black hair growing close over his skull like healthy fur.

It had been a nightmare two weeks for Nari Prasad, and this, this passing through the British customs, was to be the ultimate crisis of the nightmare towards which all the earlier preparation had been moving.

Practice had not been so bad. After all, grapes, except for the pips, dissolved almost immediately. But the actual packages he had to swallow, though roughly only the size of grapes, were rock hard. Powdered heroin compressed with great force into a substance like solid cement, enclosed in the ends of two condoms, one within the other, and secured tightly with dental floss. He had gagged at the sight and the feel of them. Having been given a moderate meal, he had been dosed with kaolin and lomotil tablets and told to begin. Each container went down with a teaspoonful of strawberry jam. He had jibbed at ten, and at twenty-five he had vomited some up again. At forty he had refused adamantly to touch another one. Dr Amora looked significantly at the hammer which stood on a shelf by the door. It was the sort of hammer used to drive iron stakes into the ground.

'Shall I ring for the two men?' he asked. 'It will take but a moment.'

So eventually eighty had gone down. He felt terrible. As if he had swallowed a load of stones. His stomach was unbearably tight, and pain shot across from one side to the other. He knew any moment he must be sick. He waited only to get outside into the open air to void them into the street, retching and retching until the unbearable load was gone from him.

But there was to be no outside for him. Once the cargo was aboard there was no release for him at all. Of course he had told Bonni a week ago that he was going to visit his cousins, the Mehtas, in Birmingham, England. She had bitterly whined that she was being deserted, and how did he find the fare and who had pulled strings to enable him to be granted a visa, and what was she to live on? He tried to pacify her by showing her that the visa was only for a month, by assuring her that he must then return, and by giving her a substantial subsidy to pay the rent and to keep herself while he was away. Her kohl-rimmed eyes grew round in surprise at the crumpled handful of hundred-rupee notes he gave her. It dampened down her complaints, and she saw by the look on his face that she dare not ask him where he had obtained the money.

He did not dare tell her that Mr Srivastavar had refused to give him leave and that when he returned to Bombay he would have to look for another job.

But that lay in the future – somewhere in the unforeseeable future. It was as if that lay on the other side of a mountain range: he could only vaguely visualise it.

To his considerable surprise Shyam came with him – as far as Brussels. At first he had thought that Shyam also might be carrying stuff like him, but not so. Nari had been warned to eat and drink nothing on the plane but to accept his tray and his liquid refreshments in the ordinary way. When the stewardess wasn't looking Shyam helped himself to Nari's share. The organisation had learned that when a person refused all food and drink on a long flight it might be reported by the cabin crew as a suspicious circumstance. Also, to fly to Brussels and to arrive in London on a short-haul flight generally made things easier at immigration.

Though the pain went away after the first six hours of the flight Nari was unbearably uncomfortable. He felt his belly must be distended, and it was so tender he could hardly fasten his seat belt. Three times on the plane from Bombay he went to the lavatory to pass water, but so far the organisation had been as good as their word and he had no desire to pass anything else.

In a way he was glad of Shyam's company, though he no longer looked on him as a friend. He slept most of the way – that last cup of coffee must have been doped – but when he woke it had been a small relief from the pressures in his abdomen to see the stout familiar figure beside him, Shyam also dozing or watching the film or thumbing through a magazine.

Changing at Brussels was of course the calculated risk. They touched down at 6.30 a.m. and didn't leave for England until 11.30. Shyam saw him off.

'Well, I wish you good luck, Nari Prasad, *bhai*. Not to worry. It will all go just as easy as landing here. No problem. No one will bother you. By this time tomorrow you will be a rich man, with four weeks' holiday and money to spend! I will hardly know you when you return to Bombay with a new English suiting and money still left!'

On the last lap he was allowed to eat a little of the light refreshment put before him. He felt hungry yet sickly, and when he put food in his mouth he nearly retched. He took another pill Shyam had given him, and that steadied his nerves.

England looked just how he had expected it to look, the weather grey and sunless as they came in over the reservoirs and the huddled houses; and when they trooped out of the plane a light rain was falling. Yet how happy and excited would he have been had he been coming in for the first time on a legitimate visit!

The passengers – only a quarter of what the big plane could have carried – were divided into three streams, British, members of the EEC, and others. Nari joined the others; but on this plane there were only twelve such, of whom a mere three were coloured. Did this not make him more conspicuous, not less? The reasoning of his masters did not make sense to him.

Those ahead of him took a long time to get through, though how quickly the British were passed! He looked with envy at the dozen or more black faces in the British queue.

It was lunchtime. This too was part of the organisation's reasoning. His stomach rumbled. It was now empty, but he felt no hunger, only terror.

His turn at last. The passport officer was a ruddy-faced young man with a close-cropped light ginger beard. He took the passport, opened it, stared at it for a while, turned to the visa.

Then he said: 'You are here on a visit?'

'Yes, sir,' said Nari, and then thought he should not have been so respectful. 'I am visiting my cousins in Edgbaston, Birmingham.'

'Could you give me their name and address.'

Nari gave it, then added: 'I think I filled that in on the form on the plane.'

'Is this your first visit to England?'

'Yes.'

'You are a lawyer by profession?'

'Yes. I work for Srivastavar, Seth and Co. of Mazagon Street, Bombay.'

'Do you intend to visit other parts of England?'

'I shall be hoping to. This will depend on how much time my cousins will be able to spare me.'

'What do your cousins do?'

'Mr Satish Mehta keeps a post office.'

Another pause. 'You left India only yesterday, I see, but changed planes in Brussels. Why was that?'

Nari looked into light brown eyes which were courteous but penetrating.

'I am bringing my nephew, Shyam Lal Shastri, to join his mater and pater who live in Brussels. Shyam is thirteen and I was asked to help him.'

Another pause. Then the passport was handed back. 'Thank you, Mr Prasad.'

Nari walked through with knees that would barely support him. He *walked through*! One obstacle over! The worst and highest peak yet to come.

The delay had been considerable and his bag was already circulating on the luggage conveyor belt. He picked it up, walked towards the green exit.

Two or three groups went through unchecked, but a customs officer stopped him. 'May I see your bag, sir?'

A tall dark fellow of about forty-five with a peculiar accent Nari did not know. Perhaps it was Scottish. Perhaps Welsh. He flushed and offered the bag, then, remembering, felt in his pocket and produced the key. The officer waved him to unlock it. Nari did so. At the same time a spasm of intense pain passed through his abdomen, contorting his thin face as it came and went.

The case came open. The customs officer riffled through the shirts, the underwear, the folded jacket and trousers, the shaving things, the toilet water, the lucky charms. When the clothes were provided for him – including the good things he was wearing – Nari had wondered at the high quality of everything. He did not know the street value of what he carried in his bowels.

The suitcase clicked shut. Even that was not the cardboard thing so often seen.

'And your other bag, sir, please.'

He handed over his small black bag. The customs officer seemed to take longer over this, as if there were something suspicious in it. In the background another official had been hovering with a dog on a leash. While the second bag was being searched he strolled round with the dog and they passed close to Nari, the dog sniffing, and then went off to the end of the room. The place was now empty, except for the officers and one newcomer who looked as if he might be Vietnamese or Cambodian. Two officers converged on him and began to ask him questions. Another spasm of pain racked Nari.

He was aware that the officer dealing with him had said something.

'Pardon? I am not hearing what you say.'

The officer was holding out the bag. 'That's all, thank you.'
'I – may go?'

'Yes. Carry on.' The Englishman turned away to talk to another officer. Nari began to force his legs towards the exit.

This was the end of the nightmare. At every step he thought he must stumble and fall.

After a long time he came out into an area where a lot of people were standing behind a barrier, some with names held up on cardboard. Another plane had just come in, and, still waiting for the hard hand on his shoulder, Nari allowed himself to be carried along towards the exits. Outside all was bustle and noise and confusion, cars and taxis and buses arriving and driving off.

They had told him he might take a taxi. He opened his note-case to see the English notes were still there, then took his place in the queue.

# Two

## I

A few days before this, an inquest on Stephanie Jane Locke, aged twenty-one, a third-year student at St Martin's College, Oxford, had been held at Oxford Crown Court before the coroner, Mr Charles Latham. Evidence of identity was given by the dead girl's father, Mr James Locke.

Sergeant Denton of the Thames Valley Police testified that on Monday the 30th April he received a 999 call and, accompanied by Constable Wavell, proceeded to number 17 Broomfield Road where they found a group of students standing in the hall of the first-floor flat, and on going into the bedroom they found the deceased girl lying on the bed. There was an almost empty bottle of pills on the bedside table and a broken glass on the floor. There was an empty bottle of gin under the bed and another in the kitchen. There was no one else living in the flat. She had been discovered by one of the students, a friend who had called to see her that morning. An ambulance was summoned, and the girl conveyed to the John Radcliffe Hospital where she was examined and found to have been dead for some hours.

Dr Felix Ehrmann, the police pathologist, was called. He said a post-mortem examination showed that death was due to asphyxia and respiratory failure caused by paralysis of the respiratory centre of the brain. The lungs had asphyxial spots on them and were very congested, and there were spots on the heart, and the stomach walls were stained. The blood showed a high level of alcohol together with a barbiturate mixture of about four milligrams per hundred millilitres. Death had occurred sometime in the early hours of Monday morning. There was no evidence of any other drugs having been taken and the deceased was a healthy young woman in a very good physical condition.

In response to the coroner, Dr Ehrmann said the normal maximum dose of Medanol sleeping tablets was two tablets, and the contents of the stomach suggested that the dead girl had taken at least twenty, in addition to about a third of a bottle of gin. The date on the bottle of tablets found by her bed was November of last year, the dispenser Messrs Boots at their Piccadilly Circus branch. There were no marks on the body suggesting foul play.

In answer to Mr Alan Webster, representing the family of the deceased, Dr Ehrmann said there was no evidence of sexual assault or recent sexual intercourse. The deceased was not pregnant and had never had a child.

Dr Jeremy Hillsborough, a local physician in practice in Burnham Road, was called and testified that in September of last year Miss Locke had come to see him complaining of sleeplessness and depression after sitting an exam. He had issued her with a prescription for ten Medanol, and presumably these had the desired effect. Two months later she had come to him again and he had written her a prescription for thirty tablets. He would like to make it clear, he said, that these were mild sleeping pills and could only be considered dangerous if taken in excess. Answering the coroner he said she had consulted him only one more time – in February of this year, for a relaxed throat.

The next witness was Miss Anne Vincent, a first-year student at St Martin's. She was a great friend of the deceased, she said, and the previous Sunday night she had been with her at a party, a 21st birthday party held for Sir Anthony Maidment, an undergraduate of Christ Church, at his family home at Sutton David, which was about ten miles north of Oxford. Stephanie Locke had left the party about midnight, saying she was going home to do some work. She, Anne Vincent, had stayed until the party was over at four, and as a consequence had slept until ten the next morning. About eleven she had rung Stephanie but there was no reply, so, as soon as she was dressed etc., she went round to see her. No, this was not a regular thing, but she thought she would go and discuss the party. Stephanie had been living alone since her flatmate went back to Australia at Christmas, and she, Anne, had been expecting to move in with Stephanie very soon.

The flat was the middle one of three flats one above the other, and had its own front door. You went up an outside staircase. When she got there she rang but there was no reply. The door was locked but she knew Stephanie had a habit of leaving the key attached by a string through the letterbox, so she pulled on the string and the key was there and she let herself in . . .

'Take your time, Miss–er Vincent,' said the coroner.

Anne put away her handkerchief.

'When I went in the – the bedroom I found her. There she was, face downwards on the bed. There was this – this pill bottle on the table by the bed and – and a broken glass on the floor. I touched her – just the once – then I don't mind telling you I screamed and ran . . . The people in the ground-floor flat were away but the people in the top flat heard me shouting and came down. Then there were two students passing in the street, and they came in, and someone – well, someone dialled nine-nine-nine. I was too shaking, too upset, I nearly passed out.'

'Did you touch anything in the flat?' the coroner asked.

'No, sir. Only the one thing. Her face. That was enough.'

'Did you know that the deceased suffered from sleeplessness and depression?'

'Not at all! She was always full of life.'

'She had many friends? I mean, apart from yourself?'

'Oh, yes, lots. She was a very popular person – outgoing, you know, generous.'

'Did she say she was worried about her Finals or give the impression that she was upset about anything else?'

Anne's big eyes roamed around the court.

'Not about her Finals.'

'About something else?'

The handkerchief came out again. 'Well, there was just this – this one thing which I suppose may have upset her a lot. She'd been having this affair with a married man and it was breaking up. She denied that it was, but you could see the signs . . . Then

113

the man turned up at the Maidment party. He and Stephanie talked together at the beginning of the evening and it looked as if they had a final quarrel because after that they avoided each other, and Stephanie left early and on her own, as I said.'

'Did she confide in you about her love affair and being upset because of it?'

'Oh, no. Oh, no. She wasn't the sort to – to weep on anyone's shoulder.'

Mr Webster asked: 'Did she ever mention that she might take her own life?'

Anne Vincent hesitated a moment. 'Heavens, no! The last thing.'

'D'you mean it was the last thing you would expect her to do?'

'Oh, absolutely. She was highly strung but not that sort.'

'Not even in the wake of a broken love affair?'

'I would never have thought it could happen. Ever!'

Sir Anthony Maidment was called, and two others of Stephanie's friends, who all agreed about Miss Locke as being a cheerful, highly charged, exuberant person whom they had never imagined was a prey to depression.

The coroner said to Maidment: 'Did the deceased in your opinion drink too much?'

'She – enjoyed drink – as many of us do.'

'And on Sunday night did you think she was drinking too much?'

'I didn't have a lot of time to look at my friends individually, y'know. I was the host, and there were over a hundred of us.'

'And drugs?'

The young man hesitated. 'Well no, sir, as it happened. You see, my mother was there, and I'd put in a special request to my friends – those who were fond of a – a snort or a drag. So I certainly didn't see any of that about. Anyway, I never saw Stephanie take anything, even at college parties.'

The coroner put much the same questions to Count Marcus Scanderbeg (Zog to his friends) who replied in much the same way.

'As Sir Anthony says, it is a party at which there is a good deal of laughter and high spirits and drink. Stephanie is a little high, yes. As I have seen her so before, no more and no less. She drinks gin and tonic, and sometimes beer and gin. They have a name for it. I forget.'

'Rat's tail,' said someone in the court.

The coroner frowned. 'Would you say she was in a fit condition to drive herself home?'

Scanderbeg shrugged. 'She is not perhaps fit to pass the breathalyser. But then she did not have to, did she?'

'What do you mean?'

'I believe Arun drove her home. Is it not so?'

The coroner frowned again, and bent to speak to Inspector Summers, who confirmed that he knew all about this.

'Call Dr Arun Jiva.'

A tall, fair-skinned Indian of thirty-odd went into the box. He had an austere expression and wore a deep white collar and pince-nez, which gave him an Edwardian look.

'You are Dr Arun Jiva, of twenty-one Caxton Street, Oxford.'

'That is correct, sir. Except . . .'

'Except?'

'I am from Delhi, sir. I am qualified to practise in India, but not in England. I am a postgraduate student at St Martin's College, and am at present studying for a doctorate in pathology at the Sir William Dunn School.'

'Is it true that you gave the deceased a lift home last Sunday evening?'

'Yes, sir. I was myself leaving Sir Anthony's party at round about midnight, for I had much work to do, when I saw Miss Locke bending over her car and went up to her. She said – if I may quote her – she said, "The flaming battery is flat." So I offered her a lift in my car.'

'Did you know Miss Locke?'

'Oh, yes, sir. I have been in Oxford nearly three years and I have known her most of that time.'

'What happened?'

'I drove her home, that is what happened. Broomfield Road,

where she lives – lived – is not very far from my house. It was no trouble at all.'

'Did she seem in any way distressed?'

'She did not seem happy. We had very little conversation on the way. I thought she was angry about her car. When we got to her flat she thanked me and got out. I sat there until I saw a light go on in her flat – then I drove off.'

'And you saw nothing more of her?'

'No, sir.'

'Did you think her the worse for drink?'

Dr Arun Jiva adjusted his pince-nez. 'I think she is a little. I saw her stumble once on the way up to her flat. I have, of course . . . It is not the first time I have seen her so. But usually she was jolly with it.'

'And this time?'

'Well, angry, as I have said. And depressed.'

'Thank you.'


## II


After the luncheon break the first witness was Errol Colton.

It was James's first sight of Stephanie's lover. Taller than imagined. Bony, with high forehead, darkly wiry hair, sensual mouth, eccentric Jack Nicholson eyebrows, intent eyes, fingers that wanted to drum on the edge of the box.

'You are Mr Errol Colton of Partridge Manor, Upper Kimble, Buckinghamshire? . . . Will you please tell the court anything you think will help me in this case.'

'I don't know that I can help you very much, sir, but I felt it was my duty to come forward and offer what evidence I can.' He cleared his throat and stumbled over a word or two. 'Stephanie Locke and I were lovers . . . We – we met at a house party before Christmas – and . . . you know. We met regularly through February and March, and in April, as I had to go to India on business, I invited her to go with me. This she did. When I came home I had what I suppose might be termed a crisis of conscience. My wife had rightly taken exception to my going on like this, and I wasn't anxious for her to divorce me. I also have a daughter to consider. My own home life is important to me.' He coughed carefully into his fist. 'Also, although *she* certainly didn't want our affair to end – I mean Stephanie didn't – I thought it would be much better for her if we broke up. She was still very young. To get permanently involved with me – or any man like me – sixteen or seventeen years older and married – would be a mistake. She needed someone of her own age.'

The coroner said drily: 'It might have been better if you had considered these matters before you entered on this affair, Mr er–Colton.'

Errol nodded slowly. 'I have thought so since. I believe I thought so at the time; but Miss Locke was a very attractive young woman – and a very determined one. She was – how shall I put it? – set on a course, and she was almost impossible to resist.'

'So then?'

'When we came home I told her our affair had to come to an end. She refused to believe me, told me I couldn't leave her, we meant too much to each other, et cetera. When I didn't go to see her she bombarded me with letters and telephone calls. I went to see her twice. On the second occasion, on the – on the Wednesday before her death she became hysterical, threatened . . .'

'What?'

'She didn't actually say she would take her own life . . . but I suppose her general threats may have included that. I'm afraid I didn't take them seriously. I thought she was too young and volatile and – fond of life . . .'

'When did you last see the deceased?'

'On the Sunday evening. I went to Sir Anthony Maidment's birthday party, and soon after I arrived Stephanie came across and spoke to me. She told me that she understood my position, and she promised to stay, as she called it, in the background of my life if I would agree to go on seeing her just once a week, at least for the next few months while she tried, as she said, to get over it.' Errol's glance for the first time travelled round the court, looking at the intent faces. 'Believe me, I would very much have wanted to do as she asked, for I could see how distressed she was – and I was very, very fond of her. This was no callous throwing over of someone one didn't care about. But my wife had stipulated a complete break, if we were to avoid a divorce . . . I told Stephanie this. Her face went very pale and I thought she was going to burst into tears. But she didn't. She simply muttered something about she would make me "sorry for this" and then turned on her heel and walked away.'

'What did you suppose she meant?'

'I thought she meant she might go to see my wife and make trouble that way. Certainly I never thought she would contemplate what – what it seems she did do.'

'We have yet to decide that, Mr Colton . . .'

'Yes, of course.'

'So when was the last time you saw her?'

'Well, then, at the party. I suppose I saw her three or four times during the course of the evening but I didn't speak to her again.'

'Did you think she had been drinking?'

'Not when she spoke to me. After that I tried to avoid her and certainly didn't notice whether she was drinking heavily or not. Most of us, of course, were taking the occasional glass of champagne.'

'What did you do when you left?'

'Drove straight home.'

'And arrived there?'

'I didn't really check. I was feeling pretty upset about everything. It took me forty minutes going, so probably it would take less on the return, the roads being emptier.'

'And when did you first hear of the tragedy?'

'About three o'clock Monday afternoon. The police had rung my wife, and she rang me at my office.'

'Did the dead girl ever complain to you about sleeplessness or depression?'

'In that last quarrel on the previous Wednesday she said she couldn't sleep because of – of me and what she called my cruelty. I never heard her complain of it before.'

After a moment's pause Mr Webster got up. 'May I ask, Mr Colton, the nature of your business in India?'

Errol's eyebrows wrinkled. 'My group is negotiating for the development of tourist facilities in India.'

'And Miss Locke went with you purely as a companion.'

'Of course.'

'Was there any event that occurred in India which could have affected her adversely – any shock, any temporary illness, say?'

'Nothing at all, so far as I know. We both kept in good health.'

'And when did you have this "crisis of conscience" you refer to? While you were there?'

'No, no. At least, not until the last day or so. It was really when I came home and found my wife determined that I should make an immediate decision . . .'

'You decided your girlfriend was the more easily jettisoned.'

'I must protest,' said Colton's lawyer, who had been very quiet until now. 'It is unwarranted to make such a remark.'

'All I can say now,' said Errol, 'is that I'm deeply grieved at this outcome.'

'Thank you, Mr Colton.'

There was a pause and a stirring. The coroner shifted in his chair.

He said: 'This is one of the most distressing and depressing cases I have had to listen to. A young woman on the threshold of her life, a person of good birth, good health, high spirits and integrity, takes her own life, either by accident or design, with an overdose of sleeping pills. That it was by design would seem the obvious conclusion, were it not for the absence of a suicide note and the unanimous testimony of her friends, who all say it would be quite contrary to her nature to do this. She had been drinking, we know from the testimony. Could she then have been in so confused a state of mind as to take a few sleeping pills, determined to forget her former lover, and then to have taken more later – even only a few minutes later – the first few not having had the desired effect? Could her confused state of mind have made her unaware that so little time had passed between taking one dosage and another? It seems on the face of it unlikely; but it is not impossible. It is not impossible that she drank more gin after she returned home – indeed, the empty bottle under the bed confirms the likelihood of this. So it is not inconceivable that she did not take her own life. I shall adjourn this inquest pending a more detailed report from the pathologist.'

## III

Three people were taking tea at the Randolph Hotel. There had been a group of five to begin with. The solicitor, Mr Alan Webster, Colonel Henry Gaveston, James Locke and Teresa and Thomas Saunders, a defensive group, warding off the press. 'Tell me, Mr Locke, what were your feelings when you were told of your daughter's death?' 'Did you know your daughter was in India with this twice-married man?' Taking refuge in the hotel they had talked business for five minutes, then Webster went to pick up his car with a commitment to be in touch again as soon as the date of the readjourned inquest was known.

Henry Gaveston left a moment later, feeling they would prefer to be alone but taking with him a galling sense of guilt that, as Bursar with responsibility for the well-being of the students of St Martin's, he had let his old friend down by not keeping a closer or better eye on his daughter. His was a virulent frustration, knowing that while he and James talked at the Hanover Club about Stephanie's life and prospects Stephanie was already lying dead in the city mortuary. He could only imagine how James was feeling. Soon he must go to see him and bitterly grieve for his own failure; but it did not seem appropriate to say anything more now.

And James sipped at a cup of tea and no one knew what he was feeling for he kept it very quiet. In the days before the inquest he had felt unable to believe anything. Even the identification . . . She had still looked pretty, so pretty and so pale lying like a broken flower. Only now and then reality broke in. This formal inquiry he had just witnessed had left him unbelieving. But there were ghastly rents in the canopy of disbelief – a sudden material one when the pathologist had been giving his evidence: his knife had cut into her body, dismembering, eviscerating, defiling, with hacksaw, chisel, mallet; James had choked and nearly left the court. And in the evidence of Errol Colton: the true defiling had come from him, through him, by his actions, by his smooth lies . . .

Eventually unable to bear the silence any longer Teresa plunged in. 'The police superintendent says they are going to release the flat tomorrow morning, Daddy, so Tom and I can go round. There's absolutely no need to upset yourself further.'

'I went in yesterday,' James said. There had been surprisingly little of her about, the most poignant things being the mortar board and gown that he had only seen her in once. (And how vividly her youth and blondeness had stood out, emphasised by the subfusc.) She had been uncaring about what she wore: there had only seemed a single rail of clothes.

'I don't know when we can move things,' Teresa said. 'Not yet, of course. But there's books.'

'Take what you want.'

'And the rest?'

'Oh . . .' James put down his cup. 'Whatever you think . . . You can bring some home – those that seem personal . . . There's her room still, more or less untouched. She never liked anyone tampering with it. She never seemed to want to feel she had really left.'

'I feel the same,' said Teresa.

'About the lease of the flat,' said Tom. 'How long does that run?'

'It's paid till July. You could tell the estate agents. I imagine they'll know . . .'

'Yes, I suppose so.'

James watched people going in and out of the room, undergraduates and their parents and girlfriends; and others not connected with the university, only connected with real life by the prosaic nature of their being alive. Two nineteen- or twenty-year-old girls, sisters probably, good-looking, well dressed, laughing and talking about no doubt the importance of the unimportant. Not Stephanie. Not Stephanie ever again. The peculiar personality, the charm, the talkativeness, the leggy elegance, the quirkiness of mood and mind; his blood, his daughter. Other girls, thousands upon thousands of other girls, all of some value, with one virtue or another, all prized by other parents, other lovers, all busy about private interests of their own, in which he had no part. Not Stephanie ever again.

He said: 'About the funeral. I was told next week. She'll be buried in Exton Tracey. It will be quite a way to go. Some of her local friends may not be able to make it. But it's the family church.'

'Of course.'

'I hope it won't be too far for you, Terry.'

Teresa looked down at her stomach. 'Lord, no. I'm absolutely fine. And being a distance away may just choke off a few of these revolting paparazzi.'

'Too much to hope,' said Tom.

'I only wish,' Teresa said, and then stopped.

James picked up one of his sticks which had slid down beside his chair. 'Wish what?'

'Well, obviously . . .'

'Don't we all.'

Teresa said: 'That man! I hope he sleeps badly for the rest of his life.'

'I doubt if he will . . . I suppose he's the type of man that impressionable young girls fall for.'

'Not me,' said Teresa. 'I didn't take to him at all! He's over life-size and everything comes too easily. I can't understand. I simply *can't* understand!'

'What?' Thomas said. 'I mean what particularly?'

Teresa turned to him. 'Maybe you thought you knew my sister. I *did* know her. Well, if you want to go wild about someone and to feel terribly with it and live everything up, it may be a fairly good idea to swan off to India for a couple of weeks with a man like Errol Colton. Great. It's a leaf in the book, a notch on the gun barrel, something to have done and be done with. Then, maybe if he is such a great lover that you can't bear to part with him, it's tough when you come home to become a single underprivileged undergraduate again, swotting for your Finals and he's not around to hold your hand and tell you how wonderful you are! Bad luck. Boo-hoo. But beyond being merely *miserable* . . . She was always more up and down than I was. But not that far down! Good God, not that far!'

James said quietly: 'More tea, Tom?'

'Thank you, no.'

Teresa said: 'Forgive me for going on about it, Daddy. I know how you must feel, just to talk about it hurts and hurts. And we've all been over this in our minds, over and over ever since we heard . . . Well, it's done. She's dead and gone. Your daughter and my sister. It's done and there's nothing we can do about it to bring her back. But I can't accept it, how it seems to have happened, not even as a possibility!'

'Nor can I,' said James. 'Nor will I.'

# Three

## I

It was called the Grove Garden Hotel and it was in Belgrave Road, near Victoria Station. It had been originally a smart town house, but unlike most of the hotels in the street it had not expanded to take in properties on either side. By dividing the upstairs drawing room three extra bedrooms had been created, bringing the total to fifteen. It was owned officially by a Mr and Mrs Daman Subarthi, who offered reduced terms for new arrivals from the subcontinent. White guests were always told the hotel was full and white staff were not engaged.

Naresh Prasad had been there four days. On the first day he had voided sixty-six packets, on the second ten; since then there had been nothing in spite of all the aperients.

At first the pain had gone – such an infinite relief – and he had thought all was well. But on the third day it had come back, not so comprehensively involving the whole abdomen, but down the left side – and just as acute. He would be free of it for a couple of hours, then it would return, gripping and griping until he groaned aloud and rolled backwards and forwards on the narrow iron bed, trying to ease it.

His hosts were waiting to know what they should do with him. Three days was the maximum any traveller of Nari's kind had ever stayed before. They had got seventy-six packets, but the letter he carried stated definitely eighty. But it was not merely the four missing packages (which represented a street value of over a thousand pounds), it was that they could not risk him becoming ill and being taken to some hospital and the remaining packages coming into the possession of the police. He knew too much. Probably he would be too scared to talk, but you never could be sure how a drugs enforcement officer might get round him.

It was possible of course that Nari had voided the four packages earlier somewhere along the way and had passed them on to a confederate in Brussels to make a profit for himself. Or the packages had caused an inflammation of the bowel which had closed on them and would not allow them to pass. A third possibility could not be considered seriously, for if the packages had burst open or leaked the carrier would be dead.

In the meantime he moaned at frequent intervals and would eat nothing. Even the castor oil he sicked up.

Nari had become aware that the people here, even the two women, were not remotely interested in him as a human being and did not care whether he lived or died. He was simply an embarrassment and a danger to them, threatening the possibility of exposure, imprisonment or deportation for them all, the break-up of a safe and profitable house.

On the fourth day in mid-morning he had a period of temporary easement and got out of bed and put on his smart shirt and long-sleeved white sweater, pulled on his trousers and shoes. From his window he looked out at the traffic in the street, the parked cars, the hurrying people. All so much more prosperous than Bombay – no beggars, no street-sellers, no rubbish, no broken pavements. But apart from that he thought there was very little difference. Civilisation created the rush, the pressure, the noise, the indifference.

On the table by the bed were the remains of his breakfast: samosas and sponge cake, and he tasted a spoonful. It was cold and unappetising but this time it went down. He finished the plate, anxious to disperse the wind in his stomach. As he did so he caught sight of himself in the mirror, his face sallower than ever, drawn, cadaverous.

Yet he was a little better. His strength was returning, even though the dread of the pain hung heavy in his mind. He must get away from here. To save his health he must get away. His fingers fumbled as he tied his smart tie. He struggled into his long-waisted grey jacket.

He must face them, demand that he should be paid what was owed him and set free to enjoy his three weeks in England. At the very least they must give him some idea of their intentions.

He turned the handle of the door and found it opened. (At night it was locked.) In the passage outside a Tamil maid was cleaning out the next-door room; dirty sheets and a towel and a pillow case were in a heap by the door. He stepped over them and went downstairs.

Subdued voices on the first floor. One was that of Mr Subarthi, the other that of Pavel, the man who usually brought him his food.

'Well, we can't go on much longer,' Pavel said, talking in Hindi. 'Why don't we call Dr Yaqoob?'

'What could he do? We have no facilities for surgery here.'

'Would that matter?'

'Well, my God. We cannot have the hotel turned into a slaughter place! . . . Personally I would like to put him on the next plane back to India, have done with him. But we must get permission first. Or send him back to Brussels – where he could be met, safeguarded.'

'If we have to, it's better to be rid of him here. Take him to that high-rise building where Miss Roberto has her offices. A convenient fall . . .'

'Like Sita Ram? But that was a different case in which his guilt was proven . . . Anyway, we must wait until instructions come through, I tell you. Meantime see he does not talk to passing guests. When a man is ill it unlooses his tongue.'

Nari crept past, his heart thumping. He was weak and light-headed but fear gave him strength. He had had no intention when leaving his bedroom of doing more than confront these men; but their answers had been plainly given him. If he once went up again he might never be allowed down. He patted his pocket. They had his passport, but the wallet he had brought with him was still there. It held fifty pounds in ten-pound notes and some English silver. Of course he had been paid nothing of what had been promised him here.

On the ground floor no one was about. The front door was closed but it seemed improbable that in a hotel it would be locked. Someone was banging about in the kitchen. A little reception desk on the right of the door had a register upon it and a board on the wall with keys hanging. No one in the hall at all.

Holding his breath, he slid behind the counter, turned the key that was in the drawer in the desk. Here were more keys and a bundle of English notes. He grabbed at them and stuffed them in his hip pocket. A voice was calling now. Pavel's voice.

When he opened the front door the light outside made him blink, and the cold air caught at his breath. His grey coat was far too thin for this climate and he had no hat. Shivering he went down the five steps and turned towards Victoria Station. Just now there were not enough people to hide him, but he had the presence of mind not to run.

## II

Thirteen five-pound notes in the bundle he had grabbed. It was largely luck that had made him take the direction of Victoria Station, but when he saw it and the signpost Underground he dived into it, and decided to take a train to Oxford Circus. It was a more or less random choice, but he had a cousin living in Oxford. He knew that that was not in London, but he thought the name might bring him good luck. After a couple of false starts and being sent back to buy a ticket, he caught a tube and sat in it hunched up and sickly until the name moved across the windows in front of him. Then he was out again and into the crowded streets, wandering and cold and lost and in pain again, but free. Temporarily free.

He walked about for a bit and stopped before a shop that offered cut-price clothing. Fingering his money, he hesitated long and then went in and bought a waistcoat, a scarf, a trilby hat and a pair of gloves.

The assistant seemed friendly enough, so Nari asked if he knew how he could get to Edgbaston, Birmingham, where relatives were expecting him.

'Birmingham? Cheapest would be long-distance bus, mate, but I don't know where you catch it. Next best is train. Euston's the station.'

'Eustons? Is that in London?'

'I'll say. From here . . . look, you can turn left and keep straight on till you get to Oxford Circus, then a tube will take you to the station. If you can afford it, you could be there in ten minutes in a taxi. Cost you a couple of quid.'

'Quid?'

'Pounds. Maybe less; traffic isn't bad today. You all right? You're looking seedy.'

'Thank you,' Nari said with dignity, 'I am very well.'

Nevertheless he took a taxi, as the pain was hovering.


# III


Satish Mehta had been living in England for twenty years. He was a kind but grumpy man of fifty-five with a thin energetic wife and five children, all born, with the exception of his eldest boy, Prem, in England. Two of the children were still at school, the eldest of them helped in the shop.

A prosperous business, for it was at the corner of intersecting streets, the side streets being so unimportant that parking in them was still permitted, and he was on the edge of a comfortable middle-class area of white people who might shop mainly in the supermarkets but found Mehta useful not only as a sub-post office but for all the shortfalls in their domestic purchases.

Before the Mehtas came an English family called Robinson had run the shop with far greater efficiency than the Mehtas and kept open just as long, but the Mehtas still made a comfortable living and slept seven in the small accommodation over the shop. They had hopes of Prem, who was studying to pass his degree as a chemist, and father Mehta had already taken a lease on the

128

shop next door to turn it into a chemist's shop when his son qualified. There were two doctors' surgeries nearby.

Prem was finding it hard work and had failed the exams once. In this he was a disappointment to his parents, chiefly to his mother who had most of the enterprise of the family. The younger children yawned their way through the days, and her husband suffered from catarrh and found the climate depressing. Sometimes she thought he only came properly alive when the subject of cricket was mentioned. His children shared this passion, and when there was a test match at the nearby county ground the shop was almost unstaffed. In a recess of the small recess given over to Her Majesty's post was a tiny television set which was always on if any ball-by-ball commentary was taking place.

One afternoon early in May there appeared in the shop a tall young Indian who looked to them like a Rajasthani, in a thin grey waisted coat and a brown trilby hat; his face was haggard and drawn and he had not recently shaved. He asked the boy behind the cheese counter if he could see Mr Satish Mehta.

The boy gestured with his knife and said briefly: 'Post office.'

At the back of the shop behind the usual counter and grille a plump balding Indian was filling up forms. After due time he looked up.

'Yes?'

'Mr Satish Mehta?' the young man said.

'Yes?'

'Mr Mehta. I am your cousin, Naresh.'

Mehta's smooth gloomy face did not change. 'Cousin Naresh? Who is that? Who are you?'

The young man's face twitched as in a spasm of pain. 'Naresh Prasad, Cousin Satish. From Bombay. I am but recently arrived from Bombay. Last Thursday I was in Bombay. I came by air, on a Boeing 747, in but a few hours. My mother . . . my mother was first cousin to your wife's sister-in-law, Ania. They send you greetings from Indore.'

Mehta's face did not relax. 'It will soon be thirty years since I was in Indore. Then I was a young man, younger than you. You must ask my wife about her cousins – I know nothing of them. She is at the main till. You must ask her.'

'My mother died three years ago,' said Nari. 'Before she died she said I must visit England and meet my cousins. She said I was to bring you greetings from Indore. I have been carefully saving up until I could pay the fare.'

A customer had come up behind Nari and was waiting for her pension.

'Go and see my wife,' Mehta said impatiently. 'She will no doubt be able to greet you.'

# IV

Nari spent the night in the storeroom surrounded by packets of cornflakes and cases of tinned soups. They had found a spare mattress for him and a blanket and a tattered counterpane.

Daya Mehta said: 'It is true he is a cousin, Sati. He knows the family and all about us, but I do not understand why he has come. He says he is unwell. I hope he has brought nothing with him from Bombay.'

'No luggage, certain,' said Mehta, stirring beside her in the dark.

'He tells me it has been stolen. I do not know how much money he has got but he seems to have a little bit.'

'If he is unwell he had better go to see Dr Brown in the morning.'

'I suggested that to him, but he exclaimed no, he did not wish to see any doctor. He thinks if he takes it quietly here for a few days he will be better.'

'He is your cousin,' said Mehta after a moment, 'and it is necessary that we should show him hospitality. But for how long? There is something fishy, girl. I do not trust him.'

There was a long silence.

'Are you asleep?' he asked.

'No, I was thinking. He tells me he has lost his passport also.'

'Oh, my God!' said Mehta, sitting up. 'This is too much! There is the question, did he ever have one?'

'Do you mean – but how could he have been allowed in? You know how careful they are nowadays.'

'Indeed, but there are holes in the tightest net. Of course, it may be that I am wrong. But I do not like his looks, his nervousness, his evasiveness; he talks much but tells nothing; he eats only soft foods; I tell you, girl . . .'

'What?'

'I do not want him to be a bad influence on Prem. Already Prem idles too much of his time.'

'No,' said Daya Mehta. 'But that is not the worst. The worst thing is . . .'

'Indeed. We must pin him down as to the truth about his passport. If he is in England legally then we must try to help. If he has come in illegally we shall be held to blame if we are found to be sheltering him. It will never do for any of us to be discovered to be breaking the law of the land. It would ruin Prem's prospects and indeed the prospects of all our children. The police keep a record and once you are on the record they will come again and again. I know.'

There was silence for a time. Mehta went on: 'Although we are living in England so long there is still a feeling among many that we are intruders. You see it so often. The last thing we must do is to be getting into trouble with the police.'

'What shall I do in the morning, then? Tell him he must go?'

Mehta grunted, struggling with his fundamental good nature. 'The boy looks ill. I think in some way he has been through it. In the morning – after we have breakfasted and the children are out of the way – let us see most carefully what he has to say. If he is truly related to you it is not seemly that we should send him away without a full knowledge of the facts.'

# Four

## I

It was Polly Colton's birthday. She was fourteen, and it could hardly have been a more inappropriate time for celebration. Last weekend the house had been in a state of siege, with newsmen pressing for interviews. Suzanne had sent Polly word not to come home, and one or two enterprising media men who went to the school were choked off. Errol had been in bed for four days. Flu, he said; but this was the obvious excuse: Stephanie's death had shaken him to his roots. Even when he came down he mooned around the house and was irritable and morose.

But a birthday party for the following weekend had been long planned, and neither Polly nor Suzanne – who often made common cause with her stepdaughter – saw any reasonable excuse to cancel it. The death was almost two weeks ago, of a woman they did not know and did not like; the inquest was over, the funeral was over; it was a nasty disreputable episode which showed Errol Colton up in a bad light, but was all better put behind one. If fools of newspaper men still hovered around and cared to make something of it, then let them.

The tabloids, as expected, had had their field days. *Last Hours of Tragic Stephanie*, one had trumpeted. *Earl's Cousin With the World at Her Feet*; *Lost for Love*; *Secrets of Oxford's Smart Set*. One had got as far as *The Travel Tycoon and The Deb*.

But in fact the siege had been raised a few days ago, at least from Partridge Manor; another scandal with a royal connection had blown up.

Even so, the birthday party was a fairly muted affair. About

132

half a dozen grown-ups and a dozen young. An unexpected guest was a new friend of Daddy's called Smith. Polly had the ability of some young people of being able to take no notice whatever of people she was not interested in, but Mr Smith interested her. He was about fifty, spoke good English and was quite smooth, but anyone less like a Mr Smith it would be hard to imagine. Polly had left Corfu at eight and had not been back since, but she had vivid memories of her childhood. There had been a lawyer in Corfu, a Greek but born in Alexandria, whose reputation was highly dubious. The mothers had whispered together when he drove along the sea road in his Mercedes, and Polly had overheard them and partly understood. Mr Smith reminded her of him. (Later she learned that this man's first name was Angelo, which seemed a better fit.)

After tea, things livened up. Everyone *knew* what had happened, and after the early hesitation and silence it was as if everyone suddenly decided it was up to them to make the party go. Simon Perry, father of two of the girls, brought a large inflatable rubber fish from the boot of the car and launched it in the pool, challenging people to jump on it astride and try not to topple over. Of course it was pretty well impossible but there was lots of laughter and splashing. The fish wouldn't last long with people jumping on it, but Simon Perry said he had another in the car.

Janice had gone for more ice, so when the front door bell rang Suzanne said to Polly: 'You answer it, will you. But don't take the chain off.' Polly put a towel round her shoulders and padded wetly to the front door.

Presently she came back. 'Daddy, it's for you.'

He looked up, eyes deep set under the knitted brows. 'Some reporter?'

'No. It's a man on two sticks. Says his name is Locke.'

There was more than a touch of malice in her voice, for she thought her father had behaved like a creep, but Errol was too much on edge to notice. He paled and muttered a blasphemy, and got up. Fortunately at that moment Mrs Perry jumped on the fish, and she was no lightweight, so attention was on her. He spoke briefly to Suzanne, who shrugged. He was not bathing today but wore a brightly coloured beach shirt – one he had worn in Goa – and fawn slacks and sneakers.

He went to the door and peered through the gap allowed by the chain. James Locke always looked shorter than his real height these days, hunched as he was over his sticks.

'Yes?'

'I'd like a word with you if you have time.'

Errol's eyes travelled beyond his visitor, seeing the other parked cars, guessing that Locke had come in the estate car nearest the door.

'What about?'

'Need you ask?'

'I don't think there's very much more to be said, is there?'

James said: 'I telephoned last week, you'll remember, but you made an excuse.'

Errol rubbed his forehead and shrugged. 'I was ill. It was no excuse.'

A shout of laughter came from the pool.

'My daughter's fourteenth birthday,' Errol said sulkily. 'This is unwelcome to me but life has to go on.'

'I remember my daughter's fourteenth birthday,' said James.

Errol's colour came and went. Without replying he took the chain off the door.

James followed him into a sitting room to the left of the hall, one of those small rather useless rooms that are a feature of some Georgian houses. The walls were full of enlarged framed photographs, chiefly of churches and picturesque foreign villages. Errol took up a stance by the window, with his back to the light.

'Yes?'

Uninvited, James lowered himself into a chair, putting his sticks beside him.

After a minute Errol said: 'Was it polio?'

'What? Oh, this. No, I had an accident in France.'

'Of course I remember now; Stephanie told me. You were quite the war hero.'

James's good-looking elderly face showed no change of expression. 'It was all a long time ago.'

'Yes, two generations.'

'In my case one. Stephanie, you'll remember, was my daughter.'

Errol was going to light a cigarette but knew his hand to be unsteady. He needed another little snort. 'Look, Mr Locke, don't think I'm not upset by Stephanie's suicide. Good God, I was very, very fond of her! She was a delightful person. I blame myself bitterly for what has happened. But it never crossed my mind! Why should it? Good Christ, if every love affair ended that way! Of course I shouldn't have started it! I'm happily married. My daughter opened the door to you. When it came to the crunch, I decided that I didn't want to break up my home. All right, I should have thought of that first. Quite. But one doesn't always do what one should do. It's a sad world. An ugly world. The media has given me a drubbing. It's no more than I deserve. So there it is. It's happened and I can't do anything more, say anything more, to put it right.'

James said: 'You may know that Stephanie came to see me in Hampshire the weekend after she got back from India. We naturally talked about the trip.'

Errol didn't say anything. He just stood and waited.

James said: 'She told me there was a likelihood that your affair was about to break up. But she gave me the impression it was to be her choice.'

'Well, she would say that, wouldn't she.'

'Why?'

'Well . . . I think it's true, isn't it: women like to feel they are in control of their love affairs – that *they* should choose, not the man. After all it's the woman who always has to say yes in the first place. It's very hurtful to feel they are being – turned away from.'

'She seemed to look on it as some sort of a major choice she had to make, something that went beyond terminating a love affair.'

There was a pause. Things had gone quiet by the pool.

Errol said: 'She may – she just may have been considering – deciding whether to do what she finally did do.'

'So you feel sure she took her own life?'

'I'm certain she took her own life! I wish I could think it was for some reason other than a broken love affair!'

'I just don't believe it,' James said. 'Everyone who knows her well thinks it inconceivable. Everyone who knows her well – except you, that is.'

Errol got his lighter out at last. 'I think, Mr Locke, you will have to excuse me now. My guests will be wondering what has become of me.' Aware of the ineptitude of such a remark, he went on: 'Believe me, I very much wish I could –'

'Tell me,' James interrupted, an edge on his voice, 'if you had broken with Stephanie and wanted to avoid her, why did you go to the Maidment party?'

'Lady Maidment is an old friend and client of mine. I wanted to be there.'

'And what was it exactly that Stephanie said when you spoke to her there?'

'*She* spoke to *me*. Asking me if it was my final decision . . . But I gave all this testimony at the inquest! I have no intention of repeating everything I said then!'

'After you had first told her you were breaking off your affair, she then bombarded you with telephone calls and letters?'

'Yes, that's true.'

'Could you let me see some of the letters?'

'I burned them! I didn't want my wife to lay her hands on them!'

'What time did you arrive home after the Maidment party?'

'Here? I've already told the police. It would have been about a quarter to two.'

'Did anyone see you come in?'

'Look, what is this? Are you implying that I saw Stephanie again after I left? For God's sake! –'

'And did you?'

'Did I what?'

'See Stephanie after you left the party?'

'I've told you, no! I would have driven miles to avoid her! My marriage was almost on the rocks. It's far from secure even now, for Suzanne blames me for this tragedy. As you do. As I blame myself!'

'You know the verdict, I suppose?'

'Of course. I couldn't be at the resumed inquest because I was too ill to come. But –'

'Death by Misadventure. That's what it was called.'

'Well, it's the kindest one there could be, isn't it? I could tell at the first hearing that the coroner didn't want to bring in a verdict of Suicide, which still carries a sort of stigma. I only wish to God I could believe he was right!'

James said: 'Stephanie's body was released to me on Wednesday. She was buried yesterday in the family grave in Somerset. A lot of people were there. She had many friends, who travelled a long way. Also the reporters and the photographers, the clicking peering intruders whose job it apparently is to pry into tragedy and grief. A pity you were not there. You deprived them of that pleasure.'

The cigarette got lighted at the third attempt. 'You'll do no good to yourself by inventing insults. I've accepted such blame as I carry, but –'

'I'm implying nothing,' James said. 'But my daughter was buried yesterday. I consider I have the right to put a few questions to the man who by his own admission bears responsibility for her state of mind at the time of her death. Was she on drugs?'

Errol stared. 'What?'

'Are you on drugs?'

'What are you talking about? Drugs never came into this! Are you out of your mind?'

'I suspect –' James began, and then the door opened. A dark, olive-skinned middle-aged man with a split left eyebrow came quietly into the room.

'Excuse me,' he said. 'Do please excuse me. I hope I am not interrupting, but Suzanne sent me to see if you were all right, Errol.' He smiled apologetically at James. 'Excuse me. But Errol is only shortly out of bed, and his wife –'

'I'm fine,' Errol said with an effort. 'Everything's fine, Angelo, thank you. Mr Locke is just leaving.'


# II

Sir Humphrey Arden said: 'Well, I'm retired, old boy. Advice is free, of course, and you're welcome to any I have that seems pertinent. But what have you got to go on? As to facts, I mean. Do you know anything the police don't know? They're pretty thorough these days when it comes to a sudden death.'

They were lunching at the Hanover Club. Being midweek, the room was nearly full, but James had got his usual table in the window.

'What do I know that the police don't know? A few little things. But mainly it's not a fact at all that I'm working on, just a tiresome emotional conviction, bred of knowing and loving a person for over twenty years. I'm sure you will tend to disregard it, as the police would – as they would be forced to do – being expected to be impartial and detached in such things. But it happens that I am unalterably convinced that Stephanie did not commit suicide.'

'Well, yes, but that was not the verdict, was it? If she –'

'If she what, Humphrey? That a girl should – no, not a girl, not any girl, *my* girl – that Stephanie, my daughter, who was a very bright young woman, should have allowed her faculties to become so muddled with drink that she swallowed about *twenty* sleeping pills *accidentally*? I ask you!'

'Well, the coroner must have felt –'

'The coroner was concerned to find the most favourable verdict he could, presumably in a wish to spare our feelings. And he didn't know Stephanie. Stephanie was very like her mother: wayward, temperamental, impulsive, hard to bridle, emotional; but under it there was a weighting of common sense that would allow her to sway quite a lot without the least risk of her toppling over. Stephanie would never topple over into suicide. All right, I can see you sighing patiently.'

Arden, who had been chief Home Office pathologist and had given evidence at most of the murder trials of the last twenty years, was a broadly built plump man with scanty hair and a hearing aid. He adjusted this.

'My dear James, I am not sighing either patiently or impatiently, because I know you have not brought me here – pleasant as it is to see you! – without very good reason.'

'The very good reason, Humphrey, is that I don't believe either of the explanations put forward. This has been both a gut reaction and a natural conclusion.'

'So what are you implying?'

'That she was in some way disposed of.'

'Ah . . . Is that so?'

'That is so.'

They paused while the sole was served. James had his off the bone, but Humphrey took the fish whole. One might have guessed his profession by the skilled way he treated it when it was put in front of him.

James told him as much as he could remember of Stephanie's conversation with him on her last visit.

'In some way, probably in India, I can only suppose that she became involved in drug trafficking. Whether she was persuaded to carry some back, not knowing what it was, or had been told or had accidentally learned that Errol Colton was involved. It is all guesswork at present.'

'Why Errol Colton?'

'She went with him. These problems I've told you of were in her mind when she returned.'

'So what are you implying?'

'That Errol Colton is in some way involved in drugs, either in taking or carrying, and when he saw her revulsion he thought she would talk. So he got rid of her.'

'How?'

'That is what I have come to ask you.'

Arden helped himself to the tartare sauce. He had delicate, manicured hands that touched everything lightly. 'Tell me what other reasons you have for suspecting Colton. You say that

Stephanie did not actually link him with her talk about drugs?'

'They were the two subjects uppermost in her mind the whole time she was with me. I don't think they could have been separate. Clearly she did not want to "give him away" to me in so many words.'

'This is all suspicion so far, James.'

'Yes. Quite. I have been to see the people in the flat above Stephanie's. Of course, they have been interviewed by the police, but they seem to have heard nothing in the night at all. They did not even hear her come back.'

'I expect most of the places you go, the police will have been there before you,' Arden said gently.

'I have also seen the people in the flat below Stephanie's. They were away for the weekend. He's a Fellow of All Souls, and she teaches part time at the Dragon School. They have a cottage in Wales and were visiting it.'

'Indeed.'

'They were away', James said, 'because a neighbour in Wales telephoned them to say that an arsonist had set fire to a nearby cottage and had tried to force a way into theirs. When they got down the neighbour said he had never telephoned them. Nor was there any damage.'

'A hoax by the Welsh Nationalists,' said Sir Humphrey.

'Possibly. From their flat, unlike the top flat, it is easy to see people climbing the outside staircase to Stephanie's flat. There might have been a purpose in the hoax.'

'Indeed . . .'

'Also when I saw Errol Colton recently I asked him why, if he wanted to break with Stephanie and presumably wanted to avoid her, he had gone to the Maidment party when he knew he was sure to meet her. He said that Lady Maidment was a friend and a client of his and that he thought it necessary to be there. Last Tuesday I saw her son, whose party this was, and put this to him. He said Colton had never met his mother and that he had been invited at the last moment because another friend had told them he would like him to be asked . . .'

Arden grunted. 'Go on.'

'I have been to see both the doctors concerned. This chap who prescribed the sleeping pills, Hillsborough; it's a partnership, father and son; this was the son Stephanie saw. He was not pleased with my visit. He seemed to think it reflected on his professional competence.'

'What did you ask him?'

'Not more than the usual things. I don't believe Stephanie ever needed sleeping pills, because all her life she was a heavy sleeper. She could stay up like a night owl, but the minute she put her head on a pillow she was out like a light. I was able to discover that he did know Stephanie from an earlier and a later visit – so it was no one using her name. But why was this prescription made up by Boots in Piccadilly Circus when she was living in Oxford and hardly went to London at all?'

There was a pause while someone greeted them as he sat down at the next table.

'Then I went to see the other man, an Indian called Arun Jiva. He's a doctor in his own country and is doing postgraduate work at Oxford. Altogether an odd character; stiff and old-fashioned; chip on his shoulder, I should think. A very serious, dedicated sort of person. Hostile, thinking, I suppose, that I wanted to involve him. He simply repeated what he said at the inquest: that he had known Stephanie some time as he's attached to St Martin's, that he gave her a lift because her battery was flat and that he left her at the door. Last week my son-in-law picked up Stephanie's Mini and took it to a garage where they told him it looked as if her battery had been stolen and an old one put in in its place.'

'It can happen.'

'Oh indeed. But it's the accumulation of little untoward circumstances that gradually mount up. I went to see Sir Peter Brune, whom Stephanie had asked about his clinic, and also a social worker who had taken her round various squats the week before. Both confirmed that she seemed concerned about drugs as being in some way related to her own life.'

'So you think what, James? Can we have it quite clear?'

'I believe when she came back from the Maidment party she

was forced to swallow the pills – perhaps physically – I don't know. Or tricked into taking them. They were administered to her *somehow*. That's why I'm standing you this lunch, to ask you to determine how it could have been done.'

The wry last sentence did not detract from the purposeful tones.

Arden half laughed. 'I think on those conditions I might prefer to pay for myself . . .'

They ate for almost five minutes in silence. James clearly was not going to utter another word.

Eventually Humphrey Arden put down his knife and fork. 'I know Felix Ehrmann pretty well. He was in line for my job when I retired but for some reason they chose Jackson instead. So you can be assured that the PM was done with the utmost thoroughness. Nothing would be left to chance. Any bruises on any part of her body would be noted and reported. Any minute puncture of the skin which might indicate a needle. Saliva, contents of stomach, bladder, even hair – they would all be under the microscope. Then her clothes; the least sign of anything exceptional . . . her shoes, her car. The fact that this looked like a straightforward case of a jilted lover's suicide would not be allowed to be the excuse for a slipshod inquiry. I assure you.'

'You're not drinking your wine.'

'I will.'

It was in this club, James thought, at this table that I was lunching with Henry Gaveston while they were conveying the corpse of my daughter to hospital and inquiring as to her next of kin. Then I drove home contentedly enough, until I saw the police car . . .

He said: 'You tell me it's not on.'

'Not really, no.'

'You mean in these days of refined techniques there is no way of killing a girl and making it look like suicide which the pathologist cannot detect?'

'No ways certainly that a man like Errol would have access to.'

'How do we know what means he had access to? If I'm right in supposing he takes drugs or brings drugs into the country he

142

cannot be working alone. All the things I have told you – the discrepancies and the deceptions – all speak of a concerted effort of some sort.'

'Provided one is not making too much of them.'

'Yes,' James said. 'All right. I'm a fanciful old man trying to concoct a murder out of a simple tragic suicide – trying to rid myself of the stigma and of a paternal guilt. We all know of the murderer's mother who says, "My son couldn't have done that!" Well, I'm in her position saying, "My daughter couldn't have done that." Whereas, of course, nobody ever fully understands any other human being, however much they think they do. Well . . . let's leave it at that. Would you like Stilton?'

They finished their meal and went downstairs for coffee and drank a glass each of the '63 port. They talked of mundane things. James had resigned from the committee of the Chelsea Flower Show. For the moment, he said, he couldn't whip up an interest in anything. In anything, that is, except his one preoccupation.

'It won't bring her back,' said Arden.

'No, but I want to know how she went.'

With the port Humphrey seemed a little ill at ease. The bar was noisy, and he screwed in his hearing aid a couple of times to adjust to it. He coughed and talked at random. Then he said he should be going.

'Don't come to the door. I know what a painful business it is. But thanks for the lunch. I'll return it within the month, if you'll come.'

'I'll come.'

Sir Humphrey tramped away and James sat silently by himself for a few minutes. It would take him an hour and a half to get home. Dreary driving, most of it. And more dreary today because he had pretty well come to the end of the road. At first there had seemed so many inquiries to make. Supported by his unalterable conviction, he had kept the grief and the loss at bay by feeding his suspicion and seeing so many people and asking questions. That now was pretty well done with. There were only a certain number of people to see – and you couldn't go back and back and back. He'd like at least another word or two with both doctors, and it might be worthwhile to tackle Errol again. But there wasn't all that much new to say, unless something new turned up. He was certain the police had closed the case. He had not even taken his suspicion to them, for they dealt only in facts.

So go home and cultivate your garden and write genteel articles about acid soils and shrub roses and F2 petunias. And forget that you have lost a daughter – that all that freshness and youth and prettiness and intelligence has been wiped off the earth by a few flat pink pills. A life hardly begun, only just blossoming, with half a century of human existence gone to waste, turned already by disintegrating processes into putrefaction and horror. Stephanie was dead. She could no longer – ever – wake in the morning and see the sun, and smell the air, and know what it was to be *alive*.

Well, there was no hurry to get home. No one was waiting there for him except the faithful and good-tempered and thoughtful Mary Aldershot. The correct thing now was to get drunk. He would get drunk and then sleep it off in the library before driving home.

He beckoned the barman. 'Would you bring me another '63 port.'

'Yes, sir.'

As the barman retreated James saw Sir Humphrey Arden lumbering back. He was looking his age. What had the old boy forgotten? (Humphrey was five years older than James.)

'Did I see you order another of the '63? I think I'll stay for another glass myself. There's too little of it left.'

The barman, it seemed by intuition, brought two glasses. Humphrey paid him and sipped.

'There was a case,' he said. 'I honestly don't think it is germane – but there were similarities . . . distinct similarities. I don't know if I'm right in telling you this – not because it is in any way secret but because it won't really help you and it may only set you off on tracks that it can't really benefit you to pursue.'

'Go on,' said James.

'Well, just before I retired, it must be about five years ago, there was this doctor in Edinburgh . . .'

144

# Five

## I

Henry Gaveston, MC, having shut up his two enormous Alsa-tians – which were an important contribution to the safety of his house – went down on his creaky knees to peer under his twenty-five-year-old Alvis Grey Lady to make sure no bomb had been placed there while he was at lunch, then started it and drove the fifty-odd miles to James Locke's house near Andover. It would have been easier from St Martin's, where as usual he had spent the morning, but he had decided to eat at home since Fred, his servant and bodyguard, would, he knew, in the absence of Mrs Gaveston, have prepared his lunch.

He found James as usual in his garden but tending some seed-lings with a functional rather than a loving care. James had lost weight since his daughter died, and his face had narrowed into new lines.

Henry walked beside the electric chair as they returned to the house. When they got in and were sipping single malt whisky he said: 'I've pulled all the strings I can but the results are not deafening. Errol was born in June 1945. His mother was from Newcastle, the daughter of a Greek importer called Lascou, his father was from London and became a rubber planter in Malaysia – came home during the war, having lost most of his money and lived in what used to be called "reduced circumstances" until he died in 1960. Mother, we think, is still alive, but Errol and she never got on. Errol went to Lockfield School and Reading University. He was sent down for "dishonesty" but there seems to be no record more specific. In 1966 he went into the travel agency business, first as a courier, then as a partner in a small firm. Later he started his own firm, which went bankrupt, leaving holidaymakers stranded. In 1969 he bought a hotel in Corfu, and the same year he married Elena Mavrogodatos; their daughter was born the following year. At some stage Errol spent a month in a Greek jail for being in possession of cocaine . . .'

'Ah,' said James.

'But that's all. About six years ago he sold the hotel in Corfu and divorced his wife. He returned to England, and started another travel agency. He contrived to bring his daughter with him. At this stage his affairs became prosperous. It's not known how he financed himself in London but my friends are working on that. In 1979 he divorced his first wife and married Suzanne Fredericks, whose mother is French. He now heads a group called Sunflower Travel PLC. There are four other directors, who may be genuine, but if anything crooked is involved those will just be nominees. He has no police record in Britain – unless it is under another name, but there is certainly no suggestion of this. He is a keen and talented photographer, and while still at Reading University won a *Daily Mail* prize for the best photograph of the year. He has an exhibition at the Megson Gallery next month.'

James tapped his fingers on the crook of his stick. 'It's a detailed report. I'm very grateful.'

'It adds up to the shadowy entrepreneurial character you might suppose, doesn't it. A chap who makes money quickly and loses it quickly and wouldn't object to a shady deal if he thought he could get away with it. But nothing actually criminal.'

'Is there more?'

'No, I wish there were. The only possibly suspicious circumstance is his quick prosperity at about the time he returned to England. But this might have a perfectly innocent explanation.'

'Or it might not.'

'Quite. But so far we really only have Stephanie's conversations with you two weeks before she died – which might be significant or of little significance at all.'

'In other words, what interpretation I have put on them. And

146

my judgment may be warped by bereavement. Is that what you are trying to say?'

Henry got up and refilled his own and James's glass.

'My dear old friend, I so wish I could help you more. Ever since this happened I've been trying to say this to you, that I feel a deep sense of responsibility and guilt, that your daughter, Stephanie, the daughter of my oldest friend, a student at the college of which I am Bursar . . . someone I should have taken special pains – to see for her welfare – that this should have happened . . . I wake most nights and stay awake wondering what I might have done.'

James said: 'I can't see that you can blame yourself over this dirty business. If she'd been taking dope, you or someone would have noticed it. But she was not. She was living high, and nothing else. How could you know, or anyone know, that it was going to end this way?'

James finished his second whisky. Henry frowned, looking over the pleasant room, his face showing an uncertainty that was rare.

He said: 'Humphrey Arden telephoned me.'

James grimaced. 'Good God, what an old boy network!'

'Well, he told me what you had talked about. He was worried about the whole thing.'

'In what way?'

'Well, he seems to regret having told you of some doctor in Edinburgh who killed his wife, there being a few – a few similarities between that and Stephanie's death. He's afraid that you may jump to hasty conclusions.'

'I'm too old and disabled', said James, 'to be able to jump anywhere. But I certainly intend to see both doctors in the case again sometime soon.'

'D'you think that's wise? What can you gain? Even in the remote possibility that one or other of them had been involved in anything shady in this matter, the last thing they would do would be to *talk* about it. To you or to anyone. Whatever the truth, you will be up against the blankest of walls.'

James moved the more painful of his ankles. 'When I went to

see Jeremy Hillsborough he was the most aggressive of all the people I met. And curt. As if I were intruding on his time. As for Arun Jiva, I went to see him for a second time last week and he wouldn't open the door. When I got into my car I saw him peering through the curtain.'

Henry took his pipe out of his Norfolk jacket, began to fill it. 'Don't you think maybe the best course is to accept what has happened? Losing anyone one is deeply attached to is a very destructive and tragic thing. If it is one's father or one's mother it can – it has to be – rationalised, looked on as the normal progression of nature – however bitterly one may resent it.'

'As Dylan Thomas did.'

'What? Yes . . . But losing a son or a daughter is an inversion of the natural process, a perversion; an insult to the fitness of things . . . Nevertheless one has to try to live through it. Your other daughter, Teresa, is shortly to have a baby, your first grandchild. I wish you could try to accept what has happened – obviously you'll never forget it, but if you could look to the future . . . I know it's the bitterest of pills, but it can't do your health any good to try to prove the unprovable, to keep on and on with fruitless inquiries, leading nowhere.'

James fixed his friend with a blue stare. 'Are you trying to put me off doing anything more?'

'I am. I am, because I want to save you from the futility, the disappointment, the fatigue and the – the heartbreak of it all.'

James wheeled his way across to the window, swivelled in his chair.

'Did you say you had the names of the other directors of that company Colton controls – this Sunflower Travel group?'

Gaveston pursed his lips, took a notebook out. 'Nothing but the names. Colton is MD. The others are Timothy Lockyer, Arthur Browning, Angelo Smith and Katrina Ellis.'

'Angelo Smith. Did I tell you when I called on Errol there was another man there who put his head round the door waiting for me to be gone? An unagreeable character who looked as if he might be playing the villain in an inexpensive movie. Errol addressed him as Angelo.'

'Well, yes. But why not? If someone called Angelo Smith is a director of his company, it's not unnatural that he should be visiting Errol, is it?'

James smiled grimly. 'Henry, you must have had much more experience than I have had at smelling out suspicious situations, but some old in-built sense is telling me that whatever Stephanie got into stinks to high heaven. And Errol Colton is at the bottom of it!'

'Certainly he is to blame for this tragedy in that, had he not existed, it would never have happened. Beyond that . . . yes, there are some situations that don't add up. I've never actually been a policeman but I know what you mean, and *they* would know what you mean. There was a thing in Cyprus . . . but I won't bother you with details. The point is that, as well as having our instinct for what is shady and unresolved, most policemen develop an equal instinct for knowing when a situation is un-resolvable. In other words, they know when to give up.'

'And you expect me to give up now, after three weeks?'

'Not give up, but husband your resources, don't squander 'em on inquiries that more or less cover the same ground. I hate to say this, but it seems common sense.'

'I might go to Corfu.'

'With what purpose?'

'Errol lived there, has an ex-wife there and spent, you say, a short term in prison on a drugs charge. If you turn over enough ground you're bound to find a few worms!'

Gaveston lit his pipe. 'Could you manage on your own?'

'I think so. I might take Mary.'

'Term time would be difficult for me. But if you'd wait till mid-June I'd be happy to come with you.'

'Thanks. I might take you up on it. We'll see.'

Henry said: 'One Saturday next month Sir Peter Brune – you know, this chap Stephanie knew – is coming to dinner at St Martin's. It'll be in Hall, but the Principal is asking a few chosen friends. Peter has helped the University with a lot of money, and, as he's a distinguished scholar as well, the Univer-sity has decided to give him an Honorary Degree which will be conferred soon after the end of term. This dinner is just a little preliminary canter to mark his having been a graduate of St Martin's and his special beneficiences to us. Would you care to come along as my guest?'

'Thank you. Thanks, but I'd rather not.'

'Ah well . . . I'm sure I would feel the same.'

Conversation lapsed. After a minute Gaveston said: 'I suppose I was thinking . . .'

'That I needed taking out of myself?'

'I'm aware of your dislike of clichés, but yes, in a sense I do mean that.'

'I'll think it over.'

'And you'd meet Peter Brune again. He may not have impressed you when you saw him last, but he's really a very good fellow.'

'I don't say he didn't impress me. He was courteous and kind.'

'He told me he'd only met Stephanie twice, at that weekend he gave, and then just before she died.'

'I know. One just . . . seeks for the clue, the unexpected remark that sets a new trail . . .'

Henry pushed at the tobacco in his pipe with a silver thimble he carried for this purpose.

'Anyway, let's leave it open. I don't need to know for another week or so.'

James pressed his button and the chair moved away from the window.

'I'm not giving up yet,' he said.


## II

Arun Jiva had been born in 1949 in the village of Kamset, near Poona, the son of a minor railway official. His grandparents on his father's side were orthodox Jainists, to whom all life was sacred – so much so that one was taught to brush carefully the seat one was going to sit on to assure oneself that no tiny insect might be crushed or injured. But his father had broken away

150

from all that. Always a man of vehement opinion and passionate temper, he had come to the fore during the communal violence which followed the British withdrawal and had become a leader of the Hindu Mahasabha movement. In 1948 he had narrowly missed arraignment for implication in the murder of Gandhi, and a couple of years later had lost his job because of his rabid anti-Congress views. His death in a riot in 1958 had left Arun to be brought up by a weakly mother and his strong-minded grandparents who tried to discipline him into accepting a pious and ascetic way of life. In this, as with his father, they had failed, though Arun, who had greatly admired his father, was a man of much colder and more controlled a temper. Helped by an uncle, who was a tailor with a substantial business and shared the views of his dead brother, Arun had been sent to the medical school in Delhi where eventually he had qualified as a doctor, with high academic honours. There was even talk of a Rhodes scholarship but it came to nothing.

So he had practised for a year or two in Bombay. Though believing in nothing but secular Hinduism, he continued to show some of his grandparents' austerity in his own way of life and in his manner of dress and stiffness of speech. Whenever possible he spoke in his native Marathi.

At twenty-eight he began to find the Indian scene less and less to his liking. He talked to English and American doctors and heard of appointments at English, American and European universities; but these were only open to men better qualified than he. A D.Phil. at Oxford, for instance, would open up the world of research for him. He had no desire to go on practising, ministering to the sick and the poor. He had only contempt for such people. Pathology interested him, as did immunology. In the end he had received a substantial grant and found a place. He had come to Oxford and he had now nearly completed his doctorate.

His house in Jericho, a district which sprawled south of Aristotle Lane, in Caxton Street just round the corner from the cinema, was rented from a rich Iranian lady who was studying Astrophysics. Sometimes a fellow countryman would stay with him for a few days, but mostly he lived alone. And now, at this highly inconvenient time in his life, he was leaving, and for an indefinite period.

He was ill-temperedly thrusting some last things into his second bag when the doorbell rang. He looked at his watch. Too early for the taxi. Surely nobody had come to pick him up – wouldn't they trust him that far?

Or was it her father again, on his two sticks, bitter pain in his face, pestering, prying? But there was no obvious car outside.

He parted the dusty lace curtain further and stared down at a man he did not recognise. He was wearing a trilby hat which hid his face, but his hand, as it stretched out to press the bell again, was brown. Arun pattered down the stairs and opened the door.

A face he vaguely knew.

'You remember me, cousin?' said the man breathlessly. 'Naresh Prasad. You remember me. We met at the Hotel Welcome last year. You remember that?'

Arun hesitated, made a movement to shut the door. Then the man gave way at the knees, stumbled, regained himself, propping himself up with a hand on the brickwork.

'Cousin Arun – I – I want your help.'

Arun recalled the fellow now – he had been in that poker game in Bombay and had lost. There *was* some connection between them, some vague relationship but he couldn't remember what. It was certainly not a close one, not one the fellow had any right to put forward as a claim to special favour now. Some aunt or other in Indore had married – he couldn't recall who and it counted for nothing anyway. But the man was obviously ill.

He stood austerely aside and Nari stumbled in, into the little sitting room, where he collapsed into an armchair. When he took his hat off it showed a forehead beaded with sweat.

'What do you want?'

'I want help, cousin. I am very ill.'

'I am not qualified to practise in England. You must find some English doctor to consult.'

'I daren't do that, cousin. I dare not go to an English doctor. Can you give me some little help, shelter for a night, some treatment? I am Indian, not English. You can help me. I came to you as a last resort. For days I have been moving about. I am looking you up in the telephone book and then walking from the station. I thought, Dr Jiva will not turn his own blood away. It is an emergency, Dr Jiva. Please help. I am very ill!'

Arun impatiently put a hand on the fellow's wrist to feel his pulse. It was thin and rapid. And the wrist was hot and clammy.

'Where have you come from, man? How have you come to be like this?'

'It is a difficult story I have to tell you, cousin. I am in great trouble. I came from India only two weeks ago . . .'

Nari retched into a damp handkerchief, gulped, rubbed his bloodshot eyes. Like the capsules that were blocking his bowels, the truth had solidified, inflaming itself with lies, subterfuge, fear, resentment, pain. Now, though the physical blockage remained, the whole sordid story spilled out in that dark little front room.

He had lied to his cousins, the Mehtas, and they had allowed him to stay some days and given him invalid food and warm drinks. One night more after that he had stayed in Birmingham in a sleazy dosshouse where no questions were asked. Then as a last chance he had come by train to Oxford and sought out the cousin he had met last year in Bombay. Now he had found him, and he was a medical man, who could surely help him in his dire trouble. He would surely understand how Nari had been trapped into this terrible mission and see that it was in no way his fault.

Arun Jiva listened unemotionally to Nari's tale, which was interrupted every now and then by spasms of colic. Jiva fiddled with his pince-nez and lifted his glance to the clock. Here was a situation, complicating things at the last moment. As if everything was not sufficiently infuriating without this!

When at last his visitor had fallen silent and had temporarily finished his retchings, he said brusquely: 'You cannot stay here. I am leaving England this afternoon and returning to India for a stay of several weeks. The house will be empty. There is no one to treat you here. You must have an English doctor. There is a man called Hillsborough . . .'

'I cannot do that: you must know I cannot! For it will be

discovered that I am carrying the capsules! Then it will be prison for me – a long term, no doubt, and goodness knows what else. Then deportation after and ruin!'

Arun Jiva took off his pince-nez and wiped them. Without them his short-sighted black eyes seemed to have no light, no expression at all, as if thought, intelligence, feeling, reposed only in the lenses.

'Open your jacket.'

Nari unbuttoned his coat and jacket and shirt, unzipped his trousers. Jiva bent over him. Nari shrank in agony when the thin practised fingers probed his swollen belly. Such treatment, he knew, would bring back the crouching beast which was only waiting to pounce.

Arun Jiva said: 'When did you last pass a motion?'

'On Tuesday a little. But just watery, nothing in them.'

'Let me advise you to take no more aperients, because they could well be absorbed into the packages and make them burst.'

Nari said: 'I was given many aperients in London!'

Jiva considered him a moment. He thought him lucky to be alive. 'Your health would not be likely to be their first consideration.'

'My God . . .'

'Quite so. But look, an enema at the local hospital would be a likely solution to your problem. I have a taxi coming shortly – in twenty-five minutes – to take me to Heathrow. I can perhaps just find the time to give you a lift to the hospital where I am studying. That will be best for you.'

'I thought *you* could do something for me! My own blood cousin!'

Jiva considered again. Here there had to be a sudden decision. It could not be something to be pondered over. He said: 'I can give you an injection to ease the pain. That is simple. But I cannot miss my plane . . . Look here, I have another idea. Perhaps I can get a friend of mine to see you . . .'

'What is this friend of yours? Is he a doctor?'

'No, but he has doctors who would treat you. He is a friend. If I telephone and ask him –'

'But as to the capsules –'

'I do not think he would feel it necessary to tell anyone in authority. If I ask him, I believe he will help.'

'How can I find him?'

'I will telephone him. You will have to stay here until he sends someone round to pick you up. You understand?'

'Yes, Cousin Arun! Now you are my friend!'

Arun licked dry lips. 'I will ring him now. You will have to stay here and wait until he sends for you. It may be some hours, it may be tomorrow; it depends how busy he is, if he is at home. But if you wait here you must promise to stay in the house. There is milk and tea. You would be well advised not to take anything else. Telephone no one. Answer the door to no one else. You understand?'

Nari pulled up his knees. 'And you will give me something to ease this pain?'

'Yes. But remember you must do whatever my friend says. I think it is your best chance.'

# Six

## I

James had been in charge of the operation, and his helpers were
two farmers, a post office boy, a medical student and an electrician. They were all in ragged clothes, which was part disguise
and part necessity; they looked like tramps and they had sabotage
in mind. Apart from James, who had had a rudimentary course
before he left England, the only one with any useful practical
knowledge was Marcel, the electrician.

They had laid the charges overnight, with simple trip fuses to
demolish the bridge at the right time. The problem was to know
exactly when their quarry was to be expected. This line was used
for passenger services to and from Lyon, business men, even
schoolchildren. It would be a calamity if the wrong train were
passing over the bridge at the time.

Their objective was a train due to leave Lyon for Bordeaux at
eight in the morning carrying tanks and anti-aircraft guns to
strengthen the defences of the Biscay coast, and word was going
to be sent through from Lyon to the farmhouse about two miles
from the bridge. Unfortunately, some other members of the
Resistance who were not aware of these plans – and it was always
the custom to work in self-contained units so that capture and
torture did not involve more than the members of a single unit
– had decided that night to cut the telephone wires out of Lyon
going west.

So no quick easy telephone message could be sent.

The explosives did not need to be touched: they were well
hidden and admirably sited. But the trip fuses had to be set.

James had been out on his bicycle as soon as dawn broke,

reconnoitring the land east of the bridge. The line ran straight for a mile, then curved through a gully, with a tunnel and cliffs. He had worked it out that if he posted one of his men at the exit from the tunnel, he could be seen – just seen – by another man standing beside a tree on raised ground near the bridge. If one signalled to the other and he signalled to James, James would have about four minutes to run along the edge of the bridge and set the fuses.

It was now well after 7.30, and a cloudy breezy morning. Undulating fields, grazing cows, a distant road lined with poplars, glimmers of a green sky and a pencil or two of sun. They waited.

And waited. It occurred to James that he would not be disobeying his general instructions if he simply blew up the bridge. This would wreck the main line west from Lyon and effectively disrupt communications. But the lure of destroying the tanks and the guns was just too great.

Two railmen began to meander across the bridge from the other side, talking and gesturing and spitting as they went. As they got halfway one stopped and pointed with the stub of his cigarette at something on the line. It was the trip fuses, roughly if effectively disguised as foghorns but not sufficiently well hidden to deceive railmen. As James started up he saw Marcel standing against the skyline with both hands raised above his head. It was the signal.

James ran along the bridge. 'Halt! *Ne touchez pas! Nous sommes le maquis!*'

The man with the cigarette was kneeling looking at the fuse wire, trying to pull off the adhesive tape.

James took out his revolver. 'Stop or I'll kill you!'

The Frenchmen looked at each other. Cigarette shrugged. 'This is for the Boche? But how do you *know*? The eight-twenty is now due. That is –'

'It is not that! I have the signal!'

'*Nom de Dieu,*' said the other Frenchman. 'Those on the eight-twenty are students, housewives, young children – *all French . . .*'

He bent to yank at the fuse and James hit him on the head with his revolver. The man collapsed on the tracks.

'Get him out of the way!' As the other hesitated, 'Do you want me to shoot you?'

The railman threw away his cigarette. '*À Dieu ne plaise!* How am I to know? This could be an outrage!' But he bent to do as he was told.

As they picked up the man they could feel a quiver in the railway line. Even then James stopped to check that the fuses had not been broken. They lugged the man towards the end of the bridge as the train snorted and rattled into view.

Somebody started firing, and bullets flew near the three men, who fell in a heap at the end of the bridge, rolling to take cover in the long grass. The great engine came towards them across the bridge, thundering, unstoppable. And it did not stop. With horrible frustration James saw the train coming safely across. Then there was a flash of light, an ear-splitting boom – the men were flung backwards – and the middle of the bridge began to give way.

The momentum of the engine had carried it beyond the collapse as it poured white smoke into the great blue-black column of the explosion; then the train slowed to a stop and with extraordinary deliberation the bridge behind it came apart, and one by one the trucks and carriages fell with the bridge into the ravine below.

## II

As he slid and sidled painfully but peacefully into his estate car James wondered what had brought that adventure so vividly back today. Perhaps it was a dream he had had last night which was that he could walk and run as easily as he had once done.

He had learned to run as never before on that morning long ago, for with twelve Germans dead and a score more injured and enormous damage to railway stock and the bridge, the saboteurs had to be found. Marcel was shot and killed early on, but the rest got away, including Captain James Locke. Somehow *he* had got away, running doubled through the tall hay. Somehow he had made it – otherwise he would not be here, bereaved of a beautiful daughter who would then never have been born, prepared to go out and persevere obstinately on this most discouraging quest.

'I'm going to see Arun Jiva,' he said. 'He's avoided me twice. If he's not prepared to answer the door I shall wait. If I draw blank there I shall try Hillsborough before I come home.'

Mary patted his arm. 'Have a care.'

'Of course.'

Since Stephanie died Mary had taken to sharing his bed more often – not for any physical contact these days but for the companionship. She knew how badly James had taken the tragedy, but he was not a man to say much about it, and she believed, rightly, that she was a valuable outlet. Often they talked long into the night: he would take the tablets to contain the pain in his ankles, but never since Stephanie's death would he touch sleeping pills. So sometimes they talked until three or even four, but when he woke in the morning she was always gone. It was as if the role of the housekeeper took over at dawn.

He had put his wheelchair in the back of the estate car, but there did not appear much likelihood of his being able to use it.

Oxford was as crowded as usual. Every time he came into the city he winced at the horrors of the new architecture. If they'd built it all in Cowley it wouldn't have mattered. What had happened here was utter desecration.

After a brief lunch he made for Jericho and Caxton Street and parked outside. For once there was room. Slide out of the driver's seat, fish for the sticks, awkwardly up the two steps. Since Stephanie's death he had used his legs much more. It didn't suit them at all but he half welcomed the pain as a counterirritant.

The bell yielded no result. He tried the knocker. He was aware that the curtain in the downstairs room had stirred. No answer. He took his stick and rapped loudly on the window.

Wait. Silence. Then the door creaked.

A three-inch gap. A stranger. But an Indian.

159

'Is Dr Jiva here, please?'

The man shook his head vehemently. 'No. Not here. Gone away.'

'When will he be back?'

'Don't know. Not now.'

'I'll wait,' said James.

'Can't wait.' The door was closing. James's heavy boot was well adapted for putting in the way.

'I want to come in.'

The thin young man hesitated.

'Are you from Mr Errol Colton?'

'No.'

'Then I must ask you to be leaving me alone!'

'I want to know when Arun Jiva will be back.' James put his shoulder to the door. The resistance was not great and he found himself in a tiny hall. The Indian had retreated halfway up the stairs. He was in a thin vest and a pair of striped pyjama trousers and was grey-faced and shivering.

They stared at each other for nearly half a minute, then the Indian said: 'Are you the doctor?'

'No. Do you want one?'

After another pause the Indian turned and stumbled up the stairs, disappeared into a room, and a door slammed.

James limped with his sticks into the room on the right, a small sitting room. It was conventionally and sparsely furnished with little evidence of Asian influence and a few books with German titles among a round dozen on anatomy and pathology. There was a half-empty cup of tea, a tin teapot, some biscuits spilled on the floor. A few drawers were open and empty – some newspapers thrown untidily into a corner. In a wastepaper basket exam papers torn across, a notebook with diagrams. A coat and hat thrown on a chair, a pair of shoes as if kicked off.

James looked at the coat. It was from Lewisohn of Carnaby Street: the material new and cheap but stained and crumpled. No shop name in the hat. He stopped and listened. This was a tiny house but he could hear no movement upstairs. He had never thought anyone else lived here but Arun Jiva. This

sickly-looking fellow could just be visiting – or he might be a
student. The room upstairs into which he had disappeared must
be the one from which James had observed Jiva watching him
when last he called.

He lowered himself into a chair, put down his sticks and lit a
cigarette. How long would Arun Jiva be, and what could he
demand to know when they confronted each other? Were you a
party to the murder of my daughter? An impossible question.
Why was he here at all?

What do you want? Arun Jiva would say. Who let you in?
Your lodger upstairs who, by the way, looks pretty sick and
appears to be waiting for a doctor. And how does he know Errol
Colton's name?

## III

Fifteen minutes later, having recovered from the effort of getting
here, James began to look round the house. He took his time,
opening drawers and cupboards, a bureau, the fridge, the cooker,
the shed outside at the back. All very normal. There was a
non-European smell in the kitchen, and the existence of so many
spice bottles on the shelves accounted for that. Moving clumsily
about, he had made a considerable noise, but there was still no
reaction from upstairs. Maybe the man had fainted. Shouldn't
one go to inquire if only for humanitarian reasons?

Stairs were not the most impossible obstacle from James's
point of view – slopes were that – but a flight was not something
he tackled lightly. He went up now, one best foot at a time, hand
over hand on the rail, and sitting down twice on the way. They
were steep, cheap stairs, relic of the jerry-builder who put up
the house a hundred years ago. Three doors, the middle one
obviously the bathroom and loo. He was sure it was the right-
hand one.

The Indian lay on the bed. His face was still drawn and grey
but he looked better, more relaxed, his expression one of content.
There was a smell of vomit in the room.

They stared at each other. 'When will Jiva be back?' James demanded.

'I have been telling you. He is gone.'

'Gone where?'

'Home to India. On the plane this afternoon. In nine hours he will be in Bombay.'

As James came into the room he saw a photograph of Stephanie on the mantelpiece.

'When will he return?'

'Oh, he does not know. When it is convenient for everybody, he says.'

'And who are you? What is your business here?'

'My name is Nari Prasad. I am a relative. His cousin by marriage, you understand. You need not wait. Arun will not return.'

'Until it is convenient for everybody, eh?'

'What?'

'That was what you said, wasn't it? That Arun Jiva would return when it was convenient for everybody.'

'Did I say that? Maybe that is what he has told me. What is that you are taking up? I do not know who you are, sir.'

'My name is James Locke. This is a photograph of my daughter, on holiday with your friend, Errol Colton.'

Nari shook his head. 'Errol Colton is not my friend. I do not think I have ever met him.'

'Why did you expect him this afternoon, then?'

'Because my cousin says he will be coming or will be sending a doctor to see me. I have been very ill. I am still very ill. I have a stoppage of the bowels.' Nari's face twitched at the memory of the pain which Arun's tablets had driven away. He was feeling altogether better, less tense, quite willing to talk to this lame old man who had called, though anxious that the doctor should come. It was two hours since Arun had left.

'How long have you been suffering from this complaint?' James asked.

'Oh, ever since I came from India, which is nearly two weeks ago, I am forgetting the time. It has been a very bad time for me, what with the pain, I can tell you, and your weather is so cold after Bombay!'

'What have the other doctors said?'

'Others? Oh, I have not seen one yet! There are reasons, which I must not explain.'

'I suppose Dr Arun has been treating you himself. It is a pity –'

'Oh no, sir, you misunderstand. He has not treated me except this afternoon before he left for India. I have only just come. Today I have just come.'

James's eyes wandered round the room. There *were* a few evidences of hasty departure: a wastepaper basket containing cotton wool, a bottle of aftershave, a tie, newspapers, what looked like an old vest. It might be useful to examine it all a bit more closely if the opportunity arose.

'Have you been staying with other friends in Oxford?'

'No, no. To begin I stayed at a hotel in London, then I visited cousins in Birmingham. Now I cannot wait to return to India.'

'When you have been cured.'

'Exactly. When I have been cured.'

'Why did Arun Jiva not tell you the name of the doctor who was coming?'

'I do not know.'

'Instead he gave you the name of someone you have never before heard of – Errol Colton. I can't believe that!'

'Well, it is true!'

'What is Errol Colton's concern in this?'

Nari edged his way up the pillow. 'I do not think I wish to answer all your questions. Nor do I think you are entitled to ask them . . . Do you know Dr Arun?'

'I know him.'

'And what is the purpose of *your* visit?'

'I wanted to put some questions to him.'

There was the sound of a car outside. In the silence they both listened to the slam of a door. Then the bell rang.

'Perhaps this is my doctor now!'

James heaved himself up and hobbled to the window.

'I believe you're right,' he said. 'They have sent an ambulance.'

'Then I will get dressed,' said Nari.

James opened the casement window. A man in a peaked cap and a white coat looked up.

'We are upstairs,' James called. 'Can you come in?'

'Right-ho, sir.'

They waited. Nari was trying to struggle into his shirt, but as soon as he stood up nausea overcame him and he sat heavily back on the bed. James went to the door. A short, slightly bow-legged man was coming up the stairs. He had a bright Cockney face but dirty hands, and his white coat was too long for him.

'Mr Nari Prasad?' he said, taking out a card and reading from it.

'Not I,' said James, and indicated the bed, on which Nari was still lying back, feebly trying to get up.

'Mr Nari Prasad?' said the ambulance man. 'Dr Jiva rang us, told us you was ill. We've come to take you to a nursing home where you'll be properly looked after, see? No more trouble, then, no more worry. That's the style . . .'

'I am very sick,' Nari whispered. 'I think I am going over.'

'Never you mind that. We'll soon have you comfortable, like . . . Who're you, sir? We was told just to collect the one gent, nothink about a second one. We don't deal with the National Health, you know.'

James said: 'Are you from the Oxford Ambulance Division?'

The man hesitated. 'No, Abingdon. 'Ere, let me help you, Mr Nari Prasad. You'll fall over wobbling about like that –'

'Where are you taking him?' James asked. Having gone back to the window, he was resisting a deep need to sit down and was staring at the ambulance.

'Newfield Nursing 'Ome. Look, mate, you'd best let me 'elp you with them trousers. Else we shall get nowhere in a long time.'

'*New*field?' said James. 'D'you mean Nuffield?'

'No, sir. *New*field. Well known round here.'

'Mr Errol Colton,' muttered Nari. 'I was told he would come for me.'

'Don't know nothing about that. We just got the word, see. At the Newfield you'll have all the best attention. Everythink's for the best there. None of your National Health.'

Nari got to his feet again, swayed. The ambulance man helped him to zip up his trousers. 'Where're your shoes?'

'Down – I think downstairs.'

'This your weskit? Put your 'and on the rail. That's it . . .'

'The Newfield Nursing Home?' said James. 'In Abingdon?'

'Just outside. Just on the outskirts. Lovely 'ome it is.'

'I never remember hearing of such a home in Abingdon –'

'Look, old man, is that your car outside? That shooting brake. Now suppose you could just move that, eh? Do something instead of asking questions. You don't want the ambulance parked in the middle of the road when we're taking a sick patient out, do you. Just you potter off downstairs and move it round the corner, eh? There's a good scout. You move it, see, while me and Jim are looking after our patient. I'll just whistle up for Jim.'

He went past James to the window, brushing him aside. Nari was fumbling with his tie, trying to get it tied, but the cloth kept slipping through his fingers. He suddenly retched but brought nothing up. Then he sat down again, lay back, his eyes flickering and frightened. It seemed that Arun Jiva's pills were having side effects.

James said: 'What is the telephone number of the Newfield Nursing Home?'

'What?' The ambulance man half turned. 'What's up with you? Can't bother about that, mate.'

James limped to the phone by the bed. 'Do you or do you not know the number of the Newfield Nursing Home? If not, I can look it up.'

The ambulance man banged on the wood of the window. 'Why in 'ell don't this open? Oh, it's the other one, I see . . . Hey, Jim, give us a hand with the patient. I reckon we'll 'ave to carry 'im.'

'What is the name of your ambulance unit?' James said in a loud voice. 'Perhaps I can check with them.'

'Look, Jack,' said the ambulance man, bending his face, no longer cheerful, close to James as he sat in the chair by the bed, flipping over the telephone book. 'Look, we've 'ad enough of you, see? We're 'ere to take this poor bugger to a nursing home, and you keep your big mug out of our way! Else we may trample on you. Eh? Get that? If I was you I'd just shut up and leave us do our duty. Savee?'

Nari was moaning and turning his head from side to side. The front door banged. Jim had got the message. James began to dial.

'What the flaming 'ell're you doing now?'

'Ringing nine-nine-nine.'

# Seven

## I

James gave his own version of events to the sergeant who eventually arrived.

He had, he said, called upon Dr Arun Jiva, who had been a friend of his daughter's, but he had found no one at home except this young Indian who was clearly very ill. The Indian, it seemed, had only turned up that morning and Dr Jiva, himself about to leave the country, had rung a friend asking that Mr Nari Prasad should be looked after while he was away.

While he and Prasad were talking an ambulance had arrived. This he thought unusual, to say the least, since it was unheard of these days for an ambulance to be called for a patient who was able to walk or to sit in an ordinary car. So he had taken a quick look through the window and seen that the ambulance not only did not belong to any of the local services but was not genuine. The engine and chassis was unmistakably a Citroën; the body more like a conventional shooting brake. It would, of course, have carried conviction to a foreigner, but it looked artificial to anyone used to living in England.

So he had tackled the ambulance man, who was at first evasive and then tried to bluster his way through. Had the sergeant, for instance, ever heard of the Newfield Nursing Home? The sergeant shook his head. Nuffield, of course. Did they mean that?

'Clearly not,' said James. 'I asked for the telephone number of this Newfield Nursing Home and the man refused to give it. Instead he called his driver up to help him take away his patient. He became threatening to me. Of course I shouldn't have stood a chance against two men, but when I dialled nine-nine-nine they panicked. They argued a minute at the bedroom door, and then when they heard me getting through they went back down the stairs together, slammed the door and the ambulance drove off.'

The sergeant wrote something in his notepad.

'D'you say Dr Arun Jiva has gone away for good, sir?'

'This man Nari Prasad said he was returning to India. But there do seem to be a number of personal things still lying around.'

'And this Nari whatever-it-is had only been in England a short while?'

'He said he only arrived in Oxford this morning. I've told you he said he was suffering from a stoppage of the bowels.'

The sergeant raised his eyebrows significantly. 'Well, no doubt we shall know that soon enough, sir.'

'Where have they taken him – the John Radcliffe?'

'That's correct. He'll be well looked after there.'

'He was very reluctant to go. I think if he'd been fully alive to what was happening he would have preferred to accept the ambulance after all.'

'Being only a short while in England, it makes you think, doesn't it?'

'You mean he might be an illegal immigrant?' James said.

'That or worse. There's no passport in his belongings. Very little of anything except a wallet. We've taken possession of the pills that were beside the bed; but he said these were left him by Dr Jiva. The question of whether Dr Jiva was entitled to have them in his possession is another matter we might go into later.'

James picked up his sticks. 'You'll let me know how the man goes on?'

'Oh yes, sir. We'll be in touch. I'm sure the Inspector will like to have a word with you. I presume . . .'

James got up. 'What?'

'I presume you are the Mr James Locke whose daughter died in such tragic circumstances recently?'

'I am – unfortunately.'

'Unfortunate indeed. I wasn't on that case. But it strikes deep – that sort of thing.'

James nodded. 'It strikes deep.'

'Do you need any help to your car, sir?'

'No, thank you. I can manage if I take it slowly.'

## II

The photograph was of Errol Colton and Stephanie; standing in a theatrical attitude on what presumably was a balcony in Goa. They were both naked.

On the back was written, 'Just Good Friends'.

James had not shown the photograph to the sergeant. Nor had he mentioned the name of Errol Colton.

He drove to St Martin's and asked for Henry. The porter said he was sorry the Bursar had just left. He was, he believed, going home.

Very well, thought James, he would follow. This was a matter for consultation, if not consultation with the police. It was also possibly a matter for confrontation, but that could follow.

He stopped at the Randolph for a whisky and a sandwich, and took his road map in with him, since he had not before driven to Henry's house from the direction of Oxford. It was straightforward enough. Go out through Headington, take the A40 for a bit and then fork left; then a sharp left turn before you got to Thame. As he was folding the map he saw the village of Upper Kimble marked – only a few miles further on, north of Princes Risborough – where someone else lived.

Where he might call later this evening or sometime tomorrow.

The sun was coming out now, what was left of it as the day ended. It was in motorists' eyes as they came towards him. His own screen badly needed cleaning, but he was not in a mood to be concerned with trifles.

As he left Oxford he passed a group of students striding along, talking and laughing, scarves flying, and among them was a blonde girl who reminded him of Stephanie. She was there, flashing a smile at someone and then she was gone. As quickly as Stephanie had gone.

169

His mind flickered back to a holiday they had all had together in 1977 – not the last but the best. The children had got over the defection of their mother, and he had not yet had that disastrous operation which, instead of curing his lameness, had made him so much more lame. They had gone with Evelyn Gaveston and young Charles Gaveston, Henry being then on active service in Ulster.

They had spent three weeks at the Hotel Voile D'Or at Cap Ferrat. James had hired a large motorboat and they had swum and water-skied and dived and eaten and drunk and laughed together, both at one another and with one another. He and Evelyn had amusedly agreed that while the boy was too young to be permanently affected, the holiday had done the girls no moral good at all. The adulation of the French boys had been heady, and lying on rocks like mermaids in scanty bikinis surrounded by admiring young men had predisposed neither of them to a return to school uniform with grey stockings and red cloth skirts and round red hats and flat-heeled shoes. It had unsettled the fourteen-year-old Stephanie more than the seventeen-year-old Teresa, partly because Stephanie, as the better looking and as a dazzling natural blonde, had been the object of the greater admiration. Latin boys automatically fell in love with blondes.

Parties for the young, held in the evenings of the sun-soaked days, were known as Booms. Largely innocent but inevitably with strong sexual undertones, these had led the girls into a new and riotous and Gallic world from which they had emerged with a view of life that would never be the same again.

Would it all have been different, he wondered, if Janet had lived – and stayed? She had always in her rather tired elegant way been the disciplinarian. He felt he had failed as a father, even though to some extent he had succeeded as a companion. It would have been better to bring his daughters up on principles that went beyond the strictures of writing and speaking good grammar. Children didn't always learn by example – they needed precept too.

At the root of it perhaps was his long-held dislike of interfering with another person's life. He had always felt that children should grow up to learn from their own mistakes . . . Well and good, but what if an early mistake proved fatal?

He was almost in Thame. It was the next turning to the left; he'd forgotten the name of the village, but anyway you didn't go there. Henry's house came first on the side road.

Then he saw a garage entrance and on impulse drew in to a space beyond it and came to a stop while the traffic swished past. He sat and thought it out. When he left Oxford he had intended to talk over all these new developments with Henry. But after only these few minutes on the road he had come to the conclusion that this was not between him and Henry at all.

He drove on.

Partridge Manor had begun life as a square and compact house; but long before Errol bought it someone had added a wing and stables and a clock-tower so that it had an impressive appearance of no architectural merit. You approached it down a long gravel drive overgrown with laurels and larches. In his time Errol had developed the back of the house, with a tennis court and croquet lawn, but had been content to leave the front untended except for the most ordinary maintenance.

When James drove up that cold May evening a few birds were singing, and the last of the sun was striking fire from the tops of the larches. There was an early light in an upstairs room. Someone was in. Perhaps everybody was in and had not yet bothered to switch on. He pulled the bell. Even after so few steps he already wanted to sit down.

A long wait. The garages attached to the house were not visible from here, so he could not see if the cars were out. He pulled the bell again.

No reply. His ankles were like fire, he hadn't stood on them so much for a couple of years. The doctor told him he should lose weight; but surely he would need to lose a couple of stone before it had any significant effect on his walking.

And in fact what else was there to lose weight for if it meant depriving oneself of one of the few pleasures left in life? It was not in any case that he overate, only that he was forced to under-exercise.

There was definitely a light on upstairs, though he could not now see it from the porch. He was getting more than physically tired of waiting outside front doors.

He tried the door. It opened onto the wide hall. He took two clumsy steps in. The light was visible on the landing above. He thought to call out and then decided he would not. The house was very quiet. He shut the door behind him.

Someone must be in. An unlocked front door was a common-place in an occupied house; but people like the Coltons would never all go out and leave it unlocked.

He tried the handle of the door leading to the small sitting room where he had seen Errol before. The room was unlit and empty.

Up the stairs? He had climbed enough stairs for one day. This was like a retake of his visit to Caxton Street. To save his legs and to make less noise he sat on every second stair and levered himself up with his hands. But with two sticks it was impossible not to make the occasional noise, and someone would surely have heard if anyone was there. At the end of a short passage a door was ajar, and the light came from there. He pulled himself up by the banister, turned the corner and hobbled to the room.

This was a big room overlooking the front of the house, and the walls were even more full of photographs than the room downstairs. In addition to the normal lights, two Anglepoise spot-lights focused on a work table which was spread with loose photographs. There was also a half-full glass of a pale brown liquid that looked like whisky, and a cigarette end smouldered in an ashtray. But no one there.

James stood by the table and looked at the photographs. Two more of Stephanie, one standing bareheaded in slacks and a jersey against some Gothic arch, the other walking across a quadrangle with books under her arm. Her happy carefree expression stabbed him like a poisoned knife. Others were of churches, Christian but foreign, he was inclined to think Indian. A number of a primitive fishing vessel on a palm-fringed beach. Another of an attractive bungalow with a frangipani tree flowering in the garden. At the end of the table was a big black folder about two feet square. On the outside was written in white paint: *Exhibition of Photographs by Errol Colton, Megson's Gallery, 1–25 June 1984.*

James raised his head and listened. House totally quiet. No one might ever have lived in it. The servants, he presumed, were day servants or hired for special occasions.

He opened the folder and began to look through it. No doubt that Errol was a first-rate photographer. Subtle gradations of light and shade illuminated every picture. James went through the seventy photographs rather quickly to see if the man would have had the cold tactlessness to include any of Stephanie. He did not see one, but as he turned the pages a slip of paper fell out on the desk. It was brief and typewritten. *The Boss says scrap numbers 22 and 49. At this time he wants no more links than need be.* It was signed *C.*

James put the paper back. Then he turned to number 22.

It was of a house, surrounded by tall pencil trees. Stone-built, large, with a portico and big windows. Certainly not a new place, might be eighty or ninety years old, not English though the style was English; just possibly Scottish, but more probably Mediter-ranean, especially because of the trees. He looked up 49. It was of the same house.

What had clearly attracted Errol Colton were the wonderful storm clouds that provided a backdrop for the house and its trees. They were angry and rent, and a halo of sun lit the ragged edges like a vision of judgment – a photographer's dream. They were among the most effective pictures in the portfolio.

James cleared his throat and looked round the empty room. A lavatory flushed. So there was someone in after all.

The pictures were loosely attached to the dark brown pages by strips of sellotape. Gently James detached the two photo-graphs. They were too big to go flat in a pocket so he folded them and slid them into his inside breast pocket.

'What the hell are you doing here?'

It was Errol Colton, in a conventional blue suit and tie. His eccentric eyebrows were contracted with annoyance, his face flushed, as if he had been drinking.

There had been antagonism between the two men – natural in the circumstances – at the first meeting, but it had been contained within the confines of a formal conversation with other people close by. It was not so in this case.

'I called to see you,' James said. 'No one answered the door.'

'Trespassing. I'm sorry my wife isn't here to greet you. She's gone to Stratford to see *Lear*. It's not my favourite play so I let her take her cousin.'

'I came in,' said James.

'I never really enjoy seeing Gloucester having his eyes gouged out, do you?'

'I prefer it off stage.' James drew a chair forward and sat in it. One of his sticks clattered to the floor.

'So you can get upstairs if you want to,' Errol said.

James said: 'I suppose you know that Arun Jiva has left the country.'

'Who? Dr Jiva? No, why? What is it to you?'

'He appears to have gone back to India. I wondered what it was to you?'

'He's a casual friend, as you know.'

'And Nari Prasad?'

Errol took up his whisky. 'Never heard of him.'

'He seems to have heard of you. Jiva gave him your name today, and a bogus ambulance came to take him away. I happened to be there . . .'

'Just as you happen to be here, eh?'

'No, here I came with intent.'

'To do what?'

'To ask you a few more questions about my daughter's death.'

'For Christ's sake!'

'Also I would like to know about the bogus ambulance, whether you really wanted to help this young Indian or whether you wanted to put him away.'

Errol's face continued to stay flushed. He was on some sort of high. He put his whisky down and went to the door, took a

174

whistle from his pocket and blew it. He came back into the room. There was silence.

James said: 'You're a good photographer.'

'Thank you.'

'Even this one is good in its own way.' James pulled out the photograph taken on the balcony at Goa.

Errol smiled at it. 'Ah, that. I sent it to her. Not a picture, I agree, to gladden a father's heart.'

'I didn't find it in her flat. It was in Dr Jiva's house.'

A flicker of genuine surprise crossed Errol's face. He drained his whisky. 'She was evidently even more of a little tart than I thought she was.'

James gripped one of his sticks and Errol backed away. 'Well you asked for it,' he said, 'you asked for the truth, coming here like a thief, breaking into my house! I'm sorry your daughter died but there's nothing more to be done about it –' He stopped.

The door had opened behind him and a short dark-skinned man came into the room.

'Angelo,' Errol snapped. 'Where the hell were you? This man came clattering into the house. I heard him even when I was on the lavatory and thought it was you. What sort of a minder are you supposed to be?'

'I hear the noise and think it is you,' Angelo Smith said. 'Anyway, he is an old man and can do no harm. Do you wish him put out?'

'I wish him put out.'

'I'll go when I've finished what I have to say.' James found himself shaking with anger. 'I believe my daughter was murdered and you had some hand in it. I believe you are involved in drug trafficking in some way. And I believe you have a boss, for you haven't the guts to run an organisation such as this. Who is "the Boss"? That's what I want to know. Who is –'

Errol had made a sharp jerk of the head to Angelo Smith. 'Take this old cripple and throw him out. Don't break his legs; that would be a pity; just put him out a little roughly and make sure he drives away in his car. Make sure he remembers not to come here again.'

Smith came up quickly behind James and grasped him by his collar. Smith was a strong man and was able to yank James to his feet so that his coat was almost pulled off his shoulders. Then he took a professional grip of James's right arm, pulled it behind his back. The sticks clattered to the floor. He was frogmarched, choking, to the door and out on to the landing.

'Do you wish to go downstairs easy or hard?' Smith asked, breathing between his teeth, for James was a heavy man to handle.

'Easy,' said James. He went limp, and Smith relaxed his grip to get a firmer one. James hit him side handed across the upper lip. Smith staggered back with a hand to his face, recovered himself, but turned at the wrong moment. James hit him with a rabbit punch behind the ear. As he reeled against the banisters James helped him over. There was a monumental crash in the dark hall and no more sound at all.

After waiting a few seconds to listen, James turned back towards the room. The door was half-ajar. His legs almost giving way, he staggered back.

'For Christ's sake, Angelo, what in the name of hell have you done! . . .'

Errol had come towards the door, and saw there not Angelo Smith but James Locke.

'Your friend – has had a fall . . .'

They stared at each other.

James said: 'It has gone very dark – out there – he must have missed his footing . . .'

Errol took a step back. 'By Christ, the police will hear of this!'

James said: 'What was it you said about Stephanie?'

Two more steps and Errol had the table between them.

'Little tart. That was the expression. Even more of a little tart than I realised.'

Errol turned and pulled open a drawer in the chest behind. Leaning on the table James picked up one of his sticks, shakily raised it.

'Little tart? You set her up in some way and are responsible for her death!'

176

Errol came up with a small black pistol. 'Now, you bastard, keep your distance while I ring for the police. You'll rot in prison for what you've done tonight!'

James threw his stick. It struck Errol a harmless glancing blow on the shoulder. Errol fired. There was no possible way in which James could have avoided the bullet had it been accurate. But Errol was no gunman. The bullet winged past and struck the pilaster of the wall between two photographs.

James was still coming. The table, only really a trestle, collapsed under his weight, and Errol, raising the gun again, was grasped by an iron hand which pulled him across the fallen table, among the photographs and the albums and the sketch books. Errol kicked and struggled to get to his feet. As he came up, James chopped him across the throat.

# Eight

## I

Henry Gaveston was writing to his wife when the telephone rang.

> And so, my dear Evelyn, this awful tragedy refuses to go away. She was a popular girl who seemed to attract attention wherever she went, and her death continues to cast a shadow over the college, and I believe to some extent over the whole university . . .

He put his pen down, brushed some tobacco ash off the table, and lifted the phone.

'Gaveston.'

'Henry. This is James.'

'My dear fellow, I was thinking of you.'

'Perhaps with reason. I have just killed two men.'

'. . . What? What d'you mean? What are you talking about?'

'Just that.'

'My dear chap, don't make that sort of joke. Where are you – at home?'

'No, at Partridge Manor. Errol Colton's house.'

A brief silence. Gaveston took the telephone away from his ear, considered it, then said: 'You can't be serious.'

'What?'

'I said, you can't be serious.'

'Oh, but I am. And Colton is one of the two.'

It had been in Henry's mind to continue his letter to Evelyn telling her of how hardly James had taken his loss and expressing the hope that he wouldn't pursue too obstinately and to his own detriment his almost paranoid belief that Stephanie had not taken her own life. But in his most pessimistic moments he had not imagined anything like this.

'James, please just tell me what has happened. Shall I come over?'

'I should be obliged. I was going to ring the police but thought I would speak to you first. If I ring the police now you should all be here about the same time.'

'Who is there now? Who is with you?'

'Nobody. I'm quite alone – except for these two.'

'God Almighty . . . There were no witnesses, then?'

'No.'

'The – the house is empty? How did you get in?'

'Just walked. The front door was open.'

Gaveston's mind was working fast. 'Who is the other man?'

'His business partner – the fellow I met before – Angelo Smith.'

'I presume – if what you say is true about them – I presume they must have attacked you? Eh? Isn't that true? You'll have been acting in self-defence?'

'A good lawyer might say so. It didn't feel that way.'

'Look – how far am I from this Partridge Manor place?'

'About ten minutes, I suppose. Might be a bit more. You take the Princes Risborough road from your place and turn left just before you get in there. Upper Kimble is only a few miles on, and you take the second or third turning – anyway it's by a telephone box. Big stone posts, and the gates seem to be left permanently open.'

'I'll come at once. And listen, James –'

'Yes?'

'Don't touch anything. I mean don't touch anything *more*. Sit in a chair and wait for me. You say the front door is open?'

'Yes. I am on the first floor.'

'There are no servants? Mrs Colton is out?'

'Yes. I believe – I think she has gone to the theatre in Stratford.'

'Well, then, I'll come right away. And James.'

179

'Yes?'

'Don't ring the police until I come.'

## II

Gaveston took his wife's Mini. It was less conspicuous than the old Alvis, and as it was double locked away in a separate garage there was less chance of its being booby-trapped.

He found the house at the second attempt and saw James's estate car parked outside the front door. There was no moon, and a cloudy sky made the evening dark. Only one light in the house, shining brightly through two windows over the front door. Henry drew on a pair of surgical gloves and went in. Whatever help he was able to offer James, it was instinct to avoid implicating himself.

Upstairs James was sitting awkwardly in an easy chair, an empty brandy glass on the floor beside him. His face was flushed and new lines showed on it.

He said: 'Well, there we are.'

Errol Colton lay on his face among the wreck of the work table. Suitably, photographs were strewn all over him. Henry's knees cracked as he stooped beside the body. He dragged off one of his gloves to feel for a pulse, to lift an eyelid, to put a finger on the skin, which was already cooling.

He drew on his glove again and stood up.

'Certainly. There we are. What *possessed* you? . . . Where is the other man?'

'Downstairs in the hall, I presume. He went over the banisters.'

Henry found a chair. 'I think I need some brandy too.'

'It's not very good,' said James. 'But it helps.'

'For God's sake.' Henry took a gulp. 'I told you I was worried about you, old friend. I *warned* you – only yesterday was it? – saying you shouldn't allow your suspicions to get – to get out of hand. But this . . . Merciful Christ! How did it happen?'

In brief jerky sentences James told him. Henry kept shaking

his head in disbelief. When he had done James looked at his watch.

'I don't know what time Mrs Colton will be back, but I wouldn't want her to find us sitting here like this. It would be better to ring the police right away.'

'This Smith man – downstairs . . . are you sure he's . . . I should take a look before we do anything else . . . He might only have been knocked out . . .'

As he put his glass down Gaveston looked at the small revolver lying on the floor half-covered by a photograph of a pretty dark girl of about fourteen – who might now be fatherless.

'Don't move.'

He left the room and switched on the landing light and the lights in the hall. James heard him going downstairs. The tension had now drained out of him, so that all he wanted to do was lie down and sleep. The acute pain in his ankles was curiously dulled, as if there were other claims on his mind's attention. It would be a new experience to sleep in a cell. Before then, he supposed, there would have to be the official warning and then the signed statement: *I, James Locke, of sound mind and body, hereby state that tonight the something of May I did feloniously kill one, Errol Colton, and also . . .* He'd had nothing to do with lawyers since Janet left him – except for the brief employment of Alan Webster to represent him at the inquest. But Webster wasn't a criminal lawyer. Henry would know someone more suitable. What would it be, manslaughter or murder? Diminished responsibility? Some hopes. He had felt no diminished responsibility at all. Regret? Remorse? It hadn't happened yet. An eye for an eye? New Testament feelings might settle in later. God, he was exhausted.

Gaveston came back into the room, mopped his forehead. In answer to James's look he said: 'Oh, he's dead all right. Whether it was the fall . . .'

James felt his bruised hand. 'Look, the telephone is over there. Or shall I just dial nine-nine-nine again?'

'James,' Gaveston said, and breathed out deeply. 'That man downstairs. I know him. I knew him thirty years ago. He's fatter

181

but there's no mistaking that split eyebrow. I knew him in Cyprus. He was a leading member of EOKA, and quite the nastiest. His real name is Angelo Apostoleris.'

'Oh? . . .'

'He was much wanted by the British. He was more ruthless than Dighenis – you know, Grivas – and much more brutal. I would have loved to have caught him.'

'Now you have.'

'Now I have. Or you have. It puts things in a different light. Coming up the stairs I've been thinking. I can't explain more but I think we should get out.'

'Get out?'

'Yes. In fifteen minutes we ought to be gone.'

'What about the police?'

'It's their problem. Let them puzzle it out. Listen, James, can you stir yourself?'

James stared at his friend. 'Oh yes. But –'

'You know, I thought your conspiracy theory about Stephanie's death was so much moonshine. But if a chap like Apostoleris is involved I can believe anything. Tell me, what did you handle in this room?'


# III


They were outside in seven minutes. Gaveston, all his bones creaking, had moved with the speed of a young man. Everything James had touched or was likely to have touched was wiped down with a damp cloth. The photographs and the folder had been gathered up and put into a pillowcase Henry had found in a neighbouring bedroom. 'We can't risk one of those – they're perfect for prints – they've *got* to go with us.' Glasses wiped, door handles wiped, banisters, chair arms, the work table, bottles, even the wall on the landing. James's legs would just get him downstairs. When he reached the bottom he listened to Henry's movements upstairs; he sounded as if he was dragging Errol across the room to the door.

He came down gasping for breath. 'We shall never deceive the police – for long but if it could be – made to look like a quarrel between them – it will help to confuse things. Now into your car and drive home. Got that?'

'Yes, I suppose so. But . . .'

The sticks went into the car first and James was shoved in after. 'I can't see that there is going to –'

'Drive carefully – and think it over on the way. Apostoleris – is no loss to the community, and I doubt if Colton is. Can you trust – your Mrs Aldershot?'

'Absolutely.'

'She will swear that you had not been out tonight?'

'Oh, yes.'

'Fred Barnes I can trust – in the same way. Fortunately Evelyn isn't – home. She is never – good under cross-examination. If there – has to be any. Now go.'

James started the car. 'My car –'

'I know. It's a risk but it's worth taking. When you get home burn – everything – those photographs – *all* your clothes, down to your shoes, socks, walking sticks. Everything. Strip yourself –'

'If I do that –'

'You have an incinerator to heat your greenhouses?'

'Yes.'

'Is it lit?'

'Yes.'

'Then use it. Goodbye.'

'Henry,' James said, 'I had no intention of involving you in this. Not in any illicit way.'

'I had no intention of – being so involved. But it has happened. I'll telephone you early tomorrow. Now go.'


# IV

At 8.30 the telephone rang in James's bedroom. He lifted it off and Henry said: 'How are you?'

'Christ, I don't know. Very sore.'

183

'Is remorse breaking in?'

'Well, I couldn't abide the thought of Mrs Colton coming home and finding . . . what she would find.'

'I appreciate that. It would have been better if a police car had been winking outside. But only marginally better. She still had the shock to be faced. Did you do what I told you?'

'Mary Aldershot was still up, so she has become an accessory after the fact.'

'Your sticks?'

'Very reluctantly. I have a spare couple, but they are not as light.'

'Old friend, I have been giving this matter some thought in the night.'

'So have I!'

'My feeling is that my attempt to fool our friends the police will not be successful for long. But the chances of *your* being traced are fairly low. Of course your car might have been seen turning in to Partridge Manor, but it's unlikely. The fields on the other side of the lane are all pastureland. Only one house is in sight, and that is on the hill.'

'How do you know? It was dark when you came.'

'I drove over this morning as soon as it was light. To continue, if no one saw you turn in, it is unlikely anyone saw your car parked there, as the shrubbery hides the drive from the lane. When I came over it was very dark, so I think it unlikely anyone saw me. So . . .'

'So?'

'I have a feeling you may yet be in the clear. I presume that is what you wish to be?'

'Well . . .'

'The urge to confess was strong in you last night.'

'It was not so much an urge to confess as a feeling that there was nothing else I could do!'

'But it seems there may be.'

James shifted his elbow and took the telephone in his other hand. The side of his right hand was painful but no bruise showed. 'Listen, Henry, you're in a position of some authority,

184

Bursar of an Oxford college, still with many contacts in the Ministry of Defence and some with the police. If Mary has become an accessory in this affair, how much more you! It would go very badly for you if this came out. You have Evelyn to think of and a still fairly young son.'

'I considered all that in the night. But by then most of the boats were burned, weren't they. And unless you decide to split on me, there's still nothing to connect me with this affair. Fred will swear in any court in the kingdom that I did not stir from the house last night. I spent the whole evening writing in the study. Fred came in twice to bring me drinks.'

'So I am now a – well, whatever you want to call me, and three more people are accessories. It is a big price to pay for a fit of temper.'

'Is that what it was?'

'Not quite.'

Henry said: 'For me, of course, everything was changed by my recognition of Angelo Apostoleris. It seems likely that your suspicions – which I didn't believe – were in some way correct. However Stephanie died, Colton was a member of a criminal organisation – by association and almost certainly in fact. We must sit this one out.'

'I haven't thanked you at all. Whatever I say seems inadequate, but – you must know what I feel.'

'I think so. Let's say it's a partnership. Have you seen the morning papers?'

'Only *The Times*. But it's surely too early.'

'Yes. I bought them all. I shall be off to Oxford in a minute or two – business as usual. Are you up yet?'

'Just.'

'Keep a low profile for a day or two. Tend your garden. You know I don't think anyone could believe what you did last night – being as lame as you are.'

James said: 'These last few years I've had to make a lot of use of my arms.'

'Well, your appearance is an added insurance. Let's keep our fingers crossed.'

'Indeed,' said James.

As he hung up he saw the police car arriving at the front door.

# *Nine*

## I

James's father, Sir Charles Locke, KCMG, after being Counsellor in Paris, had completed his diplomatic career as British Ambassador to Chile and then to the Netherlands. He had looked on his only son as destined for Eton and the Guards, but Margaret Locke said she didn't much care for Old Etonians – except the one she married – so James went to Charterhouse. Then when higher education beckoned he took a fancy to the stage, and when war broke out he was a vividly handsome young man playing in the touring company of *French Without Tears*.

Rather to the astonishment of his father who had come to look on him as a lost cause, he left the company and by pulling various strings not unassociated with his father's distinguished position, managed to get himself into the army as a humble Fusilier. After Dunkirk, which he missed, he volunteered for the Parachute Regiment but was turned down on medical grounds and instead was gazetted as a second lieutenant in the Royal Fusiliers.

However, assessing eyes had been turned on him and his application, and he was one day invited to leave Aldershot, take train and bus at the country's expense and visit a building near Trafalgar Square, where he was interviewed by a French colonel and his knowledge of the French language intensively tested. Then he was asked whether he would be willing to be parachuted into France. Having said yes he was escorted out of the back entrance and reported to an aerodrome on the Hampshire–Sussex borders on the following Monday for extra training. Three weeks later he disappeared into the unknown terrain of occupied France.

187

From there he reappeared at irregular intervals throughout the war, once recuperating from injuries to his legs. But he was soon off again, this time to North Africa where he trained other parachutists and lectured them in French.

At the end of the war he was in the Far East, preparing to lead a suicidal drop behind the Japanese lines in Borneo. Hiroshima whatever its carnage, saved many thousands of Allied lives, and incidentally James's. Then the war was suddenly over and he was back in England contemplating the resumption of a career that now seemed to belong to another man.

Although he took one or two more parts on the stage he could not find enough interest in picking up the threads of the world he had left four years ago. An aunt had died, leaving him money and the property in Hampshire; he took two extensive semi-diplomatic jobs, then married and settled to become a country gentleman. Janet, herself the daughter of a worthy but unworldly archdeacon, had found the life where – between babies – she could paint at leisure entirely agreeable, until Frederick Agassia came along.

James's interest in plants had been lifelong. When his father bought a house in Sussex to spend his leaves and settle in after his retirement, it was he, though then only eleven years old, who had planned the garden. By the time Sir Charles did come to retire, the fruits of this planning were to be seen and appreciated, and when James settled in the house in Hampshire he began all over again, reckoning that he might have forty years to watch it mature.

Well, he had had half that so far. Today green life was bursting all around him, cherries dropped their blossom, his exotic rhodo-dendrons had escaped a threatened late frost and camellias were everywhere.

It seemed improbable that he would spend the next twenty years in such agreeable surroundings. Inspector Foulsham wanted to ask him a few questions.

A small, sharp, bright-eyed man with prematurely white hair. His card said he was a Detective Inspector from the Thames Valley Police.

'Mr James Locke? How d'you do, sir. I came over early as I thought you might be going out.'

'Not today,' said James. 'Thank you, Mary; will you take coffee, Inspector?'

'Um? Thank you.' When the door closed, Foulsham said: 'A beautiful garden you have, sir.'

'Yes, it's doing very well this year.'

'I remember now seeing you on TV. Talking on flowering shrubs.'

'Once you're on television you're a marked man.'

It was not the best choice of phrase. Foulsham's bright eyes met his for a moment. 'You do, I suppose, get about quite a bit, in spite of your . . . handicap?'

'As much as I can. This electric chair is very useful for moving around the garden, but it's not a great deal of use in towns.'

'D'you drive yourself? In a car, I mean.'

'Oh yes. Automatic. I don't feel myself to be an extra hazard on the road.'

Foulsham said: 'I sometimes think a handicapped person is one of the safest of people in a car. For one thing, he drives more slowly, and I'm certain that fifty per cent of all motor accidents are simply caused by speed and impatience.'

James looked out at the cloudy morning. 'How can I help you, Inspector?'

'Oh . . .' Foulsham made a dismissive gesture. 'It's just a few routine questions. You certainly got about quite a bit yesterday, didn't you, Mr Locke?'

'I went to Oxford.'

'And later?'

'I came home.'

'What time would that be?'

'Soon after I had made a statement to your sergeant in Oxford.'

'That was after this man, Naresh Prasad, had been removed to hospital?'

'Yes.'

'Had you met Naresh Prasad before yesterday?'

'No.'

189

'But you know Dr Arun Jiva?'

James eased his ankles. 'Can hardly say I *know* him. He was a friend – or a college acquaintance – of my daughter's. When my daughter died Jiva gave evidence at the inquest. I didn't meet him then but I did go to see him a week later. That's the only time we've met.'

'Was there any special reason why you went to see him?'

'D'you mean yesterday?'

'No, in the first place.'

'I wasn't happy with the implication at the inquest that my daughter took her own life. I went to see many of her friends.'

'And was Dr Jiva able to help you?'

'No.'

'Did you bring up the subject of drugs with him?'

'Why should I? My daughter did not take them.'

'No, quite so, quite so. But I have a reason for asking.'

'May I know what it is?'

The door opened and Mary Aldershot came in with the coffee. There was a pause while she poured it out. A neat, trim person getting heavy in the thighs, quietly dressed in good tweeds, bun of brown hair, elegant hands. Only a few hours ago – nine hours ago – he had stood naked except for a towel while she bundled up all his clothes and took them down to the incinerator. In everything had gone, the photographs, the albums, the two sticks. How long had she stayed there making sure everything was burned? A cool, self-contained woman who loved him in her own cool, self-contained way. A woman, in a situation like this, beyond price. But now an accessory to murder. At his instigation and at his request she had unhesitatingly accepted that position, that burden, that risk. As unhesitatingly, if the occasion should arise, she would lie to save him from arrest and trial.

As she left the room, James remembered that there were three photographs he had omitted to burn – that of Errol and Stephanie on the balcony at Goa, and the two photographs which someone – 'the Boss' – had said must not be shown at the exhibition of Errol Colton's work at the Megson Gallery. He had folded them and put them next to his pocket book, and when he took everything from his pockets before his clothes went into the furnace he had not included these.

They were in his inside breast pocket now. If he came to be searched, would they be incriminating?

'You went to see Dr Jiva again yesterday, Mr Locke. Was it by appointment?'

'No. I just drove there and hoped to find him in.'

'Did you intend to ask him more questions about your daughter's death?'

'That sort of thing.'

'And then? Was he in?'

'Inspector Foulsham,' James said, 'I have already related exactly what happened, and everything that happened, to your sergeant. Sergeant – what is it?'

'Evans. Yes. I'm sorry. Sometimes it is useful to go over old ground.'

'Where is Naresh Prasad now?'

'Oh, still in hospital. He has been X-rayed and certain objects have been located in the upper bowel. I gather he has been given a massive dose of antibiotics and it's hoped he will pass these objects naturally. It's a little early to speculate on their nature.'

'Is that why you asked me if I brought up the subject of drugs?'

'Well, drugs certainly are the first thing in these circumstances that come to mind.'

'But they don't come to *my* mind, Inspector. They've played no part in my life; nor, as I said, did they play any part in my daughter's.'

'Quite so . . . This a – this ambulance – this bogus ambulance. How would you explain that?'

'I don't think I'm in any position to try to explain it.'

'You'll remember you gave a description of the ambulance to Sergeant Evans. Could you – thinking it over – have any other details occurred to you that you can now supply us with?'

'I don't think so.'

'You didn't see the numberplate?'

'I must have *seen* it, but I was too late getting to the window when they left; you'll appreciate I'm not a quick mover.'

191

'Nothing more about the car?'

'One of the headlamps was cracked. The nearside one.'

'Thank you. Unfortunately,' Inspector Foulsham said, 'you are the only person who saw the ambulance. We've checked with other houses in the street.'

James thought this one over. 'So actually I am the only witness that it ever existed.'

'Well, we don't question that, of course. Were both the men in it white?'

'Yes. The man I spoke to sounded like a Cockney. I could identify him easily. As I'm sure Naresh Prasad could.'

'So far Prasad has refused to talk to anybody.'

'Ah.' James sipped his coffee, careful not to let the cup rattle. 'So you've only my word about the incident altogether.'

'As I said, we have no reason to question your account, Mr Locke.'

'But from a police point of view, all you have is a lame man ringing them and reporting that an Indian whom he says he has never met before is very sick and needs attention. That it?'

'Well, if we could find the ambulance it would be a great help all round. Word has gone out, of course. If these people were breaking any law, they'll naturally be anxious to avoid identification.'

'Assuming you accept my story,' James said, 'they could hardly have not been *intending* to break the law, otherwise they wouldn't have bolted when I dialled nine-nine-nine.'

'Quite so. Quite so.'

There was a silence. Is this all there is going to be? James thought. He put his hand in his breast pocket and fingered the edge of the photographs.

Foulsham said: 'Did you know that Mr Errol Colton was dead, sir?'

Here it was. The bright eyes were fixed on him. A priest inviting a confession?

James frowned, after a moment: 'Colton, dead? When?'

'Last night.'

'Good God. He looked healthy enough. How did it happen?'

'Oh, he was healthy enough.'

'What was it, then – an accident?'

'He was murdered.'

James looked at the edge of his right hand where it was so painful. But the bruise did not show.

'I'm sorry. Though you can't expect me to shed any tears. A man like that would make many enemies. Do you know who did it?'

Another silence. They both waited.

Then James said: 'Where was it?'

'The murder? At his home near Princes Risborough in Buckinghamshire. Do you know it?'

'Yes, I went there to see him after my daughter's death.'

'That must have been an unpleasant interview.'

'It was.'

'When was the last time you saw Mr Colton?'

James frowned again, this time in thought. 'Then. It must have been about ten days ago. It was a Sunday. I'm afraid I have become rather vague as to dates.'

'It didn't occur to you to go to see him a second time, as you went a second time to see Dr Jiva?'

'Yes, I'd thought I might call later this week. But I'm sure you appreciate we were not on good terms.'

'That's what I was thinking,' said Foulsham.

'Well,' said James, 'it seems that's one question we shall never resolve now.'

'Question?'

'Question or argument, call it what you will. More coffee?'

Foulsham lowered his cup. 'Thank you, no. Did you know a Mr Angelo Smith?'

'I don't think so. Oh, wait a minute; there was somebody in Mr Colton's house the day I called. A dark chap with a scar on his brow?'

'Did you get the impression that he was there as a guest?'

'I think Colton called him a business colleague.'

'Did they seem on friendly terms?'

193

'That I couldn't say. I only saw Smith for a minute . . . How was Colton killed?'

'There was a struggle.'

## II

'Was that all he asked?' Gaveston said.

'Well, he wanted to know what time I got home last night, what I had for supper. On the way out he asked Mary the same questions, so it's as well we'd thought ahead.'

'Ah.'

'Difficult, isn't it, to say whether they were routine questions that a police officer would normally put or whether they were angled at me specially.'

'It's the business of the police to suspect everybody, and after all, you with your bitter grudge against Errol will be very much in their line of fire. But I'm sure they haven't had time to sort anything out properly yet. Did you hear the local radio?'

'No.'

'No detail but the headlines, so to speak. Two men died after fierce struggle in Buckinghamshire manor house. Mr Errol Colton, recent witness at inquest on girl undergraduate's suicide, was one of the victims. While his wife watched Shakespeare at Stratford-upon-Avon, Colton and a fellow guest appear to have quarrelled and fought to the death. The bodies were discovered by Mrs Colton and her cousin on their return. Police will make a further statement shortly.'

'You remember it well.'

'I took it down on tape. And talking of tape, James, I think after today we should not speak openly on the phone. In spite of occasional apoplexies in the House of Commons by members anxious about their civil liberties, tapping has been known to happen. I should know.'

'I seem to have landed you firmly in the shit, Henry. It was not what I intended when I rang you.'

'It was not what I intended when I came. The presence of Angelo Apostoleris changed all that.'

'He served some purpose, then.'

'Wherever Apostoleris was was organised crime. But I suppose you realise . . .'

'What?'

'I suppose you realise, though perhaps I shouldn't say this, that in removing Errol Colton from the world you are likely to have removed the most vulnerable witness to anything criminal which may have been going on.'

'Last night Errol called Smith a minder. "What sort of a minder are you supposed to be?" I think it slipped out or he was high on something. This sounds as if Smith were looking after him or protecting him.'

'Or making sure he didn't talk at the wrong time . . .'

Silence fell.

James said: 'I am at present only aware of having removed from the world the man most responsible for Stephanie's death – in whatever way it came about.'

'So be it . . .' The telephone clicked. 'That's all right, I was just checking . . . There are one or two things I might add, old friend. First, you are likely to be the object of further attention from the media. "Mr Locke, how do you react to the murder of your late daughter's boyfriend?" et cetera, et cetera.'

'I shall be strictly not available for comment.'

'And another matter, rather more serious than the media. When it once becomes established that Colton and Apostoleris did not kill each other in some drunken quarrel, the group to which they were attached – the gang, if one wants to be melo-dramatic – may put two and two together and come to the con-clusion that the police may also come to but have no proof of – that you had a finger in Colton's death, somehow. In which event there might be an attempt at reprisal.'

'Oh, come, this isn't Brooklyn.'

'Maybe I've lived myself too long in a nasty and brutish world where assassination is just another branch of politics. But do have a chain put on your door. Have you a gun?'

'No. There's a lad in the village shoots the rabbits for me.'

'I can let you have something. Better to be on the safe side. You've no licence, I suppose? We'll have to forget that for the moment. I'll bring it over probably Friday.'

'Come to dinner.'

'I might do that. Evelyn's not back for a couple of weeks yet . . . All things considered, I think this *will* blow over.'

'I'm not sure that I want it to.'

'Never mind that. Consider first the police. Unless we are desperately unlucky they will be hard put to pin anything conclusive on you, apart from motive. Nobody was killed by a gun. Your age and lameness almost rule you out where one man has a broken larynx and the other a broken back. I'm a much fitter man than you, and I don't think *I* could have done it! And second . . .'

'Second what?'

'We don't know who heads this group that Colton and Apostoleris belong to, but my feeling is they will probably do nothing which will attract more attention to themselves. This is not one rival gang feuding with another. If, as you suspect, all was not as it seemed about Stephanie's death, they will do nothing more if you do nothing more.'

'I don't at all feel like doing nothing more.'

'I'd strongly advise you to lie very quiet until the results of what you *have* done are cleared up! Merciful Christ, we have enough problems on our hands!'

'I still think Arun Jiva was involved in Stephanie's death. He was the last person to see her alive, and in view of what Humphrey Arden told me . . .'

'It's still all speculation.'

'Maybe I should have held Errol Colton over a slow fire.'

'Something like that. Oh, one other thing. You remember Anne Vincent, the girl who found – the body?'

'Of course.'

'She had a breakdown after the inquest, you'll remember. Cut tutorials and went home.'

'Yes, I tried to see her that week, but they told me she'd left.'

'She was obviously very attached to Stephanie, and the whole thing greatly upset her. She's been with her parents in north Lancashire, but the doctor there says she can come back, so she's returning Saturday. The only reason I mention this is that her father is coming with her and has asked to see me. If he has anything to say bearing on the case I'll let you know when we meet.'

# III

During that morning and afternoon James spent most of his time indoors, letting Mary protect him from telephone calls and would-be interviewers. He sat in his wheelchair and tried to read, but mainly allowed his mind to range at random over the last few days and hours. Once or twice he took the two photographs he had retained of Errol's collection and studied them. They were both photographs of the same house but there was no means of identification. Except the tall pencil trees.

Then he took out the photograph he had found in Arun Jiva's room. It still badly upset him. It occurred to him that he had never seen his daughter naked since she was two. Now he saw her, a beautiful young woman, slender, finely formed, youthful, sexually exciting. The man standing beside her, mercifully partly screened by a chair, was the man he had killed last night. James wondered who had taken the photograph; Stephanie would not have stood like that before some waiter. No doubt, since Errol was a photographic expert, he had a camera which operated itself and gave you time to walk into the picture.

Of course he knew Stephanie was not a virgin. It was just the visual presentation of it that hurt him – and that it had been in the possession of Arun Jiva. Stephanie would surely never have given it to Jiva. Had Jiva then picked it up in her flat, the night he took her home, the night he said he had not gone in with her?

Several times James had the impulse to burn the picture; each time he held back, thinking that somehow it might provide a clue to the mystery of her death.

197

Unnumbered times he had read her last and only letter from India, which poignantly – almost obscenely – had arrived a week after her death.

Dear Daddy,

Well, here we are in darkest Goa, and with a little more detail than I sent you in the p.c. from Bombay.

In fact, although we are miles from what passes for civilisation, we are in a super hotel with pretty nearly all mod cons and a view where every prospect pleases.

I came to India intending to enjoy myself but with all my defences raised to resist the oh-so-romantic pull of the Far East. The spiel of travel agents was not for me: I knew all about the other side of the picture, the poverty, the beggars, the dust and the dirt. And that's all true enough! But in the short time I have been here India has really got to me. Hard to put it into words. Of course one is impressed by the obvious things, the Taj Mahal, Fatehpur Sikri etc., which we visited from Delhi; but I think it is the people I have found so delightful, and the presence of a civilisation that's far older than ours – and different – but I believe has many of the same values. (This is prosy and pretentious, so I'll shut up.)

We are now at the hotel whose paper I'm writing on, but we are actually staying at the Hermitage, which consists of a group of about twenty handsome villas – or bungalows: one might as well use the word in its country of origin – put up last year as an extension to the hotel, and the first guests were the heads of a Commonwealth Conference held in Delhi last year, and they came to Fort Aguada to take a few days' rest and relaxation after their *labours*! I have been shown the visitors' book with the signatures of the potentates. Margaret Thatcher of course – strong bold signature as I suppose you'd expect! Mr Muldoon of New Zealand, Daniel Arap Moi of Kenya, Indira Gandhi for India etc. I notice that the Canadian PM has written his commendation in French – rather pretentious, I would have thought. And I never knew that places like Western Samoa and the Solomon Islands were in the Commonwealth!

The gardens here are just being made; many of the top bungalows are quite bare, but we have a lower one where the trees and shrubs are already grown. I met Mr Mandelkar, the head gardener, yesterday, and had a long chat. Although the Latin names are the same, thank goodness, the things we can grow they don't and the things they grow we can't, so apart from hibiscus and bougainvillaea there isn't much common ground. I've admired four types of ficus – especially *religiosa* which has some sort of a legend attached to it – gorgeous casuarina, tall ashokas, bamboos 30 feet high, jacaranda and all kinds of palms. I expect *you* would know them all!

There are 30 gardeners here. When I exclaimed at the number it was pointed out to me that for half the year no rain *ever* falls, so watering has to go on every day!

Certainly there is no sign of rain at present; since I came to India I have not seen a cloud. Errol, whom you *must* meet soon, is very considerate and very generous but also amusingly eccentric. He buzzes around leaving me often – but quite pleasantly – to my own devices. His company is developing tourism in India, but his hobby is photography, and I'm rapidly becoming the most photographed girl in the subcontinent. (Though I'm usually the human interest not the main subject.) He tells me he is hoping to get a show in the West End shortly. An opportunity for us all to meet?

Have you ever had papaya with lime? Or prawn curry with peppers? Or lassi? They're not all that exciting but they certainly make a change!

Longing to see you as soon as I get home.

Ever lovingly,<br>
Stephanie

# IV

As he put the letter away James again looked at the date: 14 April. Her letter carried no hint of strain or reservation. He knew her extrovert nature too well to suppose she could dissemble even in a letter. On 14 April and up to that date all had been fine. Whatever had happened between her and Errol had happened after. Did it help to know that? It would greatly help to know what.

That evening he said to Mary Aldershot: 'It's lucky you didn't marry me.'

She smiled at him over the top of the glasses she now used for reading. 'It would never have done.'

'That's nonsense, the way you're looking at it. But it would never have done to be married to a killer who carries his criminal instincts into his old age.'

'Not old age,' she said, 'and not criminal instincts, if I may correct you, Mr James.'

She used the 'mister' this time mockingly. Since Stephanie's death her complete concern for him, partly hidden by a spiky independence, had been clear enough.

'On consideration,' she said, 'perhaps it would have been better if I'd married you. A wife, you know, can't testify against her husband.'

James rubbed his hand. 'D'you know, over this affair I feel an utter louse, but all for the wrong reasons. I'm humiliated and angry that I have involved three innocent people – three of you counting Henry's servant – in a very nasty crime by making them accessories after the fact. I have more unease over that than over the crime itself.'

'You shouldn't have.'

'I know I shouldn't have. The self-disgust at my having involved the three of you in this should indeed be great, but it should be overwhelmed by bitterness and remorse at having committed the crime. It isn't. I ask myself why this is not so, and all the answers so far have been unpleasant.'

She put down the evening paper. 'Get you a drink?'

'I can't allow myself to escape from the situation in a haze of whisky. Listen to me for a moment.'

'I *am* listening.'

'In my life, as far as I know, and not counting people who as a result of my efforts got themselves blown up, I have actually killed only four people. Two Germans, and two last night.'

'It was wartime –'

'Exactly. And killing during time of war makes one a hero. Look at all those goddamned medals! Last night I found myself being painfully frogmarched towards the stairs by a man who was going to enjoy kicking me out. I lost my temper and threw him over the banisters. Then I went back into the room and killed the man who was responsible – in one way or another – for Stephanie's death. This was not a momentary lapse of self-control, this was quite deliberate. Quite deliberate. You understand, woman: where is your sense of horror?'

'He tried to kill you!'

'Yes. He fired and missed. So I grabbed hold of him. He didn't stand a chance then. But I could just have squeezed his throat until he passed out. Instead of that I hit him where I knew it would be lethal.'

'It was instinctive, of course,' Mary said. 'An instinct of your training.'

'I suppose,' James said, 'the Christian doctrine of Redemption shows Christ as suffering for the guilt of the world and therefore allowing mankind off the hook and able to perceive a reason for His suffering. In other words you don't get what you deserve, *He* gets what you deserve. In this way a sort of justice is done and an equilibrium achieved. What am I trying to say? That one of the basic human needs is to achieve that equilibrium. Yet one of the other basic human needs is to know satisfaction when a man gets what is coming to him. Vengeance is mine, saith the Lord. Is it because I've taken the law – and the Lord – into my own hands that I have to struggle with myself and prick myself into feeling a sense of remorse? Would I be more at ease with myself if Errol had been killed by a thunderbolt? Hardly. Even if I were a practising Catholic I don't think I could confess to something about which I feel so little remorse.'

'*I* think,' Mary Aldershot said, 'that remorse is bound up with love. If you hurt the people you care for or who care for you – or neglect them and something goes wrong . . . I hope – I pray – I shall never have to kill anything bigger than a spider; but if I did kill someone so undeserving as Errol Colton I should feel less about it than if I neglected a child, betrayed a lover, deserted a family . . .'

There was silence.

Mary said: 'Sorry, my dear. I got carried away. I wasn't thinking in personal terms . . .'

'Say no more.'

The paper rustled. Mary rubbed an eye. 'Anyway, there's nothing new in the paper, beyond what they said on the radio. It's still the same line . . .'

'Perhaps the tabloids tomorrow will waken things up.'

# *Ten*

## I

The superintendent said: 'Are you at present still allowing the media to go on that assumption?'

'Yes, sir,' said Foulsham. 'But I don't think we can carry on very much beyond tomorrow with that story.'

'A quarrel is ruled out?'

'Not a quarrel. But two deaths – there is no way, after Forensic's report, that we can suppose these two men killed each other. This man Angelo Smith died of a broken back, but before that he received a blow on the upper lip and a second one below the left ear which would have knocked him out cold. Errol Colton died of a fracture of the larynx caused again almost certainly by a single blow. His body – Colton's body – was moved after his death – dragged towards the door.'

'And the gun?'

'Seems to have been discharged harmlessly, though harm no doubt was intended. Colton fired it. Just once. Then Smith – or someone else – grabbed him and killed him. It was a very expert job.'

'Is it quite certain there was another person there at the time?'

'One or more. If Smith killed Colton, then someone threw Smith over the stairs. We can find no evidence yet who it was likely to be. The drive, as I say, is loose gravel which holds no tyre marks. No one seems as yet to have seen any car in the vicinity. The lane leading to Partridge Manor only feeds the two farms over the brow of the hill and then turns back to the main road. Opposite the house is grazing land, and the house is screened by trees and bushes. Of course we've only had a day to inquire so far. The clouds came up on Tuesday evening, but it was light till nine-thirty. Someone may yet come forward.'

'No signs of robbery.'

'Not really robbery. Mrs Colton says a lot of photographs have gone, photographs intended for an exhibition in London next month. That's all. It may have some significance. It does tend to confirm the existence of a third person.'

'How is Mrs Colton taking it?'

'She was in shock when we got there, but she seems a fairly stable sort of person. And relations can't have been too good between her and Colton after the death of the girl undergraduate.'

The superintendent rubbed his eyes. 'This I think is where we might look for evidence of motive.'

'Yes. I'm afraid we'll have to open that case again – see if the girl had other lovers or another special lover who might have been seething with a desire to revenge himself on Colton.'

'This man Smith; you say he was staying as a guest with the Coltons. There was, I think you've told me, no living-in staff.'

'No, sir. Smith had been staying there about three weeks. Apparently he's a fellow director of Sunflower Travel; that's Colton's company. According to Mrs C. he had recently become a close companion of Colton's, and usually went to London with him, though sometimes he came back alone.'

'And his history?'

'We haven't got it all yet, but Smith is not his real name. A quantity of cocaine was found in his bedroom. It's been analysed as ninety-two per cent pure Peruvian powder. There was also some – a much smaller amount – in Colton's study. Where he was killed.'

'Did either of them inject?'

'No. It was snorting. But Smith had much more than a man could want for his own requirements.'

'These are muddy waters,' the superintendent said after a moment. 'We may be looking for a revenge killing, tied up with the youngster who died in Oxford, or it may be some sort of a gang feud.'

Foulsham rose to go, but the other man waved him back to his seat. 'One more thing. James Locke. Involved in some strange affair on Tuesday afternoon with a young Indian who he turns over to us; on Tuesday evening the "betrayer" of his daughter – if one can use such an old-fashioned expression – dies. Any connection?'

'I went to see him this morning. We obviously must keep him as a possibility, but I doubt if it's more – at least so far as he physically is concerned. He's well into his sixties and badly crippled. It doesn't seem on.'

'Hell hath no fury,' said the superintendent, 'like a father bereaved.'

'He has very hard hands. I shook hands with him on purpose. And the knuckles of his right hand are dark – likely to be bruised, I'd say.'

'D'you mean they have bled?'

'No. The skin wasn't broken.'

'Pity.'

'Yes. He gardens, of course.'

'So he can get out of his chair?'

'Yes but . . .'

'And the young Indian?'

'The people in the hospital are pretty certain he has been carrying drugs into England. He's under observation. We shall know more tomorrow.'

## II

On the morrow Nari Prasad, the inflammation of his peritoneum miraculously reduced by the administration of antibiotics, was given an enema, and voided the last four packets of heroin. The condoms had withstood all the pressures and the gastric juices working within the bowels and had not burst. Therefore Nari Prasad lived to fight another day. Indeed, he recovered quickly, but he refused to explain how or why he came to be carrying the drugs. A detective sitting at his bedside pointed out certain advantages which would accrue to Nari if he gave full details of who had recruited him in India and who had received him in London. Nari said nothing. He knew that his future would not be a pleasant one in Britain and subject to British law. But he knew how much more unpleasant it would be if he returned to India (or accepted an invitation from the police to start a new life in – say – Calcutta). If he gave anything away. India is a continent. It is possible to get lost among the teeming millions. Or is it? How would one sleep at night never knowing when two men would materialise out of the darkness and beat you to death?

Sometimes he even thought longingly of Bonni and the life he had left. He had not had a woman for more than a month, and as life returned old appetites revived. It had not been poverty they had lived in – not poverty of the sort that had existed all round him: the begging priest with the tin bowl and the marigold garland round his neck; the thieving children, picking up anything they dared steal to feed their hunger; the old men in rags squatting in the gutters; the cripples edging their way along on trolleys and boards. He had never really suffered that sort of poverty; his parents had lived quietly, he had had poor food to eat and had sometimes been hungry, but not in any state of despair. He had been sent to school (where he had met such degenerate characters as Shyam Lal Shastri) and had been found a respectable if lowly position in a prosperous law firm. All thrown away! For what? It was those crooked cards! He was certain the other players had cheated him. Why had he ever gone to the Hotel Welcome? If he could roll back the last twelve months! Of course it was largely Bonni's fault for being such a complaining and exacting wife. If she had been different, more willing, more supportive, more cheerful, he would never have gone out so much in the evenings, never have been tempted to try his skill at poker. He had played often at school, for cigarettes, and often he had won. (Shyam had been in those games.) He had become skilled at bluffing the other boys, and lucky in the cards dealt him. And he had begun well in Bombay, but his luck had deserted him at the worst time, just when he was beginning to wager larger sums than he could afford.

Never poverty; a certain drudgery, a sameness to every day, fighting his way into the trains and filing letters and typing letters and hurrying and scurrying at Mr Srivastavar's beck and call, then another fight – almost literally a fight – to board the train for the long trip home, and home was Bonni, with her mother or her sister or her cousin, sitting in a corner together, whispering and complaining.

But that seemed little now. In his mind the drudgery became a gentle routine, the crowded trains an opportunity to see his acquaintances of yesterday and the day before, the two-roomed flat a symbol of safety and security and comfort. All lost. He faced the certainty of prison in England or the near-certainty of a very nasty death somewhere in India. Between them there could only be one choice.

# III

On Thursday night Henry Gaveston kept a long-promised date to dine with Peter Brune and Dr Alistair Crichton, the Principal of St Martin's. They were all old friends but they were more accustomed to meet at High Table. It was a year or more, Henry reflected, since he had been to Postgate, Sir Peter's house near Woodstock. When he arrived he saw the Principal's old Volvo already parked beside two other cars, one of them a shining black Mercedes, and wondered who else was going to be there. He thrust a hand through his untidy grey hair and straightened his crumpled tie.

Talking to Brune and the Principal were two men Henry knew by sight but could not name until he was introduced. One was Michael Somerdale, seventh Earl of Crafton and Somerdale, a cheerful, extrovert, balding aristocrat of fifty-odd with a noisy voice and a keen sense of humour. The other, Lord Worrel, an industrialist and a life peer, was stout and quiet, with a polite smile that never lost its trace of grimness.

Alistair Crichton, a tall round-faced, red-faced Scot, had a voice that was impeccably English and a bumbling manner; but he was a good administrator and an authority on European political history, on which he had published six books.

They stood drinking round the fire that burned in the grate. The May evening was chill but Henry thought the fire more for appearances than heat in this big room. But another fire was burning in the dining room and Brune said, noticing Henry's glance: 'Sorry to contribute to the smog layer but I have never been able to take to the gas and electric substitutes.'

'You were never one for anything but the real thing, were you, Peter?' said Lord Somerdale, and laughed.

'No, I suppose not. Though I accept background central heating. How could one exist in England without it?'

'Many do,' said Crichton. 'And in Scotland too!'

'Have you suffered from Royal invitations?' asked Somerdale, and there was another laugh.

They dined well. Brune had the luxury of a French chef. He told them he had only just got back in time to greet them, having lunched in London with Professor Shannon of Berkeley, who claimed to be the New World's authority on Aristophanes.

'We clashed amiable swords. Lunch didn't end till four, and then the *traffic!*'

This led to a discussion, chiefly between Peter Brune and Alistair Crichton, on the respective merits of Philippos, Araros and Nikostratos as comic poets, and then by gradual stages to the problems of the University's finances, the prospects for the new cricket season, and the forthcoming Encaenia on the 20th of next month at which Peter Brune was to be invested with an Honorary Degree. This, Peter said, was an ordeal he was both looking forward to and dreading.

It was left to Alistair Crichton to mention Errol Colton's murder. (Henry had thought it probable in this company the subject wouldn't come up at all, but he was determined not to broach it himself.)

'I believe you knew him, Peter?'

'Oh yes, quite well. I didn't hear of it until Tuesday afternoon. I rang my secretary and she told me it was on the news. I've written to Suzanne Colton. I suppose I ought to go to the funeral. It's disturbing. We live in a violent world.'

Lord Worrel was not abreast of events and had to have the story explained to him.

'But there were two, weren't there?' said Gaveston. 'Two of them. That's what I read.'

'Yes, a man called Smith. Angelo Smith. I think he was a colleague of Colton's. I see the police have dropped the idea of its being a quarrel. They think it was probably burglars who were disturbed and turned nasty.'

'Was anything taken?' Henry asked.

'It doesn't say in the account I read,' Peter said. 'But if you've just killed someone you probably don't stop for the swag.' He smiled sardonically. 'Would you, Henry? You're the expert.'

'I never actually met Colton,' Henry said. 'I saw him once, at the inquest on Stephanie Locke.'

'That was the undergraduate?' said Worrel. 'He was concerned in that? A nasty business.'

'A very nasty business,' said Dr Crichton. 'One of the nicest and brightest of our girl students. I think everyone felt it deeply.'

The next course was served and conversation became general. Then, since he could now do it without remark, Henry dropped the name into the pool again.

Crichton said: 'I did meet him a couple of times at functions. He seemed to have a liking for university life – though he was never at Oxford. I didn't take much of a fancy to him.'

'He was a contradictory character,' said Brune. 'I suppose we all are, but we don't carry it to such extensive lengths.'

'And he did?'

'Well, I'm sure he was never above turning a dishonest penny, but that isn't all the world. He was a likeable rogue, and on his day the best company you could wish for. What I did dislike about him was that he was such a shit towards women.'

'You mean this Locke girl?' said Somerdale.

'Yes, but she wasn't the only one. And he treated his first wife very badly.'

'I know James Locke,' said Somerdale. 'A good feller, with a great war record.'

'He came to see me after his daughter's death,' Peter Brune said. 'I felt a bit guilty about the whole affair because Stephanie first met Colton here; but I simply couldn't help him by giving him a sort of insight into their affair, which was what he seemed to want. After that weekend when they met I never saw them together.'

'He's taken it very badly.'

'I'm not surprised,' said Worrel.

'When I was twelve,' Peter said, 'my mother took me to Aberystwyth. We stayed at a small hotel on the front. There was an accident on the beach. A crowd of youngsters larking in the water and one was missing. The father of the missing lad called at every hotel in the town, asking if by any chance his son had been taken in and was safe. I remember him well: he was a big man in a dark blue suit and he carried a white handkerchief in his right hand and the hand and the handkerchief were pressed not to his eyes but to his heart. He had the same look as Locke had when he came to call on me.'

The meal continued in silence.

'Colton's first wife lives in Corfu, doesn't she?' Henry asked, more or less as an aside to Peter Brune.

'That's where I met them. It's some years ago. They were struggling to make a living out of a small hotel, but you know Corfu is very seasonal. You have to make enough in five months to live for twelve.'

'That was a delightful holiday Catherine and I spent with you in September the year before last,' boomed Crichton.

'Thank you.' Brune glanced good-humouredly round the table. 'You will all be welcome in your turn, if you so fancy it. I invited Henry and his wife last May but it didn't fit into their plans.'

Henry laughed. 'Well, it's a pleasure to look forward to!'

'This is a damned good wine,' said Somerdale. 'Gruaud-Larose, did you say?'

'Yes, a '66.' Brune looked at Dr Crichton. 'I've ordered a dozen cases for the college cellars.'

'You spoil us,' said Crichton. 'But you must help us to drink it.'

In such affability the meal was concluded. It was Peter Brune's fancy to follow college tradition and move into the drawing room for port and coffee and petit fours.

As they moved out, Henry said in an aside to his host: 'Locke was very unsatisfied with the verdict on his daughter, you know, and was convinced Colton could have told him more as to how and why it had happened. I believe Locke was thinking of going to Corfu to find Colton's first wife to see if she could give him more details about Colton's roots. I suppose now – I suppose with Colton dead he will have given up the idea.'

'Don't think it would have helped him,' said Brune. 'Elena, Errol's first wife, was bribed to allow Errol custody of their daughter. I think to find the roots of anything Errol did you only have to scratch the surface. He did what he pleased so long as it profited him; there were no hidden motives; he served himself.'

'I suppose you didn't actually stay at his hotel, did you?'

'God, no. It was – adequate, but very much geared to the package deal. Almost every hotel in Corfu – with perhaps one exception – is so geared, from luxury to bare boards. No, I met him at a man's house – a man called Mr Erasmus. He has – or had – a villa on Corfu near Lefkimi. Very rich man. The Coltons were there.'

'Presumably not a Greek.'

'A ship-owner, I was told, though ship-owning can cover a multitude of sins. Curious thing, nobody seemed to know his first name – unless Erasmus was his first name. Everybody calls him Mr Erasmus – even his girlfriends.'

'I take it you didn't like him.'

'Well, not sufficiently to return the invitation! I haven't seen him for years, so he may have left.'

'Ever hear of a man called Apostoleris?' Henry asked.

Peter shook his head. 'Should I have?'

Henry laughed. 'He was an EOKA terrorist in the late fifties.

211

The photograph of this man Smith in the papers reminds me of him. The split eyebrow particularly. Whatever the motive for the murders, it's clear that Colton was keeping peculiar company.'

They seated themselves round the fire and sipped their coffee and admired the port. Alistair Crichton told the story of a visit he had paid to a noble house in Cornwall, where a '67 port had been served and his hostess had inquired of her husband if it wasn't perhaps a bit over the hill? Alistair had declared it very fine, and anyway wasn't it early for a nineteen sixty-seven port to be over the hill by nineteen eighty-three? To which his host had replied quietly that what they were drinking had been put down in *eighteen* sixty-seven.

Dinner broke up at midnight.

As they were leaving Peter Brune said to Henry: 'If your friend Locke does go to Corfu, tell him to get in touch with me. I can open a lot of doors for him.'

'Thank you, I'll tell him. But I imagine with Colton dead there'll be less chance than ever of his being able to turn up anything that might be useful about his daughter. It was always a forlorn hope anyway. Stephanie never went there.'

# IV

On the Friday Naresh Prasad, an Indian of no fixed address, appeared in court on suspicion of being in illegal possession of one hundred grams of heroin and was remanded in police custody.

On the Saturday James drove his car for the first time since Tuesday. On Wednesday Mary had taken the Peugeot 305 to a car wash, but there was no unobvious way of changing its number plates, its make or its colour.

As was usually the way when he went shopping in his own village, James parked outside each shop in turn and the shopkeeper or one of his assistants would come trotting out to serve him. It saved his ankles. Most times he accepted this as a generous little convenience offered to him as an old and respected customer. Today he had doubts. 'Morning, Mr Beveridge, we need some decent potatoes, ours are going soft. Yes, whites preferred. Nobody keeps King Edwards nowadays, I suppose? Yes, Cara will do. And some apples. And a couple of ripe avocados.' By the way, Mr Beveridge, I'm not quite the genteel customer you suppose. Do you know what I did on Tuesday night?

When he got home Mary said that Colonel Gaveston had rung. Was he to ring him back? No, he said he would phone later.

James went out into his garden. In the twenty years since he had planted his main shrubs and trees some had fallen by the wayside, victims of drought or wind or heavy soil; but about seventy per cent remained and had flourished and grown to a splendid maturity. He knew them all and watched over them all. He had two men, a day a week each – Farrant was here this morning – but much of the work James did himself, dropping out of his chair onto a kneeling pad to fish out some troublesome weed or crumble the soil speculatively in his hand around a shrub which was looking sickly.

But again this morning the magic did not work. It had been gone since Stephanie died, and this week even worse than ever. In some ways he would have preferred it if Henry had not dissuaded him from ringing the police and making an outright confession. Then he would not be cowering like a criminal waiting for the knock on the door, the police car, the Black Maria. Would the average person be likely to blame him for what he had done? Certainly the average person, whatever private feelings he or she might have, would, if sitting on a jury, find him guilty of murder, and the average judge would not allow any Old Testament doctrines to prevent him from sentencing the prisoner to life. So there it was.

The gardener ambled towards him, a tall big-boned elderly man, wrinkling his eyes in the sunshine.

'Morning, Farrant. Sorry I haven't been out to see you before but there was some shopping to be done. Lovely day.'

'Yes, sir. A bit still, though, for my loiking. There might be a ground frost tonight.'

James looked up at the sky. One frost, even a light frost, would turn every rhododendron flower into a damp brown paper bag. It was a risk one always ran.

'Surely not as late as this?'

'I've known it sometoimes, sur. We're too far from the sea.' Farrant came from Weymouth.

James forced himself to take an interest in things, to act the part of himself in normal times.

Farrant said: 'Did you order more heat, sur, for the furnace, I mean? I did wonder if Harper had been up to some little game.'

Farrant disapproved of the other gardener, Harper, for being young, for being north country, and for wearing his hair long.

'I think Mrs Aldershot was burning a few things earlier in the week. Saves coke. The stove will burn most things, you know. That's why we changed it.'

'Oh, I see, sur. It was just that I wondered you should want so much heat at this toime of the year. I raked it out this morning and there was one or two things.'

'Such as?'

'Well, a brass ring, sur. Such as you might have on a walking stick. And the heel of a shoe.'

'What have you done with them?'

'I put 'em in the dustbin.'

'Good. I'm sure they're not of value. Look at that *cornus kousa*. You'd never think it was so sulky when we first put it in.'

The day passed. When Farrant was safely gone James went to the dustbin and took out the things the gardener had mentioned. They went into the compost. Then he gave the furnace another good raking through. Henry did not ring again and James, mindful of earlier warnings, did not ring back.

But Henry turned up on Sunday morning. The big grey Alvis circled the drive and stopped at the door. Henry came up the steps and Mrs Aldershot let him in. His face looked more pinched in the bright morning light, his thin body more ramshackle. His suit looked as if he had slept in it.

Discreetly Mary left them, and Henry said: 'James, when am I going to bring you good news?'

'Clearly not today by your looks. Are the police close behind?'

'No. I've heard nothing from them.'

'Then?'

'From another quarter. Anne Vincent. Her father brought her back yesterday. She'd had something not far short of a nervous breakdown and had eventually told him the cause.'

Henry took a crumpled piece of paper out of his pocket and smoothed it out, stared at it as if it might burn him.

'Anne Vincent had a crush on Stephanie; we all knew that. When she went in that morning and found her lying dead, there was this note on the bedside table. She says she felt she must try to protect Stephanie's memory and reputation, so she put it in her pocket and said nothing to the police. She said she felt it was better for everyone if the verdict could be an open one. But the responsibility of having done this preyed so much on her mind that she couldn't sleep for nights on end. So now it has come back to us. I wish I could have kept it from you. But in honesty I can't.'

James took the note and smoothed it again and read in his daughter's angular hand:

This is the end. I can't go on. There's nothing for me now, now he has gone. I'm deeply, deeply sorry to deliberately bring all this trouble and grief to the people I love and trust, and who love and trust me. But there is no other way out.
Stephanie

# *Eleven*

## I

Detective Inspector Foulsham said: 'I'm sorry to ask you some of these questions over again, Mrs Colton, but sometimes something new comes out of them. For instance, have you *no* idea why the photographs were stolen, the whole portfolio that was going to provide the material for his exhibition?'

'No idea whatever. It was only the prints that were stolen. If my husband had wanted to he could have made replacements in a couple of days.'

'Would you be able to do that for us?'

'No. He had hundreds of photographs, hundreds of negatives. He didn't consult me which he was going to choose.'

'You didn't look at the portfolio?'

'No. My husband and I were not on the best of terms.'

'Because of his involvement with Stephanie Locke?'

'Of course.'

'You say you didn't know that he took drugs?'

'No idea whatever. He certainly kept it from me.'

'You didn't notice any dramatic changes in his moods?'

'Oh, all the time. He switched on and off according to the company he was in. But he was like that all the years I knew him.' Suzanne looked dark and sultry for a moment, then shrugged. 'I suppose if you come to think of it, that may have been the reason why. But I never knew. It would have smelt in the house, surely.'

'Not in the case of cocaine, which is inhaled like snuff. A substantial quantity, as I've said, was found in Mr Smith's suitcase. When did you say you first met him?'

'I'd heard of him before, but I hadn't met him until he came to stay about three weeks ago.'

'After the death of Stephanie Locke.'

'Well, yes, I suppose so. But what has that to do with it?'

'We have found that Angelo Smith was a Greek national, but he seems to have had no passport nor any fixed address.'

'Well, surely you can trace him through the company, Sunflower Travel?'

'We've been in touch with the secretary, and the other directors. Arthur Browning, Timothy Lockyer and Katrina Ellis are out of the country. The secretary, a Mrs Chaplin, seems to know nothing much about the operation of the company, except that it is trading at a loss.'

Suzanne said curtly: 'I know very little of my husband's affairs. I only know that we were comfortably off.'

'I believe your solicitor came yesterday. This house is in your name?'

'He told me so.'

'Were Smith and your husband on good terms?'

'On the whole, yes. Sometimes Errol seemed irritated by him being around.'

'How did he explain his coming to stay here?'

'When he arrived my husband and I were not on speaking terms. Afterwards – he just said Smith was here on business.'

'Did you ever get the impression that your husband feared for his life?'

'No. Why should he?'

'Are there not people he quarrelled with?'

'None that I know of.'

'Jealous husbands? Bereaved fathers?'

'I don't know. You tell me.'

'Were you present when Mr James Locke called?'

'I was in the house, but I didn't see him.'

'That must have been a very unpleasant interview.'

'Maybe.'

'Did your husband speak about it afterwards? D'you know if there was an open quarrel?'

'No. I wouldn't think so. We had friends in at the time. It was my daughter's birthday.'

'I gather that your husband was heavily insured.'

'He didn't tell me.'

'It must be greatly to your advantage now, that he should have been.'

'Look, Inspector Foulsham,' Suzanne said, 'I was at Stratford with my cousin when my husband was killed. Or don't you believe that?'

'Of course, of course.'

'It wouldn't have been any advantage to me to have him killed, would it? In spite of his playing around with other women I was fond of him. And probably I shall be much worse off without him. Don't try to pin a motive on me!'

'I beg your pardon.'

'And may I ask when I'm going to have the house to myself again?'

'You already have, madam. I can't promise this is the last time someone will call, because we have so much to work out – dealing with Mr Colton's business activities – but we will do our best not to inconvenience you unduly.'

## II

'D'you think she's as innocent as she sounds, Foulsham?' the superintendent asked.

'No, I'm certain she knows something of his business. But she may know nothing more about the killing – or be too frightened to say. We're still sifting through Colton's papers, and he's clearly been involved in the importation of drugs. It's all carefully disguised but you can read between the lines.'

'But no nearer an arrest?'

'Afraid not, sir. The clues we have are minimal. We've so far picked up about two hundred prints. The wooden banister going up the stairs had been wiped clean, as you know. Two alien prints have been found under the rail, of a first and second finger, where a hand has grasped the rail tightly. They've not been matched with anyone yet. Oil spilled on the drive – engine oil on the pebbles – only a few drips, which indicate either a slow leak or that the visitor didn't stop long. A rubber heel mark on the outside step. A millimetre of fibre under one of Smith's fingernails; we thought he might have been grasping a coat or jacket, but it seems it came from the carpet he fell on. He didn't die instantly.'

Superintendent Willis said: 'You haven't been to see James Locke again?'

'No, sir. I rather hope I shall not have to.'

'You think he is quite innocent?'

'I don't think he could have done it himself.'

'How old is he? Sixty-five? My father was playing cricket at sixty-five.'

'Oh, it's not just age . . .'

'No, I'm sure. How good is his alibi for the night?'

'He says after making his statement to Sergeant Evans he went into the Randolph Hotel for a drink, and with his disabled sticker was able to park outside. This is confirmed by the barman, who remembered his lameness. Thereafter he says he drove straight home, arriving home about eight-thirty, and his housekeeper confirms this.'

'Anybody see him on the road? He probably had to drive through his village, and they'd know his car. It would still be full daylight.'

'Nothing's come up so far. His housekeeper looks a reliable sort of woman.'

'There's no such thing as a reliable woman where a man is concerned.'

'You may be right . . . D'you want me to bring him in?'

'On what grounds? Lord, no. It's worth printing him, of course. But unless there's something more to go on . . . Imagine him in the box – if we ever got him there. Earl's cousin. Elderly and badly crippled. War hero. Unshakable alibi. And of course a bereaved father . . . But give me a print or some other solid fact, and it'll be a different story.'

'I wonder if he could have gone to the lengths of hiring a gunman? That's more feasible to me.'

'What's troubling me about the whole thing,' said the superintendent restlessly, 'is that if it were a gang killing the two men would have been shot. If Locke had hired a gunman, ditto. Have you come up with no other suspects – lovers of the girl Locke at Oxford or anything of that sort?'

'By all accounts she had had one or two affairs, but there seems to have been nothing serious before Colton.'

'You see, Foulsham, I look on this as likely to have been a killing done almost on impulse. Neither of these men had been struck by a stick or a stone or any blunt instrument. They'd been killed by someone trained in unarmed combat. A policeman, perhaps, or a soldier, or a karate expert. In other words . . .'

'James Locke?'

'Of course it doesn't follow. But could we find a record of his activities during the war? After all, many men as brave as he was only used guns. The vast majority, in fact.'

'Seeing him as crippled as he is, it's hard to believe . . .'

'I suppose it *could* have been a friend of his. Who *are* his particular friends? Find out. Does he keep in touch with his wartime colleagues?'

'Will do.'

The superintendent grunted. 'I'd like to be able to settle for a gang killing.'


# III


That Sunday evening a man called Crane, a dropout, making his way by devious routes to Aylesbury, was picked up for stealing eggs and a chicken from the back of a public house called the Old Dray near Wendover, and in the course of interrogation early on the Monday morning it transpired that on Tuesday the 22nd he had 'happened to be passing by' Partridge Manor about nine-thirty in the evening, had seen a light burning in one of the upstairs rooms and a car standing in the drive. He could not, he

swore, *possibly* be sure of the colour in that light but he thought
it was grey or pale blue. There was nobody in it and nobody
about and he had not ventured more than a few yards inside the
gate. The only thing he could be certain of was that it was a
shooting brake.

# IV

As was his custom on Monday Henry Gaveston arrived at
St Martin's just after eight, and before breakfast walked around
chatting to a few of the scouts to see if anything untoward had
occurred during the weekend. Nothing had; but after breakfast
he was told that at dinner in college last night there had been a
little fracas in which a student called Martin (naturally known as
St Martin) had broken a chair, so Henry rang the Dean and
suggested to him that they should impose a fine. Almost immediately after, the Clerk of Works, a notoriously lugubrious character, tapped at Henry's door to tell him that the boiler heating
the library and situated under the library staircase was smoking
and overheating. They went to the library to look at the trouble,
the Clerk stout and middle-aged, the Bursar tall and sharp-angled
and stooping, one foot turning in, his voice high-pitched and
aristocratic, his thick grey hair, still showing signs of its original
fairness, flopping from time to time over his brow. The Clerk of
Works had always thought the Bursar an amiable character
despite his reputation as a soldier, but these last weeks he had
been short-tempered and uninterested in matters of importance,
such as a faulty boiler. If he was still upset by Stephanie Locke's
suicide – as they all had been – it was time he snapped out of it.
Was something else fretting him?

On his way back from the library Henry was accosted by one
of the younger Fellows, who taught Modern History, with a
request to book a room for a party he wanted to give on Friday.
Henry replied impatiently that he wasn't carrying his diary with
him and would he ring him later in the day?

Back in his room Henry banged the door, picked up the

telephone and dialled James's number. Then, after it had rung twice, he put the phone down. At this stage what had one to say?

Part of the rest of the morning, adding to his restlessness and irritability, was taken up by the chef, an Italian called Corsini, who arrived to say that one of the assistant chefs was ill, and, as they were short-staffed anyway, preparation of college meals was getting beyond him. Henry pacified him by saying he would persuade some of the other staff to work overtime, and meanwhile would the chef help him to prepare an advertisement for an assistant chef to be placed in the *Oxford Times*?

Then there was the question of half a dozen students who had not settled their battels, and three were badly in debt. Two of them were reading science, and he knew it wasn't much use calling them in, because science men always had lectures on a Monday morning. The third, Wayford, a second year PPE student, had reported sick.

Henry sat for twenty minutes filling his pipe but not lighting it, wondering how best he might approach the superintendent of police, whom he played golf with and with whom he had had various minor dealings over the students in his care. It was an unwritten agreement between the Oxford police and the colleges that minor offences occurring within a college were dealt with by the college authorities (in practice the Dean or the Bursar) and only in serious cases was police help invoked. So Henry and Superintendent Willis knew each other's territory well. But that hardly covered the sort of inquiry he now wished to make. 'The murders at Partridge Manor; what sort of progress is being made? Are you any nearer an arrest?' Willis wouldn't reply: 'What business is it of yours, Colonel?' but he might well think it. The only way in which it could affect the college would be if Stephanie's death were involved, and that was precisely what Henry did not wish to suggest.

Henry had other and more secret friends at Scotland Yard and in the security services, but the circumstances of last Tuesday night made him wary of doing anything to draw attention to himself.

He remembered with annoyance that he should have rung his son, Charles, who had been giving a concert last night in Manchester; he had promised to ring early this morning to see how it had gone. By now Charles would be on his way back to York. He'd have to remember to ring about five when Charles would be likely to be in.

Just before he went to lunch the telephone went again. It was Professor Jenkins.

'Oh, Henry, can you tell me what on earth has happened to Arun Jiva? I have tried the Senior Tutor, but he didn't know, and I thought you might.'

Henry frowned at the phone. 'Jiva? I've seen nothing of him for about ten days. Isn't he out of the country?'

'That's what I'd like to know.' Jenkins was Arun Jiva's supervisor at the School of Pathology. 'I had a brief note dated – dated the twenty-second of May – saying he had been urgently called away. Nothing more than that. It's a bit thick to work the way he has been working and then mess everything up at the last moment.'

'He didn't bother to tell me at all, but the Principal got the same sort of note. Has he finished his D.Phil.?'

'He's submitted it but the problem is his viva is due a week on Wednesday. If he misses that he'll be in the soup.'

'I suppose it's been advertised.'

'Oh yes, and we can't change that now. The external examiner is flying in from Dublin especially for this case.'

'Ah,' said Henry.

'Funny character altogether, Jiva. Don't you find him so? Monumental chip on his shoulder. But no one could accuse him of not taking life seriously. That's what makes this so strange. And he's extremely good. Shouldn't have any difficulty with his viva.'

'If he's here to take it.'

'Quite. I sent round to his house but the woman next door said no one had been near for a week. She did say the police had been there. I hope he's not run into some damn fool trouble.'

'I hope not,' Henry replied enigmatically.

'Well, I suppose we shall have to wait and see. But the examiners will be mad if he's not there . . . Mrs Gaveston home yet?'

'Week after next. I gather it's been pretty exhausting.'

'America always is. Bye.'

Henry remembered to ring Charles at five and found him in. The concert, it seemed, had been a success and Henry apologised for his delay in inquiring. Charles, being in a euphoric mood, waved this defection away, and they discussed plans for his academic and musical future. Before they rang off Charles said something that pleased his father greatly: 'Thank you for being such an understanding chap.'

That evening and the following day Henry still did not speak to James. On the Wednesday morning James rang him.

'Ah, Henry, we haven't been in touch.'

'My fault. But I'm delighted to hear from you . . . I felt I should have come over again, but it's difficult in the circumstances to . . .'

'To know what to say?'

'Well, what there was to say was said on Sunday. There isn't much mileage left.'

'There's some – of a sort. Incidentally, I'm in a call box in the village, so you must get used to the clatter of coins.'

'Good man. I hope you haven't felt that my not ringing you has shown any lack of sympathy for your position.' In fact, by private arrangement, Mary Aldershot had telephoned him every night. Henry had been afraid that the gun he had lent James might have been used to follow Stephanie's example.

'The way things look at the moment I would not blame you,' James said. 'By the way, the police came again this morning. They asked if they might look at my car. They also asked if I would mind having my fingerprints taken.'

'My God. Well, I suppose it isn't surprising. Citizen's duty to assist the police, et cetera.'

'They said, of course, it was for purposes of elimination. I didn't go out to the garage with them, but Mary went. She said they were chiefly interested in the tyres and the undercarriage. They put a sheet under the car and asked permission to start it up. Looking perhaps for an oil leak, she thought. If so, no luck for them. Has your car got an oil leak?'

'The Mini? I don't think so. That reminds me, it's due for a service and I said I'd have it seen to while Evelyn was away. I'd forgotten.'

'Get it done.' James put more money in the slot.

'And the fingerprinting?'

'They went away with a fine set. Henry, I've decided to go to Corfu this weekend.'

'Good God . . . whatever for? . . . You mean those photographs?'

'Yes. The fastigiate cypress trees almost certainly identify the place as Corfu. It isn't a very large island and there can't be many houses like that one. I particularly want to find out while I'm free, since my movements might become restricted any time.'

'I hope not. But look – this move, this visit is being taken on in spite of – of Stephanie's note?'

'Yes.'

'I think I should come with you.'

'No.'

'Will you take Mary?'

'I think not. There are wheelchairs at airports, and plenty of taxis.'

'Shall you try to see Errol's first wife?'

'I don't know.'

'I think you have to keep it firmly in mind that Colton *still* bears the moral responsibility for what happened. If not the physical.'

'If not the physical . . . I think my present intention is simply to identify the house.'

Henry hesitated. There was something about James's voice that made him uneasy. Often since he was handed the suicide note he had wondered how *he* would have felt if he had killed somebody in revenge for what that person hadn't done. If *he* was in James's position would he still be pursuing the idea of finding Errol's master – 'the Boss'? He felt not. He would be too badly shaken by the enormity of his mistake.

More coins went into the box. James said: 'Are you still there?'

'I am indeed. It seems to me, James, that if you are still intent on identifying the house, why not ask around here? Many people go to Corfu these days. Why not ask Peter Brune? It might save a long and tedious journey.'

'I have a feeling I want to look for myself.'

'Incidentally I saw Brune last Friday – before, of course, we knew what we know now. I asked him how he had met Colton, and he said at the house of a man called Mr Erasmus. Ever heard of him?'

'No.'

'Apparently Peter only met him once but judged him an unsavoury character. He's very rich and has a house on Corfu, somewhere in the south of the island. He might be worth looking up.'

'I'll do that.'

'But James, take heed of what I have to say. However one may judge or assess or regret what happened last Tuesday it's still likely that you are stirring up a dangerous group of people. Nothing of that has changed. Maybe over Errol and Smith they will be content to let sleeping dogs – dead dogs – lie. But if you still go on pressing and probing there'll be a reaction. Indeed, the more I think of it, the more important it is that I should come with you to Corfu.'

'No. You have to stay out of this – for your own sake, for your career's sake, but mainly for Evelyn's sake. Stay away from me, lovey.'

There was a pause.

'I'm on my last two coins,' James said.

'All right, by God, if that's how you see it. So go to Corfu. Ask questions. Look at houses. But *don't* go any further. Otherwise I have a feeling you might not come back.'

'Does it matter?' James said.

'Yes, it matters all round.'

# Twelve

## I

Mary Aldershot drove him to Heathrow on Saturday 2 June and he flew alone by Olympic Airways, arriving in Corfu, with an adjustment of time, at 16.50. He took a taxi and stayed at the Swiss-owned Corfu Palace Hotel overlooking the harbour and the sea. He had a word with the manager and made arrangements for a private car to pick him up the following morning. The driver, Pericles Anemoyannis, spoke good English, it was said, and would be available for the two days he proposed to stay on the island. Since it is a small island where so many people know other people's business and whereabouts, James asked the manager if he knew a Madame Errol Colton, first name Elena, though he did not remember her maiden name. The manager said he would ask around.

That night James slept badly, as usual. When he did finally fall into a troubled sleep it was to dream of his earlier days in a war almost forgotten except by a few veterans such as himself. That last year of the war he had been sent to Darwin, to train parachutists to be dropped behind the Japanese lines in North Borneo. The special group he was selected to train was a company of Chinese: Canadian Chinese from Vancouver – chosen presumably because their Asiatic faces would blend easily with the inhabitants in the districts where they were to be dropped. James had the help of a splendid Australian sergeant major called Blake, but the group had been very inefficiently trained in the technique of guerrilla warfare and all it involved, and James feared greatly for them if they fell into the hands of the dreaded Japanese Kempe-Tai.

Much was done in a short time before orders came through that they were to proceed to Morotai Island in the Moluccas, from which advanced position they were to be flown to Sandakan in North Borneo and dropped behind the Japanese lines to organise local resistance and sabotage communications. Morotai itself, which was just one degree north of the Equator, had been a Japanese military base until the previous year, when it had been captured by the Allies and turned into a strategic air base.

At these instructions there were mutterings among the Chinese Canadians, which came to a head with their adamant refusal to obey orders unless they were led into action by Major Locke and Sergeant Major Blake. Much telephoning resulted in permission being granted by the Colonel-in-Chief, a decision which did not please James, since his ankles were already troubling him a bit and he was losing his appetite for the sharper edge of war; but Blake, ever happy-go-lucky, was willing enough to go, so go they did, lying with their Chinese charges in the bomb bay of an elderly Dakota, all the way from Darwin to Morotai.

Not anxious to be short of Dutch courage for this suicide mission, James packed six bottles of gin in his case, but, in the unpressurised plane, flying over the mountains was too much for the corks, and when they landed his socks and shirt and other belongings were soaked in gin.

The following day Japan sued for peace; so instead of being dropped into unknown jungle they had a hugely noisy party at which they danced round the row of improvised lavatories (made out of palm roots) and set them on fire and got happily drunk.

There was laughter in James's mind when he woke. Young as he had been then, the end of the war was like opening the gates of a new and lovely world. The tensions and strains of the last years vanished overnight. As it turned out, the tensions and strains had left their mark on him – not only on his injured feet – but he was not to know that then. What he remembered most was the flight back – in the same Dakota and lying in the same discomfort (but nobody minded now) – and the immense feast that followed, in which they had had steak and chips and eggs and bacon and good Australian wine, and the world was preparing to live happily ever after.

But what was there to be happy about or to smile about lying in this clinical bedroom looking out over the bay in which lights were still winking though dawn was soaking up the night? He had brought Stephanie's suicide note with him. Of course he knew it was a fake – within a few hours he had decided it was a forgery.

This is the end. I can't go on. There's nothing for me now, now he has gone. I'm deeply, deeply sorry to deliberately bring all this trouble and grief to the people I love and trust . . .

His daughter would never split an infinitive. It didn't matter if she was crazed with grief and half-drunk. The way she had been taught a few simple English grammatical rules made it impossible. She might just as easily have written: 'This is the hend. I can't go hon.'

Henry would understand if it were pointed out to him. Perhaps few others. Some would be derisive. It didn't matter. All that mattered was that *he* knew; and this conclusion – this certain knowledge – had saved him from even contemplating what Henry had feared he might contemplate. Stephanie's peculiar handwriting was easy to imitate. Anne Vincent's interference had spoiled a careful plan, which would have resulted in a simple verdict of suicide and no more reason to ask questions. By his testimony at the inquest, Errol Colton took the odium but escaped any suspicion of guilt.

James had not said anything about it to Henry. He had come to Corfu alone, and if the solution lay here Henry would know in good time.

The other note he carried was the typewritten one he had found in Errol's photographic folder: *The Boss says scrap numbers 22 and 49. At this time he wants no more links than need be. C.*

Exhibits 22 and 49 were in his breast pocket. The front of a

229

house, presumably in Corfu. James had thought of producing them to the manager last night, but overcaution had stopped him. He hoped to see and recognise for himself.

The sun was up now and its light reflected from the shimmering harbour. A motorboat scored a white scar on the polished surface. Too early to get up, but James rang down and ordered breakfast.

Pericles Anemoyannis turned up at ten, and it was soon clear that his English was not as good as the manager had promised. He was a heavily built dark-featured cheerful man who claimed to speak French better than English, but so guttural was his accent that James gave it up and relapsed into English.

Before they left the manager said, yes, he had found Elena Mavrogodatos, formerly Mrs Errol Colton. She had reverted to her maiden name and was living in Corfu Town. She worked nightly at a taverna called Tripas at Kinopiastes, a few miles south of the town.

'Is it a good taverna?'

'Not elegant, sair, but the best food in Corfu.'

'Book me a table tonight, will you. And, Mr Grouas . . .'

'Sair?'

'Do you know of a man called Erasmus?'

An unidentifiable expression floated across the manager's face. 'I know of him. I knew of him. He lived in the extreme south of the island, beyond Lefkimi.'

'Lived?'

'I have not heard of him recently. It is perhaps so that he still lives there. It was his custom, I know, to come only for the summer.'

'Would you ask Anemoyannis if he knows where it is, and that I want him to drive me there.'

'Sair, he speaks English, as I have said.'

'Tell him in Greek, will you, so I can be sure he understands.'

# II

The road south from Corfu Town, if one doesn't follow the coast, leads through the least developed, most primitive part of the island. The roads are equally undeveloped, giving a fair idea of what all the island was like before the intrusion of tourism. Pericles Anemoyannis took the inland road, and they bumped and jolted and twisted through tiny villages linked by orange groves and lemon groves and vineyards, with goats and stray dogs (all apparently of the same parentage) and chickens and donkeys disputing the right of way. But above all and omnipresent the olive trees, shouldering each other, bent and gnarled and of great age. Indeed, the further they progressed the more the olive tree took over, so that approaching Argirades one drove through groves of such antiquity that one could not imagine them having changed much since the days of the Angevins. Were these Roman soldiers, caught in the moment of agonising dissolution and turned in their contortions to wood and stone?

The age of a man was as nothing to trees such as this. Even less the life of a girl who died before she was twenty-two.

Beyond Lefkimi the countryside, which had lost its mountains some time ago, became flat and featureless with low-lying earth walls and a sense of desolation. Unerringly Pericles turned down a rough track, and after five bumpy minutes cheerfully drew up before double gates leading to a big low stone-built house overlooking the sea. As soon as he saw it James knew it was not the house he sought.

# III

'Mrs Colton?'

'Yes? Georgios told me you wanted to see me.'

They were in the restaurant, a bare extension built on the side of a cottage; trestle tables, noise, clatter, mountains of appetising food banged down upon the tables, Greek white wine by the litre; it was quiet yet to what it would become.

'My name is James Locke. I wonder if you have time for a word.'

'Are you from England?'

'Yes.'

'What do you want? Is it about my husband?'

'Yes. I wished to ask you –'

'He is dead, murdered; are you from the British police?'

She was a hard-faced young woman with a tight mouth, but her eyes, though unfriendly, were not unfeeling.

'No, I'm not. Just a private individual. Your husband was friendly with my daughter.'

'He would be.'

'She died some weeks ago.'

She wrapped and unwrapped a coloured serving napkin about her wrist. 'What I want to know is what will happen to *my* daughter!'

'How did he come to have custody of her?'

'He paid me. His lawyer paid me monthly. A hundred pounds a month. But that agreement was made years ago. Prices have gone up.'

'Perhaps his second wife will come to some arrangement.'

'I am his only wife! That woman living with him is not his wife! I want my daughter back!'

'How did your husband come to be associated with the drug trade?'

She blinked. 'What? What do you ask me? I do not know anything about his later life.'

'Do you know a Mr Erasmus?'

'Down in the south. Yes, I know him.'

'I went to see him this morning.'

'You would not find him. He has been away for a long time.'

'His factory goes on.'

'What factory?'

'His house down there is used as a factory for processing olives. What else does it process?'

'I do not know. Why do you not ask them?'

'I did. There were a half-dozen workmen about but they pretended not to understand English – or French or German.'

'Why should they pretend? This is Greece. Greek is our language.'

'Do you know nothing about the factory? In a small island like this it must be difficult to keep secrets.'

She looked around at a group of ten who had just arrived and were noisily seating themselves.

'I must go. I cannot stand here idling.'

'Give me your home address. I will call on you tomorrow.'

'I wish to have nothing more to do with you.' She turned away.

'One thing more,' he said, and fumbled to produce the now creased photographs. 'Do you know this house?'

She stared at it. 'I do not recognise it. It is not Corfu.'

'Why do you say that?'

She said: 'Go home, old man.'


# IV

In the morning the taxi did not arrive. Anemoyannis, the manager said, had telephoned that he was unwell. They found another taxi outside the hotel, and the driver seemed to have a better grasp of English than Pericles. James showed him the photographs and he frowned and then grinned.

'Paleokastritsa,' he said.

'Where is that?'

An expansive wave of the arm. 'Up north. I will take you.'

As James settled in the taxi he thought of last night, when Elena Mavrogodatos had not come in again with the many good things set before him – food for a hearty man, no doubt, but of a high quality – nor was she to be seen waiting at any of the other tables. When it became clear that after some Greek songs and folk dancing, the diners were being invited to join in the revelry, James paid his bill and limped to the kitchen and asked for Elena. He was told she had gone home.

He did not ask for her home address, feeling sure he would have no difficulty in finding her if she lived in Corfu Town;

but he doubted whether anything useful would come of another meeting. She had been unwilling to talk about the things he was interested in. (Not quite the barely hidden hostility he had met with at Mr Erasmus's factory, but resentful and wary.) It was only his determination to grasp at every crumb which had taken him to see her in the first place. It had been distasteful to force himself to speak to her.

The country they were driving through was beautiful – Corfu being almost the only greenly wooded of the Greek islands – with delicious glimpses of a cobalt sea and towering cliffs as they approached the west coast. Paleokastritsa was one of the beauty spots and therefore a tourist attraction. Bronzed holidaymakers in shorts pedalled bicycles or buzzed by on mopeds. Three municipal buses crawled up the hill on their way to the other coast.

Abruptly, just before the steep descent into the village, the taxi turned off and went up a rutted road, stopped before barred gates with wire on the top. The driver got out and opened the door for James.

'Here is.'

James pulled himself out and sticked his way to the barred gate. The house was now visible round a bend in the short drive.

'There is,' said the driver.

James gritted his teeth. This might be more like the photographs than yesterday's specimen, but the colour of the stone was different and the trees not grouped aright.

He had thought Elena had been lying when she said the house was not on Corfu.

'This *is not it*. Look? Look at the photographs.' He thrust them at the driver, who frowned at them and lifted his cap to scratch his head.

'Not this?'

'Not this.'

'Ah.' The driver handed the photographs back and shrugged.

They stood in the Attic sunshine. A seagull drifted silently overhead. James wished he had never come. He wished that the years would roll back and that he and Stephanie and Teresa and

Janet were here, all together again, pedalling hired bicycles down to the sand and the sea.

'You like to go round island?'

'No. Take me back to Corfu Town.'

Should have done this in the first place. Gone to the Information Office, seen some knowledgeable person – identified the bloody photographs or not. Not careering round the island in the company of idiot taxi drivers . . .

'I take you back by Scripero? Eh? Little further. Few kilometres. Show you the eastern coast. Eh?'

James hauled himself into the car. So what? He was leaving tomorrow. Good riddance.

They set off back towards the central massif of the island, climbing away from the tourists and the bicycles and the scooters and the buses. It was warm in the car in spite of the open windows, and James found himself dozing off. He didn't normally need a lot of sleep, but the cumulative effect of so many disturbed nights, the monstrous nature of the situation, the feeling of bitter disappointment brought him to the edge of consciousness.

He woke with a jerk of the car, peered over the sunlit groves and shouted: 'Stop! Stop! Stop!'

The driver obeyed him, looked round.

He had stalled his engine. Ahead of them in the sunny silence Pantokratos loomed. They were in the mountains.

'That house,' James said. 'Drive nearer.'

'Not possible this side. No way. Fields. Look, I take you other side.'

They turned in a gate, watched by a little girl tending three wickedly bearded goats, in five minutes came round from a side road and bumped along a cart track laid with huge uneven stones. The car lurched and rattled, scattering smaller stones from under its tyres and came to a jolting stop before two ancient stone pillars which would not have looked out of place on the Acropolis. Beyond them, exactly identified by the position of the cypress trees, stood the house.

'This is it! Look, it is plain to see!'

235

The driver studied the photos again and smiled and nodded.

'*Ne*. That is so. So I find him for you, eh? After all?'

It is difficult in Mediterranean countries to be sure whether a house is in use, because shutters are always closed tight against the relentless sun; but this house did look unoccupied. Yet well kept. The grass lawn in front of the house was green and tidy and must have been watered daily.

James got out again, tottered a few steps inside the gates.

'Where is the caretaker?'

The driver did not understand this word but presently broke into Greek with a sentence that sounded like Anatole Seferis.

'Where is he? Take me to him.' And then: 'Do you know who this house belongs to?'

'*Ne*,' said the driver, nodding vigorously. 'Not here now. Not here yet. Englishman.'

'What is his name?'

The driver scowled in an effort of recollection. 'Milord. English milord. Sir Peter Brown.'

'Brown? Do you – mean Brune?'

'*Ne*,' said the driver, nodding again. 'Is so. This house. Sir Peter Brune.'

# V

James put through a long telephone call to Colonel Henry Gaveston, who was entirely and absolutely incredulous, then he rang down to confirm his flight home tomorrow. The receptionist informed him that unfortunately because of a strike of the pilots of Olympic Airways there would be no Greek flights to London tomorrow.

James exploded, undignified and angry. The receptionist said she would do what she could and presently rang back to say that all she could offer him was one tourist seat, unexpectedly available, on a charter plane to Paris. It should get him to Charles de Gaulle Airport in time to catch an Air France flight, reaching

Heathrow, with the adjustment of time, at 12.55. James told her to book it.

In the night James blamed himself for not going out to Tripas again to see if he could prise more information out of Elena. But there was an element of fatigue and fatalism in his feelings now. He knew anyway that the object of his mission had been partly if horribly accomplished.

Along with the two photographs of the house and the one of Stephanie and Errol on the balcony of their bungalow in Goa was a notebook he had carried with him ever since the inquest and the notes he had made directly after his meeting with Sir Humphrey Arden. With a good memory sharpened by bereavement – reinforced by frequent reading of the notes he had made – he remembered pretty well everything Humphrey had said.

'There was this doctor in Edinburgh, I think it was March '78. He was away for a couple of days, and the maid found his wife dead in bed just before he returned. His wife apparently drank a lot, but on this occasion she had taken a large quantity of sleeping pills. As it happened, they were Medanol tablets she took. Scotland was never my patch, but I was called in by the chap up there because there was one suspicious circumstance – a light bruising in the throat. He thought – and I agreed – that this could have been caused by thrusting, however gently, a rubber tube down into the stomach and so giving the woman a fatal dose of barbiturates.

'The police decided to take a chance and charge the doctor. I don't believe if he had stood firm they would have had a hope in hell of getting a conviction, but under persistent questioning he broke down and confessed the whole thing. Apparently he'd been having an affair with a patient and his wife had threatened to report him to the GMC. He picked his time carefully and came home when she wasn't expecting him. He found her as he'd hoped, having just drunk enough to be a bit fuddled. He told her his affair with the other woman was over, and after a reconciliation he mixed her another gin. In this he slipped three much stronger barbitone tablets. The outcome of this would be that his wife would be yawning her head off in ten minutes and after half an hour would be out like a light. Get me?'

'I get you very well.'

'Well, apparently what this doctor did then was to break open the capsules – her own capsules – of Medanol – twenty, I believe he said – and mix them in a couple of glasses of dilute gin. He then passed the tube of a stomach pump into the victim's mouth and very gradually down her gullet into her stomach. It's a tricky operation but it's done constantly in overdose cases. Difference is that in such cases a bruising of the throat is an acceptable part of the exercise. Here it was clearly not, and this gave him away. He'd been clever enough to add the containers afterwards, dissolving them in half an ounce or so of water – they're red, you see, and stain the contents of the stomach and stomach wall. Without such staining the pathologist would at once have been suspicious. Then he left the house and was careful not to come home until after the maid had discovered the body next morning.'

'Clever,' James had said.

'Very clever, but he fell at the last hurdle.'

James remembered there had been a roar of laughter from some men at the bar, and Sir Humphrey had winced and adjusted his hearing aid.

'I very much hesitated to tell you this story, James. It is all the purest speculation, and the last thing I want to do is implant in your mind a suspicion – or indeed a certitude – where no certitude can exist. You suspect foul play, and that this man Errol Colton is responsible. I almost went away, preferring that you shouldn't have this irrelevant story troubling your mind. I think it must be irrelevant for one very good reason.'

'What is that?'

'Colton is not a doctor. Only a skilled medical man could have successfully committed such a crime.'

'And there was no bruising on my daughter's throat?'

'No. After you had rung me I rang Ehrmann and got a copy of his post-mortem report. I didn't know quite what you were going to ask me, but it pretty certainly had something to do with the PM. There was no bruising of your daughter's throat.'

At this point James remembered the noisy crowd at the bar had moved off, and sudden peace and silence fell, leaving the barman polishing glasses, and three other old men muttering in a far corner.

'However,' Arden had said. 'It's the fact that Colton is not a doctor which puts the hypothesis right out of court. More so than the absence of bruising.'

'Why more so?'

'Well, the doctor in Edinburgh wasn't quite clever enough. He omitted to use glycerine.'


# VI


The flight to Paris was crowded and noisy as were James's thoughts. In an attempt to keep some balance in his mind, he tried to think of Teresa and his first grandchild. He hoped for a boy, though it would never bear the name of Locke. Teresa's attitude was eminently sensible: 'I don't in the least mind so long as it's got two eyes and four limbs.'

Had he in his heart always felt a slight preference for the younger and prettier and more awkward of his daughters? Teresa was a marvellous girl, and to save his sanity and good sense he must concentrate on her and all that he had got left.

He had bought yesterday's *Times* in the hotel before he left and he tried to read this on the plane. It was useless. England were heading for defeat in the first Test match against the West Indians. It was happening in another world. A British barque called the *Marques* had foundered in heavy seas off Bermuda while taking part in a tall ships race, with the loss of nineteen lives, including a baby. Very sad. The death toll in the Lancashire underground water treatment plant explosion had risen to fifteen. The cost of first class post was to be put up to seventeen pence. The miners' strike was going on for ever, and there was a threat of more disturbances. President Reagan was arriving in London tomorrow to attend the London Economic Summit.

James folded the paper again and again, and thrust it impatiently in the net pouch in front of his seat, took up an illustrated French magazine. There was an article entitled '*L'an de Georges Orwell*', and he tried to read it. No go. This was not quite the world Eric Blair had imagined; but it was nasty and brutal and evil and in most ways unspeakably vile. Perhaps Big Brother would have been better after all.

The DC3 put down quietly at the airport, and then it was wheelchair and bus and wheelchair again, moving from one satellite to another. The second wheelchair attendant was a negro with a cheerful face and a whistle he employed throughout the journey to the point of take-off.

Charles de Gaulle Airport is innovative in that its designers employ enclosed moving platforms to a unique degree. James found himself being pushed, or in the main simply steered – since effort was unnecessary – inside a transparent tube which was like progressing through the intestines of a caterpillar. Sometimes you went uphill and sometimes down, and alongside at varying times was a similar caterpillar in which strangers passed in the night or kept one company before separating and going off in some other direction.

People stood there like Aunt Sallys at a shooting range. In his present mood James toyed with the idea of having a gun and venting his grief and frustration on some innocent passenger travelling to Stuttgart or Madrid. His mind was still full of astonishment and enormity; it was weighed down with enormity, struggling with enormity for air and light and understanding.

And then he looked again and shouted, 'Halt! Halt!'

The wheelchair attendant stopped whistling and bent down over his passenger inquiringly, but allowed the moving platform to carry them along.

'Halt!' James shouted angrily, impotently, foolishly. 'Stop! I want to speak to that man!'

In the neighbouring caterpillar, quite close but moving inexorably away, was Arun Jiva.

Absolutely no mistaking him, black-haired, fair-skinned, austere, high white collar, gold-rimmed pince-nez. Carrying a newspaper and a briefcase and wearing a light grey tweed suit.

'No stop,' said the attendant. 'Not possible.'

Jiva was almost out of sight. James shouted again, too well aware that the attendant was right. They came out at the satellite which served the plane he was going to catch. Twenty minutes to boarding time. When he knew he was having to break his journey in Paris James had changed ten pounds into francs in case of some emergency. He now thrust fifty francs into the porter's hand.

'Find out where that plane was going! These people in the next corridor.'

'*Comment?*'

'Those people who were in the next corridor, the next tube – whatever you call it – they looked as if they were outward bound. Another fifty francs when you find out!'

'I do not understand. What is wrong?' The black man was a Senegalese and spoke French much less well than James. 'What is this? What are you at? Pray be seated. See, there is your flight.'

James got out of his chair, staggering on his sticks and almost fell. People stared, and seeing the commotion a young French girl official came over, heels tapping.

'What is wrong, sir? Can I assist you?'

'That man,' said James, pointing vaguely in the direction from which he had just come. 'There was a man in the other *couloir*. He is – he is an old friend. I have not seen him for five years. I wish specially – there is an urgent special need that I should see him, meet him, get in touch with him.'

'But, sir, you are asking something very difficult – almost impossible. What is your friend's name?'

'Jiva. Arun Jiva. He is an Indian doctor. At least can you tell me where his plane is going – the one he is taking, so that perhaps I can get in touch with him later.'

The girl shrugged and went back to the desk, picked up the telephone and had a conversation. Presently she came back, her attractive face full of Gallic impatience.

'I regret, sir. We regret we cannot help you in the way you wish.' She addressed a flood of questions to the attendant, asking in which direction the other convoy had been moving and when, and in what tube. Then she went away again and fingered through some lists with another girl. Eventually she returned.

'That flight is due to take off right now. It is the AF 902 Air France flight for Birmingham, England, arriving in Birmingham at five past one your time.'

# BOOK THREE

BOOK THREE

# *One*

When he was nineteen Arun Jiva's father had met a man called Savarkar. Savarkar was then a plump bald benign-looking Indian of fifty-six. His appearance, in a dark robe and clerical sandals, belied his reputation as one of the most fearsome advocates of Hindu orthodoxy. He opposed not only the Raj but the Congress ideals of a secular state in which all religions might live in peace. Indeed during the war which followed he went directly in the teeth of Congress by supporting the British. This was not out of love for them but because they were prepared to train and equip an Indian army in the latest weapons, a great asset, he thought, when independence inevitably came.

At an impressionable age, Jaya Jiva fell completely under his spell, gave up his work as a railway clerk and devoted himself to promoting Hindu Mahasabha as a nationwide political party. In India, perhaps more than anywhere else, the opposing philosophies of violence and nonviolence are carried to extremes. Unlike Jaya's family, to whom the taking of the life of even the smallest insect was anathema, Savarkar preached cold-blooded killing for political ends, and Jaya went along with him. Assassination, whether of an official of the Raj or of one of his own race, was a means to an end, and when Mahatma Gandhi was shot and killed by active members of the Mahasabha, as a protest against his apparent favouritism to the Muslims, Savarkar was arrested and tried with seven others for the murder. He alone was acquitted – as being far away from Delhi at the time of the crime.

Jaya Jiva, when his son grew old enough, told him all the events of those days over and over again. He had been questioned and horribly tortured by the police, but had then been released for lack of evidence. Often and often he told Arun the story of the bungling of the assassins, of the stupidity of the police who with half an eye open could have scotched such an amateurish attempt. After Savarkar's death Jaya Jiva became one of the leaders of the Hindu Sanghatan until his own untimely death in the riots of 1958.

Arun Jiva grew up with the beliefs of his father, so much the obverse of all that his grandparents held religiously dear. He saw no sanctity in any life if it was to his advantage or to the advantage of his cause to destroy it. Practising medicine in the crowded tenements of Old Delhi did nothing to alter his views.

After a few years he even became estranged from the orthodoxy of the Mahasabha party and more and more discontented with his personal position as a poor doctor in a poor nation. His prospects were as narrow as a ravine, from which the only escape was to the West.

Such advancement, however, needed money, and money he had not got. Then, providentially, on a visit to Bombay he met a man called Mr Erasmus. Mr Erasmus was condescending but gracious. Through underlings a proposition was put to Arun Jiva, which, after long consideration, he accepted. He heartily despised the trade in which he was now asked to participate, but a three-year graduate course at Oxford, England, was exactly what he needed, and this was offered him. With a D.Phil. to his name there would be opportunities open to him, opportunities especially in America. So he had come to England and had co-operated with the group who financed him. At first he thought the work he did risky, but the immunity from trouble or even suspicion gradually reassured him, and he had gone on his way until last month, obeying the instructions about reception and distribution that came to him from time to time. He looked forward to the day when he could leave this despicable trade behind him and cross the Atlantic to begin a new life.

Then suddenly this crisis. On him without warning. Although he advocated political assassination he had never himself killed deliberately, except occasionally prescribing an overdose to some

246

miserable Hindu woman bloated with cancer or bedridden with arthritis. This was altogether different, someone in the height of youth and vigour, someone he knew and against whom he had had virtually no grudge – except that she had twice rather roughly shaken off his hand when he put it on her bare arm. (Blonde white girl spurning someone of inferior race.) But his first impulse was to refuse, and with contempt.

Then the temptation. A hundred thousand dollars in his name at Crédit Lyonnais in Paris. More than he could hope to earn in any other way. When he gained his doctorate he had intended to leave England and go to live in Paris, where he had friends of his own kind, and from there write to a selected number of American universities stating his qualifications. But with this sort of money at his back he could go to the United States, having severed any connection with his 'benefactors' before he left, and live over there until the right interview yielded the right appointment.

It was that and the challenge to his medical skill that influenced him to accept. Twice in Delhi: once when he had emptied the stomach of a garage mechanic who had drunk Lysol, and once with a young woman who had tried to kill herself with turpentine, he had reflected on the fact that not only was it easy to extract the contents of the stomach, but it would be equally easy to introduce things.

In cases of poisoning, whether accidental or self-administered, the patient was too ill to make a choice. In other cases the patient would have to be a willing subject of experiment. Therein lay one of the big problems concerning Miss Stephanie Locke.

But it was a challenge, and he had taken it up. Originally it had been intended that Errol should offer to take her home from the party and go into her flat with her and persuade her to have just one more drink; but this had been scrapped because of the risk of his car being seen parked outside. So Arun had done just what he said he had done, driven her home and then let her go in alone, driven to his own flat, and walked back and waited for Errol to arrive. Errol, having parked his car three streets away, had eventually come, let himself into the flat and offered to tell

Stephanie the whole story of his involvement in drugs distribution, if she would but listen. Forty-five minutes later the corner of the curtain had been lifted to give the sign for Arun to go in. He had found Stephanie lying on the bed heavily asleep and Errol in an appalling state of fright and nerves. It had been agreed that Errol should stay and help Arun in the later stages but in spite of a snort he was clearly so unnerved that Arun told him to go home.

The plane taking Arun to Birmingham International Airport was on time, and, after the usual extra fuss at passports accorded to the coloured visitor, he was through in time to take a late lunch at the airport restaurant. There would be no food in the house and he didn't want to shop in Oxford and advertise his presence there before he needed to.

The viva was tomorrow, and a little fasting would do him good. That day in mid-May when he was rung up and told to leave the country he had been impatient and angry. The inquest was over, the girl buried, and everyone in the process of forgetting the tragedy. He had just delivered his thesis: eighty thousand words on *The Inflammatory Responses of Diseased Tissues*, and he had only a couple of weeks to wait before he was granted his degree. But the Boss had been adamant. The girl's father was still very much on the prowl, refusing to be satisfied, questioning people three and four times over, pulling strings at the Home Office, bent on making trouble. He was particularly set on interviewing Jeremy Hillsborough and Arun Jiva again. Get out for the time being, until things blew over. Go back to India for a month or two. Or go straight off to the States if he so fancied.

Arun might well have so fancied, but he wouldn't go, couldn't go yet. So far as he knew, he was in no danger of arrest or of further police questioning; and anyway, no one could prove anything now, or ever. It was a stupid condition of the Oxford examinations that he had to take an oral test before he could be granted his doctorate – but that was the way it was, and there appeared to be no way round it. Of course, if he did not turn up his years of dedicated work would not be lost, but he would not be granted his degree for perhaps a further six months, after once again being requested to attend. And how could one be certain that it would be any safer to attend then than now?

So instead of going to Delhi or New York, he had gone to Paris and awaited events there.

The death of Errol Colton, which he had seen in the *Daily Mail*, was an event which had jolted him. It seemed likely that Errol had been disposed of by the group because in his present parlous state he was a safety risk. The newspaper reported the early findings of the police, and to Arun it was evident that Angelo Smith had been appointed to get rid of him. Somehow in the process Smith had met his own death, but the object had been achieved. Errol Colton, the security risk, had been eliminated.

The only serious question in Arun's mind was how much he also might be regarded as a security risk. Certainly he could say nothing without totally incriminating himself; but then neither could Errol. Errol might have been considered to be in such an unstable condition that under persistent examination he would give way and confess his involvement, and Errol, of course, knew a great deal about a lot of things. He, Arun Jiva, also knew a lot, had come to know a great deal too much about the organisation.

Arun remembered all too many Indian legends of princes who had buried some priceless treasure and then had the workmen who buried it put to death so that no one should be able to tell where it was. But surely the people he knew and for whom he worked, Mr Erasmus, and the Boss, and the rest, would never suppose he, Arun Jiva, was a weakling who might be induced to talk. He, whose father had endured the obscene tortures of the Indian police, would be unlikely to be intimidated by a British examination.

But that was why he had come back via Birmingham instead of Heathrow. That was why he intended no further communication with anyone until he had taken his viva and flown back to Paris. From there he could telephone them and ask about the latest developments. From there he could bid them farewell.

The house in Caxton Street looked much the same when he unlocked the door and went in. Nearly three weeks of dust had accumulated, and some milk left on the draining board had long gone sour. The sickly young man who had called just as he was leaving had departed without trace. Reluctantly he had handed his distant cousin over to the organisation, and they would have taken care of him. Like every other object dangerous to them he would have been removed – or sent back to India after an operation on his abdomen to clear the obstruction.

He was just about to retire to bed when he noticed the photograph of Errol and Stephanie had gone. That night of 29 April, which seemed now months past, he had leafed through a pile of photographs in Stephanie's desk, and taken it as a memento. He was not wasting time on that dangerous night but waiting for the girl to go into a deeper sleep, before he went on with the job. Errol had met him in sweating fear. 'She didn't want another drink, for Christ's sake. I nearly gave up. I wish to Christ I had given up. I can't go on with this, you know; I can't go on!' Perhaps that young fool Nari Prasad had seen the photograph and fancied it. Perhaps it had slipped down between the mantelpiece and the wall. He would look in the morning.

He fasted right through the following morning, making do with milkless coffee and some stale tea biscuits. The viva was to be at the Examination Schools in the High at 3 p.m., so at 2.30 he put on his subfusc and mortar board and walked through the town to his appointment.

The viva took seventy minutes. They wanted elucidation of some of the obscurer points of his thesis, and they questioned him and cross-questioned him to make sure he understood the wider body of literature and scientific evidence on his subject; also were at pains to make sure his was an original work and hadn't been too much the result of strenuous efforts by his supervisor. Eventually it became clear that the thesis had gone over well.

The second examiner, after a consultation with the man from Dublin, said: 'Well, Dr Jiva, I think I can tell you that you have made a satisfactory showing this afternoon. Formally, of course, you'll have to wait until we have reported to the Faculty Board, but I think you need have no worries about the outcome.'

'Thank you, sir. When will that be?'

'Oh, I'd expect in a matter of weeks.'

The meeting was over. The stiffness, the sharpness of the examiners had gone, and they rose with a smile to shake his hand. Arun rose also, adjusting his pince-nez, his own tension slower to go. 'If I should be out of the country would a letter be sent . . .'

'Of course. Leave your address with the Graduate Studies Office. Maybe, just to be on the safe side, you could leave a forwarding address at your college too.'

Arun turned and walked out through the high echoing corridors of the Examination Schools. Outside, in the sulky grey sunlight, he allowed himself a breath or two of satisfaction, and walked home. As he went he looked with some interest at the city he was leaving for ever. Although by and large he disliked the people, the colleges appealed to his sense of antiquity, of a useful tradition of culture and learning. He remembered particularly one day he had taken a pretty Indonesian girl on a punt from the Cherwell Boat House to the Victoria Arms and what had followed. He thought of the chiming of Big Tom; and eating in Hall with one or two congenial companions who did not make fun of his precise manners and style of dressing; he thought of his supervisor, Professor Jenkins, of Brasenose, who seemed to have no aversion for Indians. He remembered slights and semi-slights through the three years. Sir Tony Maidment had once said to him: 'Forget your chip, Arun. There's no such *thing* as colour prejudice in this place. It doesn't *exist*! It's all in your subconscious. Look around you! Who the hell *cares*?' Being a baronet, he had been listened to without dissent, but Arun could tell him the other side of the story, the sly smirks he had caught, the occasional look of laughter or distaste in some girl's eyes.

Well, there was one girl who would never show her distaste for him again. A pity. There were others he could have put away with greater satisfaction. Particularly a bitch called Clara, who had gone out with him several times and led him on and then

251

turned him down, pretending she had never meant it that way.

Well, it was all over and done with. He had booked a flight to Paris tomorrow morning. Goodbye, England. There was almost time to catch a train to Birmingham tonight and try to get on the night flight. But that was rushing things.

Near Caxton Street was a garage where he kept his battered elderly Hillman, untouched for three weeks. He went in and paid the owner and told him to sell the car for what he could get. He asked him to post what he got to Professor Jenkins, who would know his address and forward it on.

There was time still to call on Mrs Velayati; but the rent was paid until the end of the quarter, and Mrs Velayati was liable to talk too long. The few sticks of furniture belonging to him would fetch very little; she was welcome to the proceeds to settle electricity and telephone bills.

He walked down his street. The usual accumulation of parked cars. No room outside his own place, of course. The Parretts next door always overlapped into his parking space.

Hungry now. Once he had taken off his cap and gown he would slip round the corner to a mini-market, pick up enough to cook an evening meal. His plane meant leaving Oxford Station at 8.15. He had an alarm clock, but would ask the telephone people to give him a call just to be on the safe side.

He went up the steps of his house, feeling in his pocket for the key. As he did so two youngish middle-aged men in grey sweaters and slacks got out from a car parked opposite. They came up the steps after him.

'Dr Jiva?'

Arun stared at them, thinking for a moment that they came from the organisation. But something in their manner told him they did not.

'Yes?'

'Dr Arun Jiva?'

'Yes?'

'We are police officers and we have a warrant for your arrest.'

'What do you mean? I don't know what you mean.'

Identity cards were thrust at him and a document which he

252

stared at vaguely, feeling for the first time a sense of insecurity and fear.

'Dr Arun Jiva,' the older of the two men said, 'we'll have to ask you to accompany us to the police station. We have a warrant for your arrest on a charge of possessing dangerous drugs.'

# *Two*

## I

Nari had spent his time in Oxford Remand Prison in the company of a man accused of burglary and another of child molesting. He did not enjoy their company or like their habits. But on the Thursday he was called out of his cell and told someone wished to see him. He followed the warder to an interview room where two middle-aged men were waiting. They introduced themselves. One was Detective Chief Inspector Hampton of the Thames Police, the second was Deputy Chief Investigation Officer Warren of the National Drugs Intelligence Unit.

'Prasad,' said Inspector Hampton after they had sat down, 'your case is not yet due to come up in court, but I expect you are aware that when it does it will be something of a formality.'

'Formality?'

'Well, you are quite an intelligent man. You must know that there can be no adequate defence you can put up to the charge of being in possession of a hundred grams of heroin. The capsules were discharged from your body in the presence of witnesses. It will save time if you plead guilty. It will not save you, of course.'

'So then – what will happen?'

'You will go to prison. The maximum sentence is fifteen years.'

Nari blinked. 'It cannot be that much . . . I – it was only a small amount.'

'You are lucky you're in England,' said Warren grimly. 'In many countries in your part of the world the sentence would be death.'

There was silence. Nari fingered the marriage ring on his

254

finger. They had allowed him to keep that. 'Why are you telling me this? I have said, I know nothing.'

Hampton pushed across a packet of cigarettes. After hesitation Nari took one. A lighter was held to it. He inhaled gratefully.

'I expect you like American cigarettes,' said Hampton.

'Yes . . .'

'My wife,' said Warren to Hampton, 'prefers Egyptian. Likes the taste better.'

The two men discussed smoking for a few moments while Nari sat and watched them with his sad, liquid brown eyes.

Hampton said: 'We look at it this way, Mr Prasad. We think you have been used, maybe against your will, made use of by an organisation that smuggles drugs into this country and distributes them. That right?'

Nari did not reply. He had not shaved yet, and his skin was itching.

Hampton said: 'We think you know something; you must do to have come to this pass. But it may not be much. You probably only dealt with underlings. You might be able, if you felt like it, to tell us about the safe house you came to when you arrived in England. You might be able to give us a few names, but they would almost certainly be false. So it isn't much you have to offer even if you wanted to talk. Right?'

Nari drew at his cigarette.

'Answer me, please.'

'I know nothing.'

'Exactly. So we shall do our best to get you the maximum sentence when you do come up in court. Have you enjoyed your time in the remand prison?'

'I am innocent. I know nothing.'

'Fifteen years is a long time. Even with remission you'll be an old man when you come out. *Old*, even if you're still only forty. I know. I've seen enough men. And you have to be tough to survive in prison at all. You're not tough. You'll crumple and break. I know your sort.'

Nari finished his cigarette in silence.

'We've been talking over your case, Mr Warren and I. He had an idea. He suggested there might be a way out.'

Nari looked at the pack of cigarettes but they were not offered him again. His fingers were unsteady as he screwed out the butt.

'Want to hear it?'

'Hear what?'

'Mr Warren's suggestion.'

Nari hesitated. 'If you like.'

Hampton said: 'We often talk together, Mr Warren and I. We laugh about things. I say he's got more power than I have. Customs and Excise can do things the police couldn't possibly do. Am I right, Mr Warren?'

'Just in a few small things,' said Warren.

'These last few days Mr Warren has been taking an interest in your case. He thinks he can see a way out for you. Instead of fifteen years you'd get three months.'

Nari looked from one to the other. It seemed that always now he was being victimised one way or another. Quite clearly these two men were preparing some sort of a trap for him.

'I don't understand.'

Warren was the heavier and the older of the two. They both had strong, hard faces, no more to be trusted than Mr Mohamed or Shyam Lal Shastri.

'I can't of course *promise* you anything,' Warren said. 'If you plead guilty it will be up to the judge to sentence you. He might give you five years. We can't stop that. But I could promise to get you *out* in three months. There are always *ways*. Mr Hampton knows that as well as I do.'

Hampton smiled and nodded. 'Let's say between us we could promise you that.'

'Top of it all,' said Warren, 'we could arrange for you to remain in England, find you a secretarial job; you could apply for naturalisation papers; we'd see that there was no obstacle raised because of a short prison sentence. It can all be done.'

A second cigarette was passed across. Nari lit it himself this time.

'You say I am an intelligent man. So please say to me what

256

you could possibly expect me to do to receive such treatment.'

'Let's have a cup of tea first, shall we,' said Detective Chief Inspector Hampton.

# II

'This is the arrangement,' said Hampton agreeably. 'You will be brought before the magistrates again tomorrow and you'll be remanded for a further two weeks; but this time you will be released on a bail of one thousand pounds put up by a friend. See?'

Nari frowned doubtfully.

'On release you will spend the night at a small hotel on the outskirts of Oxford, and on Saturday morning you will take a taxi to a house called Postgate, which is north of Oxford, near Woodstock. When you get there you'll instruct the taxi to wait, and at the house you will ask to see Sir Peter Brune. Say it is a personal message you wish to deliver. Refuse altogether to give the message to anyone but Sir Peter Brune. When you meet him – and we shall make sure he is at home before you leave Oxford – when you meet him you will ask him five or six questions. That is all. Give him time to reply to each one before you ask the next. But take no other notice of his replies. Just put your five or six questions and then leave as you came.'

Nari stared at the two men, looking for the trickery. 'Who is this Sir Peter Brown?'

'Brune. He's a highly respected philanthropist and millionaire. He cannot molest you, for he will be anxious above all to avoid any hint of scandal. He is expecting to receive an exceptional honour in two weeks' time, bestowed on him by Oxford University. He cannot refuse to let you return, with a taxi waiting at the door.'

Nari's stare was unblinking. 'And then?'

'Then you'll continue your stay at the hotel, until at the end of the two weeks you will be granted further periods on remand until the time comes for you to appear at the Crown Court for trial and sentencing. This cannot be avoided and we cannot guarantee the sentence. What we can guarantee, as I say, is that within three months of your being sentenced an excuse will be made to free you.'

At last Nari blinked. 'This is all you wish me to do? What are the questions to be?'

'We'll tell you that tomorrow, if you agree to put them. Sleep on it and let me know.'

'How can I sleep on such a possibility? How can I be sure what danger there is for me?'

'For the reasons we've told you. If Sir Peter Brune connived at an illegal act he would be socially disgraced. You can come to no harm.'

'What have you to gain by this? I do not understand why you can offer so much for what seems to be so little. It *cannot* be little. It must be of great importance to you – to the police.'

'Leave that to us,' said Warren grimly. 'We know what we're doing, that's all that should concern you.'

'And what will the police be doing while I am visiting this man?'

'They'll not be far away. We can promise you that too.'

Nari thought longingly of home. But he was not being offered a way home. Home was what he could not hope to see for ten or twelve years. What he was being offered, it seemed, was a new life in England. It was all too complex. Ever since he borrowed the money from Shyam Lal Shastri he had felt himself to be in the grip of forces too strong and brutal for him. He was being manipulated, first one way and then the other. These two men were persuasive. But who was instructing *them*?

'If – if I were to do this – this thing, how can I believe your promises? Who is to say you will keep them?'

It was Hampton who answered.

'You have probably heard the saying in India, Mr Prasad, that an Englishman's word is his bond. There are many sad exceptions, but generally speaking it still holds good. I am a chief inspector of the Police, answerable to a superintendent and above him to an assistant deputy commissioner. Mr Warren is a deputy head of Her Majesty's Customs and Excise. We cannot put anything in writing but we could not have attained our present positions if we were in the habit of giving undertakings we couldn't fulfil. We can't make this offer official, but if you do your part, rely upon it we'll do ours.'

# III

Friday the 8th was the best day of a fine week. Nari stared out of the window of his cell and thought that it was a little bit – just a little bit – like Bombay. Since he came to England the weather, to him, had been constantly cool and cloudy. And unwelcoming. He had not really seen either an English winter or an English summer. During the anxious days he had been here he had been too preoccupied, chiefly with pain, to look at the trees or the burgeoning countryside. Nor had he ever given real thought to what it would be like to start life over again, living in a cold safe country like England. Two years ago he would have leapt at the idea. As a teenager he had not been without ambition. He had done sufficiently well at school to dream of later success. He had felt himself a cut above the others – quicker and smarter even than Shyam Lal Shastri. Shyam had been the bully, the leader, up to most forms of mischief, but not specially bright. Nari had thought of himself as quietly special. What had happened? Where had it all gone wrong?

Both his parents had died quite suddenly soon after his marriage. Had this made the significant break in his life – in his luck? Soon afterwards he had failed in his first law exams: it had been a moral and psychological shock. He knew that before he took them again it would mean hard concentrated studying such as he had never had to do before. Instead he had taken to going out in the evenings and had drifted into a poker set.

During his spell in hospital and in prison on remand, he had thought more seriously about himself than ever before. He had even been self-critical, realising that it is not always the wrong behaviour of other people that is the cause of misfortune.

259

If he ever got a chance to take a grip of a new life, to try to begin again . . . Perhaps nowadays he was looking at his past existence in Bombay through rose-coloured spectacles? Anyway, as he had reminded himself before, there was not likely to be any choice. What would these men say when they came in?

They came in and sat down, and as if mesmerised he nodded and gave his consent. They then passed him a sheet of paper with eight typewritten statements on it.

'Between now and tomorrow you will have to learn these by heart,' said Warren. 'Get them off word for word. Understand?'

Nari stared at the paper.

(1) 'My name is Nari Prasad. I have come with a message from Arun Jiva.'

Pause for reply.

(2) 'I would like to speak to you absolutely privately, sir.'

Pause for reply.

(3) 'Arun Jiva has been arrested in Oxford for smuggling drugs.'

Pause for reply.

(4) 'He says you must help him. Otherwise . . .'

Pause for reply.

(5) 'He says if he comes down you will come down.'

Pause for reply.

(6) 'Arun Jiva says the police would like to know all he knows about Stephanie Locke.'

Pause for reply.

(7) 'Well, I have given you his message, sir, I can do no more.'

Pause for reply.

(8) 'I will go now. I have a taxi waiting at the door.'

Nari's hand began to shake. 'I do not think I can do this.'

Hampton said: 'Don't worry about nerves, Prasad. We can give you something to quiet them and to help your confidence. You've only to remember your lines. You've got – what? – pretty well twenty-four hours to learn them.'

Nari went over the eight remarks he was being asked to make. To a strange man in a strange house. How could it help the police – or anyone else? It must be dangerous for him to go to this house, he knew it in his guts. But ten years or more in an English prison . . .

The two men had got up, were talking together. He looked at them.

'You can come along with me now,' said Detective Chief Inspector Hampton kindly. 'We can take you straight along to the magistrates' court and get you remanded on bail for a further fourteen days.'

# Three

## I

Alistair Crichton said: 'Well, of course, it's quite *ridiculous*, Henry! It's simply not worth giving credence to such a scurrilous rumour!'

'That's exactly my feeling,' said Henry Gaveston. 'Well, it *was* my feeling when Locke rang up. Since then there have been a few things which have rather affected my conviction.'

'But good God, Catherine and I *stayed* with him in Corfu! There was no question of anything underhand going on! What the hell is Locke insinuating?'

'He's insinuating far more than I like to face up to at the moment. Peter Brune is an old and valued friend of mine. There's never been a breath of scandal about him. He's also been a most generous donor to the funds of this college, as we both know.'

'Indeed! And a *continuing* benefactor. I don't know what we should have done without him!'

'Or shall do.'

There was silence, during which Dr Crichton shifted uneasily.

'There's the Encaenia on the twentieth! Everything's published and printed! We can't possibly go back on that!'

Henry said: 'We can't confer an honorary degree on someone who is under suspicion for a criminal offence.'

'But *what* suspicion? Something James Locke has cobbled together out of his anger and grief? Of course it was a tragedy to lose his daughter, but he mustn't be allowed to traduce a distinguished and blameless man because of a few coincidences! Tell me again, what is his twisted reasoning?'

Henry pushed back his boyish grey hair. 'It isn't just his twisted reasoning any longer, Alistair. The police have come into it. I told you this.'

'But how? Have they any firm proof?'

'No, fortunately. But, as you know, learning from Locke that Arun Jiva, the graduate student from Delhi, was returning to England, they kept watch on his house and arrested him on Tuesday. Although he has so far refused to talk, they have searched his house again and also his baggage and have found evidence confirming what they had already gathered from investigations put in hand after Errol Colton's murder. Both in Jiva's house and in Colton's were references which the police think point to a drug ring located, among other places, in Bombay, Corfu and Oxford. Importing and distributing hard drugs on a big scale. It's a nasty thought. What is nastier is that they have several leads pointing to Postgate as the centre of the organisation in England.'

Crichton got up, rubbed his nose, looked at his Bursar. 'God Almighty, it's just impossible! I'll have to speak to the Vice-Chancellor, and then I suppose also the Chancellor! But for God's sake, you can't condemn a man on *suspicion*! We'd be living in a totalitarian state if we did such things!'

It was plain to Gaveston that these two meetings, if they had to take place, would be highly embarrassing for the Principal. A strong advocate of Brune from the start, Crichton in his anger reflected his own conflicts. If the rumours about Brune proved to be baseless he would lose face because he had not condemned them. If he said nothing and the allegations surfaced elsewhere, particularly in the press, he would be even more exposed and could no longer say he knew nothing about them. He clearly wished Gaveston had never raised the subject and that it would go away.

Henry said, 'One thing had occurred to me. It might be far-fetched. Or it might be the answer. That is that if police suspicions are correct – and we've no proof that they are yet – Postgate may be being used by members of Brune's staff unknown to him. He's got a confidential secretary who's very close to him and takes on a lot of the responsibilities of his business and the charities –'

'You mean John Peron? Yes. That could be! It would explain a lot.' A look of relief passed across the Principal's face. 'It might well be the solution.'

'It would be a more likely solution if Peter were an unworldly scholar,' Henry said. 'Scholar he certainly is, but he's very much of the world as well . . .'

'Whom have you spoken to among the police?'

'Superintendent Willis and one of the head officers of Customs and Excise.'

'Ah,' said Crichton. 'Customs and Excise are the barracudas of our investigative system. On their VAT rounds they can make forced entries in a way the Tax Inspector could never do, and they can take liberties with the law that the police wouldn't dare.'

'You're well informed, Alistair.' Henry would have been amused if the situation had been less serious.

'I don't live in such a cloistered world.' The Principal grunted. 'Like Brune, I'm a practical scholar. One couldn't hope to run a college otherwise.'

Henry said: 'You haven't forgotten that Brune is dining with us here on Sunday.'

'I'd not forgotten at all! It's a hellish situation. But good grief! Have we not invited James Locke as well?'

Gaveston began to light his pipe.

'I can stop that. I can ring him, ask him not to come. I'm sure he'll understand.'

'Who else is coming – Caterham, isn't it? And that architect chap. And . . .' Crichton frowned, groping for names.

'Our MP. And the Shadow Minister for Education. And Professor Shannon from Berkeley. And there's sure to be a few of our people. Mary Fisher and Martin Goodbody always turn up.'

'That's at least nine,' said Crichton, having ticked them off on his fingers. 'Hm. Perhaps in all the circumstances better to leave it as it is.'

'Not ask the Chancellor?'

'I doubt if he could come at such short notice. But no, Henry,

264

while this – this thing is hanging over us! Inviting Charles, with Peter Brune as principal guest? I should feel hypocritical, and towards both men!'

Henry frowned at his pipe, which had not lit up, put it away in his pocket. At this year's Encaenia two others were to be made Doctor of Civil Law, one of Science, one of Letters, one of Divinity. The eulogy for Sir Peter Brune, KBE, MA, printed first in Latin, in which it would be delivered, and then in an English translation, would, Henry guessed, refer to his distinction as a Greek scholar, his wide-ranging benevolences, his many gifts to the University, particularly to St Martin's, his endowment of foundations in some of the poorer countries of Europe so that scholars there could come to England to continue their studies at Oxford. This was the highest order Oxford University could confer. The ceremony was picturesque, beginning this year with a recital by the organist of Corpus Christi, followed by an assembly of the dignitaries in the Hall of Exeter College and the procession of them all in caps and gowns to the Sheldonian where the ceremony would take place.

Gaveston stirred uneasily, dusting the ash off his shabby jacket. He knew at this stage Alistair Crichton would accept his advice. He had to choose between two friends, and he had tried to take a middle course. But mainly he had acted on the assumption that James (and the police) were mistaken. Peter Brune was *sans reproche*.

Would they be justified – could they be justified in going ahead with the investiture without telling the Chancellor? Disbelieve James – who by his violent action a couple of weeks ago had put himself beyond the pale of civilised behaviour – but who was now cooperating with the police? Disbelieve the police, who presumably did not suspect James or had not enough evidence to proceed against him, but were now accepting his evidence and advice in the arrest of Dr Arun Jiva? Superintendent Willis and the drug enforcement officers thought they were on to something: Willis had told Henry that they had applied for Home Office permission to tap the telephone in and out of Postgate, but it had not yet been granted.

The Chancellor, told the situation, would almost certainly ask Peter Brune if he would consent to a postponement until next year. Brune would be deeply alienated and his benefactions to the University would dry up. No one wanted that to happen. Clearly one did not want the University to benefit from money made out of drugs; but neither could one cast such splendid gifts aside without the weightiest of reasons.

'Principal,' Henry said, and it was rare that he called Crichton by his official name, 'perhaps it would be better if we allowed James Locke to come to the dinner on Sunday.'

'What? Who? What can you mean?'

'Locke is a civilised man, accustomed to keeping his feelings to himself. He hardly knows Peter Brune, nor Peter him. A dinner where they meet casually may convince James that he must be completely mistaken about Brune. No one in his right mind would believe it.'

'And if it doesn't convince him?'

'In one way or another it might help to lance the boil. Of course it's a risk – a calculated risk.'

Crichton walked across to the window, looked down at the quad, where some students were clustered arguing.

'I would call it an uncalculated risk,' he said.

## II

Nari stayed at the Fairlawn Hotel, which was just off the Woodstock Road. A quiet fairly inexpensive place, much favoured by reps; they kept it busy during the week but at weekends went home leaving the hotel half-empty. A few new people came in, parents visiting their sons and daughters, but Nari had the dining room almost to himself on the Friday evening. He went to bed early and rehearsed his questions over and over again before taking the pill he had been given.

He did not know whether he was as free as he seemed: he thought it likely that if he chose to leave for the railway station somebody would be there to make sure he didn't catch a train. The pill he had taken had certainly calmed his nerves, and he looked on his mission with a sense of fatalism, as if this were the last act of some tragedy in which he was the central figure.

There had been no time at all in his early days in England to write to Bonni; he had begun a letter in his cell but never finished it. What was there to say?

The taxi was to pick him up at eleven, but he woke at seven and reread the two sheets he had written to her – necessarily garbled, falsely reassuring. How could he finish it now? If he successfully fulfilled his mission – and if an Englishman's word was his bond – he would not return to India at all. He would never see his wife or his flat or his friends (including, pray God, Shyam Lal Shastri) ever again. Unless eventually he established himself in a modestly successful way in England and was permitted to send for Bonni. Would she come? Would he want her to come? In spite of distance and separation having lent some enchantment, he thought not. Cringing and complaining and resentfully subservient, she would be a drag on him in England. She was old-fashioned, out of date, uneducated. In Edgbaston he had seen several very pretty Indian girls, Westernised, emancipated, coming into his cousin's shop. Even those who retained their saris had a totally different outlook. Perhaps in the end – who knew? – he might be able to marry such a girl. With a new name and a new identity, no one was to know he had been married before.

He tried the questions a dozen times more until he was word perfect, then took his second pill dutifully after breakfast. It crossed his mind to wonder what sort of justice there was in the world that the police authorities should have the freedom to administer pills that gave sleep and confidence, whereas he faced a prospect of fifteen years in prison for bringing in one of the likely ingredients.

But by the time the taxi came his mind had passed this by and confidence settled on him. As the car drove through the city suburbs and then into the green and lush and leafy countryside he compared it with the suburbs of the city he had left in India, his home and its surroundings. The everlasting smell of sweat and urine and stale cooking that came up from the flat below; the street outside down which he walked every morning to catch his train, the bolts of dyed cloth piled in an entrance, with bangles and cheap jewellery; the fruit stalls selling oranges and pomegranates and guava, the shoe stalls and food stalls; and children defecating in the gutter in the molten glare of the early sun, and further on the shacks and shanties, many of them made of packing cases and old sacks and all full of people in rags or naked, children waiting to beg, old men waiting to die. People, people everywhere, pullulating, multiplying faster than hunger and disease could take them off, all drifting into Bombay from some greater crisis of existence in the outer countryside.

A week or two ago Nari had longed to see the back of this cold orderly country, wanted to return to Bombay with all its faults and ugly memories. Now, with the prospect of a new identity and an opportunity to live here, his feelings were different. He was not unaware of the risks this interview might bring – he was not such a fool as to suppose it would all be as easy as the policemen pretended – but he knew also that if by some miracle he was found not guilty and allowed to return to Bombay he would not be permitted to resume his normal life, drab though that might be; he would still be in thrall to men like Mr Mohamed and Dr Amora. There had been a sentence he had half caught that horrible day when he had refused to swallow more than eighty of the packages. Someone had whispered: 'Eighty's only just worth while,' and Amora had said: 'It will do for a first time.' They had been talking in a dialect he only partly understood, and which they probably thought he did not understand at all, but during these last few days in prison the interchange surfaced and solidified in his mind. If he returned to India a free man, *that* might be waiting for him.

The taxi turned off down a side road, and Nari thought he had reached his destination. But not so. They came to a clearing in which was a caravan and a police car. Two men in the car, both strangers to him. When the taxi drew up one of the men got out and opened the door of the taxi. He smiled pleasantly.

'Mr Nari Prasad. Could we trouble you for a minute or two?'

Nari edged his way out, was escorted across the grass, up the two steps and into the caravan, which had in it a table and three chairs and some radio apparatus. The other man from the car joined them.

'Sit down, Mr Prasad,' said the first man genially. 'We just want to know if you can remember the statements you have to make. Shall we just go through them?'

They went through them three times, while the second man checked with what was typewritten on a sheet of paper.

'That's good,' said the first man. 'That's very good. Remember, not to get flustered. Give him time to answer. Put the questions *clearly*, then wait for the reply. See?'

'I see,' said Nari.

'Now then,' said the second man, getting up, 'just put this round your neck, Mr Prasad.'

He was holding out something on a thin black tape like a necklace, like a medallion, no bigger than an old-fashioned watch, but flatter.

'What's that?'

'Just put it round your neck. See, like this, let me; if you put the cord under the collar of your shirt just like an extra tie, then the mike will lie comfortable, hidden by your shirt. No one can possibly see it.'

'*Mike?*' said Nari.

'Yes, it's just a body mike. Didn't they tell you about it? It's quite harmless; nobody'll know you've got it; but with it we'll be able to listen to the answers.'

# III

'I wish', said Nari, 'to see Sir Peter Brune, please.'

A maid had come to the door, but a man hovered behind her in the shadow.

'What name is it?'

'Nari Prasad.'

'Oh.' She half closed the door on him and could be heard whispering inside.

It was an impressive house, and some of Nari's Dutch courage had seeped away.

The door opened and a dark man stood there. 'What is your business?'

'Are you Sir Peter Brune?'

'State your business and I will see if he is in.'

'I can only state my business to him, sir. That is what I was told.'

'Who told you? Who are you from?'

'I cannot say. I can only say it to Sir Peter Brune.'

John Peron stared at the young man and then beyond him to the waiting taxi.

'I will see,' he said, and shut the door.

Nari stood on the top step, his kneecaps trembling. A shaft of sunlight among the clouds lit up the young beech trees with a rare brilliance. It was something that could not happen in India, the much paler sun illuminating the much brighter green. Nari was not conscious of it.

After waiting and waiting and waiting the maid opened the door. 'Come in.'

A dark hall; Nari stumbled over a rug; a big, lighter room; at the other end of it an elderly man with greying hair, a deeply etched rather handsome face. The brighter light from the window behind him made his expression impossible to read.

'What is it?' he said in a deep cultured English voice.

'You are Sir – Sir Peter Brune?'

'Yes.'

'My name, sir, is Nari Prasad. I – I have come from – with a message from Arun Jiva.' Pause for reply. Could he remember anything else?

'From Jiva? Surely he's not back in England?'

'I would – like to speak to you privately – with absolute privacy, sir.'

Pause for reply. But there was no reply. After a brief silence

Sir Peter Brune said: 'You may say anything you wish in front of my secretary.'

What now? Did he hold firm or did he give way?

The dark man said: 'Come along, man, what is it you want?'

'Did you know he was back in England?'

'Who, Jiva?' Brune said. 'No. What is it to me?'

Nari got on the rails again. 'Arun Jiva has been arrested in Oxford for smuggling drugs.'

A grandfather clock was ticking in the room. It was enormously solemn.

'The damned fool,' said the secretary. 'What the hell did he come back for? He was told to stay away!'

Peter Brune held up a hand to silence the other man. To Nari he said: 'I'm sorry to hear he's in trouble. I don't think I can help him.'

'He says you must help him now. Otherwise . . .'

Brune turned his back, looked out at the fitful sunshine. 'I'm sorry. I can provide him with a lawyer; nothing more.'

Now was the big one – the threat. Nari was overawed by this elderly distinguished Englishman, by the big house, by the dark-faced secretary standing arms folded by the door.

Nari stuttered and was hardly audible. 'He says – he says if he comes down you will come down.'

'What do you say?' Brune demanded.

Nari stumbled through the words again, but more clearly.

Brune laughed. 'I'd advise him to think again.'

Peron said sharply: 'Weren't you remanded in custody? You were in hospital and then in jail! How did you get out?'

Nari was almost on the point of collapse. He swallowed hard and said in a voice made louder this time by his panic: 'He says – Arun Jiva says the police would like to know all he knows about Stephanie Locke! . . .'

Brune turned back from the window. 'If he tells them what he knows about Stephanie Locke he'll be in worse trouble than on a drugs charge.'

Peron had come up behind Nari. 'How did you get out? Who

sent you here? How did you ever see Arun Jiva if he's been arrested?'

'I was released on bail, sir,' said Nari, and then remembered his last line. 'Well, I have given you his message, sir. I can do no more.'

Peron grasped his arm. 'What the hell are you doing here? Tell me that? Who sent you?'

'Arun Jiva,' said Nari, improvising. 'I – I saw him in court . . . Sir, I will be going now. I have a waiting taxi at the door.'

The two men hesitated, looking at each other. Then Brune shrugged slightly and turned away.

'Show this man out, John. He's wasting our time.'

'If I may differ, sir,' said John Peron with a courtesy that did not ring true. 'If I may differ, sir, I don't trust him. I suggest we take him upstairs, lock him in a room and ask him a few questions. He may well be working for the police.'

'No, sir, not at all!' gasped Nari. 'I would never . . .'

The grip on his arm did not relax.

'He may have been a police spy from the beginning; the way he turned up at Arun's door just as he was leaving; then conniving with the Locke man to refuse the ambulance.'

'If you please, sir, that is not truth at all! I am terrified of the police. I will not go near them at any price! I am assuring you!'

Peter Brune was the coolest of the three. He came towards Nari, stared closely into his face. Nari smelt some antiseptic on his breath.

'Tell me this, Prasad. Why were you given bail?'

'I – don't know, sir.'

'You were not discharged? You were given bail.'

'Yes, sir.'

'After being two weeks in custody?'

'Yes, sir.'

'On such a serious charge? Who is putting up the bail money?'

'I am not knowing, sir. I must go now.'

Peron said to Brune: 'He's a spy! Good God, it stands out a mile.'

'I don't see it. No one would ever send him here – except Jiva.

The police have no reason to suspect anyone in this house.'

'Unless Jiva's talked.'

'Nonsense, he wouldn't dare. But take this man upstairs if you want to. He doesn't look as if he would be difficult to break.'

'Who *sent* you?' Peron demanded.

'No one! I cannot stay! I have a taxi waiting!'

Brune's sardonic face creased again. 'Ah yes. You have a taxi waiting . . . Tell Angie to go out and pay the taxi off, John. Say Mr Prasad has accepted an invitation to lunch and that we'll send him back in a car later. Give the taxi man ten pounds. There shouldn't be any difficulty then.'

# IV

'Hell!' said the man in the radio car, parked in a lay-by where the road was not far from the house. 'They're keeping him.'

'Never mind,' said his companion. 'He did well! We've got a fine tape. They'll be delighted.'

'Leave it on,' said the first man. 'There may be more transmitted before they discover he's wearing it.' After chewing on his thumb for a moment he added: 'All the same, I feel sorry for the poor little bugger.'

The second man raised his binoculars. 'The maid's paying Joe off now. There's nothing he can do about it. There's nothing *we* can do about it – short of a search warrant, which we certainly haven't got. Too bad. Never mind, I'm not going to be a crybaby. He's fulfilled his purpose in life.'

The receiver crackled but so far there was no further speech.

The first man said: 'I'll ring the station.'

'They won't know the first thing about it,' said the second man. 'Try this number. It's direct to Hampton.'

# Four

## I

Detective Inspector Foulsham said: 'Well, as I was in the area I thought I'd call and see you again, Mr Locke. I know I should have rung up, but after all the help you have been giving us . . .'

James said: 'Sit down. Let me see, you take coffee, don't you?'

'Very kind of you,' Foulsham said, as James pressed the bell. 'Whenever I call here I always admire your garden.'

'The weather's been pretty kind this year.'

Foulsham sat down. 'That must have been an interesting trip to Corfu. Were you on holiday?'

'It was just a long weekend.'

'But with considerable results!'

'Most of it was luck on the way home.'

'That certainly! But your time in Corfu, I gather, was not ill-spent. At least according to your friend, Colonel Gaveston.'

'Afraid I found nothing but rumour and counter-rumour.'

'The police often work with that before they can collect the concrete evidence.'

At this stage Mary arrived with the coffee. James was glad of the interruption. He had, of course, been entirely frank with Henry, but neither he nor Henry could be entirely frank with the police. Especially there must be no possible mention of photographs.

'Do stay if you'd like, Mary,' James said. 'I'm sure the Inspector and I have no secrets.'

'Thank you, no,' she said, 'if you've everything you want.'

'Mrs Aldershot has just agreed to become my wife.'

274

'Oh?' Inspector Foulsham's bright eyes went from one to the other. 'May I congratulate you both!'

'Thank you,' said Mary, who had coloured. She smiled stiffly and left them. James busied himself with the coffee.

'Let me see, where were we now?' said Foulsham. 'Oh, yes, your trip to Corfu, sir.'

'Colonel Gaveston will have told you about it.'

'Something, yes. But it's good to hear it in your own words.'

James cursed himself for not having prepared for this situation.

'Oh, a few tongues wagged. But then they are always wagging – especially in such a small community.'

'I hear there's some talk of your suspecting the existence of a drugs ring operating from the island.'

'Indeed? Do you know Corfu, Inspector?'

''Fraid not, sir. My daughter went last year but it was simply on a package deal.'

'Well, there's a quay on the south of the island which can take thirty-ton vessels that may or may not ferry illegitimate consignments. Who am I to say? And there's a titled Englishman who has a large villa in the north of the island who may or may not be involved. Guesswork at the worst. Plain unsubstantiated guesswork. And at the best, only hearsay.'

'Only hearsay . . .'

'Yes.'

Foulsham's white hair was silhouetted against the bright day.

'Well, seeing Dr Arun Jiva was not hearsay. The information that he was returning to England was of the utmost value to us.'

'I'm glad.'

'Jiva was arrested on Wednesday, and documents on him, pieced together with papers found in his house, point to a direct connection between him and an important man – also a titled man – who we have recently – that is, since Colton's death – had some suspicions of, but not a vestige of proof. All that has now changed, and we very much appreciate your assistance in the matter.'

'Delighted I was of help.'

275

'You will be, of course.' When James raised his eyebrows Foulsham added: 'Then there was the young Indian, Naresh Prasad. Had you not brought his plight to our notice it's pretty clear he would have disappeared without trace. We still haven't found the ambulance, by the way.'

'Pity, that . . . It just seems I have twice been lucky enough to be in the right place at the right time.'

'Only twice?' Foulsham said.

James looked up. 'As far as I know, yes.'

'Tell me, Mr Locke, when you were in Corfu, did you look up the first Mrs Colton?'

Curse Henry. Had he let this out, or was the policeman guessing?

'I suppose you could look on that as another lucky coincidence. She was a waitress at a restaurant I visited.'

'Did you go there on purpose?'

'Actually it was an embarrassment, meeting her,' James said, dodging the direct question.

'Embarrassment?'

'As you know, I had been on bad terms with Colton.'

'So what was your purpose in meeting her?'

'I thought she might be able to tell me how Colton first became involved in the drugs trade.'

'Presuming he was . . . And did she?'

'No. I think she was too scared.'

'What was her reaction to her husband's death?'

'Not much obvious grief. Chiefly concerned whether her allowance would continue. And she wanted her daughter back.'

'Did she say who she thought might have murdered her husband?'

'I didn't ask her. But I don't think she had any idea.'

Foulsham sipped his coffee and then stared into the cup as if seeking wisdom.

'*We* have ideas, Mr Locke, I must tell you that, but as yet there is insufficient proof.'

'I wish I could help you,' said James.

'I wish you would,' said Foulsham.

There was a rather long silence. James nursed his ankle.

Inspector Foulsham said: 'Have you ever heard of the Locard principle, sir?'

'No.'

'In effect it's a principle much used by the police these days – the theory being that when a person enters a room he brings something in with him that he leaves behind, and when that person leaves that room he takes something away with him that he did not have when he entered.'

'Interesting.' James pressed his button and the chair took him to the coffee table. 'How would it apply?'

'Well, if a murder is committed the chances are that the murderer has brought something in and taken something away – it may be a dog's hair, foreign dust, fingerprints, footmarks, threads of tweed or cotton or wool, saliva, mud, biro marks, chalk, sweatstains. When the murder has involved a struggle it is still more unusual for it not to have occurred.'

'More coffee?'

'Thank you, no, Mr Locke. I must be on my way.'

'Am I right in supposing that in the case of the murders of Colton and Smith, the Locard principle has not worked?'

'Not so far.'

'But you're still hopeful of an arrest?'

'Investigations which are still proceeding may help us to find the culprit. Perhaps someone will come along who will be as helpful as you have been in this other criminal activity.'

'Don't you think they are connected?'

'Maybe. Tell me your reasoning, sir.'

'Oh, I haven't got as far as that. But Errol was in the drug trade, Errol was connected with Jiva. If –'

'Why d'you say that?' Foulsham's voice was suddenly sharper.

'What?' James breathed out slowly. 'That Errol was connected with Jiva? Well, weren't they?'

'You are telling me that they were. How do you know that?'

Having put his cup and saucer down, James brought his chair round to face his visitor.

'On the afternoon when I found Naresh Prasad waiting for an

ambulance he told me, as you know, that he had been given Errol Colton's name by Jiva as the man who was going to help him.'

'You didn't mention this in your first statement to Sergeant Evans.'

'Didn't I? Well, no, I must have forgotten.'

'Do you think, Mr Locke, that your daughter could have been in any way involved with Colton or Jiva or both in their trade in drugs?'

'I do not.'

'You seem sure. Young people –'

'I'm very sure.'

For the first time in their several meetings Foulsham heard steel in James Locke's voice. It made more sense of police suspicion.

'Just so. Just so . . . Well, we may be able to persuade Dr Jiva to tell us more about his involvement with Colton. So far as Colton's death is concerned, it could have been a revenge killing and with Smith more or less accidentally involved.'

'Revenge?'

'It's a good motive.'

'Nietzsche had something to say about that.'

'Who, sir?'

'Nietzsche. I think he said that revenge was the sign of a noble mind.'

'I hadn't heard. I can't say I agree with him. Was he a Frenchman?'

'A German.'

'Ah, well, there you are. We're all entitled to our views, aren't we. Except when we take the law into our own hands. There's all the difference between thinking and doing. Are you a religious man, sir?'

'No.'

'Nor I. But I was brought up right. I was taught that it was almost as wicked to think evil as to do evil. As a policeman I have had to disregard those teachings. There's all the difference in the world of law between wishing a man dead and killing him.'

James smiled. 'And I suppose there's all the difference in the world of law between suspecting a man of a crime and finding evidence to prove it.'

'Just so,' said Foulsham. 'But we shall keep on trying.'

## II

When he had gone Mary Aldershot put her back to the door and said: 'How *dare* you! What possessed you? How could you tell him such a thing?'

James looked at her, his head on one side. 'It was an impulse.'

'An impulse indeed!'

'A double bluff, if you get my meaning.'

'Not at all!'

'The police suspect me of the murders but they've little or no evidence. They see me as the most likely suspect but they know they could be wrong. I think they look on me as a fairly honourable man driven to distraction by his daughter's death. An honourable man does not ask someone to marry him if he thinks his new wife is likely to become the wife of a man arraigned for murder. It seemed to me a way of confusing them, of throwing them off the scent. "He must be innocent, or sure of the lack of evidence, or completely around the bend, to make such a proposal." D'you see what I mean?'

'I think you are completely around the bend,' Mary said.

'Well, thank you.'

'You could equally be marrying me because my testimony as a housekeeper could incriminate you, whereas as a wife I could not be compelled to testify.'

'I hadn't thought of that.'

'I thought, perhaps,' said Mary, 'that you *were* thinking of that!'

'The unkindest cut! Why d'you so resent what I have said?'

'Because,' she said, 'because if it were ever even to be a possibility, the motive would have to be quite different.'

James thought this out. 'Oh, I could make the motive very different. Pity, for example.'

'Pity for me?'

'You know very well what I mean! A healthy youngish woman and a crippled elderly man.'

'You're talking of *my* motive now, not yours.'

'Well,' James said after a moment, 'there could be a joint motive, common to us both. A selfish motive, seeking affection, companionship, mutual interests, even love. But you turned me down once, five years ago. It can't be any more of an attractive proposition now.'

Mary moved from the door, opened it again and looked out. The police car had gone.

She said: 'I don't think last time you mentioned love.'

# *Five*

## I

That evening the guest of honour was the last to arrive.

'*Very* sorry,' Peter Brune said to the Principal, smiling as he shook hands. 'An urgent telephone call at the last minute from Hong Kong. It's always difficult to refuse a call when someone has taken the trouble to ring you in the middle of the night – *their* night.'

Crichton beamed to hide his constraint. 'Let me see, do you know everybody here? Herbert Norris, the member for Lewisham. I'm not sure . . .'

'We've met,' said Brune. 'At a memorial service in Cambridge, for the Master of Caius.'

'Yes, yes. Three years ago. Certainly.'

'Norris, as you know, is Shadow Minister for Education.'

'There's room for improvement, isn't there?' Brune said.

'Well, we certainly feel so.'

'You don't, I think, know Martin Goodbody, whose subject is Medieval History. Henry Gaveston, of course –'

'*Very* well,' said Brune.

'James Locke, whom I believe you met once.'

'Briefly,' said Brune.

'Briefly,' said James. When you carried a stick it wasn't difficult to ignore the half-extended hand. They stared at each other, eye to eye, for a long moment. It was like a clash of swords.

Alistair took his guest by the arm, not touching Brune's hand for his own were sweating. 'Of the others, Lord Caterham . . .'

'Yes, of course. How d'you do. Are you going to Ascot this year?'

They went round the remaining guests. Brune seemed to know what each of the others did, where they had met before, what would be a subject of particular interest to mention.

Everyone talked amiably for a few minutes. Among the guests was Bruce Masters, Stephanie's personal tutor. He shook hands with James silently, and looked as if he would like to say something but did not know quite what. They had met twice since her death, though briefly.

James suddenly said, in a voice Henry could overhear: 'Tell me, Mr Masters, you dealt with Stephanie's work?'

'Yes, of course. Indeed.'

'What was her grammar like?'

'Grammar? D'you mean English, or –'

'English.'

'Very good.' Masters smiled wryly. 'She was well brought up.'

'Did she ever split an infinitive?'

Masters' expression became slightly strained, as if he were not following the line of questioning. 'Surely not. I would have noticed. She was rather a stickler for that sort of thing.' He smiled again. 'Nowadays, alas, most people don't even know what split infinitives are.'

'*She* did,' said James.

'I'm sure. As I've said . . . Fortunately such problems don't arise in French or Spanish.'

Crichton, having seen that Brune had finished his drink, was now leading the way into Hall. A few other Fellows were already there, but places had been left for the main group. They were already a few minutes late, and the students all stood when they came in, though a few were getting restless at the delay.

Brune sat next to Crichton, with Lord Caterham on his right. James was between Henry and Martin Goodbody, a little way down the table with his back to the students. Food and wine came and went. Although they had spoken frequently over the telephone, it was the first time Henry had seen James since the Corfu visit. Henry noticed James kept his eyes on Peter Brune, who looked more relaxed than his host, with his handsome hair, hooked nose, deeply indented sardonic smile that came and went as he talked. And bright dark eyes that occasionally met Henry's, but never James's stare.

The food was no better and no worse than usual, but the wine was specially excellent. Brune probably expected some word of appreciation for having donated it to the college, but Crichton unexpectedly gagged and couldn't find the words.

They went downstairs for the customary coffee and port and grapes. According to tradition, the seating had to be changed, and James found himself next to Lord Caterham, who had been Home Secretary in the mid-sixties. Conversation at the new table was wide-ranging: congratulations on St Martin's good showing in the Norrington Scale, progress of repairs to the tower, the bitterness of the miners' strike and the tightrope that had to be walked by those responsible for law and order. Brune had his share of the talk; James was silent; Henry in his high-pitched voice contributed ever and again. At the extreme end of the table two dons could be heard arguing about the influences of the Swahili language on East African politics.

'I imagine law and order was quite a different matter in your day, Rupert,' Crichton said to Caterham.

'Well, my day doesn't seem so far away to me!' Caterham said. 'It's a different problem now, I agree, but no one is likely to forget the student unrest in the sixties.'

'Indeed not,' said Professor Shannon, 'for I was one of the protesters at Berkeley at the time! Mind, I'd say we had a lot to protest about, what with the Vietnam War and the general disillusion with American social and foreign policy. Let me tell you . . .' He went on for a couple of minutes.

'Is it true what I hear, Principal,' asked Herbert Norris, 'that students today have moved away generally from rebellion towards conformity and from drugs back to drink as a part of the social scene?'

Crichton smiled and shrugged and deferred to Henry, who said: 'At the moment we're probably producing more church-going Tories than revolutionary socialists, but I don't think it's much to do with us – more a sign of the times, a swing of the pendulum. And of course it's a relatively small proportion of the

283

students who make the change, just as a small proportion of the voters in England swing an election.'

Talk returned to the miners' strike and the risk of its spreading to other industries. An aged Fellow who had just joined the table for coffee was the only man there old enough to remember the General Strike of 1926, and he stirred his memories for the benefit of the company.

Then in the general talk James heard Norris say, almost it seemed out of the blue: 'I understand, Sir Peter, that you have unorthodox views on the drug scene.'

Brune made a disclaiming gesture. 'Somebody's been telling on me. I have to do with it, of course, as I am a director of the Worsley Clinic. And I have views. Yes, I have views. Perhaps by some standards they could be called unorthodox.'

There the matter would have rested. No one was going to pursue it further but, as if on impulse yet quite deliberately, he chose to go on, as if personally to Norris but with most of the table listening.

'D'you know, my mother was the formative influence in my life. She was a highly gifted teacher at a good girls' school who gave up her vocation – as many women did in those days – when she married my father. So she turned her attention to me. I was educated, forcibly but kindly. Every day in my bath from the age of three onwards she had records in the bathroom playing over famous men speaking in classical Greek.'

'That explains a lot, Peter,' said Professor Shannon.

'When I was fifteen she developed cancer of the pancreas.' His voice was unemotional. Then he shrugged deprecatingly and went on: 'For too much of the time she was in appalling pain. I used to hear her screaming. The fault of the damned Welsh doctors, and maybe it was partly my father's doing: he was well able to take a Puritanical view of things where he was not personally concerned. I went out into the streets – into the docks of Cardiff – and with money I had "borrowed" from my father I bought heroin and a syringe – much more difficult to get hold of in those days – and began to give her injections. The doctors were surprised and suspicious but whatever they suspected they

284

held their peace. The effect was miraculous. Not only was the pain taken away but she was at peace with herself and the world. She faced death with an almost benign acceptance. It was my first introduction to the underworld!'

In spite of the last sardonic sentence the uncomfortable silence remained. The two dons nattering at the end of the table were now talking about the Bantu tongue and its infusion of Arabic.

Crichton said: 'I knew some of your views, Peter, but not the cause.'

'Heroin, I understand,' said Lord Caterham stiffly, 'is scarcely ever refused a dying cancer patient these days.'

'Oh no, you're probably right,' Brune said. 'But if you go into it, as I have, it's not only terminal cases that show enormous benefit. If it were allowed, heroin would have a tremendously good effect on all sorts of disorders. Bronchitis, angina, shingles; and on burns, painful bowel disorders, rheumatic fever. It was some English chemist, wasn't it, who discovered that by boiling morphine with acetic anhydride this exciting new compound was created?'

'I thought it was a German discovery,' said Mary Fisher.

'No. They took it up twenty or thirty years later, called it the Wonder Drug. It's only about ninety years since it was put on the open market, like aspirin or senna pods, and recommended as a general palliative for all painful complaints.'

'That was before its addictive and lethal properties were understood,' Lord Caterham said.

'I know. Of course. But don't forget that it's less than two hundred years since tea was condemned as addictive and harmful. Someone called it "the deleterious product of China". And when it was first introduced into France it was only available on prescription.'

'Well, I suppose there's something to be said for making cocaine and heroin available on prescription in England,' Norris said. 'But that surely is what happens now in drug dependence clinics?'

'Less and less,' said Goodbody, entering the conversation unexpectedly.

Caterham said: 'It puts the doctor in an intolerable position. Whom to supply, whom to refuse.'

'Isn't that what doctors are for?' Brune replied. 'It's a matter very much under constant review at the Worsley.'

'A relative of mine,' said Goodbody, and stopped. 'Actually it was my son.' He stopped again. 'Made a hash of his life, but he's come through it. One hopes . . .' His voice trailed off.

Peter Brune said: 'Some of you may know of a man called Dale Beckett. One of our leading consultant psychiatrists. For years he's been involved in the treatment of drug addiction.'

'I've heard of him,' said Norris.

'Well, not so very long ago he wrote an article saying that when he first started treating heroin addicts he was "stuffed full", as he put it, of current newspaper myths, and that it took years for it to dawn on him that heroin was in fact "very gentle". If care is taken in self-injecting, he said, it's extremely safe.'

'Well,' said Norris. '*Chacun à son goût.* Whatever the paradoxes and contradictions of the present situation I have to come down emphatically on the side of total prohibition.'

'A significant word,' replied Brune, smiling now.

'On, indeed, prohibition as we all know created the drink barons in the States. But it's a price we have to pay for civilisation.'

James said: 'In the end most of the Al Capones were gunned down.'

Shannon said: 'Cut down the tares and more sprout, I guess. That's the way it's been in the States. There's a big campaign against drugs, but I'm not sure we're even holding our own.'

'The important thing,' James said, 'is to cut down the tares as soon as they show. Or gun them down, as the case may be.'

'That's a murderous philosophy,' said Crichton, very red in the face now. 'Of course, it's the age-old paradox: how do you defeat dictators without having to use some of their methods? How do you combat crime yet keep strictly within the limits of the law?'

'You don't always,' said Henry with a short high laugh, which

286

some of the others, knowing Henry's reputation, joined in. But Henry's laugh had not been a pleasant one.

Brune said: 'We all step out of line, one way or another, sometime in our lives. Isn't that so? Isn't it in Matthew? "Therefore all things whatsoever ye would that men should do to you, do ye even so to them: for this is the law and the prophets."'

James said: 'And would you have a man do to you what you have done to him?'

The challenge was there but now Brune refused it. 'I was brought up on the Bible, but can only quote it at random –'

'Like the devil, for his own purpose?'

'Well, yes, I suppose that's true. Aristotle says that man is either a beast or a god. "η θηρίον η θεός." Or better still, Aristophanes: "You cannot make a crab walk straight." Do you shoot the crab because he disobeys the general rule?'

The conversation went on for a while. Henry was able to whisper to James: 'No need to face him out here. There's trouble waiting for him when he gets home.'

'I'd like to believe you,' James muttered.

'Graham Greene,' whispered Henry, thrusting his hair back. 'He once said in one of his books that it's only in Europe that a rich man can be a criminal. Overstated, but there's a basic truth. Perhaps my old friend has miscalculated and thinks it applies here. My old friend, my good and amusing and long-standing friend, my generous friend, my wise and learned friend. Christ, I can't believe it! It calls into question so much of what life is about!'

# II

Parsons and the Daimler were waiting for Sir Peter Brune outside the college gates. Almost always the Principal walked out with him and saw him off. Not tonight. Crichton had muttered a bumbling excuse.

It was a chilly night for June, and as Brune got in he said: 'Drive me to Carfax, will you.'

'Yes, sir.'

It was nearly midnight, and the streets were already emptying. A few town boys lurked in a corner; a group of students linked arms on their way home.

The car slowed. 'Is this right, sir?'

'It will do.'

When the car stopped Brune got out before Parsons could do so and went to the driver's window. 'I have one or two things to do. I'll drive myself home later.'

'Er – yes, sir?' said Parsons, in some surprise. 'D'you mean – without me?'

'Without you. The bus stop is just down there in the Cornmarket. The bus passes our gates.'

'I think it might be a bit late to get one now, sir.'

'What? Oh, I see. Well, there's a taxi rank close by. Here, take this.'

'Thank you, sir.'

Parsons watched his master take his seat, finger the unfamiliar controls, then drive away. Parsons stuck his hands in his pockets and found a cigarette as he walked towards the taxi rank.

Peter Brune, KBE, MA, did not drive far. He went round a couple of streets and stopped near a phone booth. Then he waited to see if anyone was following him. When he was sure that was not so, he went into the booth and dialled his own house.

A familiar voice. 'Sir Peter Brune's residence.'

Brune said: 'This is Michael Carpenter. I rang to know if my television men have been round to see your set.' (Have the police been?)

'Yes, they have, Mr Carpenter.'

'Are they still there?'

'No, they went about nine.'

'Is the extension line on?' (Are we being tapped?)

'I don't think so.'

'Did our guest get away safely?'

'No. The ambulance was stopped outside the gates.'

'Ah. I shall be some little time, John.'

'Whatever you say.'

'Naturally you'll tidy up.' (Burn everything you can.)

'Already have done. But of course it's a big job.'

'Do your best.'

'When shall we be seeing you again, Mr Carpenter?'

'If the set is working properly I'll send you our account.'

Peter Brune hung up and climbed into the Daimler. He stopped to light a cigar, meanwhile glancing around the empty street. He was still in his dinner jacket.

He drove west.

It was a fine night, and stars sprinkled the sky like confetti. He drove slowly and was overtaken by other cars. He did not at this moment fear pursuit, and he had not yet altogether made up his mind. He had ample private money in Zurich and Luxembourg, and some in New York and Hong Kong. He could never be anything but a rich man.

But he most bitterly regretted what he was leaving behind and wondered if there was too much risk in staying to brazen it out. On the whole he thought so. The stopping of the ambulance (with the little Indian spy inside), the record of what he had said at the interview, these were likely to be final bricks in the prosecution's case.

It was a crying cursing pity. He had looked forward to the university honour with almost as much enjoyment as when five years earlier the Queen had tapped his shoulder with her sword. He enjoyed his joint position as scholar and benefactor. It was his life – one he had made for himself and believed in.

His brilliant classics career, which he had begun at Lampeter and completed at Oxford, had not fitted him for taking over a bankrupt business when his father died, and he had soon sold it piecemeal to pay off the debts. Contacts with the subworld of drug dealing had led him into a career of huge profits and quick returns, for which he had discovered a talent that surprised himself. In no time he had developed a thriving trade of which he was owner and controller until he was taken over, firmly if not quite forcibly, by a larger and more ruthless organisation led by Mr Erasmus of Hong Kong.

With profits quadrupled he had had no cause to regret this,

and by the time he was fifty much of his money was invested in legitimate and profitable enterprises – mainly property – from which he was able to extend his benefactions.

He was not self-critical of his way of living; but he very much regretted the death of Stephanie – chiefly for the mismanagement of events which made such a repulsive choice necessary, but also for the inescapable fact that was now emerging, that it had led to his own personal involvement.

When she had invited him into her flat that morning and told him that she was coming to the conclusion that she couldn't keep quiet about Errol's activities, she had signed her own death warrant. He had asked her to delay any exposure for a few days while he thought the situation through and came back to her; but when he got home he had at once rung Erasmus, who by then was back in Hong Kong.

Before even Errol and Stephanie returned from India, Erasmus had been on the phone to him, ferociously angry that Errol had taken a girl with him on such a sensitive trip, and blaming Brune for ever recruiting so unstable and unreliable a character as Colton. It was not Peter Brune's way to raise his voice or show anger, but he had replied acidly that the recruiting had already been done by a man called Lake – now dead – and by Mr Erasmus himself before he, Brune, ever set eyes on Colton. Mr Erasmus did not like his own mistakes pointed out to him, and only someone as senior in the organisation as Brune would have dared to do it.

They had discussed the measures that might be taken to correct Colton's error, to close the loophole, as it were, and there was talk of eliminating Errol himself. But that would not necessarily keep the girl quiet, and anyway by now Colton had too many contacts and might well have protected himself by leaving papers in a bank in the event of his death. (When his death did take place it seemed that in his usual casual way he had not even taken that precaution.)

So one flawed operator had brought the whole edifice tumbling down. Of course it would be built up again. It was a temporary setback. Money was the answer to everything.

It was not, however, the answer to his own future. Money could take him far out of reach of the British law. It could not, unfortunately, be used to grease the palms of British policemen. He had many friends in high places, but only one or two could be tempted that way, and none of these was in a position to influence the course of justice.

What was the future for him if he returned to face it out? The Lilliputs would tie him down. And then what? Could anything at all be proved about Stephanie? Unlikely that Arun Jiva would ever talk.

But whether or not the girl's death was involved he would be pinned down on the drugs charge. A sentence, then, of some sort. Ten years? Fifteen years? You couldn't tell. Some slow-witted arrogant old fool in a faded horsehair wig might think it necessary to 'make an example' of him, just because of his eminent position. When he came out, Postgate would still be there and all the trappings of his wealth. In prison he might begin a new translation of Aristophanes. He'd had that ambition as a young man but had never got round to it.

Supposing he briefed some brilliant counsel who got him off on a technicality, his life could not even then be resumed as he had known it. Embezzlement, with a three-year stretch? People would soon forget or overlook. Evading tax? Of course. Being a drug baron? Not quite ever.

Anyway, was he even prepared to take the chance? There was plenty of time to return home.

He went on.

He had thought a lot about Stephanie Locke over the last weeks. He remembered her open, appealing face, the wisps of fair hair falling over her forehead as she talked. But she just talked too much. That day he had focused his eyes on her pretty mouth and thought – it says too much. There were some women like that – and often they were pretty women – however much they might say they were going to be discreet, they never were. It was not in their nature to be.

Erasmus, of course, was in favour of immediate action, and drastic. The arranged motor smash – or a kidnapping and the

291

body discovered a week later in some pond. They had discussed it all one night, three of them, eight hours of coffee and talk and talk and coffee, with intermittent exchanges with Hong Kong. Errol Colton had been in favour – if he had been in favour of anything – of the arranged car smash. It had finally been vetoed because of its haphazard result and the likely injury to the other driver. Kidnapping would be followed by an unending and unrelenting police inquiry. Then they had sent for Arun Jiva.

What had gone wrong? Nothing in the execution. Except for the suppression or theft of the suicide note, nothing had gone wrong. The present crisis was nearly all due to the persistence and interference of the girl's ex-paratroop and crippled father. Better by far if he had himself become the object of an arranged accident in Corfu – if only in retaliation for the destruction of Colton and Apostoleris. Erasmus would be livid that it had not been fixed up.

But by then most of the damage had already been done – and Locke had done it.

Brune drove through a sleeping Swindon and got on to the M4, heading for the Severn Bridge. Time passed, headlights glimmering; still plenty of traffic on this road; but there were no queues at the bridge, as so often in daylight. He drove into Wales.

There would be no trouble in his getting out of the country. Although he had lived his life without apprehension, he had long ago prepared for the worst and then put it so far back in his mind as to be almost forgotten. A flat in Cardiff, a small car garaged underneath with the battery on a time-clock charger; suitcases, ample changes of clothing, valid passport in another name, hair dye, spectacles, sufficient particulars of another life, plenty of money in five different currencies.

So now a flight tomorrow morning from Cardiff to Dublin. Then Dublin to Zurich.

When he was knighted he had almost decided to close the flat. It was all too much cloak and dagger for the establishment figure, the rich scholarly philanthropist. Only a lack of decision had prevented him doing this. Fortunately now. Fortunately perhaps. He still could not quite believe he would make this move.

He drew in off the motorway at a service station and rang his home. The bell went on some time before it was answered. Then a strange voice came on, just giving the telephone number. All his staff were taught to answer 'Sir Peter Brune's residence'. He hung up without speaking. Even in the two hours since he last rang something had happened, events had moved on. He got back into his car, lit another cigar, smoked half of it in silence.

He thought over the address that was likely to be given about him at the Encaenia in two weeks' time, the summary of his life, the rolling Latin phrases.

'Of Anglo-Welsh parentage, educated in Cardiff, Lampeter, Oxford . . . brilliant Greek scholar, books on Euripides and Aristophanes . . .'

The Chancellor of Oxford University would pronounce the admission. 'Perceptive philosopher' (How did it go? *Philosopherum sollertissime*), 'scholar and philanthropist, benefactor of the University and of many deserving charities throughout the land, I admit you by my own authority and that of the whole University to the honorary degree of Doctor of Civil Law.'

He was, he knew, by choice and by temperament a gentleman. He had been born to be what he eventually made himself. To achieve that end he had overstepped the limits of what was loosely termed a civilised society. While mankind – or that part of it which made the laws – considered certain acts criminal, he was out of bounds. Now, through a hideous succession of ill events and ill judgments, his behaviour would become public knowledge. *Au poteau*, in fact.

A schoolmaster had once said to him: 'Brune, I believe you could talk yourself out of anything.' So now. He would go back and talk himself out of this. It was not in his nature to run away.

He slowed to a crawling pace as he reached the outskirts of Cardiff. He had been born and brought up here. He knew it more intimately – and with the intimacy of youth – than any other city. Handsome as the town was, with much of the capital city about it – thanks, he supposed, chiefly to Lord Bute, who had made a fortune out of coal – it held too many bitter memories for him ever to want to return to it. To be brought up a rich man's son and to become a bankrupt's son; to have so strong and deep-rooted an attachment for his mother that after her death he had not been able to form a stable relationship with any other woman; to feel himself always to be more Welsh than English yet to be unable to come to terms with his chosen countrymen; to be about to go to Eton but instead to be sent to Cardiff High School, where his educated near-English voice had been a liability; to know himself to be much cleverer than most people yet to be unable to make the impression he wanted; to be used to money as a boy but to be brutally short of it as a teenager; all these sensations merged into an amalgam long associated with this town. When he had moved out of it and turned to the making of easy money, a new life had begun.

As he came into the city he saw Llandaff Cathedral on his left, and turned into the parking bay above it. There was a light on in the cathedral, a dim light perhaps left permanently on. Was the place locked, he wondered, or had vandals not yet crossed the Severn Bridge?

His mother had been a convinced Christian, his father a casual atheist; in this respect he took after his father; but he had been to the cathedral almost every Sunday and could still recite most of the relevant parts of the Prayer Book. Some of it he also knew in Welsh.

Still in his dinner jacket and black tie, he got out and went down the uneven path to the church door. How often he had trod this way.

The cathedral was lit as if with pilot lights, but there were sufficient of them to see the whole of the great Gothic edifice including – for one could not miss it – the Majestas, Epstein's brilliant but brutally incongruous sculpture in aluminium and concrete which straddled the nave.

He walked down and took a seat in its shadow. These were the seats he and his mother had occupied Sunday after Sunday all those years ago. He knew exactly what he was going to do now. No hole-in-the-corner escape, no panic flights across the Irish Sea and a long life in exile in Singapore or Hong Kong. He would return and face it out. It was all suspicion. There was not a *scrap* of firm evidence the police could bring against him. Even the little he had said to Nari Prasad could be explained away.

All right, people would talk. The whole of Oxford University was a gigantic gossip shop. They would talk behind his back; but suppose he upped his contribution to the University to the million mark for this year? Who would refuse it on the tendentious grounds that it was tainted money? What of America? Half of the great universities of the past had been built and endowed by gangsters, men making fortunes out of the early railways, out of a corner in metals, out of a ruthless extermination of their rivals. Before they knew where they were, Oxford would be celebrating the opening of a whole new medical laboratory financed by him, or even a new college. Money in the end would solve anything. He would return to Postgate tonight and smilingly put himself into the clutches of the Lilliputians.

A clock somewhere in the cathedral struck three. He was the only person, it seemed, in the entire building. The only one alive anyway. He sat quite still for a long time. His brain was not active but he had no sleep in him. For a time he felt his mother's presence beside him, smelt the eau de Cologne which was the only scent she ever permitted herself. Then for a moment there came quite strongly to his nostrils the terrible smell that had come and gone around her when she was dying.

He stirred restlessly, and the clock struck four. In another hour it would be daylight. Time he was going. Time to return to the poised, sardonic, competent, rich and richly gifted man to whom a Doctorate of Civil Law would shortly be awarded. A few policemen, a little scandal, what did that matter?

He took out a phial from his jacket pocket and held it up in the dim yellow light. The phial was filled with a light purplish liquid, about an ounce in all. Half was a lethal dose. He drank it all. The taste was bitter but he knew the effects were quite painless.

He moved into the seat his mother had always occupied and composed himself for sleep.

295

# EPILOGUE

Evelyn Gaveston was a week late returning home, but she did so in the end, wispy-haired and flat-shoed, and clutching a large handbag in which was concealed a hamster bought in New York and smuggled through the customs. Henry, whose business it was to keep the law, at least in small things, despaired, and banished the animal to a back room for their first luncheon party.

James Locke and Mary Aldershot were among the guests, as were Teresa – looking plump and roseate – and Tom; but since there were twelve at table not much private conversation was possible. This was Evelyn's aim. Everyone steered clear of subjects such as suicides, drug taking and college scandals. Indeed, as most of her guests were from distant parts of the country, the tragedies of the last two months did not loom so large. Obviously they had all heard – or rather read – and so would exercise tact in the subjects opened, but with much less effort and constraint than if it had been a local gathering.

Tom and Teresa left fairly early, since they wanted to get back to London before the traffic built up. As they left Teresa kissed her father warmly on the lips.

He squeezed her hand. 'When?'

'Next Thursday or Friday, they expect.'

'I'll be thinking of you.' He kissed her again.

'Daddy,' she said.

'Yes?'

'Be of good heart.'

Some of the others drifted away during the next half-hour, but two sisters, maiden ladies of great wealth and little learning, stayed on and on, so Henry invited James to come out of doors and view his *Sciadopitys verticillata*, which he had got some reluctant students to guy for him last weekend.

The two old friends moved off together, one pushing the other in an unmotorised wheelchair specially kept for James's visits. They inspected the wayward tree, and James told Henry he simply had to make up his mind. The tree quite clearly needed the support to keep it steady in wind; the ground it was planted in was a moderate clay which should give it a substantial grip; but something was wrong, roots remained too near the surface, spreading rather than digging deeper. It would need this sort of support for at least another ten years, he said, and in that time you'd have to watch that the ropes didn't slip or rot. A simple choice between maintaining a distinguished invalid or cutting it down and rooting it up.

'I'll give it a year,' said Henry. 'I'll give it one more year.'

'You're wasting your time. If the guying offends you you may as well root it up now.'

Henry grunted and looked his old friend over, studiously. 'When are you marrying Mary?'

James shifted in his chair. 'Not yet, certainly. Of course not yet.'

'What's stopping you?'

'While this suspicion hangs over me I can't do anything. Maybe in a year or two.'

'Then you're wasting your time. This suspicion, as you call it, is going to hang over you for the rest of your blooming life. The police don't altogether ever lose interest in a murder, they put it on a back burner and there it'll stay, waiting for something to turn up and set it all alight again.'

'All the more reason –'

'But so what? It's another hazard in life, that's all, to add to those that exist already. You or I might have a coronary to-morrow – or a stroke or what you will. There's always things waiting round the corner that you close your eyes to and hope to dodge. This is just another, and the chances are you'll dodge it. If it would make you happier to marry – and I think it would – and I'm sure Mary would like it, don't dither about, take it on board without any more hesitations. D'you know what old George Hoskins said to me the other day?'

'I couldn't guess.'

'He said, "When you get to seventy-five any pleasure you have after that is like having a picnic in a graveyard." He was always a miserable old bugger but he had a point. So what are you? – a bit younger than I am – not yet sixty-six? With luck we shall have a few interesting and constructive and enjoyable years before we reach George Hoskins' eminence.'

James crossed his ankles, which for once had been comfortable today.

'What's happened to that Indian – Nari Prasad?'

'Oh, they found him in the ambulance – as I told you – a bit knocked about, but he's all right. The police have got him in protective custody until after the trial.'

'And then they'll ship him back to India?'

'I don't think so. Some sort of a bargain was struck. He'll get a new name, a chance for a fresh start.'

'In England?'

'If they said that. Chief thing is for him to go to some place where he can merge into the landscape.'

'When is the trial?'

'Oh not yet. Trouble is, of course, most of the main villains are out of reach. You topped two, and the head of it all topped himself.'

'The tumour will grow again.'

'Of course. But it'll leave a huge gap that'll take time to fill. John Peron is the biggest fish we've caught, but there are a dozen others. The drug squad are delighted.'

It was a warm day, and the scent of new-mown grass wafted in the breeze.

'But the case of Stephanie's death can't be reopened?'

'Depends on Arun Jiva. He'll be closely questioned for a long time. On the face of it it seems unlikely he will ever say enough, but one never knows. He has a tremendous arrogance, and he might be cleverly led on.'

James frowned. 'Did your students cut this lawn?'

'Yes. Chap called Harrington. Reading PPE. Quite a good job, but he left the machine in rather a mess.'

'Most things are left in rather a mess,' James said. 'I hope I'm not a specially vindictive man, but I'd like somebody to be tried for the murder of Stephanie. Not just to see him get a few more years in prison but to clear her name.'

'I think Death by Misadventure has been pretty well accepted by everyone now. What did you do with the suicide note?'

'Burned it. But Anne Vincent might talk.'

'She won't. I had a long session with her.'

After a silence James said: 'The stigma remains. A girl who killed herself because she'd been rejected by her lover. Or a girl who drank so much that she didn't realise she'd taken an overdose of sleeping pills.'

There was not much Henry could say, so he said nothing. There was another long silence.

Eventually James said: 'Well, I suppose Brune's self-disposal lifted the problem of the Encaenia out of Alistair's lap. And out of the Chancellor's too.'

'It was a near thing.'

'If Errol had taken up with some other girl none of this would have happened.'

'Indeed. Which could devoutly have been wished.'

'Probably Brune would have received his doctorate and the University some further big donations. And no one the wiser. And perhaps no one the worse.'

'I don't know. I wouldn't say that.'

'Brune certainly would.'

'Nemesis followed him,' Henry said.

'What?'

'Nemesis. With you in the title role.'

'I would have been happy not to have played it.'

'Of course.'

In the distance four ladies were walking in the garden: the two rich spinsters and Evelyn and Mary.

Henry said suddenly: 'Colton and Apostoleris were rubbish –

299

better out of the way. But I would have liked to hear what Peter Brune had to say for himself, how he could have explained everything – *anything* – apart from what little he said at that last dinner party. A personal friend I've known for upwards of a quarter of a century . . . Fortunately I never talk to anyone on security matters . . . Although no one has accused Brune of being connected with terrorism, one never knows where one criminality ends and another begins.' He stooped to pluck up a thistle which seemed to have grown overnight. 'But we have talked often of college problems and the like – life in London, charitable ramps, police discipline, Welsh miners, grubby politicians, Middle East madness; you know, the sort of things *we* talk about. He's even advised me on investments, usually very well. I would have trusted him as much as I have trusted you. Yet he has, it seems, not only been head of this organisation but instigated – or condoned – Stephanie's death. That is the most horrifying thing of all.'

'I too would have liked to talk to him,' James said.

Henry looked down at his invalid friend. 'Perhaps it's as well you did not.'

A pack of clouds obscured the sun. They had drifted up unnoticed like an unexpected frown. The four ladies were approaching. Evelyn, wearing a shapeless frock, hair lifting in the breeze, was talking animatedly and making Mary laugh. A shaft of sun pursued the women with deliberation like an arc light on a stage.

James looked up at the broken sky. He did not cavil at the thought of the life ahead of him, if only he could have forgotten the past. Memories of Stephanie would never go away. No more, for years, had thoughts of Janet. Yet one could only try to live for the day. *One moment in annihilation's waste, One moment of the well of life to taste. The stars are waning and the Caravan starts for the dawn of nothing. Oh make haste.* For the relatively short time left, would the well of life always be sour? He did not know. But he had one charming daughter and an agreeable son-in-law, and a first grandchild expected next week. And a housekeeper called Mary who seemed resigned – even willing – to be his wife.

Even if one couldn't be happy oneself, was it not a pretty thing to try to make others happy?

Henry gave the chair a push towards the ladies. 'Right ahead?' he asked.

'Right ahead.'